It's a Privilege Just to Be Here

It's a Privilege Just to Be Here

♦ A NOVEL ♦

EMMA SASAKI

alcove
press

Published in the United States by Alcove Press, an imprint of The Quick Brown Fox & Company LLC.

Alcove Press and its logo are trademarks of The Quick Brown Fox & Company LLC.

Library of Congress Catalog-in-Publication data available upon request.

ISBN (hardcover): 978-1-63910-783-4
ISBN (ebook): 978-1-63910-784-1

Cover design by Alcove Press

Printed in the United States.

www.alcovepress.com

Alcove Press
34 West 27th St., 10th Floor
New York, NY 10001

First Edition: June 2024

10 9 8 7 6 5 4 3 2 1

*This book is dedicated to my daughters,
who amaze and inspire me every day.
Remember: Confidence creates miracles.*

*And to my husband, who told me to write
a novel. You've helped make all my dreams
come true.*

AUTHOR'S NOTE

M UCH OF THIS STORY is true.
Names have been changed to protect the innocent.
And to keep the guilty guessing.

DECEMBER

◆ 1 ◆

"Why would anyone pay so much for a private school when you can get the same thing for free at a public school?"
— Confused in the Burbs, dcparentzone.com

*P*RIVATE-SCHOOL PARENTS. THEY'RE *just like other parents, only with shinier teeth, alternative energy cars, custom-built firepits, and multiple board memberships.* This is what Aki Hayashi-Brown thinks as she surveys the scene before her. Eight of the DC area's most affluent and academically oriented parents, all gathered together for the annual auction parent committee meeting.

Aki knows a private-school parent when she sees one: she happens to be one. But today, she's at the meeting as a teacher, not a parent. She takes a languid sip of the organic, West Coast–roasted small batch coffee that's been brewed especially for the day's meeting and sighs. It's not always easy being both a parent and teacher at a high-priced, overachieving private school in Washington, DC, but *at least the coffee is good*, she thinks to herself as she takes another sip, wondering how many cups she can drink without looking openly cheap. If she's being honest, the brew really is the highlight of these inane meetings.

She inhales the aroma and closes her eyes; it reminds her of the Ferry Building in San Francisco. Aki is from the Bay Area, though she's taught—and her daughter has been a student—at Wesley Friends School for thirteen years. Though it needs no introduction within the sixty-eight square miles of Washington, DC, Wesley Friends School is the country's oldest Quaker School and arguably the most prestigious, being able to boast having educated four sets of presidential children, various cabinet-level offspring, not to mention multiple *Post* editorial writers, and the army of K Street lawyers who bill $1,000 per hour to all of the above. Known as "the Harvard of the Washington, DC, private schools," Wesley Friends manages to attract the best students, the brightest teachers—and more than a fair share of intolerable parents.

"Can we please call this meeting to order?" directs Holly Henderson-Hines, mother of Zach, Cody, and Ellie (because all private-school parents are identified first by their children, second by their place of occupation—in Holly's case, she's the CEO of their household, otherwise known as a stay-at-home mom). Holly is also the newly selected chair of the annual auction benefit, having recently dethroned Liz Everett (parent to Sibley, Simon, and Chase, and former party planner, who managed to raise over one million dollars at last year's gala). Holly is in her usual uniform: white button-down shirt, expensive-but-not-too-trendy jeans, cashmere sweater draped over her shoulders, and her dark hair swept up into a perfect-looking messy bun.

"For those of you who don't know her, I'd like to start by thanking Aki Hayashi-Brown for volunteering to serve as teacher liaison to the auction this year. Thank you, Ms. Brown," Holly says officiously as the other women—and one man—in attendance clap politely.

Of course, the truth of the matter is that Aki didn't volunteer. She was forcibly hoisted into the position by the head of the upper school, Ousmane Gueye. ("I've given your name to the parent association you'll be great, good way to network, thanks.") Ousmane is famous for his run-on sentence fly-bys.

Ousmane Gueye started as a French teacher at Wesley back in the '90s, left for graduate school to complete a PhD in French history, but instead of going the professor track was wooed back to Wesley to be the school's first-ever person of color to head any of the three school divisions (lower, middle, upper). Ousmane is the ideal private-school administrator: tall and handsome, he has the polish of a star, the guile of a politician, and armor made of Teflon. After all, 95 percent of his day is spent fending off well-heeled parents and their eloquently executed and feverishly demanding emails, and being yes-man to the head of school, Harrison Neal III. The other 5 percent is spent in the one class he teaches, a section on World Civ with a focus on former French colonies. This technically makes him part of the history department, which Aki chairs, not that Ousmane ever shows up to their meetings. "Auction committee meets before classes, I know you have first period free, thanks for doing this, you'll be great," Ousmane had told Aki as he flew past.

"Excuse me. Welcome, Ms. Ha-ya-shi Brown. We're thrilled to hear your thoughts and added *diversity*," Holly emphasizes.

Points to Holly, yup, I'm a minority! Aki feels like joking. But DC private-school parents have no sense of humor, and the sticks up their butts are plated in titanium and studded with ethically sourced diamonds. Instead, she just nods and smiles at the parents around the table. After all, the Wesley Friends School is all about *Diversity, Achievement, Collegiality*, as any brochure or hand-picked commencement speaker reminds those who wander the reclaimed-wood hallways. Never mind the last four out of five parent association presidents have been white women.

"Let's get started so that people can go about their day, and so Ms. Brown can go teach," Holly declares.

Ms. Brown, Aki thinks. *Why is it that people feel like they can use multiple versions of my name?* She's of course used to the Anglicized, shorter version by now. "Too long!" Her mother had admonished when she hyphenated.

Holly starts again. "This is just a check-in, so it won't take long," she promises.

At 7:45, it's criminally early to be holding a meeting, and Aki's seventeen-year-old daughter Meg was sideways with irritation when she heard she would have to get to school at this hour if she wanted a ride that day. Taller than Aki, with lighter hair and inky black gumdrop eyes, her daughter is more attractive than her as well. Unfortunately, like most teenagers, she is also allergic to early mornings.

"I don't know why you have to go to these stupid things," Meg had grumbled as she got out of the car that morning. "Auctions are predicated on an elitist principle that the wealthy willingly engage in the public allocation of money."

Aki had to bite her tongue; she knows how the trees feel when the hurricane of a patronizing adolescent lecture is about to make landfall.

"What gets auctioned off in that particular marketplace?" Meg asked, giving her mother a sideways glance. "Things with no rights. Cattle, land, *slaves*," Meg continued, suddenly awake and indignant.

Aki sighed at her daughter's soliloquy. She didn't want to remind her that at schools like Wesley, auctions are not only proms for adults, they also help subsidize students who can't otherwise afford to go there. Students like Meg.

"Ugh, whatever. I'm going to get some sleep in the student lounge," Meg finished, looking tired and rumpled. "Have loads of fun getting nothing done as usual," she spat out before disappearing down the hall.

Holly coughs expectantly, bringing Aki out of the memory of her conversation with Meg from earlier that morning. She looks at Holly and blinks.

"Ahem! Our first order of business is to fill these seats." Holly declares, clasping her hands together and placing them in front of her, as if she's actively praying for increased parental membership. Everyone looks around the table, multiple conference room chairs yawning with emptiness. Aki knows without asking that the auction is a heavy lift for the parent community and the call for volunteers seems to have faltered.

"It's such a shame that we have to go hunting for parents to contribute their time to something as important as *serving their school*," Holly intones, looking at Aki as if to say *See, I'm a good parent!* "But let's try to brainstorm some names and ask them directly." She looks around the table expectantly. Crissy Stone (parent to Clara and Jack, curator at a high-end gallery) raises her hand obediently. Holly nods in her direction.

"How about Priya Gosh?" Crissy asks timidly. It's hard to believe two hell-raisers like Clara and Jack Stone have a mother as quiet as Crissy.

"Oh, that would be good, we need some minorities," Sally Rose-Allen (mother of Eli, civil litigation attorney) exclaims before looking at Aki and the other lone minority—and father—at the table. "I mean, you know what I mean," she says somewhat defiantly.

Aki swears she can hear the father, Travis Jones (father to Edwin, vice president of the area's NFL team), mutter "Jesus Christ" under his breath. She tries to keep from laughing as she watches him clench his jaw and shake his head ever so slightly.

"Will you ask Priya?" Holly asks Crissy quickly, eyes darting between Travis and Aki. "Priya would be *such a great* addition!" Crissy dutifully scrolls through her phone, ostensibly looking for Priya's contact information, and Aki can't help but think about the time Jack and Clara decided to steal all the toilet paper from the boys' and girls' bathrooms. She remembers the custodial staff scurrying about, hurriedly refilling the stalls while Clara and Jack

were ceremoniously hauled into the middle school head's office
for a stern warning. Nothing more than that, of course; everyone
knew that their father (Crissy's husband) is the CFO of one of
the country's biggest energy companies and a major donor to the
school. Aki found their prank pretty funny, but given the school
population, she was probably the only one.

Holly continues. "Great, next order of business, Dr. Gueye
and the advancement office have asked me to make sure that all
auction planning this year is *inclusive*," she intones. The advancement office, Aki knows, has nothing to do with the advancement
of anyone or anything beyond the school's own wallet. Basically, a private-school term for "People We Hire to Raise Lots of
Money for Wesley."

"Inclusive? What does *that* mean?" Liz Everett screeches. The
Everetts, who made their fortune in online gaming, are two of the
few openly conservative parents in the school. They live in a $4.5
million house in Kalorama, sandwiched between the Obamas
and Ivanka's old house, a fact Aki learned thanks to the parent
directory and Zillow. Who knew online zombie games could buy
three private-school tuitions topping $51K each and so much real
estate? Rumor has it that Liz was not at all pleased to step down as
the chair of the auction committee this year, and Aki wonders if
this is the start of a turf battle between Holly and her predecessor.
Suddenly Aki wishes she had brought some popcorn. Her phone,
which she has tried to covertly place in her lap, lights up with a
text message from her husband, Ian. Aki knows that although he's
on a research vessel somewhere near Greenland, the text is not an
SOS or work update but most likely a joke of some sort. Whenever
he's away from home, he sends her a funny meme every morning.
Yesterday's was a photograph of a man in outdoor gear standing in
a snowy field with a caption that read: "Ladies, please know that
our job of being the man of your dreams and the reason for your
daily ire is exhausting." She had to laugh at that one.

"Rog and I," Liz continues, "we think that the point of any auction is to raise as much money as possible." She purses her lips. "Which is what we did last year." Squat with a perpetual grimace on her face, Liz is the type of person who never has individuated thoughts, only those conjoined with her loudmouthed husband. Of course, they also donated a whopping $50K to the endowment last year. Not to mention a hefty check to the school's current campus expansion project, which is probably why the school tolerates Roger's annual drunken tirade against the "libtards" at the school's annual fundraiser and makes sure the Everetts are on all the parent committees. "So whatever this *inclusivity stuff* is, just remember, the school doesn't run on the latest buzzwords." Liz crosses her arms and stares at Holly, who looks openly and uncharacteristically wary.

Aki has known Holly for years, mainly because her son Zach started in kindergarten with Meg. Holly, Aki acknowledges, is the perfect person to preside over any sort of parent committee. A former management consultant, Holly is always looking for her new fiefdom to rule over. Holly is also always looking to claw her way to the top of the anonymous parental heap littered with wannabe players, first by volunteering for the parent association, and now presiding over the auction in order to one day serve on the board, which she suspects is Holly's ultimate goal. But Holly is also the most conflict-averse parent Aki has come across during her time at Wesley. Luckily, someone else steps in to save Holly from Liz's scathing comment.

"I think," Travis says quietly, "what we should remember is that not everyone can pay the price of admission." Tickets to the auction cost close to $200, though teachers' tickets are comped, which is a good thing since that's the only reason Aki can attend. Travis clears his throat and continues softly, "And not everyone can bid 10K on a trip to the Cape. So, we just need to be mindful of everyone's budgets."

Holly nods vigorously at Travis. "I think we can all agree that Wesley always strives to move forward into the light," she adds.

Aki works hard to keep from gagging. *Move Forward into the Light* is the school's motto for the year, shamelessly borrowed from the various Quaker-themed apothegms it bandies about. Last year it was *Let Your Inner Light Shine.* Meg looked at the banner, sniffed and said, "What are we, light bulbs?"

"I also think we can agree that the school always collaborates to make movement in significant areas such as these," Holly concludes, smiling brightly at everyone.

It amazes Aki how Holly can just throw out a lot of words that sound great together but ultimately say nothing.

"I'm sorry I'm so late!" A loud voice punctuates the room. "What did I miss?"

Lulu Miller, mother to Luke, Lucy, Graham, and Sweetie, and CEO of a wildly successful chain of "online beauty apothecaries"—otherwise known as "the Amazon of overpriced face junk," as Meg likes to call them—rushes to an empty seat. She flings her wildly expensive fur vest (faux of course) over the chair before pulling it back with great zeal, artfully sweeping her perfectly blown-out hair behind her. "I'm sorry I'm so late!" she repeats, then explains, "I was on the phone with Zurich."

Holly nods her head a little too vehemently as though Lulu had actually been speaking with an entire city.

"No problem at *all*, Lulu. We were just talking about some changes to the auction, but we really need to get more names to fill out the volunteer roster," Holly says while motioning to the remaining empty seats.

"I'm sure I can do some arm-twisting," Lulu winks. "Consider it done."

"Ah-mazing," Holly says a little too loudly. Aki notices that Liz wrinkles her nose when Lulu talks, like she smells something bad.

"No problem. Great coffee, by the way!" Lulu says as she takes a noisy sip. Holly looks as if she is about to die with pride.

"Thanks to Lulu," Holly beams as she shuts her notebook, "I think this meeting can adjourn!"

Aki swears she hears Travis sigh with relief, or maybe that's just her. She gathers her cup and folders, thinking about what she needs for her second-period class when she realizes what the morning's meeting has really accomplished.

Absolutely nothing.

She hates it when her daughter is right.

$\star$ $\star$ $\star$

Though many of the parents stayed to chat, Aki escapes Holly's meeting as quickly as she can, practically racing down the shiny, perfect hallway, its floors lines with environmentally responsible planks of reclaimed wood. Aki tries to ignore the walls adorned with banners announcing, much like Holly, that they should all strive to *Move Forward into the Light*. If it wasn't bad enough that every wall is plastered with the slogan, she had noticed that morning that the school decided it was so important that they all *Move Forward into the Light* that they painted it along the walls of the underground parking lot as well. Aki sighs. Despite its insistence that the "foundational pillar" of the school is "inward knowledge of the Spirit"—a basic tenet of the Quaker religion—anyone paying a cent of the $51K tuition will tell you the real currency of Wesley is prestige wrapped up in achievement and topped with a bow of success.

There is no more obvious sign of these three things than the shirts worn by a select group of seniors that day, the not-so-humble declarations of their early admission to college. For an institution that doesn't assign class rank or compile GPAs (because it's "un-Quakerly," which is the school's handy reason for whenever they don't feel obliged to do something), they don't seem to mind this tradition, which is simply called "Senior Day"—not that all seniors got in early, but those who do get to flaunt it every year. Aki is so busy scanning the names on the shirts of passing students (Harvard! Yale! Amherst! Williams!) that she plows into what feels like a brick wall, only to realize looking up that it is Aaron Wakeman and Holly's son Zach.

"Hi, Ms. Hayashi-Brown, how are you?" Aaron asks politely.

If ever there was a Golden Boy at Wesley Friends, Aaron Wakeman would be it. A perfect smile on a perfect face, a lush tangle of chestnut hair on top of a tall frame, athletic and smart, he is every teacher's dream student and every student's imaginary best friend. He is also from a long line of Wakemans who entered the Wesley halls before him. Reid, the eldest, graduated from Princeton and later Harvard Law School. Next was Max, a preternaturally gifted runner who was recruited and admitted early to Princeton thanks also to his perfect SAT scores and love of economic theory, now a graduate student at the University of Chicago. Third was Dave, who, though not as academically inclined, managed to start three clubs and help found a business nonprofit that matched DC businesses with student interns from lower-income wards, and was now a junior at, yes, Princeton. All of the Wakeman brothers went to the same school, all in their father's footsteps (Cash Wakeman being a Princeton '84 man).

Aki imagines that it must be an emotionally unmanageable task to come after such gilded brothers, but Aaron is so well liked that perhaps he manages to define success on his own terms. She swears she once watched an ocean of underclassmen part like the Red Sea as he walked down the halls—and if she needed further testament to his likability, she had never even heard Meg say two negative words about him, despite routinely calling the rich kids of the school "the Anti-Bolsheviks." It might have to do with the fact that they had been friends in lower school, or maybe the hype was real, and Aaron really was as nice as he seems.

She remembers him as a fourth grader, slightly chubby and very sweet, and even when middle school brandished its unforgiving sword, rendering most kids socially and physically awkward, she would see Meg and Aaron joking in the hallways every now and again. He had really blossomed in upper school, and often had a trail of girls following him like the tail of a kite.

The faculty wasn't fully immune to his charm either, which is why Aki can't help but stare at the lack of an early admission shirt on Aaron, and she hastily reminds herself to greet the boys, both of whom are in Wesley athletics warm-up jerseys.

"Aaron, Zach," she nods officiously. "You all had a good season," she supplies, knowing that the soccer team had managed to win the league that past fall. If she can't talk about colleges, she might as well talk about sports.

"Seven and one," Aaron says proudly. "Thanks to this guy right here," Aaron bumps his shoulder against Zach's in a show of affection. Aki vaguely remembers Aaron being named all-league first team himself. "How is Meg?" he asks politely.

"She's doing well, looking at colleges, gearing up for the whole process, you know, like the rest of the junior class," Aki watches as Zach casts his eyes downward at the topic. Having taught Zach in her Ancient Eastern Civilizations course, she knows him to be an alarmingly mediocre student, and she assumes that having a parent like Holly must make Zach's life miserable. Not that Aki is immune from her own parental insecurities. Just yesterday she asked Meg about applying early to college in order to improve her chances of being admitted somewhere, only to have Meg fling her arms up with exasperation and refusal, decrying the practice as "Unfair to financially disadvantaged seniors who have to wait for scholarships." This fact is true, and Aki said nothing to her morally upstanding daughter, while feverishly hoping that she will apply early somewhere next year, if only to ease her own maternal anxiety.

This is going to be a long year, she thinks.

Just then, another group of seniors streaks past in shirts that announce their acceptances to Pomona, Duke, and Michigan. She watches them gallop down the hallway as Aaron hits Zach with his elbow and asks, "Dude, can you imagine having to root for Duke for four years?" The two boys laugh, Zach throwing his head back as he guffaws, his grin reminding Aki of Holly when she occasionally taps into the little humor she has, then deliciously remembering that Holly is a proud Duke grad.

Aaron smiles at Aki again and genially says, "Is Meg still gunning for Berkeley? I wish she'd at least consider the East Coast. I remember her telling me way back in the seventh grade how she wanted to go to Cal." He stops and laughs, then says, "She told me Princeton is for losers."

Aki has to smile; that seems like something Meg would say. She then clears her throat, feeling suddenly nervous about a college choice that isn't even hers and is at least a year away, but that's Wesley for you: parents start thinking about college admissions in lower school. "Yes, we'll see," she says and laughs, feeling anxious about the topic of college but also impressed with Aaron's memory. Just then, someone jumps up on Aaron's back, startling both Aki and Aaron, judging from the expression on his face. He turns his head to see who is on his back. It's Yeardly Ward, junior class president and one of the editors of the paper. All Aki knows of Yeardly is that her father is a Republican senator. "But at least he's a moderate," Meg had sniffed.

"Hey, Yeards," Aaron laughs as she hops off his back.

"Where's the Princeton shirt, Aaron?" she chides. Then she looks at Aki. "Oh, hi, Ms. Brown."

Aki gives them both a tight smile, realizing it's time for her to exit, and says, "Have a good day, kids."

"Have a nice day, Ms. Hayashi-Brown," Aaron says graciously, as he, Zach, and Yeardly turn to continue down the hallway.

"Why are you talking to *them*?" Meg asks, suddenly appearing in the doorway of the history department, watching Aaron, Yeardly, and Zach's retreating figures with a look of disgust.

"I thought you liked Aaron anyway," Aki says, raising her eyebrows in surprise, thinking how the two of them used to pretend to be Percy Jackson characters and play during recess in lower school.

Meg lets out an exasperated sigh and, as if reading her mind, tells Aki, "We're not ten anymore, you know," then pushes past her mother and into the hallway.

◆ 2 ◆

*"Be real, there is frankly never going to be much diversity at a
school charging over 50k for tuition."*
—A parent with two kids in two privates, dcparentzone.com

Meet me in the parking lot.

AKI LOOKS AT THE text and smiles. As ominous as it sounds,
one look at the name, and she's happy for a break. After
grading papers nonstop in the morning and teaching one senior
seminar, it's almost eleven but not quite lunch and Aki is hanker-
ing for a snack, and there's a bag of cookies in the back of her car.
She hurries to the lot, unlocking her door with the fob and rifling
through a large canvas bag in the trunk. She knows she should
take advantage of the organic meals provided by the female-run
local business that operates Wesley's cafeteria, but right now she'd
really rather have some unrefined carbs and white sugar.

"I am loving that top, Hayashi! Let me just go grab my stuff!"
A voice calls out with a distinct Southern twang.

Aki looks up to see Jules's slight figure in the far corner of the
garage. Her best friend on the faculty at Wesley. Petite, blond,
and generally happy to clap back at anyone, Jules is the yin to
Aki's yang. Jules is as direct as they come and doesn't believe in

"nonsensical bullshit," as she likes to call it, whereas Aki is mostly dutiful and hopeful, for better or for worse. Aki remembers her first day of work, which was also the first day she met—or rather, heard—Jules.

"Look at yew, we're gonna be besties," Jules declared in her Southern accent after looking Aki up and down.

During their combined twenty-five years at Wesley, Jules has become a hard-nosed cynic when it comes to the school and has adopted some strange-bordering-on-paranoid rituals, like these lunchtime tailgate sessions, which she instigates, insisting, "You never know, they probably bug our offices." She even refuses to use the school-issued computer, doing all her work on an air-gapped laptop her husband bought her. She also has a policy on where she parks her car: "If I'm in a corner, I know that I can only be attacked from the front," a reference to last year's spate of stalking incidents. It made the DC gossip circuit via dcparentzone .com, a mean-spirited online bulletin board where parents go online to anonymously spew vitriol and malicious gossip.

Aki looks at it from time to time to see what people are saying and usually ends up rolling her eyes. A typical post reads something along the lines of "If my dd [darling daughter] is in the 98th percentile for testing and has all As, will she get into pre-K at Wesley?" followed by a response that snipes, "If she's as annoying as you, I hope she's not in my dd's class!" The fortitude it takes not to reply with equal snark leads Aki to try to stay off dcparentzone altogether, but in an unfortunate turn of events, the gossip that was birthed from the Wesley parking lot via the site morphed into actual news in the *Washington Post*: "Entire Staff of Wesley College Admissions Office Quits Over Allegations of Parent Harassment."

Aki didn't need to read the rest of the article when it was published; for one, the incidents happened just as they were spelled out in the title, not to mention in various threads on dcparentzone.com. Multiple parents had either accosted staff in the parking lot or phoned the admissions office during the day, either about their own child's chances of getting into *insert-name-of-Ivy* or, even worse, making unfounded claims about other families' children in the hopes that the admissions officers would push their child over another's during the application review process.

It's an open secret that college admissions officers routinely take the advice of Wesley college counselors in terms of which candidates the school thinks are best suited for each college. This unofficial "push list" is rumored to affect where kids land, and parents jockey to make sure their kids are on the list. Aki has borne witness to more than one of these Overprivileged Parental Episodes, first when a father mistakenly called the history department extension and let off a tyrannical diatribe about their child's application to Brown without even asking if he had reached the college advising department. On a separate occasion, Aki had been walking in the garage with Jules when a car screeched into the lot and then in an equally dramatic manner, stopped abruptly behind the parked car of Willow Sanders, the then-head of college admissions, preventing Willow from moving her vehicle. When Willow exited her car, her first unwise decision, she was— and there really was no other word for it—*accosted* by Stephanie Steele, mother of Stanford and partner at a lobbying firm.

"Why did you drop Stanford from the Stanford push list and put him on Georgetown? I told you Georgetown was his safety!" Stephanie's hysterical cry reverberated in the concrete structure like a malfunctioning siren. Aki and Jules laughed at the idea of Stanford going to Stanford, but poor Willow, at least fifteen years Stephanie's junior and a reserved, thoughtful individual, stood in terrified immobility at Stephanie's tyrannical outburst. Aki bets that poor Westport-bred Willow never thought she'd be attacked by someone in an M.M.LaFleur wrap dress at five PM on a Thursday. Two more parking lot incidents ensued, by differing parents; one was in fact an unfortunate nanny who had been tasked with asking a bullet-pointed list of questions while trying to record the answers on an old iPhone. After multiple anonymous letters to the admissions office containing "threatening words," the school wiped all telephone extensions from its website, made everyone swap physical offices to confuse future combatants from infiltrating their offices, and planted a permanent security guard at the entrance of the garage. These measures weren't enough to keep Willow and her two assistants from executing a dramatic exit; like soldiers who went AWOL from Guantanamo, they all simply disappeared in the night, desks cleared and computers wiped. Later, the teaching staff would find on dcparentzone that Willow and her crew had in fact been recruited en masse by a boarding school in Connecticut, their housing paid for a period of two years. Wesley credentials don't just work for the students—they carry weight when you're a staffer in need of an escape hatch.

Ever since the incident, Jules jokes that she wants to be able to see the enemy when they attack, though it makes Aki wonder if she is serious because she really does vie for the corner parking spot like her life depends on it. She watches as her friend shuts her car door and click-clacks back toward her in her tottering heels.

"Girl, did you hear about Tyler Kominsky?" she crows, eyes looking like fireworks. Tyler is Jules's protégée, "the best musician Wesley will ever see, period, end of story, no more paper, no more ink," Jules liked to say. Aki shakes her head. Another early decision notice, she assumes. "Early to Columbia, cross-registered with Julliard!" Jules is so excited that Aki wonders if she's not trying to cover up some disappointment that her own son Felix is in the same boat as Meg: on a slow boat that doesn't dock until next April. Felix, unlike his mother, is quiet, large, and "unoffensive for a jock," as Meg describes him. Aki remembers him as a lumbering fourth grader who was always "it" in tag because of his lack of speed, though now he is the leading scorer on Wesley's varsity lacrosse team. He and Meg don't interact very much, and he always casts his eyes down in embarrassment when he sees Aki in the hallways, probably because he knows that his mother talks to her about him.

Watching Jules's ebullient expression, Aki says, "How amazing for Tyler, and for you, congratulations!" while still feeling somewhat deflated herself. Aki opens her trunk's hatch, and they hop onto it as if tailgating, only drinking coffee and eating.

Jules gasps, almost dropping a carrot. "Oh, my gosh, girl, did you hear about Aaron Wakeman?"

"No. Tell me. Did he really not get in early?" Aki asks.

"Adonis has *fallen*," Jules says solemnly as she bows her head. "Deferred from Princeton, bless."

Of course, Aaron's deferral is hard to believe not only because of his envious test scores, grades, recommendations, and legacy status but because of his lineage. Cash Wakeman, his father, is one of the wealthiest real estate developers on the East Coast, making a drive from DC up to Maine without seeing one of his projects an impossible task. More relevant to their fair city is the tangled network of ties and connections he has within the world of politics. Given Cash's stature—and deep pockets for future donations—it's hard to imagine any school turning down his son. Rumor has it that college admissions offices ask college admissions counselors at schools like Wesley just how likely families are to donate. In the case of the Wakemans, it is to the tune of seven figures.

"Well, a deferral isn't a no," Aki says, sounding like a good Wesley college advisor counseling a sobbing senior.

Jules clucks. "Well, you know who *did* commit early to Princeton," she raises her eyebrows. "Double."

"Really? Wow. Princeton?" Aki asks a little incredulously.

"I *know*," Jules responds.

The surprise is not that Dennison B. Lukes, or "Double," as he's called by almost everyone at Wesley, was admitted to Princeton but that he'd want to go. As the president of the Wesley Council for Social Justice and a senior member of the Black Student Union, one can most often find him orating *against* such elite, traditionally WASPy institutions like Princeton. Double is *the* prototype for the ideal Wesley student: intellectual, driven, politically engaged, but possibly more important, he is the spawn of socially desirable parents in line with the Wesley mission. His father is the museum director for the Smithsonian, and his mother is the nation's current poet laureate. If the Wakemans are the old guard of Washington, DC, private schools, the Lukes are what is *in*. And it didn't hurt that Double was a preternaturally gifted athlete to boot, boasting double-digits in both scoring and assists in lacrosse across multiple seasons, hence his nickname.

"It's binding, right?" Aki asks, still surprised at the decision and thinking of a recent *New York Times* article alleging systemic racism at Princeton and an ensuing civil rights investigation.

"Maybe he's going to change it from the inside. I wouldn't put it past him," Jules says, snapping a carrot in half.

Aki thinks about this. Despite being a year apart in school, Double and Meg are good friends, with overlapping social circles and common concerns about school and the world beyond it. She wonders if both of them being biracial plays into their mutual interests too. Meg leads the People of Color at Wesley (PoC@Wesley) student group and works with the Council for Social Justice on shared events. The image of Double bent over their kitchen table in their small apartment making posters, spray-painting banners, and working on speeches that he and Meg planned to give at a rally makes her think that Double is definitely not going to let some eating club *bruhs* get in the way

of his making serious institutional change. Even at a place as tradition bound as Princeton.

"Double, double, toil and trouble," Jules jokes. "I hope
Princeton knows what they're in for. If I were them, I'd take
Aaron too, you know, even out the whole feel of the place."

Jules is just one of Aaron's many faculty admirers, Aki knows,
because Aaron adopted Felix as one of his best friends in middle
school when Aaron was on the rise and Felix was still an awkward twelve-year-old. "Double can be a little intense," Aki says,
thinking about how Meg characterizes him. "He's the next Cor-
nel West," she often said. Jules and Double, on the other hand,
had a more complicated relationship. And it all stemmed from the
annual holiday concert.

Jules, like most of the faculty, is used to the broad freedom
provided to all private-school teachers in deciding her curriculum, not to mention specific musical pieces. When Double and
the Council for Social Justice sent her a formal letter asking her
to be more inclusive in her choices, she initially chafed at the
idea of moving away from traditional Christmas carols and the
works of Cole Porter, things she had been teaching since her
arrival at Wesley, fresh from a Master of Music program in South
Carolina.

"I get it, I get it," Jules had said. The school had started to
overhaul certain long-standing traditions in the name of equity,
such as the "numbers change." They were the first school in the
area to get rid of numbers and terminology that suggested rank:
grades were no longer to be referred to as ninth, tenth, and so
on. French 3 or 4 was now French X or Y. Bio II was now Biological Inquiry. Advanced placement courses were eradicated
and renamed at the same time, creating a brew of consternation
and hysteria from the parents, most of whom were concerned
that college admissions officers would no longer fully understand just how difficult the Wesley curriculum was without the

long-standing generic gradients. It was probably just the start, the faculty realized, of the school taking issues of equity more seriously.

For her part, and after reading through the student suggestions and consulting with the chair of the department, Jules made concessions in response to both. But Aki knew that Double continued to take it upon himself as a member of the chamber choir to approach her and the chair at the start of every term to look at their selections, which Aki found to be an overstep, not that she would say anything. Double was a force to be reckoned with, which meant he was destined for social greatness, coming from a place like Wesley. She once mentioned this to Meg, whose feathers immediately ruffled in indignation.

"Mother, the dominant paradigm replicates itself if you simply leave change to institutional decision-making!" Meaning, of course, that Meg did not trust the school to make the right decisions. At the time, Aki had struggled with trying to make her friend feel better while also supporting her daughter's beliefs, which was certainly not as heart-wrenching as *Sophie's Choice* but felt a little treacherous nonetheless.

"Man, lunch goes quick as a slippery toad, doesn't it? We'd better get back!" Jules yelps as she swipes the last of her hummus with her fingers and throws her Tupperware and mug into a canvas bag. "Do you have next period? Can I just keep these in here? I don't want to walk back to my car," she asks as she throws her bag into Aki's trunk.

Aki nods and shuts the door before they both make their way out of the parking lot and to the high school building. As they walk up the stairs to the courtyard, they see that a small crowd has gathered in front of the arts building.

"I smell trouble," Jules says. "The last time this many people cared about what was going on in our building was when we had a bake sale for some new handbells and someone slipped in a batch of pot brownies. Why Wesley can't just pay for it with their 100 million dollar endowment I don't know, but I guess they have a new science center to build," she grumbles.

As they draw closer to the arts building, they see the crowd growing larger by the minute, students running closer, all with phones in hand, craning their necks to see something on the doors.

"So much for the no cell phones on campus rule," Aki sighs, watching several high schoolers raise their phones up above their heads, trying to take pictures of something that neither she nor Jules can see. Finally, Jules gets annoyed and starts pushing through the sea of students.

"Everyone aside, move aside, management coming through," she jokes loudly, pushing bodies out of her way. Aki watches as her tiny frame gets swallowed up by a group of juniors. From inside the throng, she hears Jules's panicked voice. "Holy *shit!*" her friend cries out, followed by shouts of "Right?" and "Seriously, bruh" from the students. Aki then sees Jules's arm thrust out from the crowd, reaching, she supposed, for her. Aki grabs hold of her friend's hand and migrates through a tight corridor made up of gathered bodies. When she finally makes it through, she stands abruptly still in front of the arts building doors, her own anxiety curling around the five words spray-painted in a harsh shade of turquoise:

Make Wesley White Again

♦ **3** ♦

"Wesley didn't integrate until the late 60s. That was a conscious decision, you realize."

—*A Wesley alum, dcparentzone.com*

From the Desk of Harrison Neal III

This is not who we are.

Move forward into the light,
Harrison Neal III

THIS WAS THE FIRST brief, if insistent, message from the head of school, Harrison Neal, that arrived in faculty email inboxes after *the incident*, as it came be called. The message was echoed with a statement consisting of the same words but with the added "Emergency faculty meeting tomorrow morning," from Ousmane Gueye. Both came the evening of the incident, and the faculty, despite the collective number of advanced degrees and general tech savviness, or perhaps because people simply didn't know what to do, hit the Greek chorus Reply All to Harrison's and Ousmane's emails with messages that ranged from "Outraged but standing strong!" to "Weeping for our community" (insert crying emoji). By the time Aki woke up in the morning, the inbox was a waterfall of message and replies from Wesley about Wesley.

Then again, this was de rigueur for how things worked at Wesley after a crisis: a glib note from Harrison followed by a serious talking-to from Ousmane, chased—invariably—by dozens of emails from teachers to one another before the school's director of communications, Amanda Nutley, stepped in to purge the mess like a top-of-the-line Dyson vacuum cleaner.

Perpetually clad in J.Crew suits, Amanda Nutley presided over every email that left Harrison Neal III's desk. She also arranged for "puff" stories in the style section of the *Post* about the school coaches and athletes, and increased the budget for the alumni magazine, arguing it was a good way to drum up donations. Amanda deftly warded off inquiring journalists like a too-short lob to her commanding overhand, and it was rumored, canvassed dcparentzone.com at night, posting messages to dispel people from thinking that Wesley was anything other than perfect.

Parents started crowing that Amanda was more effective than the White House press secretary, and Ousmane and Harrison began tapping her first before making any decisions, which Aki found somewhat questionable since Amanda's LinkedIn profile showed that the last position she had held was as a marketing assistant at an overpriced furniture company. But Amanda was certainly effective. Case in point: When a certain overachieving senior sued Wesley for violating her civil rights when she was not accepted to any Ivy League schools, several media outlets immediately seized upon the case like a pack of desperate hyenas. Before the story could reach the bastion of professional gossip on Page Six, Amanda threw down a gauntlet of Thor-like proportions, promising exclusive behind-the-scenes photos of one of Wesley's presidential children at a varsity softball game, making any mention of the lawsuit all but vanish.

But this crisis—a disgusting hate crime erupting like a blemish on the side of their pristine and newly built arts center? Even Amanda couldn't just scrub this one away, and Aki wonders how the school will erase what will undoubtedly become an indelible scar on the school's pristine reputation with every Google search.

Aki is used to everyday racism. Growing up, she had been teased because of her name and regularly subjected to customers in her family's store who mimicked her parents' heavy accents. Aki had grown an extra layer of skin—helpful for fending off both casual remarks and racism and critical private-school parents—but she honestly never thought something like this would happen at a place like Wesley. Despite its faults, the school prides itself on listening and learning from diverse voices. At the very least, Aki had thought her own daughter would be shielded from daily teasing. From hazing. From hate. Apparently, she was wrong. In one of the multiple emails flying about, someone had suggested that the front gate had been unlocked and that an outsider could have been responsible. That, of course, put the security staff on the defensive, saying there had been no "breach of the security perimeter" on the morning of the incident.

"Earth to Aki?" On the other end of the phone is Aki's husband, Ian.

Aki shakes her head. She's in the car with Meg on their way to school an hour earlier than usual because of the hastily called faculty meeting, and she's taken the opportunity to call Ian, who has been on a research vessel for three weeks, part of his job as an oceanographic researcher for the National Oceanic and Atmospheric Administration (NOAA).

"I'm assuming the school's idea of a resolution for the graffiti was a maybe well-intentioned but possibly completely off the mark missive from the Desk of Harrison Neal III?" Ian isn't a fan of Harrison's and thinks his emails are pretentious. Ever since Harrison's arrival ten years ago, Ian decried him as a terrible fit for a Quaker school, with his slippery politician vibe and insistence on farming out as many decisions as possible in order to fend off potential criticism. Why make a hard decision when he can fire someone else for making one in his stead? Whenever Ian marvels at Harrison's decade-long tenure, Aki reminds him that the board loves him because he raises money like Alaska produces snow.

"Right? See, Dad knows where it's at," Meg nods in agreement while slumping further down into the front seat. The emergency meeting means that Meg has to be at school earlier as well, since unlike many of the other students in her class, she doesn't have a car at her disposal. "Watch, they're not going to do anything meaningful," Meg scoffs as she whips her phone out of the hoodie pocket and starts jabbing at it with her thumbs.

"We'll see. I mean, maybe the school will look inward a little," Aki says quietly, wishing Ian would be a tad less honest about his feelings for Wesley in front of their daughter, if only to quell the growing fire of rage against the school mixed with what appears to be the onset of way-too-early senioritis. "How's Greenland?" she asks Ian.

Ian ignores Aki's segue. "The only gazing Wesley does is at its own perfect naval," he scoffs.

"Preach," Meg mumbles from inside her oversized hoodie, looking like a disgruntled Sith Lord from Ian's favorite movies. Aki peeks over to see what her daughter is looking at. Instagram, naturally.

"At least Meg is out of there in a year, and they gave her a good brain," Ian concedes.

Out of there in a year. Aki still can't believe it. She still remembers walking Meg to school the first day of Kindergarten, leaving her with an older teacher with kind eyes and sensible shoes.

"Gummy can always just live at home with us forever if no one deems her academically acceptable," Ian jokes, referring to

Meg by his favored nickname, a fusion of Meg's given name, Megumi, and his favorite candy. "Remember how long it took her to understand the difference between Washington state and Washington, DC?" he jokes. "Was it, like, freshman year she got the difference? Poor kid told everyone our nation's capital was Seattle."

"West coast is the best coast," Meg replies, though with a small grin on her face. Ian has always been her favorite parent.

"Listen, I have to run, we're drilling on an ice bed this morning," Ian chirps.

Aki is about to say goodbye when her phone beeps, indicating another call. It's her mother.

"Is that your mother?" Ian asks, ever intuitive. "Tell her I said hi, love you both!"

"Bye, Dad!" Meg responds quickly.

Aki sighs and pushes the green button on her phone.

"Aki-chan? *Genki*? How are you? How is Megumi-chan? And Ian?" She says his name *Ee-aahn*, which always makes Meg giggle.

"They're good, Mom," Aki says patiently. She can predict what's coming next.

"*Gakkou daijoubu?*" (Is Megumi doing well in school?) Her mother only speaks to her in Japanese, even after forty-some years in this country.

"Yes, Mother," she dutifully replies. She can feel Meg rolling her eyes next to her.

"*Me-ru ni henji ga naikedo.*" (Because she hasn't responded to my last email.)

"OK, I'll ask her to check her inbox. Kids really prefer texting these days." Meg nods her head vigorously as Aki says this.

"*Okaasan sonnano wakarimasen yo!*" her mother shouts. (I don't know how to text or do that TV thing in the phone!)

"FaceTime, and OK, Mom, I'll remind her."

"*Kareshi ha genki ka douka kitte ne!*" (Ask her how her boy-friend is doing!)

"Boyfriend?" Aki asks.

"*Obachan, kareshi inai yo!*" Meg responds. (Grandma, there is no boyfriend!)

"Boyfriend?" Aki asks again, peering over to Meg. It wouldn't surprise her if she had one and didn't bother to tell her. At the same time, she'd be mildly shocked if her daughter was in fact dating someone without her knowing since she sees her in school all the time.

"There is no boyfriend," Meg whispers again to Aki, who nods in response. Anyway, if Meg had a boyfriend she's sure someone on the faculty would have told her.

"OK, bye-bye!" her mother says abruptly and hangs up the phone.

"Bye," Aki says mostly to herself and thinks about her mother. After Meg was born, Aki had summoned the courage to tell her mother that the baby was not, in fact, Ian's. Her mother looked at her with a blank expression, waved her hands in front of her face as if to disagree, and asked when the two of them would get mar-ried. Her mother never asked about Meg's father and Aki never brought it up again. True to form, her mother was only interested if Meg was smart, how she was doing in school, and what she would do with her life. When Aki complained to Ian about how single-minded her mother was, Ian would laugh and say, "Fuji apples don't fall far from the proverbial trees, do they?"

Aki sighs as she turns off of McComb Street, drawing closer to the school. Her mother condoned Aki's choice of profession only after she explained that it meant that Meg would receive a top-ranked education at a fraction of the price. This was some-thing her mother could get behind, she knew. "At least you mar-ried a PhD," her mother said when Aki left her own graduate program while pregnant.

"Can you drop me at Starbucks? I'm going to meet Aiko," Meg says suddenly. They are four blocks from Wesley, waiting at a light on Wisconsin Avenue, but before Aki can say anything, Meg jumps out the door and scurries to her best friend, who is waving at them from across the street.

Aki remembers when Meg came rushing home from school in fourth grade, feverish with excitement and announcing, "I have a new best friend! She just moved here! Her name is Aiko!" The mention of the name made Aki assume that Aiko must be Japanese, a thought that tickled her. Would Meg no longer be the only Wesley student within three grades of her to have a Japanese parent? Though a common Japanese name, it turned out that Aiko was half Nordic and half Ghanaian, and her name was derived from her Swedish mother's father's name, Ekke, and a common West African surname. Meg and Aiko had been best friends since the day the family moved from Paris, where Aiko's father worked for BNP Paribas. Her mother was an artist whose works had been commissioned by the likes of Diane von Furstenberg and a Kardashian or three. They always seemed far too glamorous, but Aki and Ian grew close with them over time, even having the couple over to their cramped condo for dinner.

Aki watches as Meg and Aiko link arms and march into Starbucks as the car behind honks to get going. Having rid herself of her grumpy daughter, Aki turns the music on to her favorite, the Dave Matthews Band ("Whiny indie rock pop of the '90s, fuuun," Meg likes to say), and makes her way to the school parking lot. She laughs as she spies Jules pulling into her favorite far corner spot before exiting her massive SUV and click-clacking her way toward Aki with a sour expression on her face.

"Do we really have to deal with this right before Christmas vacation?" Jules demands.

"Is it a surprise that this place sucks?" Percy Bishop grunts as he makes his way past Jules and Aki. Percy is the upper school art teacher and an all-around grump, though no one can deny he is easy on the eyes. He reminds Aki of Alfred Enoch, an English actor that Meg and Aki had seen on stage in London a few years ago.

"Come on now, it's not *that* bad, Perce," Jules admonishes. Jules often ping-pongs back and forth between contemptuous criticism and protective praise for Wesley, making Aki wonder if her friend doesn't suffer from some sort of distorted form of occupational Stockholm Syndrome.

"Anyway, we don't say 'Christmas' at Wesley, we use the word 'holiday,'" he shoots back darkly.

"I know, I know, Perce," Jules coos, trying to smooth things over. Jules digs through her bag. "Here, honey, I made you some rice crispy treats with the Fruity Pebbles like you like them," she says, handing him a stack of goodies wrapped in parchment paper and tied with festive ribbon.

Percy munches on the treat, looking thoughtful. "Those words spray-painted on the building, though? They aren't just words, they're a threat," he says, looking serious again. "Hayashi, those words were meant for you, too" Percy says to Aki, looking at her expectantly.

Aki pauses. She's not sure what to say. She knows Percy wants a reaction, but her immediate response to this kind of thing is to be quiet, something ingrained from her since childhood.

"Remember what happened two years ago?" Percy reminds them.

Immediately she knows what he's talking about. Aki had gotten to school early on a Friday morning and walked to her office to see a poster hanging on the history office door. Students regularly posted announcements on it, but there were people in the administration who felt strongly that no one should tape posters up because the renovation of the upper school had cost $300 million and the structure was made of reclaimed wood too beautiful to mar. That morning Aki had looked at the poster and at first thought nothing of it—just another basketball player in a Lakers jersey—but then she saw that the jersey had a picture of a banana on it. She thought about just tearing it down and throwing it in the trash, but she knew there were probably similar posters everywhere (there were). Instead, she took a hard right down the hallway to find Ousmane and the head of the language arts department holding up what Aki presumed was a copy of the same poster.

"Do you remember the school's bullshit response?" Percy demands.

Percy is right, it was a bullshit response. Very much like an NBA ref, the school reviewed its security footage and promptly hauled Foster Billings into Ousmane's office while calling for an all-school "meeting of reflection." Teachers and administrators hustled all the kids into the meeting house, where a student would sporadically rise and talk about their feelings regarding the incident, even though from what Aki could tell, only a few students had actually seen it. Of course, those who did manage to witness the actual posters took pictures and uploaded them onto their social media sites of choice, and from there the rumors spread nimbly. Aki wonders now if this is what instigated the school's policy of banning phones on campus.

As for Foster, he insisted that it was all just a joke, that he had done it because he hated the Lakers, and didn't think about the loaded reference. In Foster's case, it was hard to know where idiocy ended and prejudice began. Everyone knew that Foster was never going to suffer any real consequences; his father was once the ambassador to France and served on at least a dozen corporate boards. He was untouchable. True to form, Ousmane suspended Foster from classes for a single week and asked him to write an essay of apology (read by whom, Aki never found out). But possibly the most effective punishment was suspension from the boys' lacrosse team for the remainder of the season with the justification that the school "shouldn't be represented on the field by one of unsportsmanlike character." Incredibly, the incident never got leaked to the press. Maybe sometimes Amanda was worth the money—at least this is what Harrison Neal would say, anyway.

Thinking back on it, it wasn't that Aki hadn't cared about the posters; they were immature, not to mention racist. Her refusal to respond the way Percy wants her to, with indignation and fury, was because she had been groomed to ignore such incidents. Daly City, California, where Aki had grown up, was majority Asian, though mostly Chinese and Filipino, but it wasn't resistant to prejudice. She remembers when her father came home from the golf course, agitated and lashing out, sputtering how an older white man had rushed at him with a club shouting something about Pearl Harbor. Her father had yelled back at the man, explaining that he was American and that his own father had been interned, but it did no good. It hadn't made him feel better—as her mother pointed out, it only riled him and his antagonism up even more.

For every snide comment from a passerby or even a direct confrontation like the one her father had on a public golf course, Aki's mother would just cluck her tongue and say, "Ignore it. Fighting only means hurting yourself." Was this true? Aki had wondered at the time. Since then, both consciously and subconsciously, Aki adopted her mother's passive approach. When she saw the poster taped on her door at Wesley, she felt the familiar flash of anger, which she gulped down.

"We all know how this is going to end," Percy declares, as if reading her mind. He kicks a stray pebble across the garage, which is so empty you can hear the tiny stone skitter across the asphalt.

"Then *why* do you stay, Percy?" Jules asks, her tone not mean but curious. They both like Percy, who is not only a teacher but a well-established local artist. He's also never afraid to call out the school on their behalf, his worst characteristic merely being that he's a grump more often than not.

"Because it's my school too," Percy explains, and Aki finds herself nodding along with him on this one. "Thanks for the treats, Jules," he says, giving her a small smile.

"Maybe the security footage will turn up something?" Jules suddenly suggests, but Percy just shoots her a look that says, *Sure, uh-huh.* "What? It did before!" Jules insists.

Percy gives both of them a hard look before saying, "The posters were inside the school. The graffiti is on the news. Mark my words, the school is going to try to sweep this one under the rug."

Jules and Aki don't say anything as the three of them make their way slowly through the garage and up the stairs, filing into the auditorium and taking seats in the back. The moment they sit, Jules whips out her knitting needles while Percy unfolds a copy of *Art in America*, noshing on his rice crispy treat. As much as she hates faculty meetings, the A student in her won't allow Aki to do anything but fold her hands in her lap and listen to whoever is talking.

She watches as Ousmane walks across the stage to the lectern. Aki remembers when Ousmane started as head of the upper school. He quickly endeared himself to the faculty by listening to them without talking down to them—and admitting when he was wrong. Two things that were apparently beneath Harrison, who was more likely to plow past a member of his staff on his way to wine and dine high-profile donor parents.

"Faculty, thank you for gathering so early in the morning," Ousmane starts, his velvety voice rolling though the assembled crowd, some grumbling under their breaths. "We," he says as he extends his hand toward the front row, occupied, Aki assumes, by Harrison, Amanda, and possibly members of the board, "are here to act as a sounding board and provide our faculty with the tools to report and address harms caused by these latest events."

Percy grunts, though his eyes remain on an article about modern Iranian art.

"First, we want you to know that we are investigating yesterday's *incident* to the fullest degree possible, and we have not ruled out the possibility that an individual outside of our community may have breached security and vandalized the school." Ousmane gazes out at the crowd, hands clasped in front of his chest.

"You have got to be shitting me," Percy says under his breath, flipping the pages of his magazine. "Who is getting into a locked campus during the day?" he adds while bending over his satchel to retrieve another of Jules's treats. As he noisily opens it, Grayson Manne, the history department's newest hire, rushes into the auditorium and noisily claims the empty seat next to Percy.

"What did I miss? Did I miss anything?" Grayson asks while taming the flyaway curls near his ears. Grayson is as young as she was when she started Wesley, and as much as the school likes to tout its diversity, it also has a hard time turning down a Yale-by-way-of-Saint-Paul's grad who is clearly trying to find himself by teaching about the great civilizations of Rome and Athens. After working as a ski lift operator in Aspen, of course. Gangly and good-looking, Aki suspects that he's already caught the eye of some of the seniors. Jules has adopted him as her pet, but now she shushes him while leaning over Percy to hand him a rice crispy treat.

Grayson shrinks in his seat while noisily unwrapping the snack. Ousmane scans the crowd. "As many of you know, the stature of our institution makes it ripe for criticism, and it is an unfortunate reality that we do receive quite a bit of scrutiny from the outside world."

Jules leans over abruptly. "That's Ousmane's way of saying the Proud Boys send us hate mail," she snorts, and Percy growls "Mm-hmm" in agreement. Aki wonders if there is any merit to Ousmane's claims.

"However, an important facet of navigating through this difficult *incident*—"

"Why don't we just call a spade a spade?" Jules demands.

Grayson pipes up. "To call a fig a fig and trough a trough," he says, looking up at the bewildered expressions. "Erasmus translated the saying from Greek to Latin, but some believe he changed *trough* to *spade*."

"That's nice, honey," Jules says.

Percy interjects, "The word *spade* was used colloquially by Black writers in the 1920s to refer to other Black folks. But it slowly morphed into a word with discriminatory connotations through the end of the twentieth century."

Jules opens her mouth in surprise. "I honestly didn't know that."

"But now we do!" Grayson says kindly.

Percy nods at them and settles back into his seat, casting a wary eye toward the stage where Ousmane continues his speech. "We must unite as a faculty in our response. And now I will turn to Amanda Nutley, our director of communications." Ousmane bows slightly and backs away from the podium as Amanda strides with great purpose on her nude patent heels, slamming a pile of manilla folders on the lectern, making the room jump from the loud thump emitted through the microphone.

"These are really good, Jules, thanks!" Grayson says cheerfully, appearing almost ignorant of what is going on around him.

"Hello, Wesley faculty. I have the unfortunate task of educating all of you on the basics of crisis management," Amanda says crisply. "First, the correct answer to any inquiry from a journalist or media outlet is 'No comment.'"

"And so it begins," Percy says with a scowl.

Amanda looks out at, or rather, down upon, the assembled faculty members. "I'm sure none of you wants to put the school into the position of being liable for this . . . *incident*," she warns, as Jules rolls her eyes and snorts. "Second, we have temporarily blocked all outside calls from coming directly to any faculty phones. I know that all of you are used to this." Amanda is clearly referring to the Willow Jones debacle, when not only were phone numbers expunged from the school website, but a central operator was tasked with answering every phone call and connecting callers to offices, but only when deemed absolutely necessary. "Finally, we will be monitoring emails."

A groan comes up from the crowd. Though Wesley made it perfectly clear that student emails from school accounts were privy to continual monitoring, Jules has always suspected that the school reads faculty communication going in and out of the school as well. She never uses her school account when she can avoid it, and usually ends up communicating with people, including parents, from a personal email account and using the cell service on her phone. "Just call me Hillary Clinton!" she likes to say.

"It is important to us, and to your reputation as faculty of this school, to create a united front," Amanda says, meaning, of course, a *silent* front. She collects her items and starts to walk back to her seat when she remembers one more commandment. "And please, faculty, nothing on social media."

"That is where I draw the line! I need to update my stories. I want to regram Stanley Tucci's rendition of 'Paris in the Springtime,'" Jules retorts. Aki isn't sure if her friend is joking or not. Wesley strongly discouraged teachers from having public social media accounts, not that this applied to Aki, since she was still using an old AOL email account, something Jules and Meg liked to deride. "Lordy, how much more of this do we have to listen to? It's not like we're the ones that did this!" Jules complains.

"They have to make it seem like they're doing *something*," Percy explains. "And forget voicing an opinion, they don't even want us to have one."

"Like the Great Purge," Grayson says. "Stalin stopped the presses too," he adds, munching on his snack and looking chipper, in contrast to the faculty around him. "Civil liberties are a dangerous tool for the oppressed."

As if on cue, Harrison Neal rises from his seat and walks to the stage. He is in his late fifties with graying hair, and if Aki's feeling charitable, she might say that on a good day he resembles Greg Kinnear.

"Well, if it isn't Caligula himself," Jules mutters, making Grayson sit up.

"He died of syphilis, you know," Grayson whispers.

"Naughty *and* evil," Jules quips.

"Friends," Harrison starts, "this is not who we are." Harrison concludes gravely and lets the room go silent for what feels like a very long time.

"That's . . . it?" Jules whispers incredulously.

"Let's hope so," Percy responds, barely looking up from yet another article.

Aki thinks about Harrison's email that was sent out to the student body the night before. Meg read it out loud at the dinner table, her voice dripping with sarcasm.

"'To the student body at Wesley Friends, Move Forward into the Light means acting as a role model not only for your peers but for all students in our community and beyond. The way you act will reflect upon your generation, and as future leaders and thinkers, we implore you, think before you speak, question before you act, stop before you anger.' I'd say it's a little late for that," Meg huffed before stuffing the rest of her empanada into her mouth.

Aki watches as Harrison paces the stage, clearly thinking about the next cheesy line he can drop in the faculty's laps.

"Let our silence show our strength," Harrison announces, looking out at the auditorium before giving everyone a small wave. Grayson dutifully waves back, making Aki giggle.

Jules bends over Aki's lap and announces, "That's Harrison-speak for shut the F up, y'all," returning to her knitting needles, making them clitter-clatter away.

Then Harrison adds something that makes Aki open her mouth in surprise.

"Faculty, we will *not only* unearth the individual who has done this, we will make sure to *purge* them from our community." He stares at the crowd, his gaze fanning out across the assembled teachers before stopping, unsettlingly, on Aki. Then he closes his eyes, clears his throat, and takes a breath before finally announcing, "Faculty, this is a promise I will see through."

★   ★   ★

The faculty begin a slow exodus from the auditorium, forlorn in their realization that they still have a full day of teaching ahead of them.

"Uh, so what was with the dramatics?" Jules asks, poking Aki in the back with a knitting needle as they file out. "I didn't know Harrison took anything that seriously other than his golf game."

Aki feels unsettled and doesn't know how to respond. Between the actual vandalism, Amanda Nutley's curt instructions of a communications lockdown, and Harrison's uncharacteristically emotive response, she wonders if the school is actually taking the incident seriously. Despite Ian and Meg's suspicion that this incident was going to end up as yet another embarrassment that the school would simply sweep under the rug, Harrison's stern proclamation makes her think otherwise and, for reasons unbeknownst to herself, also makes her nervous.

"I hope they mean it," Percy says, looking back at the two of them as they make their way en masse up the midcentury-modern theater aisles. "It's the first time—"

"They sounded legit? I agree," Jules pipes up. "Let's take it one step further! Let's give back the family's money once we figure out who did it! Then we'll really know the school means business!"

"Are you serious?" Aki asks. She has a hard time imagining Harrison writing a check for anything other than the new campus expansion plans, his latest passion project.

"Like I think the school is serious about anything other than its college matriculation list!" Jules shoots back. "Gotta go sort out the risers for the choir performance since I'm the only one who cares about the *arts* around here." She looks at Percy and adds, "OK, one of two who care. You coming with?"

Percy nods and after a brisk wave, Jules zooms across the courtyard with him in tow, leaving Grayson and Aki in their trek back toward the upper school building. When they enter the wood-paneled, blond-colored, and tastefully redone hallways, they immediately notice something odd. Though the senior hallway is filled with students, some sitting on the floor with backs against lockers, others standing in small clusters, they hear only silence. It is as if they've entered a hermetically sealed world, no one making a sound, which stands in great contrast to the usual chaotic babbling that permeates the hallway on any given morning.

Grayson and Aki stop in their tracks. They look at the students, then at each other, then back to the seniors. Then they realize that the students are all looking at something on their phones. Aki stares in wonderment at their heads bowed in unison as if engaged in collective prayer, with a sinking suspicion that they are all looking at something they possibly shouldn't be. All of a sudden a swell of voices—some laughing, some gasping, others saying "Damn" or "Ouch"—rings through the hallway. Aki is desperate to reach out and grab one of their phones. It's not lost on her that none of them are supposed to have their phones at all, but it's not a surprise that they would be flouting the rules with the entire faculty corralled in a meeting.

"Is it just me, or does this feel like the usual Wesley overreaction?" one student says. Aki recognizes Felix's deep British voice, and their eyes meet briefly before he averts his gaze.

"Why? They're not wrong," a female voice responds.

"Really? Do you think so?" Felix argues back.

Aki can't tell from their debate what either student is talking about, or which side they are arguing. She can't help but stare at Felix, now tall and muscular, but still one of the more elusive students. Plenty of faculty have children in the school, but unlike Meg, most of them try to disappear into the background, like Felix.

"Please, it's not like Wesley is ground zero for right-wing extremists," another shoots back.

Aki's head jerks toward the last comment. She and Grayson exchange looks, and Grayson leans over to one of the girls and asks in a bright voice, "What are you all talking about?"

She looks up and smiles at Grayson. "Oh, well, a local television station interviewed some Wesley students about the graffiti," she explains, a blush coming across her face.

"Can I take a look?" Grayson asks cheerfully as the girl smiles and places her phone in front of him.

"My parents are so sick of this woke stuff," Aki hears a student say as Grayson takes the phone from the student. "They say the school should just focus on academics." She thinks its Holly's son Zach, but she can't be sure.

"How can you say that?" another student demands. Aki forces herself not to try to identify the voices for fear they'll stop talking if they notice her listening. "You know it's probably some dumb jock who did that shit!"

"I am offended by that comment," Felix says, but he has a smile on his face as he does.

"Take it seriously, man, it's messed up!" another student protests.

Do they mean the graffiti? Aki wonders, furtively looking around the hallway to identify the voices.

"Well, I will say, all of this makes the school look bad, and it makes *us* look bad," Felix points out. "And I didn't get into Penn early so I'd like to keep looking good, thanks."

"It's going to take a lot of makeup to keep you looking good, King Charles," a boy jokes as Felix takes a pretend-swing at him, as Zach guffaws.

"Um, Aki . . ." Grayson starts slowly as he looks up from the screen. "I think you better take a look at this."

◆ 4 ◆

"DD came home and told me that kids use racial slurs all the time.
How can this be going on at a place like Wesley?"
—Concerned Wesley parent, dcparentzone.com

DECEMBER IN WASHINGTON, DC, can be a chaotic mélange of weather: warm enough to rouse the plum blossoms on one day only to be chastised by frost and snow the next, followed by weeks of a low-hanging gray ceiling. Today's sky is a depressing dove color that reminds Aki of growing up in Daly City in Northern California, minus the snow, of course. Sandwiched between two of the wealthiest communities in the world, San Francisco to the north and Woodside to the south, Daly City is the stretch of Interstate 280 that is perpetually shrouded by fog. Woodside and its sister, Palo Alto, felt like Daly City's beautiful stepsisters. Sunny and lined with cyprus and palm trees, not to mention multimillion-dollar houses, their public schools filled with not just overachievers but hyperachievers. No one went to private school around there—she remembers reading the local paper about how Henry M. Gunn, one of the public schools in Palo Alto, sent eight students to Harvard, twelve to Princeton, and ten to MIT in a single year. Palo Alto High School sent close to a dozen to the Ivies, not to mention ten students a year to Stanford.

Aki knew all of this because she was once a teen obsessed with getting into college—and by virtue, out of Daly City. Her mother was a stereotypical Asian mother in that there was no acceptable grade other than an A, and Aki, in turn, worked like a stereotypical Asian student, which meant in constant overdrive. She lived less than a mile from her high school, on Westridge Avenue, a steep, meandering road lined with fifties-style bungalows, boring two-storied stucco homes built over a one-car garage, all built in rows snaking up and down the hills. Whenever she sees the cover of Joan Didion's *Where I Was From*, she can't help but think of ascending and descending those very hills to school every day. Her parents had scraped and scrimped to buy their modest three-bedroom stucco house, which on the rare clear day had a view of San Francisco, a sliver and a slice from the top of the Presidio and the Golden Gate Bridge, just enough to be a daily reminder of the existence of something more beautiful, and possibly more important, than Daly City.

Westmoor High School was no Henry M. Gunn, and there was no express elevator to Harvard or Princeton. Her parents were thrilled when she got into Berkeley on a scholarship, but Aki had been disappointed to land so close to home, though she did eventually learn to love the East Bay with its aging hippies and old standby of Telegraph Avenue. But every time she crossed the Bay Bridge and disappeared back home into the dense fog of Daly City, it made her even more determined to find her way to the East Coast and to an Ivy League school. She was not immune to the images of heavy wool sweaters, leaf-covered gothic buildings, and brick pathways dense with undergraduates from places like Exeter and Wesley. Her romanticized notions of centuries-old libraries and apple-picking season came partially true when she eventually secured a graduate spot at the University of Pennsylvania. When she finally arrived, however, she discovered that though it was part of the Ivy League, Penn was also very much in a part of Philadelphia that was more an episode of *The Wire* than *Love Story*. Though the terminus of her graduate career came more quickly than anticipated, it was there she met Ian, and, she knows, what helped her land her job at Wesley.

Though she sold the school to her skeptical mother as the best way for Meg to access a top-ranked education, the fact of the matter was that Wesley ended up as an unplanned salvation in the contorted road that was her own educational experience. She spent her youth longing for the trappings of a private school, then passed her time in college dreaming of an elite doctoral program. What ended up warping her aspirations for that PhD?

Meg.

An unplanned pregnancy a year into grad school and barely being able to juggle her coursework with a baby, Aki somehow figured out that if she could find a job where her child could also be cared for, she might be able to eke out a living. Exit dreams of the academe and enter Wesley and its heavily subsidized childcare for teachers and subsequently reduced tuition for enrolled children. Aki paid so little in fees that never in her thirteen years at Wesley has she told anyone the price tag of her child's education. During that time with the school, she has seen various teachers come and go, a different head of school, one cheating scandal, and various firings, but she was so desperate and grateful for what Wesley had provided her and Meg that she'd never dare leave.

She remembers her first year of teaching, being so incredibly intimidated by the parents that she actually let one of them rearrange the chairs and desks in her classroom during a parent-teacher conference. "Darling, this just makes much better sense," the mother clucked as she sweated and rolled up her sleeves while hauling chairs from one corner to another. "You can't expect these kids to learn if they're distracted by things," she commanded Aki, never fully explaining what she meant by *things* or how those *things* would distract the students. Aki just stood and gaped, hoping that would be the end of the meeting and that she wouldn't have to inform the mother that her son had been caught plagiarizing another student's paper. Even still, the school has always been a calling, a master, and a salvation merged into one.

Now Aki stands in her faculty office with her twenty-something coworker in the school she has called home since she herself was a young parent and her seventeen-year-old was but a preschooler, as Grayson's words ring in her ears: *Aki, I think you better take a look at this.*

The walls begin to fade away the moment Grayson clicks on a YouTube link. On the screen she sees what looks like her daughter, standing on Wisconsin Avenue, the school directly behind her, being interviewed by local reporter Joanna Javier-Hernandez. A chyron travels across the bottom of the screen with the words, *"Hate speech roils White House private school."*

Aki can barely contain her panic as Grayson turns up the volume.

"I'm *glad* the school got vandalized!" Meg says boldly into the mic.

Aki can feel herself shrivel. *Where is Meg? What is going on?* Panic rises upward from her stomach.

"Why?" Joanna asks hungrily. "Why would you want to see your school disfigured like this?"

"The graffiti forces the school to admit it's not perfect. That it needs to change, and that there are some very bad people within the school itself—"

"What do you mean?" Joanna interrupts. "Teachers? Are they doing things to provoke this?"

Aki groans, feeling herself sink a little lower into the floor. She realizes that Meg must have seen the cameras on her way from Starbucks to the school and made herself available for this impromptu interview.

"No. Not teachers. *Students*." Meg intones. "The chosen ones with the right last names—"

Just then, the camera swings wildly as Ousmane enters into the picture. Aki watches intently as he bends down and whispers something into Meg's ear, then stands up straight and stares into the camera sternly. Meg, for her part, looks off into the distance as if she's waiting for a Metro bus to arrive.

Joanna pushes the mic into Ousmane's face. "Ousmane Gueye, head of upper school, do you have any comment on the racial slur that's been scrawled on your building?" Aki is impressed that Joanna knows his full name. Then again, he's probably as important as the Speaker of the House by virtue of being part of the Wesley administration.

He stares at her with a blank expression before saying, "No comment."

Aki thinks she can hear Amanda Nutley cheering somewhere in the building.

Joanna turns her attention back to Meg. "Even students have the right to free speech! Is there anything else you'd like to add?"

"No, she does not," Ousmane says decisively, then clears his throat. Meg meets his gaze and turns on her heel, heading back toward school grounds. Aki wonders what he said to her to make her so quiet.

As the clip ends, Aki realizes she's been holding her breath and exhales, staring at the blank screen, wondering what she should do. Grayson removes his Patagonia vest and places it over the back of his chair before asking kindly, "Are you doing OK? That was a lot for one morning."

Aki can't stop thinking about how unbelievable it all is, starting with the graffiti, the hateful message serving as a sharp spear of reality piercing their privileged bubble. She knows how the inside of the Wesley bubble can actually feel: pressurized, rumor-filled, rife with indignation, and despite the occasional Foster Billings, it usually also feels *safe*, especially from the out-side world. Right now though, Aki is scared that Meg is going to get into trouble for speaking to the press, the first cardinal sin of Wesley Friends. While some presidential offspring who attended other schools regularly made headlines when they skipped a cur-few or got drunk at a party, Amanda had managed to keep the child of president number forty-two out of the spotlight until she herself arranged for a puff piece in *People* magazine when the girl was an Amherst-bound senior. Meg's unauthorized interview, on the other hand, is sure to replay at 5:00 and 11:00.

"Hey, can I use your computer?" Meg bounds in, hair wet from the snow and pant hems dirty from standing outside all morning. "Hey, Mr. Manne, how are you?" she asks Grayson affably, as if nothing out of the ordinary has happened. Aki gawks. *What happened to all that anger?*

"That sure was some TV interview," Grayson responds.

"Ugh, Joanna Javier-Hernandez is such a wannabe Hoda, but at least we got the word out," Meg responds.

Aki watches Meg and Grayson banter, feeling her anxiety mount. "Meg!" she says sharply, unsure of what to say next. It's not like Meg can go back in time and undo her interview.

"Mother." Meg responds dryly, nudging Aki out of her seat and planting herself in front of her mother's computer. "Just a sec," she insists as she starts typing.

"Why do you have to use my computer?" Aki complains as she moves to the empty chair next to her own desk.

"No cell phones during school hours!" Meg chirps while clicking away.

Just as Aki is about to say something along the lines of *You really need to be careful about what you say*, Meg pipes up again. "Hey, Mr. Manne, word to the wise, I'd make your social private because I know for a fact some freshmen were ogling you the other day." Meg then opens Aki's desk drawer, takes out a bag of popcorn and tears it open, eating hungrily. "There are some hardcore Manne stans out there," she says, raising her left eyebrow with a small grin and making Grayson nod gravely.

"Meg! No social media!" Aki admonishes, realizing what her daughter is doing on her computer. "And don't spill!" she adds, watching her daughter eat messily at her desk, popcorn kernels jumping from her lips like sailors abandoning ship.

"Well, if they didn't block it on our computers, I wouldn't need to use yours," Meg says before tipping her head back and emptying the rest of the popcorn into her mouth. She flings her bag over her shoulder and stands to leave, saying "Bye, Mother," without a backward glance. "See ya, Mr. Manne," she calls as she opens the door.

Grayson, who is now clicking away at his own computer, looks up at her with an uncharacteristically concerned expression on his face and says to her solemnly. *"Optimum est pati quod emendare non possis."*

Meg stops, propping the door open with her foot. *"Si vis pacem, para bellum!"* She declares, smiling at him and exiting the room.

"What did that mean?" Aki can't help but ask, craning her neck to watch Meg in the hallway screeching with delight at something Aiko is showing her on her phone.

"Optimum est pati quod emendare non possis," Grayson repeats. "It means 'best to endure what you cannot change.' The kids here are smart, aren't they? I didn't learn this stuff until college."

This, of course, is an understatement; the students at Wesley are unequivocally brilliant, single-mindedly focused, and also somewhat terrifying, particularly in the high school, where the brightest kids from the area public schools and beyond come with their perfect GPAs, perfect SSAT scores, plans for world domination (and, natch, assumed Ivy League acceptances). The "lifers," the kids who start in nursery school and continue in the school through graduation, like Meg, or Felix and Zach, are more of a mixed bag. Some of them turn out to be high achievers, others not so much. The kids who really can't cut it are "counseled out," private-school parlance for "asked to leave due to bad grades," since the school doesn't want to have to deal with anyone who might inadvertently lower their average SAT scores or cheapen their college matriculation list.

"If you want peace, prepare for war," Grayson declares, expression darkening.

"What?" Aki asks, returning her attention to Grayson as Meg disappears down the hallway.

"*Si vis pacem, para bellum*," he repeats gravely. "That's what Meg said. If you want peace, prepare for war."

Aki wrinkles her brow. The last time Meg took Latin was as a freshman before quitting and declaring it a "dead white dude's language" and picking up Chinese. Aki moves back to her computer, wondering what Meg was looking at, but of course the screen has been closed. Her phone pings again, this time with multiple !!!!!! and emojis from Jules.

"Aki?" A deep voice makes her jump, and her phone goes clattering on the floor. Aki dives down to retrieve it. "Shit! I mean yes! I mean, yes?" Aki lies on the floor feeling very stupid as she stares up at Ousmane, who is standing in the doorway of their office.

"We would like you to join us in the conference room," he says, the corners of his mouth twitching upward.

"Of course," Aki says, standing up and smoothing out her clothes, the words *Am I in trouble?* running through her head. "I have class—"

"Mr. Manne will cover your next period," Ousmane says, motioning to the door. "If that is OK," he says to Grayson in a way that conveys *But of course that will be OK.* Grayson nods solemnly.

"Oh, you mean come right now. With you," Aki says, feeling very stupid.

Ousmane's expression remains unchanged. "Thank you. Quickly, please," he says, waiting patiently. Aki's phone continually pings with notifications, probably more texts and links about Meg's up-close-and-personal with Joanna Javier-Hernandez. *Shit.* Aki places her cell on the desk and mentally runs through Wesley's Student Code of Conduct. Meg spoke out of turn, but surely it's not against school policy.

Aki's feet are heavy as she slinks forward, and she can feel herself shrinking as she follows Ousmane out of the office like a caboose trundling behind a self-assured locomotive, mouthing "Thank you" to Grayson.

Aki overlapped with Ousmane on the teaching staff for several years before his six-year graduate school absence and subsequent return as upper school head. While they had been friendly, he had always been somewhat reserved, not just with her but with everyone, putting professional distance between himself and the other teachers. She supposes this inborn trait also made him perfect for academic administration, boundaries being the most important protection against the litany of daily parental complaints and faculty demands. That and his ability to stay unruffled.

In the past few years, however, Ousmane had opened his emotional doors to her in bits and pieces, occasionally asking for advice on school matters or insights on certain students. "I trust your judgment here," he would say to her when he sought her counsel. "We need to stand together," he would often say.

Today, however, feels like she's being *sent* to the principal's office, instead of walking down the hall with Ousmane as a peer. They hang a left into the conference room, a large space echoing the Shaker aesthetic found everywhere on campus, decorated

only with black-and-white photographs of the old school buildings and a portrait of Thomas Wesley, the founder of Wesley
Friends. When Aki enters, she sees Amanda Nutley, who flicks
through her smartphone making *tsk* sounds and looking vexed.
She looks up at Ousmane and Aki as they enter the room, her
hazel eyes aglow with agitation.

"Oh, good. I just off the phone with the board," Amanda
declares. "It's important they're in the loop."

While some in the community cling to the belief that
appointment to the board of governors at a school like Wesley
is a reward for being a major donor, this is not the only ticket to
becoming part of the inner circle of decision-makers. The fact
of the matter is that rich parents cost less than a dime a dozen at
a place like this. The school, and certainly Harrison Neal himself, likes to populate the board with people who will serve it in
some way, not simply as a reward for an annual fund donation.
Hit with a lawsuit from a disgruntled parent whose child did
not get accepted to enough elite schools? Make sure you have
enough lawyers on the board. Racked with repeated bad press
like when the school announced it was breaking ground on a
campus expansion that meant kicking senior citizens out of an
assisted-living home? Make sure to have a PR guru on the board
that Amanda can tap. Need to send a message to the alums that
diversity is a top priority? Have a school board that looks like the
UN (never mind that the school has never *not* had a white male as
a head of school). Of course, if you need your contract renewed
by the board? Fill it with your rich pals.

The school seemingly dangles board seats over the heads of
parents as some sort of reward, and the people actually on the
board may feel like they get to be part of a crucial vote in things
like the approval of a soccer field—but only if they do their time
and provide an in-kind service. Aki also knows that Harrison

Neal III's ideal board members are the ones who are well connected *and* available, making them more accessible to his whims,
and to Amanda's midday phone calls, apparently. Aki looks
around the cavernous room and is surprised to see Percy sitting at
the end of the long conference table looking downright agitated,
slumped in his seat like a student about to be reprimanded.

"Great, let's begin," Amanda announces as Aki and Ousmane
take seats across from her.

"With what? I know you might think that an art class can
run on any old sub, but they can't. They aren't artists," Percy
says pointedly, making Aki nervous. It's not in her genetic code
to challenge authority. She hears her mother's voice in her head:
Respect those above you, teach those below.

"I'll just cut to the chase then," Amanda says in a clipped
tone, ignoring Percy, who scowls so deeply that Aki is afraid his
face might crack in half. "We've got a PR problem on our hands."

"You think?" Percy responds.

Amanda's expression remains neutral as she continues. "As part
of our response, Harrison has decided to establish a task force."

Task force. The last one Aki was part of was in response to a
raft of cheating among the students. When it appeared that some
seniors were getting off while others weren't (read: spawn of the
wealthy and influential, or at a place like Wesley, the *more* wealthy
and influential), the school convened a task force to address equity
in the school's response, which ended up being the usual slap on
the wrist. Someone correctly pointed out that a task force is just a
junior varsity committee, meaning it was a slapdash organization
cobbled together to make people feel better, and here is Amanda
Nutley proposing that Aki and Percy lead a task force together
somehow, but on what, Aki is still not sure.

Percy lets out a sarcastic laugh. "Right, the two nonwhite
folks have to represent, right?" He says, patting his fist on his

chest, "Keep Wesley a Little Nonwhite, huh?" He laughs, shaking his head.

Aki looks at Percy then back to Amanda and Ousmane, feeling both relieved that the meeting doesn't seem to be about her daughter, the student-agitator, but disappointed at the same time. *This can't be what Harrison meant by "making a promise" to address the incident, can it?* she thinks incredulously. *Scraping up a few minority teachers on staff and parading them in front of God knows who?* She supposes that Amanda's line of thinking is: if the school is being accused of housing racist students, who better to head a task force than two minorities? Then again, this type of hackneyed response is almost knee-jerk. Aki thinks about how many times she herself has been on the marketing materials for the school—on the application pamphlet, the alumni magazine, the posters in the admissions hallway. It's so obvious that she doesn't even notice it anymore, though Meg loves to point it out whenever she can: "Aw, look, there you are, poster child for Woke Wesley! Maybe some nice family will adopt you!" Then curtly reminding her, "The school is exploiting you, Mother."

"I'm not sure how comfortable this makes me feel," Aki starts slowly, but what she's really thinking about is how Meg will have an absolute field day with this. "Shouldn't we focus more on who actually spray-painted the building? Has anything turned up on the security footage?"

Ignoring Aki, Amanda raises one eyebrow at them before peering back down at her phone and reading whatever is on the screen with great seriousness, a sign, Aki supposes, that Amanda's part of the conversation is finished.

"I am almost certain that Harrison Neal cannot tell the difference between me and Marshall Price," Percy responds. Marshall Price is an upper school math teacher and one of three young

Black men on the teaching staff. "I'm the one that doesn't coach football," Percy adds with snark.

"Mr. Bishop, that is enough," Ousmane reprimands, though in a frankly lackadaisical tone, lending partial credence to Percy's claim. "You've been chosen because you both have *ideas* about how the school should run, and as such, we'd like to see you rise to this challenge."

Aki has no idea what Ousmane is referring to—Percy might have ideas, but she really doesn't.

"That said," Amanda interjects, looking up from her phone, "we need you both to follow a script."

"No, thanks, I'm out," Percy says, putting both hands on the blond oak table, about to push his seat backward.

"Not a script," Ousmane says smoothly, glancing at Amanda then back at Percy and Aki. "An outline. We have a rough idea of how this task force should run, and if we implement any programmatic or policy changes, they would be for the purposes of refocusing the future of the school's philosophy on matters of this nature."

Aki looks at Percy, whose expression reads *Wuh?* She almost laughs. Ousmane's play-both-sides, weekend leadership-seminar-speak works well on the parents, but she's pretty sure it will have a zero-to-negative effect on the millennial sitting next to her. True to form, Percy cocks his head, raises his eyebrows, looks at Amanda then at Ousmane, and says quite simply, "No." Then pushes back from the table and exits the room.

Ousmane and Amanda exchange a wordless glance, then refocus on Aki. Her chest tightens as Ousmane zeroes in on her.

"Regrettably, what Percy did not stay to hear is that we are seriously considering altering the way the school addresses harm as a result of these incidents. And we want you to be in charge," he declares simply.

Aki feels Ousmane and Amanda watching her, waiting for her response, when suddenly she hears two voices quarreling in her head: Ian saying, "Don't do it!" and her mother, telling her, "Your bosses are asking you, of course you will do this." Even before she can respond she feels her head bobbing up and down ever so slightly. Yukiko 1, Ian 0.

Aki suddenly stops nodding, making Amanda and Ousmane freeze in their seats. "You aren't asking me to do this because my daughter is—" she trails off. If by some miracle Amanda hasn't seen the interview with Joanna, she doesn't want to be the one to bring it up. She thinks about it another minute, then understands what is going on in the room. Her daughter accuses the school of racism on TV. The school's response? We can't be racist, her own mother is leading our task force! Aki stops nodding her head and starts shaking it.

"Who is your daughter?" Amanda asks, looking up from her cell, tapping her nails impatiently on the oak table.

"It's just a coincidence, Aki," Ousmane inserts quickly, clearly understanding what Aki was about to say, while Amanda goes back to scrolling without another word. Aki feels like grabbing Amanda's phone and throwing it against Thomas Wesley's portrait on the wall.

"Aki," Ousmane says, leaning on his forearms. "We feel you are the best person for the job and that you will work well with those in the administration. *I* feel like you are the best person," he emphasizes, making Aki feel momentarily chuffed. She hates to admit it, but praise from a superior still affirms her. "The school will, as promised, address the incident and reprimand the person involved fully. But we are asking you to be the public face of our community response."

Amanda suddenly sits up straight while letting out a violent, "Shit!" Amanda's usually imperturbable expression is replaced with what looks oddly like fear. Ousmane and Aki sit in silence for what feels like an eternity before Amanda looks up from her screen to explain, "Someone's set up an Instagram account."

No one says anything. Then suddenly Grayson's voice runs through Aki's mind: *If you want peace, prepare for war.* Trying to keep the trepidation out of her voice, she finally croaks, "About what?"

Amanda's eyes are wild with worry. "About *this*," she hisses.

♦ 5 ♦

"Overheard in the hallway: A popular white girl called her Black guy friend 'her slave.' WTF"

—*Anonymous student, PoC@Wesley*

"MEGUMI ALICE BROWN!" ALL Aki sees is red as she opens the door to their condo and tears through the living room. "SHOW YOURSELF!" she yells as she makes her way down the hallways, flinging doors open and feeling like a character from a movie, like a masked killer hunting for prey. "WHERE ARE YOU?"

"SURPRISE!" a deep voice booms. Aki screams in fright, tumbling to the floor.

"Oh, honey!" Ian cries as he bends down.

"Ian," Aki looks at him and swears she sees stars orbiting his face. "What are you doing here? Why aren't you in Greenland?"

"Research vessel sprang a leak and we had to get towed! Got lucky and caught a flight home from Kangerlussuaq."

Aki sucks in a breath. "What do you mean, sprang a leak? Did you guys sink?" She slowly sits up and he crouches down to hug her. She always worries when he's away.

"Nothing that dramatic, but NOAA thought we should have another vessel brought in, so we have two weeks off."

Aki is so grateful for his words that she starts tearing up. She realizes with her reaction just how tired and anxious she's felt in his absence. Always her mooring, life is easier with Ian at home.

"What is this? No crying now, the boat is fine!" he jokes.

Aki laughs, then remembers why she's so stressed: Meg. "MEGUMI! WHERE ARE YOU?!" She jumps up off the floor, knocking Ian back on his behind.

"Gummy will be back soon—I sent her out to pick up Thai food for dinner as a treat," Ian explains.

"Does she have her phone?" Aki demands.

"Isn't it tethered to her soul at this point? I am my phone and my phone is me," Ian jokes. "Come on, let's have a glass of wine and stare into one another's eyes," he says as he pulls her into the living room. Aki uses her free hand to try to retrieve her phone from her bag to call her daughter when the door bursts open, revealing Meg, struggling with two bags of takeout.

"Despite fully understanding that eighty percent of Uber drivers use the platform as a second job to supplement what is probably an unsustainable first job, and that Uber drivers are afforded no protections as contractors, why could we not have just gotten all of this from Uber Eats?" Meg asks half-jokingly as she hauls the bags onto the table. Aki can tell Ian ordered dinner because it's pretty clear there is way too much food. Her irritation and anxiety begins to bubble up again alongside the hunger in her stomach.

"Megumi!" Aki says a little too loudly.

"Geez, Mother, what?" Meg has never been one to call Aki anything other than "Mother." There was no "Mommy" phase or even "Mom." Meg's first word was "Ian" and her second, "Mother."

"Let me see your phone!" Aki demands. Meg hands it over, grumbling under her breath. Aki struggles to find Instagram, and Meg snatches it back from her.

"What are you looking for exactly?" Meg snaps.

"Oooooh, tone," Ian warns lightly.

"Instagram!" Aki snaps back. *I never should have let her have that account*, she thinks. *Too late*, she knows.

"I only really use TikTok, Mother," Meg says snidely.

"Instagram. Now." Aki says through clenched teeth.

"Oooooh, tone," Ian chides as they both ignore him.

Meg gives a few swipes before placing the phone under Aki's nose. "Happy?"

"OK, that's not cool, Gummy," Ian warns as Meg pretends to pout.

Aki snatches the phone from Meg, but all she sees are photos and videos of golden retriever puppies. Her face must register confusion, because Meg sighs and explains, "That's the search page—do you know what that is?" She sighs again at Aki's blank expression. "Never mind, anyway, I got caught in a wormhole of puppy videos. Now all it wants to give me is puppies. What are you looking for?"

"PoC@Wesley," Aki says tersely.

This is of course the Instagram page that Amanda had discovered, the one Amanda kept scrolling through and pointing at hysterically while simultaneously muttering, "I manifest my success, I manifest my success."

Meg wordlessly reclaims her phone as Aki searches her daughter's expression for any admission of guilt. Meg types in a few letters before handing the phone back to her mother.

"Is this you?" Aki says, pointing at a post.

"What does it say?" Ian cranes his neck to look at the small screen. He takes the phone and reads, "When I was at Wesley back in the '90s . . . OK, I'm going to guess that one isn't you. Which one?" He asks as Aki enlarges the posts she's referring to. Ian clears his throat and reads, "Wesley doesn't even understand the term antiracist."

Aki and Ian look expectantly at Meg, who has opened a box of pad thai and is eating it with the restaurant-supplied chopsticks. Meg is the current editor of the opinion page for the school newspaper, and her first article for the *Quaker Newsman* was a reflection on a book about antiracism, and whether Wesley would ever be able to live up to its own ideals. The title of the article had been "Does Wesley Know What an Antiracist Looks Like?" Ian and Aki raise their eyebrows in concert and look at Meg, who shrugs. "What? They don't."

"Know what it means to be an antiracist?" Ian supplies as Meg rolls her eyes and nods.

"So, the post is clearly yours. What about the account? Did you start it?" Aki asks again, thinking about the ramifications if it was indeed Meg in charge of the account. Amanda would surely try to get her suspended.

Ian continues scrolling through the posts and reading from them out loud. "Once I was in science class with Ms. Bryson and she said that if we didn't shut the hell up, a big Black man would come and get us. I think she was talking about Ousmane." Ian sucks in his breath. "Geez, spare no one," he jokes, but Aki's gaze is fixed on Meg, who stares past her mother at an invisible spot on the wall while slurping noodles.

"Are you responsible for all these posts?" Aki demands, her voice getting higher, and if she's being honest, she's not even sure what she is trying to get at—she's just upset that Meg might somehow be involved in something she is *sure* that Wesley will hate.

"No, Mother, I did not set up the account," Meg responds drolly. "I did send the account a DM about Wesley not knowing what an antiracist is because it's true." Meg closes the pad thai box and opens the box of spring rolls. "I guess they found the info worthy of a post," Meg declares with a look of satisfaction on her face.

"Not so fast!" Ian shouts, grabbing the box from Meg's hands. "Don't think you can divert our attention from spring rolls by pointing out the blatant hypocrisy of the school!"

Meg guffaws, but Aki looks at Ian in surprise. "What do you mean?" she asks as she extends her hand for a spring roll. If you can't beat them, join them.

Ian shrugs. "They love to talk about how they value diversity blah, blah, blah, but the head is a white male, right? And Ousmane is the first minority head in the school's two-hundred-year history? What about the faculty?"

"Thirty percent minority," Meg shouts. "They fluff the numbers by hiring minority admin, not teachers! And even then, it's not that racially diverse," she sniffs. "Wesley doesn't really understand that *diverse* means *of many races*."

"What about the board of overseers?" Ian asks, fanning the flames.

"Governors," Aki corrects him flatly.

"Ten percent!" Meg cries out. "Even worse! And it's not a democratically elected board!"

"But the student body is pretty diverse, at least in the upper school," Aki says slowly.

"Is there any real economic diversity though? Diversity of thought? How many Latinx students are there? Or East Asians?" Ian is on a roll. "The school seems to think all Asians are the same."

"Preach, Dad! Harrison apparently never got the geography lesson about India being part of *South* Asia or South Korea being part of *East* Asia. I wonder if he can even figure out where Malaysia is on a map. It's in *Southeast Asia*."

Aki pauses at Meg's comment. Her daughter referring to Ian as "Dad" never fails to buoy her spirits, and Aki feels her irritation soften. What is she so worried about, anyway? So what if students are airing their feelings on a social media platform. If the school wants to respond to it, is that a bad thing?

"Aren't you worried that everyone will know that post is from you?" Aki asks, though she knows that if anyone is fearful, it's *her*—after all, fear is the chronic state of parenthood.

"Nope," Meg shoots back calmly, pouring green curry onto a plate of rice. "No one read that article anyway, Mother. It has wider play on social." She takes a too-hot bite and lets it drop from her mouth back onto the plate.

"Elegant," Ian jokes, then takes a bite and spits it out just as quickly. He and Meg start giggling. Watching the two of them, they act so much like two peas from the same pod that it was hard to ever believe Meg isn't genetically related to him.

"You did this to get a reaction?" Aki asks. Then she realizes that the school *is* reacting to the site.

"Duh, Mother, that's the power of *social*," Meg repeats, as if speaking to a toddler. "Look, if the *Quaker Newsman* says something, the only people who read it are the students, and maybe some administrators, right?" Meg asks, as Aki nods. "But on social, literally anyone and everyone can see it. It's *public*."

Aki ignores the sanctimony and focuses on her daughter's declaration: "It's public." Of course the school will react to that, protecting its manifest destiny: Thrive, expand, and prosper. Not to mention it has to shield its reputation, one that is worth as much as its $100 million endowment. "Wait, so what does the school account say?" Aki suddenly asks, assuming Wesley has also made an equally public response.

Meg's face lights up as she scrolls through her phone and thrusts it in front of her mother's face. It displays a picture of a smiling Harrison Neal III and Ousmane Gueye standing in front of Hartwell House like a team of friendly real estate agents. The caption underneath reads: "We at Wesley are committed to the fight for justice as we stand together as antiracists." "Read the comments," Meg says, eyes sparkling. "They haven't gotten around to deleting them yet."

Thomas Garrett and Tom Loker twinning in khakis

Aki blinks at the reference, which appears to be about *Uncle Tom's Cabin*. "But Thomas Garrett was an abolitionist," she says quizzically, looking up at Meg, ignoring the uncomfortable reference to the slave and owner relationship suggested by the comment.

Ian clears his throat. Aki knows that this is his tell when he feels like the conversation is going in an errant direction. He takes the phone from her and focuses on the screen, probably in an effort to drown out Aki and Meg's ongoing quarrel.

"Mother," Meg starts dramatically. "The point is that even the empowered minorities at Wesley are seen as needing a white savior." She throws up her arms. "Do *you* even know what it means to be antiracist? God, Gen-Xers literally know nothing, do they?" she declares, looking at Aki's blank expression.

Aki, for her part, gets the feeling that now is not the time to inform her daughter about her new position within the school.

"Who is in charge of the PoC@Wesley account then?" Aki asks, needing to know now more than ever.. With barely over a hundred students in Meg's class, and a hair over four hundred in the whole upper school, Aki is confident she either has taught them or knows them. She feels like an operative for the Stasi, but she is seized with the feeling that she has to know and is feverishly hoping this isn't part of Meg's idealistic plots for an upper school revolution. "I also saw your interview with Joanna Javier-Hernandez," Aki remembers out loud.

"Is our little girl local-news famous?" Ian looks up suddenly and applauds as Meg pretend-curtseys in her seat. "Was Joanna doing one of her hard-hitting pieces on corruption at the local 7–Eleven?" he jokes.

"What is your endgame here, Meg?" Aki asks, figuring she can fill Ian in on not just the protest but the interview later. She can't help but worry about all the potential blowback, and she hates to admit that she's worried about Meg being too distracted from her studies and college visits.

"There are more important things than homework and college," Meg retorts, as if reading her mind.

Ian whistles. "Is this what was spray-painted on the side of the building?" He has been scrolling through PoC@Wesley while Meg and Aki argued. The three of them bend their heads over the small screen, all of them looking at the stark black-and-white photo of the words that had been hatefully scrawled on the school building. Aki looks away quickly, closing her eyes. She remembers the feeling of confusion and helplessness the day her father came home after being attacked on the golf course. His elbows were scraped, and dirt had splattered across his new golf shirt from being pushed to the ground. But it was more than that. He was not just angry, he was deeply saddened too, colliding with her mother's voice saying "Ignore it." As Aki's mother cleaned off and bandaged his bloody elbows, he looked smaller. Even frail. Aki can understand now that her mother was trying to make things better, but by not addressing it, she inadvertently made Aki feel smaller too.

Even so, Aki can't help herself when she hears the words come out of her mouth: "Meg, we need to figure out how to keep you out of this mess."

Meg looks at her mother with anger in her dark eyes. "Don't you mean," she says, her voice tense with a barely contained fury, "*we need to figure out who did this?*"

♦ **6** ♦

"Can Wesley please get back to the business of teaching?"
—Worried parent of Wesley 11th grader, dcparentzone.com

Meg and Ian left for a run early the next morning, Aki waving at their retreating figures as she marveled at their similar running gaits, both of them loping, easy runners with long legs, something that Meg didn't inherit from her mother, but clearly couldn't have gotten from Ian, either. She thinks about this as she waits for her chai at Starbucks. Aki had gotten pregnant her first year in her master's program by a faculty member—a married, older faculty member no less. She hated thinking about it, even now, seventeen years later. Chats after class became extended office hours, which lead to evening walks, which led to . . . Meg. Aki knew that it wasn't love, but she also didn't know what to expect when she told him she was pregnant. Would he tell her to get rid of it? Instead, he sputtered an excuse about having to leave for the day, shut the door, and never contacted her again. She had steeled herself for an angry denial, but in the face of complete disregard, she did the only thing she knew to do: carry on. She dropped out of the professor's class, ignored the whispers of her classmates. She hated to admit it, but she had been attracted to his stature and the fact that he had thrived in a world that was both enigmatic and romantic to her; she didn't even know him. These days, she knows, he would have been considered a predator. Back then, Aki didn't feel there was anything to do, and that is where the narrative ended.

Then she met Ian.

Ian and Aki's first encounter was at the Graduate Student House, which sounded like a large and welcoming gathering space but was really just a room carved out of an administrative building that offered free coffee for graduate students. Aki went there once a day, making sure to limit her caffeine intake while also minding her budget. She was on a stipend from the school as part of her program and luckily as a full-time student also received free medical care. But she still counted her pennies, knowing what lay ahead.

Grad House, as they all called it, sometimes had leftover pastries and bagels from seminars or faculty meetings, and she often circled the space like a shameless vulture looking for food. She and Ian had the same schedule, not to mention shared miserly ways, and she began to look forward to seeing him and exchanging friendly banter. It took her mind off her pregnancy, that was, until the day when Ian joked, "Hey, are you pregnant?" Aki surprised even herself by saying, "Yeah, I am," since she had spent the last five months in denial, not even telling her parents. She didn't even stop to think about how awkward it was that he asked—his awkwardness, she would find, being an enduring and endearing quality of Ian's.

Upon her admission, she figured she'd never see Ian again and that he would shut a figurative door on her, just as the professor had shut a literal door on her face. But the next day he appeared at Grad House with mug of decaf and handed it to her. "You probably should switch from caffeinated. But I bet your husband tells you that already." To which she told him quite directly that there was no father in the picture, again assuming that was the end of their friendly run-ins. He surprised her by asking her out to lunch the next day. Two months into dating, Aki fearfully asked Ian if it bothered him that she was pregnant. He looked at her and said, "I love kids!"

Aki never questioned him after that, though she did eventually tell him the story of how she ended up seven months pregnant and unmarried. Undeterred, Ian was not only loyal, he managed to talk his way into the delivery room and moved in with her at the lowest point in her life, when Meg was a month old and Aki was overwhelmed, sleep-deprived, and near collapse. She thought it was crazy that a twenty-seven-year-old chemistry PhD would take on a girlfriend with a baby, but she tried not to question it, fearing he would disappear. She finally told her parents she had a baby when Meg was two months old, and let her mother assume it was Ian's. It was only at their wedding a year later did she confess to the truth, and only because by then, Meg's biological father had suffered a heart attack and had passed away. Aki read about it in the student paper.

After dropping out of her grad program, Aki, Ian, and Meg moved to Washington, DC, a year later when Ian received a fellowship from NOAA and she accepted the job at Wesley. As happy as she currently is, life's "what ifs" nag at her from time to time: What if she hadn't gotten pregnant? What if she had finished her PhD? What if, what if, what if? She wishes she could push these questions out of her mind, but here she is at Starbucks, where she ends up most mornings either with or without Meg. This morning Ian had agreed to drop her off after their run, and Aki tries to enjoy the conflict-free time as she thinks about the graffiti and questions if Wesley is still the right place for her daughter—not to mention herself.

"Aki, is that you?" A familiar voice calls out. Aki looks behind her and sees India Bradley, the senior admissions officer for the Payet School, a small and equally exclusive private school down the road from Wesley. India used to work at Wesley but left after two years. "How are you?" India asks, moving in for a hug. They had been friendly while at Wesley. India grew up in San Francisco and attended UCLA, and the two had bonded over their love of the North Bay and comparing war stories about the UC system. "How are things at Wesley? Still finding the light?" India chuckles.

Aki thinks about the headlines that had been splashed over the Internet about the graffiti: the *Washington Post*, "Elite Private School Vandalized" (the tamest); *Politico*, "School to Children of Senators and Presidents Sees Hate Crime" (the truth hurts); *Page Six*, "51K to Learn How to Hate!" (clever); and Fox News, "Liberal School Loved by Democrats Not So 'Woke' After All!" (expected).

What did Jon Stewart say about the media? That it peddles in sensationalism and laziness? Don't they have something better to report on, you know, like climate change? Aki sighs and wrinkles her brow.

India laughs at Aki's expression. "OK, so I guess you all are in the hot seat right now. Glad it isn't us! We're up twenty percent over last year!"

"Do you think this stuff will affect applications to the school?" Aki asks. She hadn't thought about that angle.

India lets out a deep, loud guffaw. "Ha! Are you kidding? Harvard on Wisconsin Avenue?" She looks at Aki while grabbing a drink that has been placed on the counter behind her, taking a long swig. "I'm sure the school will scatter some PR pixie dust and make it all go away."

"Chai latte!" A voice calls out. Aki turns around to quickly retrieve her drink, hoping India will enlighten her further.

"That place, I swear," India says nostalgically but not without a hint of disgust. "Payet is really different, you know," squinting at Aki while also looking like she's choosing her next words carefully. "They really want to make sure the parent community is a congenial one." India looks at her watch and gasps. "Ooh, gotta go! Lots of admissions tours today. Hey! It was great seeing you; we should catch up. Better yet, come work for us at Payet! It may not be Harvard on Wisconsin Avenue, but it's nice!" India calls behind her as she rushes toward the entrance.

"Bye!" Aki says somewhat pathetically as she watches India exit the store. She lets a few minutes pass before she leaves as well, thinking about what India had said. Wesley is mind-bogglingly difficult to get into these days, the Harvard of prep schools, as India joked. The acceptance rate floats somewhere near 6 percent, even lower in the years when presidential children are enrolled. But did it really warrant such popularity? The teachers at comparable area private schools were just as well-trained and highly educated, and the students are just as smart, the parents just as accomplished. What was it that made Wesley shine so brightly, at least on the outside? She wishes she felt more of a sense of pride working there, but lately it's been something of an embarrassment, especially when people raise their eyebrows, lower their voices, and say, "Oh, you work at *Wesley*," in a tone that suggests both awe and pinch of judgment. She always feels like telling people she and Meg started at the school before Wesley was Wesley—when it was just a good prep school with a sprinkling of rich parents. That was before all the presidential children, of course, and feels like it was a million years ago when it was only a decade. India took a swipe at Wesley with her comments—but she's right, it isn't the same school it used to be. With the extra prestige comes extra baggage.

Aki parks her car just as her phone alerts her to an email notification. She takes a sip of her chai and opens a message from Amanda. After Aki had reluctantly agreed to become the head of the equity task force, Amanda sent her a peppy email filled with directives; today's was bolded and underlined: "**<u>Convene future parents task force meeting</u>**." The school had, literally overnight, tapped a group of parents ("the Wesley Parents Equity and Diversity Advisory Task Force") that would help Aki "guide future conversations with the school with regard to equity and inclusions issues," but really, she suspects it's a way to include the more influential parents and convince them they're part of a solution, even if they're not. She also knows that if the school has handpicked this group of parents, they are Wesley boosters, not haters. Aki wonders nervously if they've all seen the Instagram account and are gossiping that somehow Meg is involved.

Aki opens her car door, holding her latte in one hand and her bag in the other, when she hears a familiar screech.

"Bye, hon, have a good day, don't offend any Yankees!" she hears Jules yell at Felix, who looks like he can't get out of the faculty garage fast enough. "Hey, Hayashi!" Jules yells again as she speed-walks toward her. Jules is always this chipper: she says it catches her students off guard. "Oh, Lord, you won't believe the shit that is going on with the musical revue!" Aki realizes that her friend, for once, is behind the curve on the social media news. "These people!" Jules continues, strangely cheerful, and Aki knows right away it has to do with a parent and not the administration. One of the reasons that the school is so sensitive to parent appeals is because the parents have grown more demanding over the years, which in turn makes the school increasingly responsive to their complex requests.

"What now?" Aki asks, hoping Jules's gossip will get her mind off of Meg, the Instagram account, and her mounting general anxiety. The musical revue is a short performance put on by the upper school right before spring break. She personally loves the revue, especially since it feels like Wesley increasingly places an emphasis on sports over the arts ever since they had their first ever NBA player go twentieth in the first round of the draft. Never mind the kid was placed on academic probation for poor grades, only to be put back onto the team in order to win the league championship.

"Well, Addison Lane called about Maddy," Jules starts. Addison is famous among the faculty. She is a grade-A complainer and winner of the award for worst parent-teacher conference. She is famous for refusing to sit with her back to the door *or* the window, and whatever desk she sits at has to be pulled up against a back wall before she launches into a loud missive about how whichever teacher sits in front of her is doing their job incorrectly. "Miz Lane wants Maddy to have a solo, probably so she can put it on her Wesleyan app, right? I guess she didn't get in anywhere early decision. Anyway, I point out that Maddy has a documented anxiety disorder and will likely crumble into a million pieces before she would ever perform a solo for four hundred people."

Aki nods, remembering when Maddy was a freshman singing in the choir and ran off the stage and threw up in the wings.

"Anyway, her mom insists that Maddy needs to do this in order for her to 'fulfill the challenge of self-agency,'" Jules says, using air quotes. "Which really means she wants something to pad the girl's college application with. Anyway, when I pointed out that I didn't think it would be good for Maddy emotionally, mom says that—and I'm not kidding—she's had the doctor prescribe some clozapine so she'll be all ready to go. The woman is doping up her kid with an antipsychotic so that she can have a shot at singing 'Memories'?" Jules shakes her head and shouts the last part as she raises her hands to the sky, and Aki can tell she's on a roll. "And lady, why in the world are you heading up this racial task force thingy?" Jules demands as they make their way to the entrance of the school.

"How did you know about that?" Aki is shocked. Ousmane and Amanda had tapped her just two days ago.

"You didn't see this morning's email from Harri-poo?" She pulls out her phone and puts it in front of Aki's face.

From the Desk of Harrison Neal IIII

It is with great pleasure that I announce, by unanimous vote of the Board of Governors of the Wesley Friends School, the appointment of Aki Hayashi-Brown as the newly created Interim Director of Equity and Diversity to oversee program implantation and make recommendations on behalf of the Office of Diversity, Justice, and Community. Wesley Friends strives to promote open dialogue amongst our faculty, students, and the wider community and address their concerns in a constructive and positive manner.

Aki brings a wealth of knowledge as a steward of Wesley culture, having taught at the school for over fifteen years. She is a graduate of University of California at Berkeley and holds a Master's degree in history from the University of Pennsylvania. Aki also brings a wealth of administrative knowledge, having managed the Wesley Upper School history department for close to five years.

We at Wesley at honored and lucky to have Aki step into the enormously important role. Please join me in welcoming Aki in her new directorship.

Move forward into the light,
Harrison Neal III

"This is your cruise director, Aki Hayashi-Brown!" Jules squeaks, saluting with her right hand while quoting *The Love Boat*.

"What the actual fuck," Aki says in a tired voice, making Jules whoop with delight, since unlike Meg, Aki rarely swears in public.

"I take it you didn't know?" Jules says, bouncing in her heels.

"They asked me to head a task force, but—" Aki starts before being cut off by her friend.

"What sorts of fun things do you have in store for us, Director Aki?" Jules salutes again. "Bingo on the Lido deck at fifteen hundred?"

"Interim director," Aki corrects her glumly, reading the email again. She knows that Ian is on the parents listserv and is probably reading it and wondering why she never said anything to him. *Interim Director of Equity and Diversity.* What happened to the junior varsity task force she was temporarily heading up?

Jules can't keep herself from bouncing around. "Watch out for the *firing squad*," she squeals, her pet name for Wesley's parent population. "Okeee, gotta run! See ya later, sweets!" She blows Aki a kiss.

Aki, realizing that she too is late, rushes through the hallway, eyes darting about and trying to avoid everyone when a tall figure blocks her path. Ousmane. She narrows her eyes and is about to say something when he holds up his hand.

"I did not know that was going to happen," he says slowly. Referring, she assumes, to her newfound title. "I appreciate you accepting this mantle until we figure things out."

She looks at him seriously, hoping her expression doesn't give away how vexed she feels. How was she expected to head an equity and diversity role when the way she was raised to tackle racism was by ignoring, denying, or deflecting? She tries to remember a time when she felt supported at school or at university and comes up meaningfully short; her entire PhD program had only two minorities. In Daly City, where the population included a large number of East and Southeast Asians, their classes and textbooks were never focused on them. When Meg complained that Wesley glossed over Japanese internment during World War II or only had one Asian author as part of junior year English, Aki's first thought was *But that's progress*. Meg told her that she was happy with too little, and maybe her daughter is right. Which still begs the question: should she be the one running a diversity and equity program, even if it's only temporary?

Ousmane takes her elbow and guides her to an empty classroom. "I will be honest, Aki, I did not know that Harrison would send out such a public announcement," he says, knitting his brows. "I'm afraid it's too late to cancel the town hall we have scheduled for tomorrow, but I have confidence in your ability to fulfill this role until we can find a suitable replacement."

"Wait, *what*?" Aki raises her voice, ignoring Ousmane's attempt at assuaging her anxiety and focusing on his words. "What town hall? Tomorrow?"

Ousmane clears his throat and bends down over Aki as if telling her a secret. He drops his voice and explains, "Yes, well, Harrison feels that time is critical and that the school needed to involve the parents quickly, before winter break. We don't want them to discuss things *elsewhere*," he intones, and Aki understand he means places like dcparentzone, the op-ed in the *Washington Post*, or maybe even the recently launched PoC@Wesley account. But she feels like asking him, what's the point? Not everyone will be able to attend on such short notice, and even if they did, there is absolutely nothing to keep them from gossiping online.

"Ousmane, this is insane. I didn't expect to—"

"I know you'll be fine," he says, standing up straight and peering down at her. "We will support you," giving her a tight smile. "And we have something we need you to take care of today, unfortunately."

Aki feels a familiar tightness in her chest, like when her mother would tell her to do something unpleasant, like approaching a teacher about an unfair grade or rewriting an already labored-over paper for the tenth time. She swallows the ball of frustration that has quickly built up inside her, as she is so used to doing, and croaks out an "OK," dreading whatever request he is about to make.

"Good," Ousmane nods. "Please follow me." Aki follows with a growing sense of dread. She gives Ousmane's assistant a feeble hello as she passes through to his office and sees who is seated—none other than Meg and Double. Seeing her daughter in the room, Aki can't help but narrow her eyes and glare at Ousmane, telepathically sending him a message that says *I knew you picked me for this very reason to do a job I'm healthily unqualified for.*

Ousmane sits behind his desk and motions for Aki to be seated as well. "Ms. Hayashi-Brown and Mr. Lukes have a request on behalf of several student groups at Wesley."

Aki stiffly turns to Meg and Double.

"Mrs. Hayashi-Brown," Meg starts with a detectable whiff of sarcasm. "The Wesley Council for Social Justice in conjunction with Women's Action at Wesley formally request the creation of an official safe space at the school."

Aki can feel herself blinking rapidly, knowing she can't very well say *Huh?* out loud.

Double fills in the blanks. "We would like a dedicated space within the school where members of historically oppressed members of society can gather and feel safe. We know that some of our peer institutions have done this already, and we would like to see Wesley honor its commitment to creating a tolerant and equitable environment within the school."

Aki blinks again, then looks at Ousmane, who has his hands clasped and his pointer fingers resting on his lips, looking thoughtful. Seeing that she isn't getting much verbal support from him, Aki gulps and responds, "What did you have in mind?" hoping the question will create some time for her to think.

"There aren't that many open classrooms available for something like this, and we want it to be *permanent*," Meg says. "But the one space we know we have, and think we *should* have, is the senior lounge."

Aki looks quickly at Ousmane to see his reaction, but the master poker player that he is gives nothing away in his expression. She can only think about the vitriol that will ensue if they take away the senior lounge. At the same time, it would make quite the statement to turn it into a "safe space" dedicated to the minority population of the school.

"Well . . ." she starts, "any decision we make will have to take into account—"

"*Mrs. Hayashi-Brown!*" Meg interjects angrily. "Some neo-Nazi just spray-painted the side of the building. How is the school going to respond? Or is Wesley going to pretend like everything is OK?"

Thankfully, Ousmane steps in. "As you are both aware, Mrs. Hayashi-Brown is part of a multipronged response to recent events, including a parents task force and all-school town hall. She will also start the appropriate inquiry into the feasibility of your idea. In the meantime, we thank you both for your passionate advocacy."

"You should know," Double says, "there are students in this institution who are not *advocates*."

Meg snorts.

Ousmane raises an eyebrow.

"They need to be told they're not welcome," Meg intones.

"The school will begin to construct a formal mechanism by which students can file official complaints of this nature in the appropriate manner," Ousmane responds. "And Mrs. Hayashi-Brown will get back to you about your proposal." He rises. "I believe you both have class now?" His way, Aki knows, of dismissing them from his office.

"Thank you both for your time," Double says, extending his hand to Ousmane, then to Aki. Meg rolls her eyes at Aki and follows Double out of the office.

Ousmane turns to Aki. "Thank you for your commitment to this role," Ousmane says quickly before she can say what she is thinking, which is that her appointment was obviously not just a coincidence.

+ 7 +

"Thank you so much for making this page. I feel like no one wants to talk about how awful it can be to be a POC at a place like Wesley."

—*Current Wesley student, PoC@Wesley*

THE NEW GYM, WITH its overhead indoor track and four side-by-side basketball courts, now holds countless rows of folding chairs that look like a battalion ready for combat. On each seat is a fat, spiral-bound packet with a Wesley logo pen. On the stage is an oversized screen set up behind a lectern, and flanking both sides of the setup are huge white banners with the words *Move Forward into the Light* written in black. Aki wonders how Amanda and her team could have whipped up such an impressively involved town hall in a day, then remembers that managing egos, reputation, and crisis is Amanda's raison d'être.

"Looks like they're hosting a presidential debate," Jules's voice reverberates behind Aki. She turns around to see that her friend has changed since work this morning and is now dressed in a pink-and-white checked shirt and khaki pants, with a headband in her blond bob, and raises her eyebrows. "I thought I'd try the WASP look tonight, you know, see if it scares off the pretend-liberals," Jules jokes. She's long been suspicious that the parents aren't actually as liberal as they sell themselves to be, if only because they're all so rich. She alleges that they're liberal mainly because of the guilt brought on by years of tax credits.

"Where's Jasper?" Aki asks as she gives Jules a little hug. Jasper is Jules's London-born, manor-raised, polo-playing husband. She's not sure how the two of them ended up together. Jules is brash and loud, not to mention small, whereas Jasper is a tall, wry former banker turned business school professor at Georgetown.

"Dealing with the rug rats—making them watch *football*, you know, the British one where they play with their *feet*?"

Aki giggles.

"You're presenting, right?" Jules asks as Aki suddenly grows nervous again. "OK, Imma sit in the front and cheer you on," she says, sashaying away.

"Please don't," Aki pleads after her.

"Aki Hayashi for president!" Jules yells out as a sprinkling of early and undoubtedly confused parents watch Jules, who stops abruptly to trot back to Aki. "Wait, did you see the latest post from PoC@Wesley? And the number of followers?" Jules asks, taking her phone out of her Tory Burch satchel. Aki doesn't want to know but is also curious enough to look. On Jules's screen is a story from PoC@Wesley that flashes the words "TONIGHT," then "18." The number of followers has ballooned by several hundred.

"What do they mean by 18?" Jules clicks on different posts and videos, but all Aki feels is a mounting sense of dread. Meg had informed her earlier that evening that she and Aiko would be at the town hall, and she knows in the pit of her stomach that her daughter must have something planned. She hopes these recent posts aren't a reaction to Aki's new leadership position, which Meg has not said anything about. At least not yet.

"Oooh, it's filling up, better go!!" Jules squeals, seeing parents filing in, as she trots off. Aki shakes her head, knowing well

enough that when Jules is this excited, it's because she thinks
there is going to be some drama that she's not involved in,
ready to unfold for her own entertainment. Aki looks around
and sees that the seats are indeed filling up, row by row with
concerned-looking parents, many of whom she recognizes. In
the front and middle of the audience are Liz "What Does Inclu-
sivity Have to Do with the Auction" and her husband Roger.
The Everetts are one of the few openly conservative families in
the school, and they are happy to let the entire community know
it. Aki had heard rumors of trying to convince the Everetts to
leave to no avail. Instead, the Everetts appear hell-bent on staying and making Wesley change its ways. Maybe at the Episcopal
school down the street, they just wouldn't get noticed as much—
they'd just be yet another registered GOP member who likes to
talk about how great Reagan was.

"Are you ready?" A terse voice asks at her shoulder. Aki turns
to see Amanda, dressed in a taupe suit and tan patent heels, looking very much like a flesh-colored baton, blond hair ironed to a
straight sheen. "You have the notes I sent you? We don't antici-
pate you having to speak, but just in case you get questions, stick
to the script."

"Are we allowing questions or comments?" Aki asks suddenly. Often times at town halls, a microphone is set up for Q&A
after the main speaker.

Amanda lets out a loud guffaw. "Oh no, no, *no*," she stops
laughing as her hazel eyes bore into Aki. "Why would we ever
let them do *that*?" she asks as if Aki had proposed giving away
weapons of mass destruction. "We can't control the narrative
with parents involved. When we have the discussion circles, we'll
let some of the parents talk." She pauses. "But only parents we
choose to come, of course," as if the idea of allowing the parental
participation in a discussion about school matters was the most
ludicrous idea ever conceived. "Come with me, you need to be

seated on the stage with Ousmane," Amanda says as she turns on
her heel.

Aki follows her to the stage, wondering what in the world
Amanda means by "discussion circles," and sees Ousmane and
Harrison standing next to one another, heads bent in discussion,
both wearing dark trousers and crisp white shirts. Aki thinks
about the comment on the Instagram post that labeled them
twins and then cringes as she realizes that it could very well have
been Meg who posted it. Amanda gives her a stern look as Aki
plants herself in a folding chair at the edge of the stage and looks
out at the assembled crowd, feeling awkward and out of place.
She watches as Harrison claps Ousmane on the back, then takes a
seat of his own on the opposite side of the stage, but not before he
waves and shakes hands with several parents: Sylvia Burress (parent to Tyrell and Delilah, former White House social secretary,)
Jackson Lyle (father to Lisa and William, founder of a hugely successful venture capital firm and underwriter of the science labs at
the upper school), and a few others who serve on the board. After
exchanging greetings with Harrison, the parents sit in a tidy row
in the front like the clergy around a pulpit, their placement befitting a school board, she thinks.

"I'd like to thank everyone for gathering tonight," Ousmane
starts, making everyone turn their attention toward him. "If
we can please start with a moment of silence," he adds, and the
room settles into a hush, a customary start to any gathering at the
school. Everyone bows their head. "Thank you," Ousmane says
as he raises his head after a few seconds. "I appreciate all of you
gathering here on a school night. I know that many of you have
come directly from work, and we appreciate the generosity of
your time."

Aki tries not to squirm as she sits, feeling like a cross between
a mannequin and a wall plaque. Jules gives her an encouraging
wink.

"Recent *incidents* have asked us as a community how we can come together and address the harms caused in recent days," Ousmane starts again. Aki sees fixed expressions and terse mouths on the parents in the audience, quiet only for now, she knows. Ousmane clears his throat. "We hope to open dialogue with everyone in the community and will start by convening a parents task force, as well as holding discussion circles within the community." With his last comment, the crowd starts to murmur. Aki watches Roger Everett lean over to his wife and whisper something to her as he rolls his eyes. The usually unflappable Ousmane's lip twitches ever so slightly, most certainly because he cannot tell if the murmuring is supportive or not. He clears his throat again before continuing. "We will also conduct a thorough review of the student code of conduct to address the consequences for hurtful speech—"

"Can I ask a question, please?" A voice rises up from the crowd.

So much for no questions, Aki thinks as Ousmane looks out toward the voice, squints, then points to a raised hand. Evelyn Goode (parent to Rhea, partner at a K Street law firm specializing in financial crimes) stands up without being asked and has a look on her face that says, *go ahead, try.* Evelyn is one of the parent reps from the Black Parents Association and someone Wesley probably shouldn't cross. Rumor is she eats Senate aides for breakfast.

"So, you're going to have some *task force*," she says sharply, "and you're going to have 'talk circles'—"

"Discussion circles," Amanda mutters under her breath.

"—and that's *it*?" Evelyn demands.

Ousmane stands a little straighter and grips the sides of the lectern. "The parents task force is an important—"

"I am *sorry*, but this all sounds like performative antics to me!" Evelyn retorts. "Someone *inside* this school wants to make it *white*. Do you honestly think I feel comfortable sending my child here until you figure out who did this and kick them out? Is the task force going to do that for me?" The crowd murmurs its response, with some people cross-talking and others applauding, albeit politely.

Aki knits her brows. Of course parents should feel concerned. Having been raised to ignore overt—or covert—racism, she wonders if she shouldn't be more afraid herself. Instead, she mostly feels paralyzed. Nothing in her life, she realizes, has adequately prepared her for this.

"I must agree," another voice calls out. Heads swing to the other side of the room, where Esther Green (parent to Julian and Rufus, NIH scientist) has risen. "We have to do more," she insists. "We need more discussions!"

Aki watches as Evelyn shakes her head. "That's not what I mean—" she starts, though she is cut off by chants of "Yes!" "More!" Abundantly clear is that the school's proposals are being considered too superficial but somehow not enough all at the same time.

Harrison rises abruptly from his seat, momentarily causing the growing swell of parental voices to calm. He approaches the podium, and Ousmane steps courteously aside, motioning to the microphone.

"As I expressed to the faculty earlier this week, we will find the individual who did this, and we will make an example of them. You have my word." And with that, Harrison nods to Ousmane and reclaims his seat behind the podium. Even if Ian and Meg have their suspicions, hearing Harrison say this twice makes Aki believe that he means it.

Ousmane, resuming his place, sticks to his script. "We will also establish accountability mechanisms through antiracism work and a stringent review of biases within the current curriculum," clearly sidestepping Evelyn's comments and focusing more on what the Esthers of the parent community think is the answer. The silence that Harrison commanded is quickly dismantled with loud murmurs.

"Wait, wait. What exactly are we talking about here?" a different voice yells out. It's Roger Everett, his plump face becoming an unadulterated and unattractive shade of eggplant, his jowls drooping over his collar like overflowing lava. "Because I've got *problems* with indoctrinating my kid with mumbo-jumbo about all white people being racist," he shouts. "And I know some of these other cowards won't say it, but they do too!" He makes a circle around his head with his oversized paws.

Ousmane pauses, then without changing his expression, looks at the front row of the audience, the clergy, his supporters, then back out to the assembled parents. "We will further discuss any integration of racial awareness and sensitivity into our daily lives, including any recommendations as it relates to curriculum. This will be part of the work of the newly formed Faculty Task Force on Equity, Diversity, and Inclusion, headed by Aki Hayashi-Brown, and she will work in partnership with the Wesley Parent Advisory Committee on Diversity and Equity." He extends his hand to Aki, who almost jumps out of her seat at hearing her own name, not to mention all the words strung together that seem to say the same thing, which is "how is Wesley going to deal with this racism stuff."

"Woo-hoo! Go, Aki!" Jules smacks her hands together and cheers. It never ceases to amaze Aki just how unselfconscious her friend is. Jules might as well be at Cirque de Soleil while all the other parents act as if this meeting is the next Bretton Woods.

"So are you planning on dumbing down the curriculum and alienating other groups in the school?" Roger yells out. "Because that what it sounds like when you say 'changing the curriculum'!"

A hand shoots up, but the woman it's attached to doesn't wait for permission to ask "How is this going to affect AP courses?"

"Ahem," Ousmane gives an annoyed look before continuing. "Ms. Hayashi-Brown will head this important initiative until we find a permanent director for this role. We have hired a prominent consulting firm by the name of Elliot Associates, and they will be directly involved in the search to fill this position, and will assist Ms. Hayashi-Brown and the parents task force as well as meet with teachers." More whispers permeate the gym. Aki knows that there are some parents who will view a place on the task force as a power move, and she thinks about Amanda's insinuation that the parents have already been chosen. "Aki, would you like to say a few words?" *No, I definitely would not, are you insane?* Aki thinks in panic. She doesn't move from her seat, and Amanda kicks her ankle to get up.

"Ow!" Aki yelps as she stands. She hobbles toward the podium and looks out at the audience, who watch her in a stony silence.

Aki shoots Ousmane her best death stare before standing behind the lecture and gripping the sides. She takes a breath. This is the first she's heard of any curriculum changes and certainly the first time she's ever faced such a large number of parents. *Fake it 'til you make it*, she thinks to herself before opening her mouth.

"Wesley Friends is dedicated to prioritizing equity as a core value," she starts, amazed that the line slips out of her mouth so easily. "But of course, any alterations to curriculum or otherwise will be done carefully, with community input, and over the long term," she finishes, knowing that of those three, only the last one is probably true. Someone once said that at Wesley you can't buy pencils without an unanimous vote by committee after an excruciatingly long deliberation.

"First order of liberal business, cancel Shakespeare!" Roger yells, laughing at his own joke.

"You should be ashamed of yourself!" a voice retorts.

"I assure you, I'm not," Roger calls back, smiling. "None of you wants to admit it, but most of this sensitivity stuff is just crap. Someone show me research to say it actually works. I dare you."

Evelyn stands up again, looking angrier than she was just ten minutes ago, "*This* is the problem, don't you see?" She waves her hands around, probably trying not to point at Roger directly. "*This* is why we have spray paint on the side of the school! Are you going to try and figure out who exactly did this?"

Evelyn's point is met with louder murmurs, and someone calls out, "What about security footage? What's the point of a huge security team if they can't catch the person!" Of course the community wants to know who did it. Ousmane has been repeating the same line about not wanting to interfere with an open investigation, but Jules, the perpetual gossip that she is, took matters into her own manicured hands, not necessarily due to an undying sense of justice but rather a deep-rooted suspicion that the school was trying to cover something up. She worked her sources in security, but the security staff claimed that the tapes are erased every forty-eight hours and there was nothing to show. And to Percy's point, no one in the administration seemed to be pursuing the surveillance, which was curious in itself.

Aki looks to Ousmane, trying telepathically to draw him back to the podium. Ousmane, however, appears completely unaffected by the rising dissatisfaction and vocal clamor. Instead, a sharp sound cuts into the room. Parents look around at one another. There is a muffled sound, then a blast of noise.

Suddenly, the room is filled with the blasting sounds of N.W.A.'s "Fuck tha Police." Parents swivel their heads to see where the music is coming from, and people in the audience start talking louder but are drowned out by the music, which gets turned up even more loudly.

"Look!" a voice comes up from the crowd, and Aki sees fingers pointed to the elevated track above them that encircles the gym.

Aki gasps. She sees what looks to be dozens of students, all in hoodies with the number 18 crudely taped on them in masking tape. They loom over the audience, swaying to the music, silent and watchful. Aki gasps again when she sees Percy standing among them, arms folded, a smirk on his face. He must be how the students were able to hijack the sound system for the entire complex. Aki looks back at Harrison and Ousmane to see their reactions. Harrison sits with his mouth agape, while Ousmane's expression, heretofore one of control and restraint, has morphed into open stupefaction.

She looks up again as two rows of students above them on opposite sides of the gym abruptly unfurl two large white banners, making many in the seats below recoil in surprise, afraid of what is about to fall down on them. The students hold up the banners silently, forcing the audience to crane their necks in order to read the writing:

CULTURALLY SENSITIVE TEACHING—
EQUITY AND INCLUSION—RESTORATIVE JUSTICE NOW

Against the calamity and mix of still-blaring music and parent voices, Aki suddenly feels very sick to her stomach. She recognizes the song, one of Ian's favorite rap tunes. "Rap music used to be about social change! Tupac, N.W.A., they were the original social justice warriors before anyone started paying attention. These new artists, all they care about weed," Ian once rhapsodized to her. She gulps as she scans the students for Meg and Aiko, but it is too dark up on the indoor track to distinguish clearly which faces are encased by which hoodies, something, she knows, they must have planned.

Aki listens as the song keeps reverberating around them.

"Fucking with me 'cause I'm a teenager . . ."

★   ★   ★

"I'm Joanna Javier-Hernandez, reporting from outside the *exclusive* Wesley Friends School, the scene of a recent hate crime, and tonight, a dramatic student protest."

The screen switches to video filmed on an iPhone, and it pans the inside of the gym, where dozens of students in hoodies

raise their fists to the words of N.W.A. Then the screen cuts back
to Joanna, who speaks into her microphone. "Allegations that the
recent vandalism of the school was perpetrated by a fellow student have shaken the community."

The next shot shows the same microphone being pushed
into the face of Susan Rose-Allen (mother to David, tech
entrepreneur) as the screen reads, "Wesley community reacts
to hate."

"No," Susan says in a nasal voice. "I don't believe for a
moment that a Wesley student did this. I send my son to this
school because it stands for justice." She leans into the microphone. "Because of the *diversity*," she adds, as if no one understands what she means. Then again, Susan is the type of woman
who wears a cashmere sweater with a black fist raised under a slogan of Black power but rolls up the windows of her Range Rover
when she crosses to the wrong side of Union Station.

"Thank you," Joanna says to Susan seriously as she turns to
face the camera and resumes her stand-up. "Questions linger,
however, as to why these students felt compelled to stage a protest about the recent *incident*." She turns to someone standing to
the left of Susan and places the microphone near their face. On
the screen is none other than Wesley senior and president of the
Wesley Council for Social Justice, Dennison Lukes. "What does
the 18 stand for?" Joanna asks.

"It represents all that is wrong with our school community.
We demand action from Wesley. We demand these students be
extracted from the school, and the school show us that character
matters more than pedigree," Double says calmly as he stares into
the camera, which cuts quickly back to Joanna.

"While there has been no official comment from the school,
we will continue to report on this hate crime as events unfold.
This has been Joanna Javier-Hernandez, reporting in front of the
Wesley Friends School. Back to you, Tiffany."

Aki turns off the television and looks at Ian. There is no question that both Double and Meg have sharpened their spears and are aiming at a fellow classmate. For right now, she's just glad that Joanna didn't come after her for an interview as well, since undoubtedly Amanda Nutley and her PR machine have told everyone who will listen that Welsey has appointed an interim director of equity and diversity.

"Who am I?" Ian asks her animatedly, pretending to choke himself while banging his head against the back of the sofa. He then stands up and runs out of the room screaming before making a U-turn, straightening out his shirt, and grinning. "I'm Amanda," he chuckles as he sits back down at the coffee table, returning to cracking walnuts with a nutcracker.

Aki sighs. They've been sitting in the living room, waiting for their daughter who has yet to materialize and has frustratingly turned off "find my friend" on her phone. Aki repeatedly looks at her phone screen, hoping for a text from her daughter.

"She's OK, just out doing age-appropriate things," Ian supplies, reading her mind. "A late-night diner run is definitely called for after terrorizing suburban parents and giving them a virtual middle finger on the local news," he jokes.

Aki is about to respond when the door bursts open, Meg standing in the frame and struggling to take off her Dr. Martens boots.

"Meg!" Aki jumps up, bumping her knees against the coffee table and making the nuts and shells scatter across the floor.

"Mother!" Meg calls back, throwing her boots in the closet and her hoodie on the dining room table.

"Hey, kiddo! Overthrow the government while you were at it?" Ian jokes. Meg raises her eyebrow and gives him her patented look of annoyance.

"Meg," Aki starts, stopping suddenly when she realizes she doesn't know what she wants to say. *Aren't you worried about what people will think? Have you even been thinking about college visits and early applications?* But those are her own concerns, or ones her own mother had for her, Aki realizes. She swallows as she watches her daughter dig through the refrigerator. "Meg," she starts again. She can feel Ian eyeing her.

"Mother, I'm really tired, I'm going to bed," Meg responds, taking a bite of string cheese. "Night, Dad—"

"Wait!" Aki demands, much more loudly than she intends. A sudden sense of urgency washes through her. "What is 18?"

Meg stops and looks at her mother. "Seriously?" she says snidely.

"Hey! Tone, kid," Ian interjects.

Meg looks at Aki and shakes her head while grabbing her phone from her back pocket. Why does it seem like all of life's answers have to be found on a phone? Aki wonders. Meg punches and swipes, then strides over to Aki and places the phone squarely in front of her face.

On the PoC@Wesley Instagram page, she sees a grainy black-and-white video. Aki squints and realizes she's looking at the arts building on the Wesley campus. Suddenly a tall figure darts into the frame, stopping abruptly. The person's head, shrouded by a light grey hood, looks quickly to the left and to the right. Over their hoodie, the person on the screen is wearing a Wesley warm-up jersey, with the number 18 on the back. Aki gasps. She realizes now the significance of the number.

"Where . . . where did they get this video?" she asks softly, still in shock.

"You all have been so fooled," Meg says tersely. She turns on her naked heel, making the wood floor squeak as she retreats to her room.

◆ 8 ◆

"I don't understand. For a school that sells itself on diversity why aren't more people angry? We still don't know who did this."
—*Current Wesley student, PoC@Wesley*

WHEN AKI WAS IN high school, she was invited to attend a seminar for gifted and talented students at a university in the South Bay. She remembers feeling excited and nervous when her parents dropped her off on the sprawling palm-lined campus, promising they'd be back in two weeks to pick her up. She arrived with two bags and a sense of pride that she had been chosen from several thousand to meet with renowned professors and students from across the country. She shared a double room with an Indian girl named Sruthi, who had flown from Texas and wanted to become a doctor. When Sruthi asked Aki what she wanted to study in college, she remembers Sruthi's shocked expression when Aki told her that she wanted to study history. "But why?" Sruthi asked with the incredulity of a well-trained child of an Asian immigrant. "You can't do anything with that."

Nonetheless, Aki and Sruthi stuck together that week. There were only a few female minorities, and it seemed natural to band together rather than be alone for the next fourteen days. They sat together at meals, walked together to classes, and though their divergent interests meant they didn't share classes, they became close. Being sixteen, they also bonded over boys, though many at the camp seemed more childish and awkward than either of them. There was one that they both noticed, and his name was Thomas Feller. Thomas was one of those kids who attracted people to him, like a politician in a small town. He was brimming with confidence and funny stories, and would talk to anyone who hovered near him.

"Once my mom was in an elevator with former president George Bush, and he told her if he was her age, he'd pick her up, and my dad said, 'Don't let me get in the way!'"

His stories felt so *adult*, like what Aki imagined people at cocktail parties sounded like. He was on the crew team at his New England boarding school, and she would hang on his every story. "Parlor is awesome," he said offhandedly one day as they waited for their humanities teacher to start class. She remembers asking him breathlessly what that was. "All the fourth forms will go to the headmaster's house on Thursdays and just, shoot the shit, you know?" She didn't know what a fourth form was, or what he meant by *shoot the shit*, but it strengthened her resolve to one day move to the East Coast. She would pepper him with questions, and eventually told him about wanting to move east. "You'd totally fit in. You're cool, Hayashi." She still remembers the tingle up her spine when he complimented her.

"I don't know why you hang on him like that," Sruthi said to her one night. "He's a jerk." Before Aki could defend him, Sruthi looked her straight in the face and said, "I overheard him talking. He said, 'Aki? What kind of name is that? More like Yucky.'"

Aki was stunned. After that story, she avoided Thomas for the rest of the camp, though he tried to talk to her on occasion. She would shrink away and avoid eye contact, and he would shrug as if to say, your loss. As much as she wanted to hear his stories, she felt embarrassed, convinced he was still making fun of her behind her back. When she first met him so many years ago, she was convinced he was the next JFK. But when she looked him up one lazy, rainy afternoon when Ian was on a research trip and she was stuck at home, she was mildly disappointed to find that he simply ended up as an investment banker in San Francisco.

She thinks about Thomas Feller today as she shifts uncomfortably in one of the many padded seats in Ousmane's reception. Thomas Feller would probably clamor and kill to get his own child into Wesley. *They're all like Thomas Feller*, Aki thinks as she wills herself not to look at the people in the room with her: Aaron Wakeman and his parents. *The students and the parents*, she realizes.

When Meg showed her the video on the PoC@Wesley page the night before, Aki had immediately recognized the significance of the number 18. In sixth grade, when Aaron joined the manga club, Aki split proctoring duties with another teacher. Once a week she would sit at a desk and ignore the kids as they talked about manga, and once a week the kids would bring in books to exchange while throwing M&Ms at each other. Aaron was incredibly friendly and would inevitably end up by Aki's desk to talk to her; he was a typical people-pleaser and someone who wanted to be liked and complimented. So she tried to be accommodating, even if she was busy with grading or other schoolwork.

Aaron's favorite topic at the time was football, and she remembers feeling somewhat sympathetic to his short and squat stature, assuming then that he would never become a quarterback (neither of them knowing then that he'd eventually become a star soccer player). His favorite player was Peyton Manning of the Indianapolis Colts, and he wore Manning's number 18 football jersey to school every week. "My dad is from Indianapolis!" He told her. "Peyton chose that number because it's his brother's number, and his brother is his hero. My dad always tells me that my brothers and I are a team. That we have to stick together!"

Aki peeks up at the Wakemans. Claire Wakeman is, in a word, beautiful. Dressed like a Hellenic statue in all-white, her auburn hair is coiffed to perfection and her skin appears translucent. She must be well into her fifties, but the only lines on her face are a furrow of worry between the eyes. Aaron's father Cash sits with a stony expression. Once blond, his hair is now mostly gray and neatly groomed, and he's dressed impeccably in a suit and cashmere overcoat. Aki remembers a ninth grade parent-teacher conference when he arrived in a chauffeured town car and sat in a student desk in the very same overcoat.

"Your son is doing quite well in my class," Aki had started.

"Reid? I thought I was here for Aaron's conference," Mr. Wakeman responded.

"I am speaking of Aaron," she told him, and he raised his eyebrows in surprise. He looked down at his coat and removed several pieces of invisible lint before looking up at her again.

"If Aaron spent the same amount of time on his studies as he did watching the Colts play, he'd have his brother's GPA." The rest of the conference was mostly Aki informing, and on some level trying to convince, Cash that Aaron was in fact doing well in her twentieth-century history class. After a firm grip of her hand and a curt goodbye, she watched the elder Wakeman leave, thinking how difficult it must be for Aaron to live with someone who had that little faith in his abilities but boundless compliments for his siblings.

Aki sneaks another peek, this time looking at Aaron. His usually upbeat expression is replaced by a pitiful hangdog look. Is she seeing another Thomas Feller? A collegial, popular, two-faced, moneyed, old-school bigot? Was Aaron capable of the casual racism that Thomas was? It was hard to believe, if only because he seems so genuinely nice, and she has a hard time believing he had anything to do with the graffiti.

"Please, come in," Ousmane says as he opens his office door and steps into the reception area, extending a hand to Cash Wakeman. "I'm sorry to have kept you waiting." Cash shakes Ousmane's hand, then motions to his wife and son to enter the office first. As Aki takes up the rear, she shoots Ousmane a look to say *What exactly am I doing here?* Ousmane gives nothing away as usual, his expression both placid and pleasant, nodding to her and closing the door behind him. Upon entering his monochromatic and austere office, she sees four chairs spaced out evenly before his desk. Aki sits in the one closest to the door, thinking about one of Jules's patented quotes: "When Dave Grohl was in Nirvana he said the first thing he would do when he got on the stage was look for the exit just in case he needed to escape an angry mob." The quote seems befitting of this moment; Cash Wakeman looks very angry and all Aki can do is think about a quick exit.

"This is slander, pure and simple," Cash Wakeman starts as soon as he is seated. "We will not stand by while our son is accused of something he did not do!" His voice rises.

Aki feels her shoulders cowing involuntarily as she looks up at Ousmane. Unlike her, Ousmane has been handling the Wakemans of the DC world for far too long to be intimidated. "While I can see that you are upset, there have been no allegations, libelous or otherwise, actually made against your son," he responds calmly as he clasps his hands on his desk.

Acknowledge his feelings, correct the term "slander" and replace with "libel," then minimize the situation, Aki thinks. Ousmane is much smarter than the parents can begin to comprehend.

Cash lifts a finger and points it at Ousmane. "You cannot seriously sit there and tell me that they aren't all pointing the finger at my son after that stunt at the town hall? The interview? And now the video on social media! That's his jersey and his number, everyone knows that! We need to find out who posted this BS. They're clearly waging war against him!" Cash raises his voice again.

If you want peace, prepare for war. The words enter Aki's mind unbidden. Was this Meg, waging a war? She searches her mind frantically to think of a reason why Meg would suddenly hate Aaron so much, the boy who joined the manga club with Meg and asked her daughter to read passages to him in Japanese. The energetic and clumsy fifth grader who befriended all, ultimately becoming the king of the school. Aki's chest burns as she ponders an alternate hypothesis for her invitation to today's meeting: Is the school mad because of Meg and Double's flagrantly inflammatory interview with Joanna Javier-Hernandez? Or Meg's equally obnoxious post on the Instagram account?

Cash continues angrily like a dust cyclone sweeping through a ghost town. "Even if they aren't coming out and saying his name, he's being bullied! Didn't Wesley come out with some grand statement about being an antibullying establishment or some BS like that?"

Aki watches as Cash—not looking unlike a bully himself—lays into Ousmane. She tries not to look obvious as she shifts her gaze toward his wife. Claire Wakeman sits calmly, in great contrast to Cash, who looks like he's about to blast off into the stratosphere fueled by the twin turbo engines of outrage and indignation. Claire's earrings, two large, bright aquamarine stones encompassed by at least a dozen winking diamonds, shine like a lighthouse beam. They complement her equally bright and piercing blue eyes as she looks at Ousmane, worried but silent.

When Claire finally opens her mouth to speak, what she says surprises Aki. "I don't claim that my sons, any of them, are perfect." This strikes Aki as a strange way to defend her son. Claire continues, "But I am here to try and sort out what has and hasn't been done, so that we can all move on." Rather than sounding angry, like her husband, Claire appears as any mother

would in the same situation: concerned. Only with more expensive jewelry.

Aki now looks at Aaron, who sits between her and his parents. She searches in her mind for any hint of an off-color joke
or remark, but all she can remember are the volunteer grocery
drop-offs he undertakes for seniors and the diaper drives he orga-
nizes with the soccer team. She looks at his profile, which hangs
lower today, his usually handsome face dejected. She wonders if
his expression is one of sadness at being wrongfully accused or
one of guilt. His profile is the collage of his parents' facial con-
tours behind him, and she notices now how closely he resembles
them both, with Claire's wide eyes and Cash's strong features.
People always say that Meg looks so much like her and Ian, and
Aki never bothers to correct them.

"Aki is here in her new role as interim director of equity and
diversity," Ousmane declares, shaking Aki out of her thoughts.

"Well, that's all well and good, but where does that leave us?"
Cash demands, not even looking at, much less acknowledging
Aki. She imagines Thomas Feller, now probably a father himself,
standing on the sidelines of a game or defending his own children
in an elite institution much like Wesley. He is undoubtedly still
acting in his subtly bigoted ways, just as he did so long ago, Aki
thinks, watching Cash act out in all his privilege. She knows it
should bother her more, how Cash is ignoring her. Instead, she's
nervous that someone is about to bring up Meg's name in connection with the post.

Ousmane counters Cash with a calm expression. "Mr.
Wakeman," Ousmane says courteously, "Civil discourse will be
at the heart of any initiative Wesley adopts as it works through
these issues. We understand that harm may have been done to
Aaron—"

"*May have?*" Cash interjects. "Has been. Has been done. Anyone who looks at that social media garbage knows that they're

pinning it on Aaron! Don't think for a second that Princeton hasn't seen that video!"

It's more than a little presumptuous of Cash Wakeman to think that Princeton actually knows what number is on Aaron Wakeman's jersey. But his arrogance and paranoia are explained by the simple fact that they are talking about a Wesley senior in the middle of college application season, and his son hasn't gotten in anywhere early.

Ousmane's face slowly spreads into a thin, tight smile. "At the end of the day, and though I realize this is of little consolation, no one has actually said Aaron's name or made any direct allegations in connection with the actual incident."

"*Come on*," Cash growls. "Do you really think it's a coincidence they chose that video to upload?" He turns brusquely to Aaron and nudges him with his elbow. "Son, tell them what you told us," Cash says loudly.

Aaron clears his throat. "That warm-up jersey. I don't have it. I haven't had it for a while," he says quietly, looking up at Ousmane. "It's missing."

The adults sit in silence, considering Aaron's statement. Aki feels something akin to relief, if only because it feels so uncomfortable sitting in the same room as someone who is being accused of such a heinous act.

"I see," Ousmane says. "I see." He appears to be considering Aaron's words.

"What else?" Cash prods. "Come on, Aaron."

"Coach said he'd have to order one if I wanted to have the same number, so I've been wearing a different number," he offers.

"So, as you can see," Cash interjects feverishly, "not only has my son been wrongly incriminated, we have definite proof it wasn't him. Whoever has his warm-up jersey obviously wanted to frame him!" Cash declares with a flourish like Perry Mason closing the case.

"I think the real point here is that," Claire says quietly, "my son is not a racist."

Aki wants to agree with Claire, but she also knows that Wesley seniors are not just two-faced, they are four-faced: one face to their friends, one to their parents, one to their teachers, and one to college admissions officers.

"Wesley needs to get off its ass and find out who's in charge of that Instagram account," Cash growls. "So that our son's name doesn't have to be associated with this nonsense for another minute longer!" Cash's voice crescendos into a yell as pushes his seat back and stands up in one aggressive motion. "We are *done* here. And I *will* be speaking with my colleagues on the board about this!"

"As Harrison has promised, we will be putting every effort into rooting out who vandalized the school, of course. As for these allegations that have been made online, we will speak to the students about expectations around respect for our community members both on and offline. This will lead our agenda in the new year after break. You have my word," Ousmane looks at Claire, who nods in return.

For her part, Aki looks at her feet, still uncomfortable in her new role and unsure how much trouble Meg could be in for sending that DM to PoC@Wesley and for her general rabble-rousing. Then, like the click of a lighter, an image pops up on Aki's mind: Meg, stomping around their apartment fueled by anger, informing Aki and Ian that they are *"all so fooled."* Meg sneering at her mother when she was talking to Aaron and Zach at the start of the year. What is clear to Aki now is that Meg obviously has a problem with Aaron, and she needs to find out why.

"Come on, let's go," Cash says gruffly as Aaron and Claire stand.

"Aaron," Ousmane says, making them all stop. "Given what is going on, I think it may be wise for you to," he pauses, trying to find the right words, "lay low for a bit."

Cash looks like he's about to rebut when Claire places her hand on his forearm, giving him a silent look. Cash merely grunts and turns on his heel, leaving in a huff as Claire gives Ousmane a polite smile. She then stops suddenly as if remembering something, leans down to Aki, and says, "Meg is lovely."

Aki, taken by surprise, responds with an elegant "Er, thank you?" But what she really feels like saying is, *Nice outfit. Love the jewels. Get out of my face.* Aki really just wants to be anywhere other than Ousmane's office.

Claire smiles serenely and takes Aaron's hand, leading him out of the office. Aki watches open-mouthed as Claire breezes out of the room, the scent of gardenias following her soft footsteps, then shakes her head and turns back to Ousmane, squinting her eye at him with equal parts irritation and fear but unable to open her mouth. *If Meg was here she'd know exactly what to say,* Aki thinks.

Ousmane looks at her with a blank expression on his face.

"Aki," he starts slowly. *Why did he have to choose such uncomfortable chairs? Was it to make sure that people didn't stay too long?* "It's important that you learn about the various administrative responsibilities that go on in the school," he says. She can feel her face contort with confusion. Before she can say anything, he continues, voice smooth as freshly laid asphalt. "But I would administer the same advice to Meg as I did to Aaron."

Lay low. He doesn't have to say it out loud.

"We made it through a difficult two weeks," he says, looking cheerful and not like he just exited treacherous diplomatic talks with one of the school's most reliable sources for their annual fund donations. "When we return, I look forward to working with you to implement some of the recommendations from the consultants, address the proposal for a safe space, and hearing what you learn from the parents advisory task force."

Aki groans inwardly. She remembers now that Amanda scheduled it for after winter break.

"Happy holidays to you and Ian," Ousmane says cheerfully. "Hello, Ms. Hamish," he says without taking a breath.

Aki whips around to see Jules in the doorway, eyes wide, hair somewhat wild. "Heya, Ousmane. Can I steal Aki from ya?" She stomps into the room and grabs Aki's upper arm. "Come on girlie," she says, dragging Aki out of her seat. "Happy Festivus!" She calls back to Ousmane.

"Does he celebrate Festivus?" Aki asks Jules incredulously. She seems to recall Ousmane being Muslim and his wife being Quaker.

"Sure, don't we all at Wesley?" she jokes, a nod to the all-inclusive holiday calendar that the faculty tries to pretend to understand. She pulls Aki into an empty classroom and turns around, waving her hands excitedly. "Did you see that video? The one of the person actually, you know, spray-painting the building?"

Aki nods, tired from the meeting and not wanting to talk, not even to her best friend.

"That video." Jules repeats, "it's a surveillance camera. They keep saying they don't have the tapes, but they clearly do."

Aki crinkles her face in confusion.

"Think about it," Jules says, dropping her voice. "They must have known about this for a while now."

Aki feels herself deflating, a long sigh emanating from her nostrils. Jules is right.

"Aki," Jules intones. "Did you see the comments on the video?"

Aki shakes her head. Her fears that Meg was the one who uploaded it had kept her from viewing it more than once. She hadn't even thought about the comments.

Jules stops scrolling and thrusts the phone in front of Aki.

@megummy no one is safe not even you

JANUARY

◆ 9 ◆

"Someone in my English class asked me if I spoke Ebonics."
—Current Wesley student, PoC@Wesley

From the Desk of Harrison Neal

To the School Community:

Our first step in addressing this incident, one that has left me deeply saddened, is to prepare our faculty for the challenges we face. Elliot Associates, a renowned consulting firm, will begin a preliminary round of equity and diversity training for our teachers.

As such, the first day after break, Monday, will be a faculty training day with no classes for students. In coming months, we hope to have student listening days, further widened to parents as well.

We appreciate your support as we move forward into the light.

Harrison Neal III

Aki sighs as looks at her phone. She knows she shouldn't, but she can't help but gloss over yet another glibly crafted Harrison Neal email on her screen.

"Cell phones away, please," says one of two women who stand before her and the rest of the upper school faculty, both in dark suits.

Aki nods. "Sorry," she sputters, putting her phone—and Harrison's superficially plaintive email—away.

The two women smile languidly, their hands clasped in front of their wrinkle-free shirts. One is Black with light, almost golden eyes, and the other is white, with her dark hair tied back into a tidy ponytail.

One of the two consultants, Aki can't remember their names, counts the assembled teachers under her breath. Aki calls them Consultant One and Consultant Two in her head.

Percy swivels his chair toward Aki and Jules, who are seated next to him at the long conference table. "*This* is how Harrison is going to figure out who did it?" he asks incredulously.

"OK, thank you, everyone!" Consultant One says, raising her hands like a conductor. "If you can please look at the screen—" motioning to a slide titled, "Pro-genda."

"You may be wondering," Consultant Two interjects, "why we call it a 'pro-genda.'" She looks around expectantly.

"I am one hundred percent sure I am going to disagree with at least ninety-eight percent of what she has to say," Percy declares.

"*Agendas*," Consultant Two says dramatically, "*are racist.*"

"Lord," Jules says and closes her eyes. "Give me strength."

A thin arm waves wildly in the air. "How are they racist?" A young woman from the math department, Rebecca Hinds, pipes up. "This is *fascinating*!" she exclaims.

Aki is having a hard time concentrating. The comments from the video marched through her mind all through vacation:

@megummy no one is safe not even you. What was Meg not safe *from*? The question had nagged at her at night, keeping her awake. It bugged her during the day, when she was supposed to be grading or writing letters of recommendation. Should she and Meg be on watch for more overt acts of racism? That is what the comment seemed to suggest. She involuntarily yawns, then looks up at the consultants to make sure they haven't seen her.

Consultant One, for her part, either not noticing or ignoring Aki's exhaustion, gives a victorious smile before announcing, *"Agendas* are a structure *infused* with the language of hierarchy and," she pauses dramatically, *"white supremacy."*

Aki can feel her face blanch.

Two hands shoot up in the air: Rebecca and Percy. Consultant Two points to Percy.

"Excuse me," Percy says in a tone that suggests he is trying to exhibit more patience than he feels. "There are words that are degrading and hateful, ones that suggest that Blacks like me aren't human, words that are tied to early slave trades. There is consensus in the academic community and in the media that these types of words simply shouldn't be used. And I think it actually devalues the hate they represent when we suddenly decide that words like 'agenda' are equally vicious."

"Go, Perce!" Jules says under her breath.

Consultant One points to Rebecca without even pausing to acknowledge Percy's point. Percy throws up his hands in irritation.

Rebecca pipes up, "If words like 'agenda' are racist, then wouldn't that mean that much of our everyday language would contain this type of biases?"

Consultant One gazes at Rebecca proudly, like a mother whose child has just brought home a report card full of As. "It is nice to see that we have *allies* who instinctively understand their own prejudices."

"Math, though, wouldn't be subject to this," Rebecca continues, making Consultant One frown ever so slightly. "Because numbers are not biased!" Rebecca crows triumphantly.

"Well," Consultant Two squints. "In fact, math is *incredibly* biased." Rebecca looks horrified. "Given the disproportionate number of white practitioners in the field, the entire field of mathematics maintains white supremacy and values one racial group over other historically repressed groups." She pauses. "It is an institutionally white space."

Rebecca looks crestfallen as Consultant Two clicks to another slide.

"Isn't that all from an article in the *Atlantic*?" Grayson asks, scratching his head, looking at the bullet points on the Power-Point slide.

Consultant Two glares at Grayson and starts again. "We, as white people, must accept that our natural state is that of prejudice, and this practice will help us all identify the denial of our own deep-rooted racism. We must start at this place," she repeats, "that we, as whites, are racist."

Aki sees Rebecca's head bobbing up and down.

"I feel," Grayson says, gulping, "like a criminal."

"You should," Rebecca says, almost gleefully. "We all should!" Then noticing Aki, she corrects herself, "*White* people, that is."

Aki tries and fails not to sigh exasperatedly. To her, this all seems like an incredibly myopic way to view racial issues.

Consultant One changes the slide to one that lists a number of groups: "Asian," "Black," "Latinx," "Muslim," and "White Allies."

Consultant Two announces, "Now we will break into groups, or what we like to call 'Humanity Resource Groups.'"

A hand shoots up. Aki cranes her neck: Monica Stein, head of the English department.

"Excuse me, but if you have one religious group, shouldn't you have another? I'm Jewish so—"

Consultant One interrupts with a smile. "We prefer to use these groups as they are historically repressed—"

"I'm out," Percy declares as the room erupts into a squabble of voices, all in dissent over what is unfolding. He starts gathering up his things. Aki wishes she had the courage to do the same, and she hopes that people know that she had nothing to do with today's training.

"Excuse me?" Monica responds, her hands on her hips. "So because I'm half Black and half Jewish, only half of me counts as a repressed group?"

Aki thinks about this. Her own daughter is mixed heritage, and she feels instinctively uncomfortable that a workshop like this would force her to choose one identity over another. Can she get up and leave like Percy? As interim director of equity and diversity, she knows how it would look.

Consultant Two quickly clicks to the next screen, which reads "Restorative Circle Processes."

Percy grunts under his breath, gathering up his things. "This is what happens when you try to make money off of racial prejudice. Instead of having meaningful discussion you get fancy words and people telling you to think about the wrong things. See you guys," he closes his bag and starts down the aisle. "Call me when Harrison gets real."

Aki thinks about the exchange that she, Jules, Grayson, and Percy had at the assembly right after the graffiti had been discovered. When confronted with a problematic phrase, they had discussed the history and the current meaning, civilly, intellectually, and as friends. This seminar was something altogether different. It felt like the consultants were there to divide and shame.

Consultant Two continues in a silky voice, trying to soothe the rising discontent in the room, "Hello?" she calls to Percy.

"We will convene in our Humanity Resource Groups to discuss harms that have been done to us, and prejudices that we believe we hold. For our white allies, we will discuss how to become *collaborators* instead of *conspirators* against the process."

"Excuse me for being a dumb blond, but isn't she basically saying we shouldn't be racist?" Jules whispers loudly, then stands abruptly.

Oh no, Aki thinks.

"Excuse me," Jules starts. The consultants both look at her with curious expressions. "Look, I *get it*. I'm from the South. People I grew up with said terrible things. I did not always stand up to those bigots and tell them to take a hike. But—"

"Actually," Rebecca interrupts, "I think the appropriate way to diffuse a racist incident is to empathize with the victim rather than take on the aggressor," eyeing the consultants, clearly fishing for praise.

Jules gives Rebecca a look before continuing. "Well, look, these days I'm not one to back down from a fight. But I really wonder if it makes sense to separate us like that," she points to the slide. "But maybe I'm crazy."

"I agree," Percy says, returning to stand next to Jules.

"But—" Consultant One says, eyeing Percy up and down.

"Yes, that's right, I agree with her," he states. "How about we all talk about how we've felt minimized, either as women or as Blacks, because we're mixed race or heritage, or because we have a disability," he says angrily, "and then we really try to listen to one another as colleagues and friends, and learn more about each other and validate one another's feelings, rather than be subjected to this bullshit parade through a thesaurus of racially adjacent terms? Can that be on our 'agenda'?"

Aki stares up at him. Not in a million years could she be that openly confrontational, and she hates that about herself. But she loves her friend for saying what she wished she had the courage to say. The faculty in the room begin to murmur more loudly.

Percy continues. "And how exactly is this going to help us figure out *who did this*? Until we do, no one is safe."

Of course by *this*, Aki knows he's talking about the vandalism. Still, *@megummy no one is safe not even you* flashes through her mind again. She feels frightened but also hates herself for being so still, emotionally unable to speak out freely like her friends.

Consultant One's mouth widens into a satisfied smile. "In fact, we are assisting the administration through recommendations on how to properly investigate the hate crime on your campus."

Aki can feel her heart beating. Why does an investigation make her so nervous? Because of Meg's involvement in the Instagram account? Or something else? Then she feels herself jump to her feet.

"As my friend Jules has said, I'm not sure it makes sense to separate us." Aki knows that she's thrown her support out to the group because part of her just wants the consultants to back off the topic of searching for the perpetrator.

Consultant Two purses her lips. "In our professional experience, we have found that *no true conversation* can happen in an integrated group."

The room falls silent.

Aki cocks her head. The consultant's statement makes her momentarily forget about Meg and finally focus on what is being said in the room. After a lifetime of people misspelling her name, ignoring her in lines and helping other (mostly white) customers, dismissing her credentials ("affirmative action"), and making racially based assumptions ("you must be so good at math!"), she wonders why she has to sit and listen to these consultants tell her how it feels to be marginalized and also be told who she can talk about her feelings with. In fact, she feels more comfortable telling her white friend Jules about being called a racial slur than she does with these two consultants, that is for sure.

Aki feels herself walking toward the front of the room, wedging herself between the consultants and the teachers. She makes eye contact with Grayson, who gives her a little wave, then looks to Percy and Jules, who watch her silently.

"I propose that we break into working groups of our own choosing, and we come up with our own *agenda* for how we'd like to discuss race. We're pretty smart people. I think we can figure this out," she says with more confidence than she feels. Then she sees many of her peers smile at her, and many start snapping their fingers at her suggestion. She looks at the consultants and adds, "I think it makes sense for you to take into account our interests as well."

"I'm afraid—" Consultant One starts.

"We haven't even discussed curricular changes," the other consultant bleats. "We have a full list of recommendations for Wesley to adopt, starting with the eradication of the hegemonic Anglo-Saxon voice—"

"I think that means *me*," Grayson whispers.

Aki clears her throat. "As interim director of equity and diversity, I take responsibility for what happens today. Please speak with Ousmane if you have any concerns," Aki declares, feeling a newly formed sense of confidence growing.

★ ★ ★

After hours of battling back Elliot Associates and the endless nature of their meeting, Aki grows somehow more exhausted when she sees the surprise waiting for her in the foyer when she gets home from school.

"*Aki-chan! Megumi-chan wa?*" (Where is Megumi?) Her mother stands in her years-old striped apron, hands on her hips and feet in slippers.

Aki opens her mouth but nothing comes out. What is her mother doing here?

"*Yasui kippu attakara Megumi-chan ni ainikitanoyo!*" (I found a cheap ticket so I came to see Megumi!)

Aki scratches her ear. *Sounds about right.* She sighs and enters, taking off her shoes, her mother hovering over her as she does.

"*Ian-san mo iruwayo!*" (Ian is here too!) Aki assumes she is incorrect about Ian's whereabouts, since he's on a boat in Greenland at the moment. "*Shinshitu de neteruwayo. Megumu-chan wa?*" (He's sleeping in the bedroom. Where is Megumi?)

Aki opens her mouth again and forces herself to speak through her surprise. "*Megumi wa mousugu modottekuruhazu. Chotto Ian no yousu wo mitekurune.*" (Megumi will be home soon. I'm going to check on Ian.)

She looks at her tiny mother, hair perfectly in place, dressed in her usual uniform courtesy of the Chico's sale rack, then scurries down the hallway to her bedroom like a prisoner on parole. When she opens the door she finds Ian lying on the bed with a folded towel on his face.

"What's going on here?" Aki asks as she starts changing out of her work clothes.

"Your mother told me to lie down with something cold on my eyes," Ian says without moving.

"I see, and what, pray tell, is this a prescription for?" Knowing that her mother is undoubtedly doling out one of her nonmedical fixes for a bodily ailment.

"Headache," Ian says.

"And do you actually have one?" Aki asks, pulling on a light cotton sweater, knowing that if she puts on a hoodie her mother will accuse her of looking like "one of those dirty-looking teens at the mall."

"No, but it feels nice. She froze it for me," Ian explains as he removes the towel and sits up. "Why didn't you tell me she was coming?" he asks, not annoyed but curious. She arches her eyebrow and cocks her head. "Ah, I see," Ian realizes. "You didn't know either."

This was not the first time her mother had flown across country for a surprise visit. She uses a travel agent—an actual person, not a website—some ancient woman who manages to find open seats from SFO at cut-rate deals. She suspects it's some sort of airline employee scamming their company and selling empty seats, but if there's one thing for sure, her mother definitely got a deal.

"Wait, why are *you* here?" Aki asks. Ian was scheduled to be back in Greenland.

"Called back to Silver Spring again," Ian says from underneath his towel.

"Why?" Aki asks. NOAA headquarters are in Silver Spring, about a half hour from their apartment, but Ian is rarely ever in the actual office.

"Big Man wants to talk with me tomorrow," Ian says.

"The director of NOAA wants a meeting with you?" Aki asks, surprised. NOAA has over 10,000 employees; Ian is, as he likes to put it, "Just a wee researcher of the sea."

"Head of the Oceanographic division," Ian says, finally taking the towel off and sitting up to face her. "Just shop talk, nothing serious," he says.

"So he called you back here?" Aki asks again, not sure if she's more surprised by her mother's impromptu visit or Ian's sudden U-turn back to DC.

"*Aki-chan, gohan wo yoi shimasuyo!*" her mother calls from the kitchen. (Aki, I'm starting dinner!)

Aki is being summoned, she knows. Ian merely nods and motions for her to go.

"I'll see you at dinner," he says and lies back down. "I'm here for the week," he adds.

Aki returns to the kitchen to see Meg peeling carrots. "Didn't know you could do that, kiddo," she jokes as Meg ignores her.

"*Meg-chan kara kiitakedo, gakkou taihen mitaine*," her mother says, holding up her knife and tracing circles in the air. (Meg tells me things are difficult at school.)

Aki looks at her mother, dumbfounded. How is it that Meg is more open with her grandmother than she is with her? Aki had spent her life trying to avoid her mother, the glare of criticism and the pernicious sermons, yet here Aki is, perpetuating the same relationship with her own child.

"I was just telling Grandma about everything going on, you know, with the PoC@Wesley page," Meg explains, now julienning the carrots into thin rectangular strips, which means her grandmother must be making *kinpira gobo*, braised burdock root. Savory and sweet at the same time, it's one of Meg's favorite dishes.

"I'm sure she doesn't care," Aki says, taking a carrot and nibbling on it.

"*Ara, nande? Meg-chan tadashii to omoukedo!*" (What are you talking about? I think Meg is right!)

"You do?" Aki is again stunned. She doesn't even bother to respond in Japanese. "But you never cared about that stuff when I was growing up. You told me to ignore it, that it wasn't worth fighting!"

Her mother puts the kitchen knife down and wipes her hands on her apron, which she never forgets to travel with and won't cook without. "*Aki-chan, sekai wa kawarimashita yo!*" (Aki, the world has changed!)

"Yeah, Mother, the world's changed," Meg parrots, looking pleased.

"But, but . . ." Aki sputters, looking at her mother, who has resumed sautéing the burdock, and Meg, who beams back like a solicitor general who's just successfully argued the government's case in front of the Supreme Court. "You always said not to fight battles we can't win!" Her mother doesn't bother to turn around, so Aki continues. "Whatever happened to 'you can't convince people that you're right when they're clearly wrong'?" She recites another saying her mother liked to calmly deliver in the face of obvious racism.

Meg snorts. "Mother, seriously, if we believed in that line, nothing would *ever* change," she says drolly. Typical Gen Z: Not only happy to take on the role of arbiters of change, they're also willing to shame everyone around them into their revolutions too. A soy-licious (as Meg would put it) aroma wafts from the cooktop as Aki's mother turns around and wipes her hands on her apron. "And I heard you led some sort of revolution yourself this morning," Meg says, giving her mother a knowing expression. "How were the consultants, by the way?"

"How did you hear about—" Aki is about to ask when her mother interrupts.

"*Yononakaha mikka minuma no sakurakana.*" (As quickly as the cherry blossom changes, so does the world.) She looks at Aki (and Aki swears she sees a tiny grin on her face), then takes Meg's cutting board and empties the contents into the frying pan. "*Tsugi wa gyoza ne!*" (Next is dumplings!) She cheerfully hands Meg a package of dumpling wrappers and a bowl of filling.

"Gyoza? I *love* gyoza!" Ian appears in the kitchen, holding the hand towel in one hand and a mug of tea in the other.

"Eeeee-aaaaa-nnnn!" Aki's mother cries, jumping up and collecting the towel from Ian while offering him more tea.

"Thank you, Yukiko-san," Ian says, bowing slightly, a habit Aki's never been able to break him of. "You don't bow when you're conversing, it's a greeting!" Aki had explained on numerous occasions, but something in his subconscious always made him genuflect, probably because at his core, he's afraid of his mother-in-law.

Aki's mother washes the towel in the sink, then folds it carefully before placing it back in the freezer. She sits back down with Meg as they scoop small spoonfuls of meat and chopped vegetables into the thin dumpling skins, folding the edges to make them look like delicate shells. Ian sits down to join them, and Aki watches Meg happily folding dumplings, chatting with her grandmother and father, switching back and forth between Japanese and English about college and school. Aki knows she should feel comforted by this domestic vista but instead feels annoyed.

"*Megumi-chan boyfriend genki?*" (Megumi, how is your boyfriend?)

"I'm sorry, *what?*" Aki almost shouts.

"Not a boyfriend, Grandma!" Megumi quickly corrects. "I told you that before," she adds gently.

Aki thinks back to their conversation in the car when Meg insisted she didn't have a boyfriend. But now looking at the flush on her daughter's face, she's not sure she believes her. Meg averts her mother's gaze as she and her grandmother work swiftly like an assembly line, forming perfectly plump dumplings and lining them up in neat rows.

"*Owarine! Sate yakimashou!*" (We're all done, let's start frying!) Her mother takes two platters to the stove and turns on the gas flame. Aki wonders if her mother is trying to guide the conversation away from added drama, but then again, that would be quite unlike her.

"So, kid, how's it been being Insta-famous?" Ian jokes, giving Meg a wink.

"The school has video of Aaron Wakeman defacing the school and no one has done anything about it! He's still walking around like he owns the place," Meg says, angry all of a sudden. "He and his stupid lacrosse posse. The next time I see Zach and Felix in their stupid jerseys and backward baseball hats following him around like puppies I'm going to smack them!"

"So, wait, why hasn't he, Aaron, been expelled?" Ian asks, used to playing catch-up when it comes to school matters.

"The video doesn't show Aaron defacing the property, it shows someone wearing a warm-up jersey that apparently was not in his possession at the time," Aki explains calmly, feeling like Amanda as she does.

"Why are you defending him? Obviously, it was him!" Meg insists. "Did he say it wasn't him? Did he?" Meg is bordering on hysterical. "I thought for sure if we posted the video to the PoC page it would get some reaction, but the school just can't seem to believe its perfect darling did this!" Meg spits out.

"So it *is* you running that account? Where did the video even come from, Meg? Did someone hack into the school's security system?" What Aki desperately wants is to ask why Meg is so angry, but all she can manage to croak out is, "Was it Double?"

Meg throws her another look of disdain. "Double doesn't even have a smartphone, mother. He's anti big tech," as if Aki should know. "And how many times do I have to tell you I don't run the account?"

"*Sate!*" her mother interjects cheerfully. "*Gohan ga dekimashi-tayo!*" (There! Dinner is ready!) Aki's mother has a smile on her face and a full tray of Japanese entrees. Ian's face lights up just as Meg jumps up from her chair. If this is her mother's way of steering the family away from sticky issues, it seems to be working.

"Meg, come back please," Aki commands. *Tell me why you think it's Aaron*, she thinks to herself. *Tell me you didn't do something stupid.*

"I have to go do something, I'll be right back" is her daughter's terse reply.

"Meg!" Aki calls after her. "You're being rude!"

Aki's mother sits and picks up her chopsticks. "*Musume no itteiru koto yori ittenai koto ni kiwo tukenasai.*" (Pay more attention to what your child doesn't say instead of what they're telling you.)

Aki stares at her mother, wondering where such a cryptic message is coming from, considering tact and subtlety are not usually in her mother's arsenal. "*Oishee desuka, Eeann-san?*" (Is it good, Ian?) Her mother is either ignoring Aki's stares or is not concerned by them at all.

"Oh yes, Yukiko-san, delicious!" Ian says blissfully, concerns about the school or their daughter wiped away by pork gyoza and sweet and savory vegetables.

Meg reappears looking flushed, but sits quickly, puts her hands together and says *itadakimasu*, the traditional Japanese saying before meals, before hungrily attacking the dumplings.

"*Ashita wa futari de odekake shite kudasai ne!*" (Tomorrow you and Ian go out together!)

"Thanks, Mom," Aki mumbles through her rice, her mind still on Aaron, her daughter, and the assorted vandalism plaguing the school.

"Mmm, this is amazing!" Meg says loudly, smiling at her grandmother. "What are you going to make tomorrow, Baba? Should we watch *Wheel of Fortune*?"

Aki looks at Meg's obvious adoration for her grandmother and feels a flash of jealousy.

"*Sentaku mono tatandoita wayo,*" her mother says to Aki as Ian and Meg battle over the few remaining dumplings. (I folded the laundry for you.)

"Thank you, I think I'll go put it away now," feeling increasingly annoyed as she watches Meg tease her father and be so helpful with her grandmother.

"Mother, you're being rude," Meg says, smiling at her.

"Don't you want some more?" Ian says, oblivious to her mood.

Aki shakes her head and takes her plates to the sink, turns on her heel, and though she would never admit it out loud, is happy not to be in her daughter's presence.

◆ **10** ◆

"The racism is as entrenched as the privilege at a place like Wesley.
Why are you people so surprised?"
                    —*Someone who left the school, dcparentzone.com*

Pls meet me at the Senior Lounge

AKI IS HUSTLING THROUGH the parking lot, late as usual, frazzled by the text message just sent her. She wanted to spend her free period grading the papers she promised her seniors, and being beckoned by Amanda's text is going to ruin her plans. She rushes through the senior hallway to the end of the corridor and takes a left into an open space that the seniors claim as their unofficial hangout spot. The "lounge" is essentially an awkwardly shaped foyer that three hallways empty into, but it is large enough to house four sofas and is tucked away from classrooms, and more importantly, the eyes of administrators. It is a preternatural mess and in a constant state of chaos: backpacks strewn on the floor, the carpet littered with bits of food and empty coffee cups. The only reason no one says anything is due to the unwritten rule that most people choose to avoid the area, taking major detours within the school to get to where they need to go.

Today, however, Aki sees that the far hallway has been blocked, and a temporary wall of sorts has been erected to create

a separate "room." There is a swinging door set into the temporary wall and a placard on it that reads: "Wesley Multicultural
Work Space."

Amanda stands in front of the door, looking all sorts of crisp
in a gray wool suit and black heels. She dramatically opens the
flimsy door and motions for Aki to enter. When she does, she
sees that the four stained sofas that used to house lounging seniors
have been replaced with a large conference table and ten ergo-
nomically correct desk chairs that sit atop a large maroon area
rug. On the walls are photos of past Wesley faculty and students,
all faces of color. Though it is clear that Amanda wants some sort
of reaction, at first Aki doesn't know what to say other than *nice
use of school funds*, which of course come from an endowment that
rivals many colleges, including the discretionary funds set aside
from the endowment. Then the light bulb goes off in her head.

"Is this in reaction to the town hall and the social media
page?" Aki asks. Displacing seniors with free time makes a definite statement. She also understands it has less to do with Meg
and Double's demands as it does *how the school looks*. Aki can
already tell that despite the fancy new furniture, this isn't going
to begin to placate Meg's or Double's anger.

"Well," Amanda starts, then coughs a little. "I didn't study
semiotics in my PR major for fun," she says in a flat voice. "But
Elliot Associates seemed to think it was a good idea, and the
board didn't blink, so here we are. We're going to have an infor-
mal ribbon-cutting," she explains. "And by the way, we're getting a better door," as if that was the only problem with the
space.

Aki stares at the pathetic swinging door. The whole space
feels more like one of those temporary offices housed in a con-
tainer on the side of a construction site rather than a serious space.
She really hopes that Percy never sees it. *This is just . . .pathetic*,
she thinks, trying to conceal her exasperation from Amanda.

"Here, help me," Amanda says impatiently as she hands Aki an enormous roll of electrical tape. "I have to put up the ribbon."

Aki holds the tape and watches Amanda unfurl a thick red ribbon.

"Cut me off some," she demands as Aki struggles with the thick tape, finally handing Amanda two strips and watching as she sticks the ribbon up. "Good enough," she announces.

Aki notices a slow trickle of students filtering into the space. "Are we the only faculty here?" *Please don't let Percy be here*, she thinks again as Amanda nods.

"We had to pull this together quickly, not a lot of planning. We just need to show the students we actually care about . . ." she waves her hand at the door, "this." Suggesting, of course, that *she* certainly doesn't.

Double, Meg, and Aiko walk through what is now a sizable crowd. Aki can tell right away that Meg is dubious, since it's an expression she's so used to seeing on her daughter's face. She averts her glance so as to not make eye contact with Meg.

"Good, let's get started before first period," Amanda barks. "Gus, are you ready?" she asks.

Aki looks at Gus Hoover, who works part time in the admissions office and is a semiprofessional photographer. Watching him crouch before them with his oversized camera, Aki realizes that he's here to cover this hastily planned event.

"Here you go," Amanda says, handing an oversized pair of scissors to Double and Aiko. Aki realizes that Amanda doesn't know their names. "Aki, a few words before we begin?"

Aki tries not to panic as she looks out at a growing number of students, some clearly here out of curiosity more than anything, "Yes, well, thank you all for gathering here today for the opening of Wesley's—" she cranes her neck to read the placard correctly. "Wesley Multicultural Work Space."

"We'd like to thank the faculty and administration for working with us to create a safe space for minority students," Aiko says graciously, saving Aki from further embarrassing herself.

"On the count of three, let's cut the ribbon," Amanda says loudly. "One! Two! Three!" she cries out as Aiko and Double carefully cut the ribbon, its two pieces falling limply to the side. "And don't worry, we're getting a new door," Amanda promises again, ripping the ribbon off and taking the scissors back as if she was cleaning up after unwrapping Christmas presents. It's not lost on Aki that Amanda probably doesn't care what it is she is there to do so long as it looks good on the school website. And as if to prove Aki's point, the next words out of Amanda's mouth are "Gus, let me take a look at those pictures."

Aiko, Double, and Meg enter the room and peer around. She's relieved when she sees the three of them exit looking satisfied, heads bobbing in agreement. Aki wonders if she can escape to her office and grade papers when a group of boys walks up to the new space. They are all wearing Wesley warm-up jerseys and, curiously enough, all holding Chick-fil-A cups.

"Hey, Double, what's up?" one of them says as he raises his drink in greeting.

"Hey," Double says back quietly.

"Wait, they've taken away the senior lounge for this?"

Uh-oh. Aki looks to see who said this particular line and sees Yeardly Ward, who has several boys from the lacrosse team hanging on to her every word. She also sees Zach, Felix, and Aaron hanging in the back of the group drinking noisily from their cups.

"Isn't this racist against white people?" someone asks, drawing laughs.

"Get the fuck out of here," Meg steps in between the boys and the doorway, as if to shield Double, Aiko, and the space from being encroached upon. The gathered crowd starts to laugh and talk, making the space seem smaller and more chaotic. "You're the reason we need this space!"

"Who, us? We're just a little old lacrosse team," someone jokes, making the other boys laugh.

"Damn, she's like a pit bull," one of the boys shouts. "Aaron, think you can get her back on a leash?"

Aki is taken completely aback. Do they not notice a teacher standing among them, not to mention Meg's mother, or do they not care? She's about to say something when Aaron takes a few steps out of the crowd and puts himself between the group and Meg. Aki almost pulls Aaron back, afraid of what will happen.

"Get. Out. Of. Here," Meg says, her voice seething.

"Wakeman, get your dad to build us a new lounge! This is some bullshit!" someone yells out as a few students clap.

Aaron looks back at the voice, a lazy smile on his face, when suddenly Meg launches forward and slaps Aaron's drink out of his hand.

"Awwww, shit!"

The students react as Aki watches in horror. She slaps her hand over her mouth, keeping herself from crying out. She's about to say something to her daughter when Aiko speaks up.

"Meg, it's OK, calm down," Aiko begs from behind her.

"Yeah, Meg, stop making a big deal about this," Aaron says, though Aki can't tell if he's being serious or taunting her. She feels afraid, and with good reason, because the next thing Meg does is raise her hand and slap Aaron across his face.

"Meg!" Aki cries out. She had suspected that any affection that Meg used to have for Aaron waned as they entered upper school, but what she is seeing now is out of control.

"Holy shit!"

"What the fuck!"

"Enough!" Amanda roars. "Gus, take her to Ousmane's office," she says, pointing to Meg. "And all of you, get to class."

She watches as the crowd disperses. "Thank God there's no faculty here," she says under her breath. "You!" she points at Aaron. "Go to the nurse, and I don't want to hear about it!"

Aki feels like her jaw is coming off its hinges as she watches Gus walk Meg toward the front office and Zach and Aaron make their way to the nurse. What in the world prompted Meg to act so violently? She is at a loss, and this makes her feel inadequate as a parent.

"Kids are such drama queens!" Amanda rages. "At least we got some good photos," she declares, acting like what has happened is nothing but a children's birthday party that went a little sideways. "Thanks for your help. I'll send you an agenda for the parents task force," she says in her usual no-nonsense voice. "Was that your daughter?" she finally asks as Aki nods dumbly. "Good luck with that," she says as she turns on her heel. "She looks like you!" she calls back as she disappears down the hallway, the red ribbon under her arm and trailing behind her like a flame.

*   *   *

Aki knew she'd better make an appearance in Ousmane's office since it was inevitable she'd get called in after what had just happened. She was too shocked at the time, watching everything unfold so quickly, but now as she makes her way toward his office all she can think is *why*? Meg is certainly impetuous and emotional, but she'd never known her to be openly violent, and what in the world had Aaron done to provoke such a strong response? From what she had witnessed, he hadn't been doing anything too terrible when Meg launched herself at him. Everything Aki knows of Aaron is that he is a polite, smart kid with plenty of friends, though she supposes in that moment, Aaron didn't do much to quell the nasty language coming out of his friends' mouths. Is that what Meg was reacting to, or had he done something to her? Aki is simultaneously dying to know while realizing she'll regret it when she finds out. She knocks lightly on Ousmane's door.

"Enter," comes his stern reply. "Ah, Aki. Thank you," he says.

For raising Raging Bull? You're welcome, she thinks as she takes a seat next to a sullen Meg, who refuses to make eye contact with her.

"I am afraid, per school policy, that Meg will be suspended."

Aki closes her eyes and tries not to flinch. A suspension as a junior. She knows how this will look to colleges. Then she catches herself. She really should be worried more about why her daughter reacted the way she did.

"Would you care to explain what happened?" Ousmane says in a quiet voice.

"Aaron is what happened," Meg shoots back.

"I'm afraid that is not much of an explanation," Ousmane says, shaking his head. "Meg, part of the process of returning to campus is meeting with me to explain your actions and how you will act moving forward."

"Why is it that students like Aaron can get away with any-thing and never get punished?" Meg spits back.

"What is it that Mr. Wakeman has done?" Ousmane asks placidly.

"We all know he did it," Meg says. "The graffiti," she clarifies.

"Meg," Aki intervenes, "that's—"

"Do you have proof?" Ousmane asks directly.

Meg slumps in her seat. "There is so much that he *has* done that is equally as awful," she exclaims, soundly sadly like a small child tattling on their sibling. "Everyone knows it!" she insists. Even Aki has to shake her head at Meg's petulance before feeling a twinge of anger at her daughter for being so careless.

Ousmane stares wordlessly at Meg and recites, "As clearly stated in the student handbook, physical altercation is an automatic suspension pending a satisfactory discussion with the division head upon return." Meg begins to rise out of her seat as Ousmane continues. "Meg, please never let anything like this happen again, because it won't end with just a suspension," he says sternly, and Aki understands that this is a serious warning about her daughter's place in the school.

"Wesley is just another name for an affirmative action program for rich parents."

—*Sad Quaker, dcparentzone*

*A*ND HERE WE ARE, *yet again, ready to discuss the merits or demerits of printing sponsor names on cocktails napkins and whether or not embroidered blankets will be a hot ticket item this year,* Aki thinks to herself as she gulps down her quadruple shot Americano.

She can't believe she's being dragged into yet another auction meeting, though she knows that this is her fate until the big day, which is always on the coldest evening with the crappiest weather on the last weekend of February. *If the school really wants people to shell out money at the auction, they should set up a fake beach and ply them with piña coladas on a warm Saturday in May,* she thinks. She tried to point this out but was informed quite sternly that the school has henceforth renamed it the *scholarship fundraising gala.* When she pointed out that the live and silent parts of the "gala" were still called "auction," she got a silent stare and a thank you for her time.

"Hello, everyone!" Holly nearly shouts from the head of the table. She's wearing her favorite cobalt blue cable-knit cashmere sweater and can't-believe-they're-$275 jeans.

Aki averts her gaze. She's sure that Holly—and everyone else in the room for that matter—has heard of Meg's suspension, but she has to pretend like nothing has happened as the group votes on this year's gala theme. Will it be "Under the Sea" or "Wizard of Oz" for the win this year? Jules likes to cackle about how every year the theme sounds like a bad prom night, and Aki has to agree.

"I know everyone is so excited to hear about this year's theme!" Holly exclaims excitedly.

Can't wait, Aki thinks, feeling dead inside. Meg hadn't spoken to her since their meeting with Ousmane, and all she could think about whenever she passed Meg's closed door was *I hope she's not planning an insurrection from inside that bedroom.*

"Last year's theme was a little tricky, I think we can all agree," Holly starts. All heads swivel to look at Liz, who had spearheaded the last auction.

Oooh, things just got interesting, Aki thinks. Holly's comment was clearly a shot across the bow.

"The World Cup in Qatar was a little too sports and niche, I think we can all agree," Holly starts coolly.

"We had that amazing travel agency donate a five-day vacation in Doha," Liz sputters defensively, but Holly keeps prattling on.

"Yes, well, and though it was nice that you and Roger dressed up in matching outfits as Neymar and Casemiro—"

"Who?" someone asks, confused by the Brazilian soccer names.

"*Exactly*," Holly says smoothly, not letting Liz interrupt. "And since I know everyone is dying to know what this year's theme is . . ." she trails off for effect, "it's . . . the light!"

Holly's words land like a *thud* in the room.

Liz cackles. "Like a light switch? Can Rog and I come as light bulbs? Incandescent is illegal on campus, I'm assuming."

Holly purses her lips, and Aki can tell she's about to launch into a lecture. She remembers this face from when Zach was a kid and they would go over for playdates, the face that looked like she was chewing on a lemon while trying to do a math problem in her head. "As you know, the school's theme is 'move forward into the light,' so we will play on these words and ideas!"

Silence meets Holly's enthusiasm.

I wonder if I should curtail Meg's social media use, Aki suddenly thinks to herself, then realizes that as a seventeen-year-old, Meg would easily be able to get past any superficial parental barriers she tried to throw up. *And I wonder why she is so incredibly angry at Aaron.* She can't help but think there's something she's missing between the two students. What happened between them to set off such off-the-chart rage?

"Ms. Brown, what do you think?" Holly asks.

Aki feels like she's been publicly assaulted and scrambles for a coherent set of words. "Uh, well, that might be nice" is all she can pull together.

"As nice as your daughter," she hears Liz mutter under her breath. Aki knows she should be mad, but she can't blame Liz for the swipe. Meg *was* in the wrong, at least when it came to hitting Aaron.

"Who paid for that new multicultural work space?" someone in the room suddenly asks.

Holly smiles serenely. "Though a wonderful and timely topic of discussion, I'm not sure it's relevant to our—"

"I heard it was the Wakemans," someone else says.

The ultimate irony. That can't be true, Aki thinks, trying not to look too interested in the conversation going on around her while hoping it continues.

"Obviously it deflects attention from Aaron being a bone-headed ra—"

Holly raps her knuckles on the table like a mob boss. "I'm afraid we really must—"

"I heard a brawl went down in the room on its opening day," another voice calls out.

Aki wants the earth to open up and swallow her whole. At the very least, she feels herself sinking into her conference room chair.

"The school has done an exemplary job of handling issues like these, and I think we can let them decide how to mediate whatever transpired," Holly offers like the perfectly trained mouthpiece in the hand-picked parent army that Wesley likes to employ for its volunteer work force. For once, Aki is glad Holly is handling the situation and not someone like Liz, who would be flaming the fans of rumor if only to make as many people feel uncomfortable as possible.

Holly clears her throat. "Now, we really must move on to discuss how many of us can ask our business and personal contacts to help underwrite the gala this year. We're trying to have an open bar with premium spirits."

"Only reason to attend!" Liz quips. "Casamigos or bust!"

Aki looks at the clock. Would it be reasonable to leave the meeting early, begging off in order to prep for class? *Definitely*, she thinks.

"I'm so sorry, but I have to run and get ready for my senior seminar," she says, knowing that no parent of a college-bound senior is about to object. Can't let a bad grade get in the way of a future freshman orientation at Yale, obviously.

"Of course," Holly says graciously. "We'll send you the meeting notes to review."

Which I will most definitely not read, Aki thinks as she waves and exits.

★ ★ ★

So much for being ready for class, Aki thinks as she sits at the front of her senior seminar. Though she'd left the gala meeting early, she got caught up in grading and never bothered to look at her discussion notes.

"Ms. H?" A voice punctuates her thoughts.

Aki looks up to see a Wesley senior named Ethan Charlip raising his bear paw of a hand. A defensive lineman for the football team, she knows he's been recruited to Syracuse.

"Where's Mr. Manne?" he asks, "Not to be like, rude," he adds quickly.

Aki had received a note from Ousmane earlier that morning: "I have gotten word that Grayson is out due to emergency dental surgery. I am hoping you can cover his class today. Thank you." This week is going to be long. Meg is on her third day of a weeklong suspension, and Aki is still digging herself out of the work that has been piling up on her desk, thanks to the additional responsibilities Amanda has been shoveling her way. Every time a student looks at her, she's assuming they're wondering what's going on with Meg. She's wondering the same thing. Why in the world would she attack another student so violently, not to mention publicly? At the end of every day, she returns home with the hope that her daughter will be willing to talk to her about her anger toward Aaron and how she plans on returning to school. And every day when she returns home, Meg is out, either at Aiko's house or running a mystery errand. It's unfortunate, Aki realized, that "suspension" doesn't mean home detention.

"We were supposed to have Roman Empire Trivia Bowl today," Ethan explains. "He promised we'd do it the first day back from break."

For a moment Aki has a crazy thought about canceling class altogether and surprising Meg in the middle of the day, forcing her to come clean about what is bothering her. Grayson hardly seems like a teacher who would mind going off the syllabus. Just then, Double enters the classroom.

"Doubbbllllle!" some of the boys call out as he takes a seat.

"Sorry, Ms. Hayashi-Brown, I had a doctor's appointment," Double says, handing her a note with his doctor's name on top. "Are you subbing today?"

"No problem, um . . ." Aki trails off, looking out the window. She sighs and looks back to the class. She's never had some of the students, the most notable being Double himself. "So, guys," she starts.

"You mean *people*," Tyler Kominsky corrects Aki kindly. "We respect the nongendered."

"Ah, yes, so, everyone," Aki corrects herself. She is about to look at Grayson's notes when another student enters the room late. "Mr. Manne is sick," Aki repeats formally in a clipped tone. "So, for today's agenda—"

"Can we talk about the fuu—I mean, messed-up shii—I mean the messed-up crap that is going on in this school?" Ethan announces as everyone sits still to watch her reaction. When she nods to signify her approval of the topic, everyone starts talking in a swoop and a rush.

"Sus, right? Totally sus!"

"Completely shook."

"When they told us to stay off TikTok and the gram, that was extra."

"Like, why so salty about the protest? We were totally in the right."

Aki stares at them, understanding that they have a lot to say but realizing that she needs some sort of dictionary to interpret it. At the very least, she feels their anger, and she realizes that this is just as important a topic to cover than whatever was originally on the agenda. She clears her throat. "Maybe one at a time? So we can think about what we all have to say?" *And in English, please*, she wants to add. She can feel herself avoiding Double's gaze, embarrassed that Meg is at home and in trouble, though she knows he probably doesn't care.

"They're just words! Don't give the douche who did it any attention!" someone calls out.

Double raises his hand quickly. Aki nods to him, trying to ignore the pressing feeling that things are already spinning out of control and she has no plan to rope them back into place.

"It's a hate crime and violence against people of color," he says simply.

Can anyone argue against that? Aki thinks.

"I wonder," Tyler says thoughtfully, "if this can't be used to open a better dialogue about inclusion. And about gender as well," she adds.

Then, Nathan Richter raises his hand. Aki hopes that her expression doesn't reveal the surprise she feels, because she can't remember the last time Nathan Richter said a word in class other than to ask to be excused. He's a perfectly sufficient student, a "master of Bs," as she privately refers to him, and the only thing she really knows about him is that he was recruited to play basketball for Wesley as a sophomore. He commutes from the inner folds of Maryland and often can't make it to school if there is heavy snow or an accident on the Beltway. She nods at Nathan.

"Do any of you know what it feels like to be poor?" he says suddenly and without a trace of self-consciousness. The class quiets and looks at him, waiting for him to say more. Aki is afraid he won't proffer any further information when he exhales exasperatedly. "Look, am I grateful that I get to go to a school like Wesley? Sure. Do I know why I'm here? Yeah," he says, again without defiance or insecurity. "But like Tyler says, it's crazy how the school talks about equality and never thinks about anything beyond race." He sits back in his chair, apparently at the terminus of his brief yet striking commentary.

Aki looks to see how the class might react. She feels a surge of empathy with Nathan since she's been in his position. Her parents run a small Japanese grocery store in Daly City, frequented by all sorts for the imported treats and staples, but it was particularly popular for her father's takeaway sushi business. Though they couldn't compete with the fancy sit-down bars in the city or suburbanized bourgeoise fusion joints in Palo Alto, her parents' little storefront was always bustling with customers who appreciated a deal. It paid for the mortgage and a trip a year to Japan, but it didn't offer much more. Aki can remember that whenever she would ask for something that she considered reasonable: a new pair of sneakers or money for a concert, how her mother would respond with a raised eyebrow and interminable silence. Aki was lucky, though, because Westridge High School was filled with families and students like herself from first- or second-generation families who didn't have much other than a work ethic. For someone like Nathan Richter, Wesley is a daily reminder that he is not like those who surround him, even without graffiti scrawled on the walls.

Jenni Pai clears her throat. Everyone turns to her, probably relieved to be liberated from the naked truth that Nathan has laid at their feet: Wesley likes to talk about equity but rarely discusses privilege. "Well," Jenni starts, "if we're talking about being insensitive, maybe we should address the fact that race relations at Wesley is an exclusive discussion of Black and white?"

A rancorous debate resumes among the dozen students—yes, Wesley ignores Latinx and Asian students, but wait, Black and white relations are prominent for a reason. Ethan's hand shoots up, and Aki hopes she doesn't look grateful for the intervention as she nods to him.

"What do you think, Ms. H?"

Aki is taken aback. It is rare for a student to ask her opinion, and she blinks at Ethan, unsure of whether or not to tell him she can't say, or if she should just ignore him. She's always found it funny how he calls her Ms. H; most people, like Holly or the other parents, call her "Ms. Brown," and very few call her by her full name. Percy asked her once if it bothered her. "I guess I never thought I had a choice," she responded. He shook his head and told her she always had a choice, and from that day on Percy called her Hayashi. She's always had a soft spot for Percy and for Ethan, but she never connected it all together. Maybe it's because they actually bothered to consider that she might like to be called by her Japanese name.

"Ms. H, you're one of like two Asian ladies in this joint. How does that feel?" Ethan prods.

"Honestly?" she says impulsively. The kids nod at her, eager to hear an adult admit to scorn. "It makes me feel invisible."

"Like your opinions get ignored?" Jenni asks. Aki feels an ache, since she knows Jenni is probably speaking from personal experience.

Aki nods. "I'd be lying if I said I didn't." She thinks of the many times she's been asked—expected—to do things other teachers aren't, to participate on committees, be on the cover of the alumni magazine, or be part of the admissions open house like a model minority. To make white families feel like they are being racially sensitive by choosing a school like Wesley. To be the interim director of equity and diversity. All the while knowing that never once has the school asked her opinion about anything substantive. "Most of the time people can't even figure out if they want to call me Ms. Brown, Ms. Hayashi, or Ms. Hayashi-Brown, and you know what? I just stopped trying," she says matter-of-factly.

"Is the school actively trying to figure out who did it?" Josh Fayer waves his hand wildly in the air, asking the obvious question.

Aki bites her lip as she wonders what the consultants are actually doing to "assist" the school. *Just another expensive Band-Aid the school likes to slap on problems*, she figures.

"There's that video," Ethan pipes up. "Can't they do something with that? Like look at the reflection in the glass analysis, you know? Mission Impossible that shit?" He puts his oversized hand over his mouth. "Sorry! I mean, you know what I mean," he says, smiling.

Aki tries not to react, thinking about Jules's assertion that the school knew about the video long before anyone else did. Why are they not trying to ferret out the suspect?

"There are surprisingly accessible programs out there," Josh says thoughtfully. "You could use Amazon Rekognition API-type software to capture and analyze images, but from what I gather, Wesley is boycotting Amazon right now," he concludes, referring to Wesley's Buy Local campaign.

"Props to Mr. Bishop," Rhea announces. "He's been super supportive."

"Ooh, Zaddy!" someone says. "Stanning Bishop *hard*!" Referring to Percy, she assumes, as the class dissolves into giggles.

"Mr. Bishop understands," Double speaks up again calmly, "that as Jean-Paul Sartre said, *par tous les moyens nécessaires*." He looks around. *By any means necessary*, Aki realizes in translation.

"Well, it's *not* who everyone says it is!" Yeardly Ward claims suddenly. The other students look at her, some with looks of surprise, others with disgust. "It's not!" she insists, tossing her mane of blond hair behind her shoulder and exhaling in a literal *huff*. "Anyway, maybe *some* people are *jealous* and just trying to be *extra* about all of this," she concludes, raising her eyebrows.

"Here's what I think," a crisp voice enters into the conversation. "If the school can prove who did it and punish them, it is an important step toward showing the students that Wesley actually cares about what it says it stands for," Scott Glanzel explains while giving Yeardly a look that says, "Please, girl." Scott is senior class president, part of the LGBTQIA alliance and on his way to Brown next fall. "Put up or shut up, amiright?" he exclaims as a conclusion. Students respond by applauding and laughing at his directness.

"Are you afraid of Aar—" Aki trails off before starting again. "Are you afraid of the person who might have done this?"

Silence falls in the classroom, allowing inside the shouts of students on distant playing fields and the tick-tock of the analogue clock passing time on the wall. Aki looks at the students, willing them to respond. Finally, someone speaks.

"I think *they* should be afraid of *us*," Double declares. Aki wants to probe his comment further when the bell rings to announce the next period. Students scramble to gather their belongings and make their escapes, and Aki starts gathering her own things.

"Ms. Hayashi-Brown?" She looks up to see Double standing before her. "Can I speak to you?" She nods.

He glances around, waiting for the students to exit the room before starting. "Before you became the DEI head, a group of us went to speak to Harrison Neal about some ideas we had for the school." Aki nods, thinking about Jules and choral choices and realizes the group must have more on their agenda other than Christmas carols. "We appreciate that they agreed with us that they needed an official head of a diversity program, and we think you're doing a great job as interim head—" he pauses to look up at her, scrutinizing her face for a reaction, she knows. Aki forces a smile, trying to encourage Double to keep going despite feeling like she's just been cut from the team. "But, well, when we asked about having a search and making it a priority to find someone for a permanent position, they said they couldn't hire anyone because of budgetary restrictions."

Oh, did they now? Aki thinks. *I see. I'm free labor.* Anger starts bubbling up inside of her, thinking about the two consultants and their *pro-gendas* and wondering how much they cost.

"But the thing is," Double continues, "we looked on the school's own website and they're hiring for three different advancement positions as we speak."

Advancement, i.e., the fundraisers. The majority of private schools in the area have eight, even upward of ten-person advancement offices, mostly led by middle-aged white women. Wesley's own office is headed by a dark-haired older woman who had a frankly inexplicable amount of power for someone whose main purpose appears to be a glorified party-planner. Rumor was you could bring her to the auction gala and blindfold her and she could still recognize who the moneybags were at the school. She still cannot, however, spell Aki's last name correctly. That said, Aki is slightly afraid of, and also unfortunately indebted to, Wesley's own advancement office since Meg receives reduced tuition.

Double continues. "Annual giving, individual gifts, major gifts . . . they're also hiring a young alumni outreach coordinator," Double elaborates. "These are all full-time positions. Not even the Latin teacher is full time with benefits. What about all the money going toward the new campus expansion that could be used for equity programming? Do they not understand that we see through their actions where their priorities are?"

Aki looks up at Double. She guesses that he is about six feet tall, with an amazing head of hair and large dark eyes boring into her. His expression is as honest as his beliefs, and what she sees in his face is the collision of idealism and innocence. She sees the same earnestness and hunger in Double as she does in Meg and understands why the two are so close. She also doesn't know what to say. The school *is* clearly laying out what it needs and thus illustrating its values; apparently, she was put in this position as a placeholder to make people happy in the interim. The old Aki would have told Double that something like a director of diversity, equity, and inclusion wouldn't help make an elite institution any less blind to its own racist tendencies, so why bother? But the new Aki wants to support people like Meg and Double who are going to right the wrongs she experienced growing up, to address the hypocrisy that she herself has helped to perpetuate, she realizes. She wishes she could stop living with a foot in two different territories of thought, and she wishes she could do more, but she can still feel her upbringing holding her back.

As if reading her mind, Double speaks again. "DEI programs, people to help teachers put programs in place, it's an important start. I know it might not make sense to you, us making a big deal about this stuff—"

"No, it does," she interrupts, and she means it. This version of Double is softer, less assertive, than the one being interviewed on-air by Joanna Javier-Hernandez. She wonders if this is not the real him.

Double smiles, which she knows is a rarity for him. "'We have the obligation to protest unjust laws,'" he says. "Martin Luther King," he elaborates.

"'If an elephant has his foot on a mouse, the mouse does not appreciate your neutrality,'" Aki quotes back to him.

"Desmond Tutu," Double replies, his eyes lighting up. "Meg is right, you know," he says. "It *is* good the school got vandalized. It's the wake-up call it needed."

Was it though? Aki wonders. To have something so terrifying scrawled so publicly? To have parents and students honestly frightened about who was in their school community? When Meg made the same public declaration—on television no less—Aki was worried about the backlash her daughter would receive from the administration, reflecting Aki's own upbringing. One that never questioned authority and was always wary of reprimand.

Double shrugs and says again, "*Par tous les moyens nécessaires.*"

By any means necessary.

$\bullet$ **12** $\bullet$

*"Hello, my name is Sasha and I'm a reporter for CNN. If any
of the posters on this account are willing to speak with me on the
record, please DM me."*

—*CNN reporter, PoC@Wesley*

THE BUZZER TO THE entrance of the condo announces the
presence of a guest, and Meg and Aki exchange glances
over their silent dinner of *chahan*, Japanese fried rice, that Aki
has whipped up. With Ian back in Greenland after what seemed
like an uneventful meeting with his boss and her mother's quick
U-turn of a visit, every dinner that week of Meg's suspension has
been a morbidly quiet affair, not to mention the only time Meg
seems to be willing to be in the same room as her mother. As the
buzzer sounds again, Meg gives an exasperated sigh and walks to
the monitor as if weighed down by an anvil, pushes the button to
open the door, then returns to her seat.

"Meg!" Aki scolds. "Did you even bother to see who it was?
You shouldn't just let anyone in!" she says worriedly.

"Well, the odds the one serial killer I let in the building
finds our unit is pretty small so I think we're good. *Gochisousama
deshita*," she says in conclusion, the traditional thanks at the end

of a Japanese meal. She stands and rinses her dish and puts it in the dishwasher, then disappears down the hallway and back into her room.

"Thanks for saying more than two words to me tonight!" Aki can't help but call after her.

There is a light knock at the door, and Aki stops to think. Who could it be on a Friday night? When she shuffles over to the peephole, she can't help but give a little gasp. Standing in her condo hallway is Ousmane.

"Oh, Ousmane," Aki stutters as she opens the door. "How are you? Come in," she says as she beckons him into their home, realizing that in any other school, this might seem odd, but she and Ian have had Ousmane over to their home many times, and she realizes that it must be something very important for him to show up like this.

Ousmane steps inside but declines a seat. "I'm so sorry to bother you at home," he begins, then clears his throat. "However, this could not wait until after the weekend, and I did not feel right merely discussing it over the phone," Ousmane adds, making Aki worried. "It has come to light that Meg has been in violation of our social media rules," he states plainly.

Ousmane and his wife didn't live far from them, and Aki has seen them while out hiking in Rock Creek Park. She knows this trip wasn't out of his way but understands the seriousness of whatever transgression Meg has involved herself in if he is here after school hours.

She tries to swallow back her mounting anxiety and squeaks, "What are we talking about, exactly?"

Ousmane pulls out his phone and scrolls through the screen. When he stretches out his hand she sees the PoC@Wesley account with a picture of Aaron in his warm-up jersey on the sidelines of a home game, with the number 18 emblazoned on the back, with a caption that reads, "Suspect number one."

Aki peers down at the photo and then like the *ding!* of a bell, she realizes that this blazing sign pointing straight at Aaron Wakeman has Meg's fingerprints all over it, as evidenced by the frankly perplexing amount of anger her daughter has toward him, not to mention her hints that she is somehow involved with the account. Despite this strong suspicion, Aki's reflex to protect Meg emerges quickly. "Is there proof that Meg uploaded this photo?" she asks, trying to keep any accusatory tones out of her voice. It is, she thinks, a perfectly reasonable question given the anonymity of the Internet. "Anyone can submit photos to that account," she points out.

"Yes, well, ahem," Ousmane starts, looking uncharacteristically flustered. "The person in the photo—"

"*Aaron*," Aki iterates, suddenly irritated. Why is Ousmane dancing around this?

"Yes, well, it appears there are . . . certain allegations that Aaron has made against Meg," Ousmane starts. "Perhaps we can clear this up. Would it be possible for me to speak to Meg directly?"

Aki hesitates, then realizes she has no real choice. It must be serious if he is at her home, and it does seem like he's here with honest intensions. She motions for him to wait while she goes to fetch Meg.

Aki knocks on Meg's door. No response.

"Meg!" she hisses. "Meg!" she whispers loudly.

Suddenly the door swings open. "What?" Meg looks like she's been sleeping.

"Ousm—I mean, Mr. Gueye is here and he has some questions for you."

"Ugh, seriously?" Meg asks, unperturbed by the fact that the head of upper school has materialized at her house during her suspension. She sighs exaggeratedly and follows her mother back to the foyer.

"Hello, Meg," he greets her formally, bowing his head slightly.

"Hey," Meg says as if nothing out of the ordinary were happening.

"Meg, I was hoping you could explain the appearance of this post on social media," he says, holding his phone out to show Meg what is undoubtedly her handiwork.

"Ew," she says as she wrinkles her nose. "Aaron."

Aki closes her eyes. Why is her daughter like this?

"Let me be direct, then," Ousmane says quickly. "Meg, did you send this picture of Aaron to the social media account called PoC@Wesley?" Aki is so taken aback by Ousmane's bluntness— he, the weaver and bobber, the man of diplomacy and opaque explanations—that she misses her opportunity to signal her daughter to shut up.

"Yes," Meg says without a hint of apology.

Aki feels her body deflate.

"Mr. Wakeman says that you posted the picture as a way to get back at him," Ousmane explains to Meg, and by extension, to Aki.

"Why would I do that?" Meg asks Ousmane. Aki stares at her daughter. On the one hand, she hopes that her daughter has legitimate proof of Aaron's involvement so that she can explain this social media post, which appears to be taken so seriously by the school that it warrants an in-home visit. On the other hand, why would Meg be so . . . *vengeful* isn't the right word, but it feels like it might be.

Meg continues to stare at Ousmane with a blank expression. Ousmane reveals nothing in his face either, leaving Aki to feel like she's watching two master poker players at a high stakes table in Monte Carlo.

Finally, Ousmane speaks. "Do you know who runs the account? Perhaps they can comment on the veracity of the claim with corroborating evidence."

Check, thinks Aki. This is his way of trying to find out who is responsible for the pesky social media proclamations. Maybe he's more interested in finding out about the account owner rather than punishing Meg, she hopes feverishly.

"Why is it that the school seems more interested in finding out who runs a social media account, one that exposes the racial injustice of the school, rather than trying to punish the person who spray-painted a hate message on the side of its own building?" Meg shoots back.

King captures rook and gets out of check, thinks Aki, wondering suddenly if she even needs to be in the room, since Meg seems to be self-advocating just fine, one of those skills that Wesley loves to instill in students from day one. She swears she sees Ousmane smile, if only a tiny bit.

"May I see your phone?" Ousmane asks, making Aki snap to attention.

"No," Aki interjects forcefully, surprising even herself. "Did you ask the same of Aaron Wakeman? I'm assuming his father would say no as well."

Ousmane crosses his arms. As he has risen in the ranks of seniority at the school, his dress shirts reflect this gravitas, and today's blue and white shirt has his initials embroidered on the cuffs. "You are correct, his father did say no. However, I wanted to give Meg the opportunity to clear herself quickly and voluntarily," he says affably.

"Asked and answered," Aki says curtly, suddenly feeling less intimidated by the situation, realizing belatedly that Cash Wakeman undoubtedly steamrolled Ousmane and that has resulted in his little after-hours drop-in. If Aki has learned anything in her thirteen years at Wesley, it's that the richer the parent, the more protected the kid, and the only thing that serves as protection for Meg is Aki. "I'm curious," she asks, no longer able to keep the undercurrent of cynicism out of her voice, "*has* the school tried to figure out who did it? The graffiti? Or do you need a picture of someone with a machete in one hand and a severed head in the other to actually do something? It's pretty clear from the leaked video that the school knew what it was looking at." This is as close as she's gotten to being openly combative with Ousmane in her entire time at Wesley. Out of the corner of her eye, Aki sees Meg smile at her. Like any parent of a teenager longing for recognition from their child, Aki feels like she's gotten her gold star for the day.

Ousmane, true to form, simply smiles at Aki and says, "Even if someone had a machete in their hand, I would still dust for prints. My job is not to assume that my own students are guilty. My job is to protect all the students and the school." He does not, she notices, address the allegation that the school had seen the footage long before it was leaked.

"So, have you asked Aaron about the graffiti?" Meg asks Ousmane pointedly.

Aki wonders why her daughter keeps pressing this question when she knows he won't answer, and he doesn't.

"Everyone knows it was him," Meg says flatly. "He does awful thing after awful thing, and you all just keep looking the other way. You know that he was part of the slave trading game on Snap at Tilden Prep, right?" Meg narrows her eyes at him.

During the fall, an all-boys school in the area had been ensnared in a national controversy when it was found that a group of students created a fake "slave trade" in an online chat forum where students of color were "auctioned" off at prices based on their athletic ability or looks. The Tilden Preparatory School said that because the online activity had taken place after school hours and not on school property, there would be no official disciplinary action, but as a nod to the problem, they did require three days of sensitivity training for the whole student body. It was rumored that the online group also had students from other area private schools, rumors that were, of course, unsubstanti-ated, given that no one had used their real name. The only reason that Linden even found out about it was because someone in the group made a screenshot of the exchange and sent it to Linden's head of school and the parent association. Aki wonders if Meg has any actual proof that Aaron had been part of this group or if she's just throwing things at the wall to see if they stick.

Ousmane looks at Meg and slowly recites, "'I'll tell you what's walking in Salem—vengeance is walking in Salem,'" quoting *The Crucible.* "We cannot punish anyone without undeniable proof."

Meg scoffs, always happy to challenge authority. "But Aaron *is* Abigail, Mr. Gueye. That's what you don't get. I bet you don't know half of what he does," she says, clearly challenging him to prove her otherwise.

"You would be surprised, I think, Ms. Brown, to see things from my perspective," Ousmane replies, neither angry nor irritated.

Aki can't help but give a frustrated sigh. Why wasn't being a teacher just about making learning interesting and helping kids acquire knowledge? More and more it felt like their days were taken up by things other than what they were actually teaching: The primacy of college admissions. Counseling upset parents. And now, hate crimes. Was this a manifestation of modern-day parenting or something to do with the school itself? Having spent the bulk of her adult life at Wesley, she can't say for sure. All she knows is that she wants her daughter far away from a potential disaster.

"Well, Ms. Brown, unfortunately because you are in viola-tion of the school's social media policy, you will be suspended for an additional three days starting next Monday."

"What?" Aki says loudly before placing the palms of her hands on her temples. A week with a surly Meg at home was bad enough; she was just starting to see the faint glimmer of hope and light at the end of the tunnel only to be slammed with another three days of being held emotionally hostage by her teenage daughter. Ousmane was tacking on extra days of suspension for her daughter who would be applying to colleges in less than a year.

Ousmane looks at Aki calmly. "She has clearly taken a photo of school property while on campus and uploaded it onto a public site *by her own admission*. This is a violation of Wesley's privacy standards with clearly stated penalties. Not to mention Meg's second offense in an alarmingly short span of time."

"But—" Aki starts before Meg cuts her off.

"As usual, Aaron commits the worse crime, but it's the one who points it out that gets punished. Whatever, Mother, it's just three days," Meg says.

But Aki knows that any suspension will live on in her daughter's transcripts—and it's something exactly like this that could drastically alter her daughter's chances at Berkeley, or any school for that matter. She's also never felt more like a Wesley parent than she does in this moment when she says haltingly, "But she's a junior . . ." before trailing off.

"Meg, I do hope that you and Mr. Wakeman can work out your differences," Ousmane finishes, ignoring Aki and looking squarely at Meg, who is more than happy to take the bait.

"I don't know what Aaron told you," Meg exclaims, "but I have nothing to 'get back at him' for, in case you both were wondering," she says, using air quotes and looking at Ousmane and then at her mother.

The lady doth protest too much, Aki thinks, wondering again what could have provoked her daughter's ire so much. Meg is known for her marathon grudges—after all, she still refused to forgive Aki for accidentally revealing that the Easter Bunny wasn't real when Meg was ten. "That was the death of my childhood, Mother," Meg still says. But even if Aaron did what Meg was alleging, something felt personal about Meg's comments, like she has been wounded by him somehow.

Ousmane stares at Meg steadily. "Meg, before we are all excused," he says and pauses, "if I were you, I would consider explaining your involvement with the social media account, in order to—"

"No," Meg replies firmly, cutting him off. "You don't seem to realize that if the school did something substantial to address what is actually *on* the account, it wouldn't need to exist. That's our point."

Aki can't help but look back and forth at Ousmane and her daughter, feeling guilty for not being wholly on Meg's team, as it were. Who does she mean when she says "our"? She has to imagine her daughter is referring to Double.

"There are other ways to have grievances addressed," Ousmane responds simply.

"But not ones that get this much attention. So, I'd say it worked. Maybe the school should focus on the graffiti now," Meg shoots back. Aki feels herself sweating at the passive-aggressiveness of their exchange, though she would be lying if she said she wasn't impressed by her daughter's ability to stand up for herself.

"Rest assured, we are certainly looking into everything," Ousmane replies, making Meg scowl. He pauses before continuing. "Meg, please know that this is a very serious matter." He pauses again, in order to drill down his point. "Considering your first and more alarming offense involving Aaron Wakeman, I am afraid his parents really do have grounds upon which to claim a pattern of bullying."

"What does that mean?" Aki asks, alarmed at the insinuation.

"It means they want the school to get rid of me," Meg says snidely. "Go for it," she says, glaring at Ousmane, then her mother.

@megummy no one is safe not even you

Is this what the post was referring to? At first, she thought Meg wasn't safe from racism. But now she's wondering if it means her daughter isn't safe from *Wesley*. Aki feels like she's short of oxygen.

Ever cool, Ousmane turns to Aki with a genial expression. "Aki, have a good weekend. Please give Ian my best," he says amiably. "Meg, as with baseball, there are only three strikes before the player is out," he warns.

Meg merely sniffs and turns on her heel, leaving both adults in the foyer.

"Aki—" Ousmane starts before she cuts him off.

"I know, Ousmane. I know," she says as he nods and turns to leave. Although Meg had gotten so angry at her when she had said it the day the graffiti had been discovered, Aki can't help but think again, *how do I protect my daughter from all of this?* Then she thinks to herself, *and what should I be protecting her from?* She can't decide if it's Aaron, his parents, or the school, but she knows she's the only thing that is probably able to protect Meg from her worst enemy, which appears right now to be herself.

13

"There are two Asian girls in my grade and the teachers can't keep us straight. WTF Wesley."
　　　　　　　　　　　—*Current Wesley student, PoC@Wesley*

"I GUESS WE SHOULD call this meeting to order," Aki looks out at the twelve assembled faces and reminds herself once more: *Private-school parents are just like other parents.* She smiles encouragingly at them. "Thank you so much for volunteering your time today." *Go ahead, try me, people,* she thinks, knowing she has exactly zero patience for the Hollys and the Lizes of the world today. In fact, she hopes she can remain civil.

"It's great you're leading this up," Holly Henderson-Hines says earnestly. "How was your weekend?"

"Uh, quiet," Aki says vaguely, thinking back to the assorted and abridged conversations she had with her daughter:

Meg, can we talk about what is going on at school? Answer: Silence.
Meg, can we talk about the Instagram account? Answer: Not really.
Meg, can we discuss Aaron? Answer: Doors slamming.
Meg, do you want to go visit some colleges? Answer: Eye roll.

"How was your winter break, Holly? I haven't seen you in a while," Aki inquires politely, and Holly recites the various insulting delays and inconveniences she and her family endured on their trip to Park City. Aki tries not to sigh and nods distractedly as she watches parents file into the conference room.

At Amanda's behest, Aki has finally convened the Wesley Parent Advisory Committee on Diversity and Equity. When she suggested to Amanda that the consultants should run this meeting, then argued that she wouldn't even know where to begin with such an endeavor, Amanda merely waved her hand and informed her, "It doesn't matter if you know what you're doing, it matters if they think you know what you're doing!" then handed Aki a bulleted list of questions compiled by the consultants. "You're the interim director. Record their answers. We're just taking temperatures." A glorified secretary or a glorified nurse, she's not sure which she is, but she's definitely sure she shouldn't be doing this. More notably, she is a glorified *minority* secretary-nurse, which is of course what the school wants. She thinks about what Double said with incredulousness, that the school was much more interested in hiring a fundraiser than paying her for whatever she is about to do today. Meg, never one to let an opportunity to criticize her mother slide, snidely announced as Aki left for her task force meeting, "Enjoy being a pawn for the Man."

Aki looks at the assembled parents, clears her throat, and, sounding like an automated answering service, announces stiffly, "The school has asked me to gather your thoughts as we plan out Wesley's future dialogue on these important issues. We will also send out an all-parent survey pursuant to these discussions."

"I'm so sorry I'm late!" Lulu Miller arrives breathless and completely overdressed as usual, with glowing skin no doubt thanks to her face-gunk empire.

"No problem," Aki says, startling at Lulu's grand entrance, this time in velvet and wool gabardine complete with statement necklace and platform heels. Aki tries to find her bearings while wiping her daughter's criticisms of her out of her mind. "I think we're all here, so let's start. Thank you again for agreeing to be part of the Wesley Parent Advisory Committee on Diversity and Equity," Aki recites.

She had felt proud of herself standing up to Elliot Associates the day of the faculty seminar, yet here she is, doing their—and Wesley's—bidding. She sighs and looks around the table at the deliberately diverse faces before her: four white, two Indian, one Latinx, one East Asian, and four Black. Amanda has clearly and carefully curated this committee through the delicate calculus of skin color plus added value to the school's bottom line. Parents like to be asked to sit on committees. No matter how menial the task, parents understand that committees like this make clear whose voices are the most important within the school community, though Jules always says the school just chooses the compliant ones to join, *you know, the baa baa sheep parent*, she likes to joke.

They may be sheep when it comes to school matters, but at the table today are a collection of the one percent: a former CFO of the region's largest hospital chain, a former White House advisor, several entrepreneurs, and multiple lawyers (antitrust, intellectual property, civil litigation). If a bomb exploded on the Wesley campus right now, it would wipe out half the bolded names in the party section of the *Washingtonian* magazine. Sometimes Aki has to remind herself that she's not just a teacher at Wesley but a parent as well, and that her ideas are just as important as the ones offered up by the wealthy and connected whose salaries are easily ten times hers. She remembers once at a school gala when a very drunk Gordon Lewis (father to Charlotte, CEO of an aerospace company) asked her how it felt to know that she'd never make enough to send her own kid to Wesley, not realizing that she, in fact, had a child at the school. She merely nodded and said something along the lines of "It's a privilege just to teach here," then thought about spitting in his drink.

Aki looks down at her prepared papers, which are crisscrossed with highlighter and exclamation points, Amanda's way of being in the room without being able to speak. "Let me begin by asking all of you how you felt when you learned about the graffiti," Aki reads from the questions as she poises her stylus on her iPad, ready to capture their thoughts. *Is this question for real?* she thinks to herself. The graffiti was, as Meg said, the most f-ed up thing she had ever seen at Wesley.

Holly places both her hands in front of her as if in prayer and starts slowly, "Well, I think that the most important thing is how we deal with this tragedy moving forward, rather than looking backward." She looks around the table for a moment before continuing. Then she drops her voice and leans over to Aki conspiratorially and whispers, "I heard about Meg being suspended. I'm really sorry. I'm sure it's just a misunderstanding."

Really, bitch? Aki thinks to herself.

Who was Holly kidding? In a school this small, there was no way everyone in the room hadn't heard about Meg smacking Aaron and her being suspended as a result, and Aki is sure that the news of Meg's suspension has gone around the parent community at least twice. She can feel herself narrow her eyes. Holly is just digging for extra tidbits of information, or maybe even a humiliated stammer from Aki, so she instead says stiffly, "Thanks, Holly, let's move on with this meeting, right?" Refusing to make eye contact with Holly or the other parents in the room, her gaze finally lands on a potted ficus plant.

"As a woman of color," Julia (parent to Joseph, former White House advisor) begins, drawing everyone's attention toward her, "I was shocked, of course, but we have to protect our children, and I think the most important thing is not letting this spiral out of our hands," she says smoothly as if being interviewed during a primetime news special, where lots of words are strung together into a nice-sounding paragraph that ultimately says nothing.

Aki nods, writing on her iPad quickly. She looks up at the table and sees Chloe Chen, who smiles serenely back at her. Chloe is the founder of an all-natural deodorant company loved by Gwyneth Paltrow, which has made her a multimillionaire. Her two sons, Alex and Caleb, are in seventh grade and are chauffeured to school. Whenever Ian sees the deodorant in a Target or CVS, he inhales deeply and says, "Smells like a new gym for Wesley!"

Aki once asked Chloe if she'd like to participate in the school's Asian American and Pacific Islander upper school assembly, and Chloe cocked her head and said something along the lines of "I didn't get to where I am by highlighting my race." Aki was shocked at the time, but Meg merely growled that Chloe Chen and her sons were those Asians who really just wished they had been born white. It made Aki sad to think about, but she realized later that it is Chloe's way of dealing with racism. By ignoring race, it didn't exist for her.

Liz Everett's hand shoots up like a newly sprouted bamboo reed. "Rog and I have a question," Liz starts, making Aki groan inwardly. "Is it true these 'consultants' or whatever they are," she says using air quotes, "that they're going to completely change the curriculum? Because Rog and I think the curriculum is just *fine*," which Aki knows is private-school parent talk for *don't fuck with this*. She thinks about the Elliot Associates recommendations that were sent to her email and says nothing.

"I, for one, am totally for this being an inflection point on what our children are being taught," Beth Morgan (mother to Trudie, installation artist, and rumored heir of the Morgan Stanley Morgans) says while staring openly at Liz, who purses her lips and sips noisily on her coffee. "The school has focused too much on the hegemony of the white male voice—"

"Excuse me," Liz barks, "but you're sounding a little racist there—"

"How so?" Beth snaps back.

"Because being white doesn't mean being racist," Liz nearly shouts across the table. "By the way, isn't it also a little racist to have a whole room dedicated to making sure the *white* kids can't use it?" referring to the multicultural work space that has taken over the senior lounge. She narrows her eyes and casts an evil-but-gleeful look at Aki. "Though I guess you can *hit* someone in a so-called safe space and nothing will happen to you."

Aki feels like murdering Amanda "You don't need to do much, just take the temperature" Nutley. After thirteen years at Wesley, Aki is used to soothing parental qualms, but right now she feels downright surly. Maybe Meg is rubbing off on her. She gives a loud "Ahem" and ignoring Liz, says sternly, "Decisions made at the administrative level take into consideration what our peer institutions are doing as well as recommendations made by curricular experts," though what she really thinks is *Why is the school so busy gathering these shiny-toothed parents in a room rather than finding out who painted the side of the arts building?*

"So is that a yes or a no on the course changes?" Liz persists. "Are our kids going to be learning about how someone should have shot the Mayflower before it made it to Plymouth Rock?"

"What I've been told," Aki starts, *which Amanda explicitly told me not to share,* "Is that Elliot Associates has a proposal for curricular reviews," *that has been sitting in my email, ignored,* "that will be implemented only after thorough vetting by the school." She stares Liz down. "Anything else?"

"Instead of 'sensitivity training' and 'hearing sessions,' maybe they should just go back to helping our kids get into college," Liz shoots back, using air quotes. "Forget all these ridiculous changes!" she insists. "Some people that should have gotten in early didn't, and that looks bad for the school," she adds.

Aki decides to change the subject. "Let me ask you all a question. Can you all name three books you read in high school?"

The clamor that was in the room settles a little as people stop to think.

"*A Tale of Two Cities.*"

"*Lolita.* Man that was messed up in retrospect," someone says, making everyone giggle.

"*Portrait of an Artist as a Young Man.* I have to admit, I really hated it," Lulu says, blushing.

Aki looks around the table. "Not much diversity, huh?" she offers. "I grew up in California, so we read Pearl S. Buck, but that was it. That and *Roots.*" She sees Liz ready to say something probably along the lines of *Well, there's a reason we read Hemingway* and decides to plow ahead. "The thing is, the world is changing, and the curriculum needs to reflect that. The students know it, and we adults are just playing catch-up." Aki wishes that Meg were in the room to hear her admit to this.

"I'm sure the school will be deliberative in any changes it proposes," Holly says loudly, giving Aki a look to say, *I'm here to help!*

"Yes, it will. Anything else?" she asks, instantly regretting the fact that she's opened the door to more comments. She should have cut her losses.

Lulu raises her bangled arm. "Sorry, I know this is a little off-topic, but when is the next auction meeting?"

Holly sits up straight and her expression brightens. "Oh, that's easy, it's next month, can you join?"

"I'll try, but if I don't have time, I just wanted to offer the chalet in Telluride," Lulu says, smiling.

Holly's face lights up and she mimes clapping. "Oh my gosh, that's so generous, thank you!" She then alters her expression back to one of solemn contemplation as if suddenly remembering why they are all there. "Aki, I know you want to adjourn, but is there anything else anyone would like to say?" Holly clearly can't help herself in meetings; as with most things in her life, she must be seated at the center console of mission control.

"What is the school going to do about all that ridiculous social media nonsense?" Priya Gosh (parent to Riann, former CFO of a hospital group) interjects. "It's an embarrassment!" she declares as the parents around her nod in agreement, and the table swells again with murmuring.

A surge of adrenaline shoots through Aki's body and the rising swell of anxiety makes her feel like she may vomit on Holly's Mansur Gavriel tote.

"Can't the school just take down the account?" Beth asks.

"My civil liberties law is dusty but I don't think so," responds Elsa Mansanares (mother to Marco and Lucia, IP lawyer and partner). "Unless there is threat made, or the school can actually prove the student is doing it on school property, Wesley has no real standing," she explains.

"They should just kick the little shit-poster out," Liz announces, and Aki swears she's looking right at her as she says it.

Before she can help herself, Aki blurts out, "Does anyone else think Aaron sprayed the graffiti on the school?"

The parents collectively look at her silently, then at Holly, since everyone knows how close she is to Aaron's mother, Claire.

"It *is* his jersey!" Liz crows. Aki has known the Everetts long enough to know that they are loyal to no one.

"But it wasn't him on the video," Holly says pleadingly. "And we shouldn't be talking about this."

"Oh, but we should be talking about ski chalets?" Liz shoots back. Every once in a while, Aki reasons, maybe Liz can be useful to have in a room.

In response to the obvious shot across the bow, Lulu responds brightly. "Aaron is such a sweet kid," as if her word should be the final one on the topic.

"They should boot out the shit-poster," Liz repeats again, "and the idiot with the spray paint. They're probably the same person."

Aki is about to interject how that doesn't make sense when Holly finally puts everyone out of their misery. "Well, I for one would like to thank Aki for gathering all of us here today, and I know we look forward to the discussion circles the school will be holding with other stakeholders and community members," Holly recites. Aki half-expects Holly to rip off her clothes to reveal Amanda with her clipboard and highlighter. "Can we officially adjourn?" she asks, though what she is really doing is telling Aki.

"Yes, of course, thank you," Aki says, as the parents begin to file out of the room, some talking to one another while others, like Liz and Lulu, quickly get on their phones.

"Aki?" Holly draws her Herman Miller chair closer toward her. "I wanted to invite you over to my place," Holly says with a wide smile.

Aki is taken aback; she hasn't been to Holly's place since the kids were in elementary school.

"It's been too long," Holly says as if reading her mind. "I'd really love to catch up," she says.

Aki can tell that there is no other answer than "yes," so she quickly nods and makes a note in her phone.

"This is great!" Holly exclaims as she picks up her tote and pushes the chair under the table. "I'll text you the details!"

14

"You people do know that most of these posts are written by bored students who want to stir up trouble, right?"
—*Laughing at All of You,* dcparentzone.com

PERHAPS OUT OF POLITENESS, or possibly because Meg and Ian get along so well, nobody had ever questioned who Meg's biological father was. Aki's close friends, like Jules, know of course, but Aki never discusses it with anyone otherwise. She thinks of her affair fleetingly, usually only on Meg's birthday or sometimes when she sees her alma mater in the news, but otherwise she doesn't let it rest in her memory. When her daughter was little, Aki girded herself for the day that Meg would ask about her biological father. Then she realized that because Ian had been her father since she was born, and because there was no time in her memory or nary a scrapbook that didn't contain images of Ian being her father, Aki would one day have to tell Meg directly. She remembers agonizing over the timing. Too young, and she wouldn't understand. Too old, and she risked anger and resentment. Aki finally settled on age seven, for no real reason other than it felt like the right time. Or maybe it was just the right time for Aki, and not necessarily for Meg.

Sundays were slow days, everyone rested and caught up on sleep, so she took Meg to get ice cream and a walk on the canal.

"Honey," she said to Meg as they stood and watched a group of turtles sleeping on a tree limb in the canal. "I want to talk to you about your father," she said.

She remembers Meg looking up at her and saying, "Daddy?" before Aki explained to her that while Ian was her father, Aki had her with another man, someone who passed away. Meg had turned back to the turtles sunning in the middle of the water. "Was he nice?" she asked.

"He was brilliant and kind, but *daddy* wanted to be your father and he was there when you were born. He's always been your father and he always will be," she promised. Aki left out the part about her advisor abandoning her, how he had cheated on his wife with her, and how she had surprisingly little baggage attached to it, though she probably should. She figured that discussion could come later.

But in times like this, when her daughter acts elusive, shutting her out as if she were a mere stranger, she wonders, *is this her father?* She knows she should be ashamed for not having known him well, other than his name was on the spine of many books she had read. She had been seduced by the prestige of his position and the wealth of his knowledge; he was also an inspiring lecturer, able to mesmerize even the most arrogant and jaded of graduate student. It was abundantly clear that Meg's academic prowess, and her ability to focus singularly on one topic or project, was something that should be credited to him. For whatever reason, Aki didn't mind attributing her daughter's strengths to him, a man she once respected. But when Meg did things that alluded Aki, it was trickier. Blaming him should have absolved Aki, but it simply served as a reminder of what she didn't know—about her daughter, and about her daughter's father.

Thinking about Meg and how hard she is to reach emotionally these days, Aki sighs as she sits in her parked car, gathering up the courage and energy for the social call with Holly. Why didn't she just decline? Aki silently berates herself as she looks up from the steering wheel. Holly Henderson-Hines's house is as perfect as Aki remembers it to be: a large white clapboard house with black shutters, double car garage, and an expertly mani-cured lawn, all within a tidy half acre in one of northwest Wash-ington's most desirable enclaves, Forest Hills. Whenever Aki sees it, she wonders how it must feel to have so much house, because as beautiful as it is, all she sees are gardening and heating bills. A wreath made of wooden hearts hangs on the large door, an early nod to Valentines Day, she presumes.

She exits her car with a bottle of rosé, Holly's favorite, and straightens out her sweater. She knows that even on a week-end, Holly will be dressed snappily, though not ostentatiously, since that would be antithetical to the Wesley way. True to form, Holly flings open the door wearing a white cashmere sweater and light denim jeans, dark blue flats on her feet, and holding an armful of white lilies. She looks like an ad for a feminine hygiene product.

"Aki! Oh, my gosh, it's so great to see you!" Holly's cheeks are flushed and her dark hair is pulled back into a neat bun at the nape of her neck. "It's been too long," she insists, even though she and Aki obviously see one another at various parent meet-ings. Aki holds out the bottle of wine.

"My favorite!" Holly's eyes light up. "And it's chilled, so thoughtful!"

Aki can't help but warm to the compliment; she's always been that way, since praise was rare and impactful as a child.

"Come in, come in," Holly motions with one arm, shifting the large white blooms to the other. Aki enters the foyer, which is an airy open space with an antique gray table in the middle. Holly places the lilies inside the oversized metal pitcher on top of the table, shaking off the bits of leaves from her sweater. The family cat, Sparkles, comes down the central staircase, mewing. Aki wonders if you can forget all your worries in a house like this. She vows to try not to worry about Meg for one afternoon.

"Come, let's sit in the sunroom," Holly picks up Sparkles and walks down the hallway toward the back of the house. Aki remembers it well: that is where they would sit while Zach and Meg romped around the backyard, which at the time had an oversized jungle gym and swing set. Meg used to call Holly's house "the park," though it was much more beautiful than any public play space, surrounded by light blue hydrangeas and concealed completely from the DC traffic and noise.

There have been some upgrades to the furniture, or the expected evolution in interior design as their children moved into spill-free ages. The sunroom, which has low, white built-in bookcases and tall windows on three sides, used to be filled with overstuffed blue Pottery Barn chairs. The current iteration of the room is more worthy of an *Architectural Digest* spread, with a circular white marble table and cream velvet chairs all sitting atop a wildly unruly white shag carpet that Aki just wants to roll around and perhaps nap on. Sparkles appears to agree, burrowing in a corner as Holly motions to a chair. On a table there is an elegant pile of French macarons in an array of pastel colors, a large bowl overflowing with berries, and bone china cups waiting to be filled with Holly's favorite *Mariage Frères* tea.

"This is really beautiful," Aki marvels with genuine awe. Holly beams, and Aki remembers how Holly likes nothing more than to be acknowledged publicly.

"Sit, sit, come on, let me serve you," Holly says as Aki sits across from her. She looks out into the yard, which is unchanged in its splendor—even in the February chill—and sighs a bit. Money may not buy happiness, but it can get you a view. Aki takes a bite of one of the macarons which taste like heaven, slightly chewy and crispy at the same time, light yet flavorful.

"So, Aki," Holly intones, making Aki look back at her hostess. "I'm really sorry to hear about Meg's resignation from the paper."

Aki almost spits out her dessert. She tries to compose herself but starts coughing and grabs the tea mug, gulping down the hot tea and making herself gag in the process.

Holly looks at her first with open shock, then jumping to help her. "Let me get some napkins!" she says, running out of the sunroom and returning with a stack of paper towels. "I take it you didn't know?"

Aki shakes her head, and all she can think is, *two suspensions back to back, now her only real extracurricular.*

"She was a true tour de force on the paper, I mean that piece on the museums was simply college-worthy!" Holly says clucking her tongue. "What a loss!"

Holly is referring to the piece that Meg had written earlier in the year to great public reception. Why were major artworks displayed in museums predominantly by white artists, and what could Wesley do about it? *Not much*, Aki thought at the time, but the art department quickly convened to unveil a program in response that focused on works by indigenous and ethnic minorities. In the piece, Meg pointed out that the only major Asian Art museum in the entire country was in San Francisco, and how despite a history of exclusion and erasure, Asian Americans deserved their own national museum on the Mall in Washington, DC. After not one but two glowing newspaper articles on Meg's piece ("Local Student Asks, 'Where Is My Voice?'") and a local television spot on the revamped art curriculum and ensuing exhibit, the music department was next in announcing its plans to vanquish Requiem in C Major by Johann Adolph Hasse for a modern take on Chinese opera (this garnered less press attention, to the dismay of the choral director). The drama department soon followed, where *The Heights* replaced *The Music Man*, though to be honest Aki was pretty delighted with that alteration. Aki thinks about Meg's article and all the attention it got and sees now that it was but a mere precursor to all that has transpired since.

"And how was her . . ." Holly trails off, taking a sip of her tea before resuming her line of questioning. "Was she OK while she was suspended? I heard about the . . ." she trails off.

The smack? The photo? Aki thinks as she resumes eating the macaron, reasoning that no good dessert should ever go to waste. Upon hearing about Meg's extended suspension, Ian excitedly took her on a camping trip, despite Aki's insistence that it was too cold.

"It'll be fun!" he insisted. When Aki pondered if Meg should learn a lesson from the double suspension, Ian grunted and said, "If anyone needs to learn a lesson, it's the school," then happily packed up his camping gear and whisked Meg off to the one camping ground on the Eastern Shore that is open year-round.

"She was fine," Aki responds simply.

"Does she really think Aaron is involved in all of this?" Holly asks with obvious faux innocence.

I see, Aki thinks, *I have been invited over for gossip.* She takes a languid bite of the decadent meringue, but Holly is on a roll.

"Is it true she's dating Double? I heard he got into Harvard early."

Aki can't help but look up at Holly and tries not to give anything away in her expression. "Princeton, I think." This must be who her mother had been referring to when she asked about a boyfriend. How does Holly know? Does Zach talk to her about things like this? Zach's absent-looking expression and overgrown bangs pop up in her mind; he barely seems like he can remember his own address much less inform Holly of the social dynamics at school. She gulps down her macaron and reaches for another as the doorbell rings.

"I'll be right back," Holly says, winking at Aki.

Aki closes her eyes and inhales the fragrant mélange of berries and leaves. Just as she's a sucker for an expensive cup of coffee, she loves nothing more than a bougie cup of tea. She wonders if her parents talked about her this much when she was a teenager, or worried about her, for that matter. She suspects that grades were used as a proxy for how things were going generally: getting good grades meant everything is fine, and following a similar rationale, bad grades meant there was something wrong in a kid's life. How then, do kids at Wesley keep up the veneer of perfection with the tumult going on simultaneously in their personal lives? Maybe it has to do with the culture of student achievement at Wesley, and she suddenly feels guilty, as if she too has fostered this type of overachieving denialism.

"Look who I found!" Holly exclaims delightedly as she reenters the room holding a box of cookies from the new bakery in Georgetown. Aki's eyes light up. The bakery has three stores in New York City and the cookies are as huge as her fist and she's been dying to try them. "Given how long all our kids have been in school together, I can't believe you two haven't hung out!" Holly trills as she steps aside to reveal the third guest at the day's tea: Claire Wakeman, Aaron Wakeman's mother.

★ ★ ★

Aki jumps up out of her seat, flustered and instantly nervous. Holly doesn't know that they've "hung out" recently, and under tense circumstances. Someone once asked her how it feels to teach the offspring of such important parents, and she responded truthfully, which is that as long as the kids hand in their papers on time, she doesn't care what their last name is. Aki tries as much as she can to avoid the parents, but since her own daughter attends the school, it's impossible to cut off all interaction. When she started teaching at Wesley, someone had given her a pearl of advice: being a teacher means loving the students and tolerating the parents. She never thought she'd be part of a social call with the mother of a student who has been outed as a possible racist by her own daughter.

Claire Wakeman presents herself exactly as she did that day in Ousmane's office, which is to say, perfect. Around her neck is a fuchsia scarf atop a pale pink short-sleeved sweater paired with a stiff khaki skirt, and Chanel flats completing the look. She would look almost matronly if it wasn't for her bright blue eyes, perfectly cut and colored chestnut hair, and line-free face. Claire is thin, and Aki can see her collarbones jutting out from underneath her sweater top.

Claire extends her hand, "It's so nice to see you under much more pleasant circumstances," she purrs.

Aki is taken aback. Was Claire being honest, or was this just *nice rich people speak*, as Ian calls it? Not one month ago, and in repeated incidents since, Meg has declared Aaron to be nothing short of the spawn of a white nationalist. "You too . . ." Aki trails off, not sure what to say and shooting Holly desperate looks. Holly, ignoring or not noticing Aki's distress, guides Claire to the open chair and smiles at the two women.

"Claire and I know each other through our husbands," she explains. "They've worked on many development projects together." Holly pours a cup of tea for Claire, who beams at Aki, making Aki feel more uncomfortable and self-conscious than she already is. Holly continues to chatter. "I wanted to get the two of you together officially," she states, speaking like a matchmaker, looking back and forth between the two of them, "and away from school," she adds.

Why? Why? Why? is all Aki can think.

"How nice to see you away from your official capacity," Claire says with cloying sweetness. "I'm so curious about the initiatives that the school is undertaking so I asked Holly to set up a tea for us," she explains pleasantly.

Aki instinctively clamps her mouth shut while eyeing the cookies that Holly has laid out on one of her decorative Spode plates. Nothing good ever comes from teachers mingling with parents.

Claire, either ignoring or not caring about Aki's reserve, continues. "I'm also still quite curious how the school is going to rectify the claims made against Aaron," she says, eyeing Aki steadily. "He is a senior awaiting college acceptances, and I have to admit, it was a real shock when he didn't get in early."

Like a frightened cat darting out from underneath a car to retrieve a treat, Aki snatches one of the cookies off of the plate, stalling for time.

Claire persists. "Have the consultants discussed how exactly they are going to assist the school to ascertain the identity of the vandal, or the person who runs the Instagram account? I believe this will go a long way in clearing my son's name."

Aki takes an oversized bite of the chocolate peanut butter cookie, gulps down her cooled-off tea, and looks at Claire, trying to control her annoyance. "The school is dedicated to investigating the matter fully with the assistance of appropriate parties." *And not the parents*, she fumes silently.

"Let me go refresh this tea!" Holly jumps up, suddenly looking nervous.

As soon as her willowy figure disappears, Claire's luminous smile turns into a cold stare.

"It would be so much better for us to be friends than enemies," she says while offering a thin smile, but behind her eyes is a dead, cold look that makes Aki feel immediate chills. "If you can help me, I'm sure I can help you," she says coolly.

"Help me with what?" Aki spits back. She wills her hands to stop shaking, but not wanting to look as unnerved as she feels, shoves them under her thighs.

"I think we both know that Meg is behind the account and the posts about Aaron," Claire hisses. "Make her stop, or I will make things unpleasant. It's bad enough that your daughter attacked my son at school, but now Aaron has to wait until regular decision to hear back from Princeton, and I don't want him getting tangled in any of your daughter's ridiculous escapades."

Aki can feel her mouth open involuntarily. "Did it ever occur to you that your precious son might have actually done it, and that Meg is just making that inconvenient truth public?" Aki finally spits back.

Claire gives her a condescending laugh. "You think this is about the graffiti?"

Aki wrinkles her brow with confusion. What else could it be about?

Claire continues. "I'm sure you'd love to think that your darling, righteous daughter is doing the world a great favor by outing a racist, but that is outrageously far from the truth." She watches as the lines in Aki's face etch further into an expression of confusion and laughs again. "They were a couple. Meg and Aaron. It was a fling. Aaron dumped her, and now she's angry. This is all about revenge."

Aki recoils and puts her hands on the table. "That is *not* true! She's dating Double!" she exclaims, knowing that this really has nothing to do with Claire's accusations.

Claire continues, the sneer on her face morphing into one of satisfaction as she informs Aki, "Aaron dumped her for Yeardly. That's probably why Meg quit the paper too. Such a shame, during her junior year." she says, clasping her hands in front of her teacup. "But Aki," her voice drops to a growl, "tell her to back off."

"Are you the one that posted on the account? Telling her that she isn't safe?" Aki demands in a croak as she sees the words float through her mind's eye: *@megummy no one is safe not even you.*

Claire's face reveals nothing as she folds her napkin primly, placing it on the table before standing up and smoothing the wrinkles from her skirt just as Holly returns with a new pot of tea.

"Are you leaving already?" Holly's face falls.

"We've had a *wonderful* time, thank you *so* much for hosting us, Holls," Claire says while giving Holly a half-hug. "It was *great* catching up with Aki," she says, bending over to retrieve her bag. She stands and winks at Holly, then looking steadily at Aki says in a cold voice, "Best of luck to Meg," before slipping out of Holly's sunroom.

★ ★ ★

Later, Aki collapses on the sofa, splaying her legs out and sinking into the cushions, letting out a loud sigh.

"Life in the mines not turning out like you imagined?" Ian quips as he places two plates of leftover Chinese food on the coffee table. "What are we going for today, the cultural phenomenon otherwise known as *Below Deck* or should we watch something emotionally meaningful like *Love Is Blind?*" he asks as he sets up his laptop in front of them.

The morning's excursion to Holly's house had left Aki not only blindsided but exhausted. She was shocked but not surprised at Claire Wakeman's antics: a private-school parent ambushing a teacher is to be expected. To be so openly threatening and have another parent conspire with them is altogether a different beast. On her way back from Holly's house Aki had called Jules from the car. Without going into the details, she asked her friend what she thought of Claire. She knows what Jules thinks of Holly: *Social climbing wannabe having an existential crisis about the midi-length dress she saw at J.McLaughlin last week.* Jules always gives Aki a hard time for even speaking to Holly, but Aki can't just cut off a parent of a child she teaches, and as she explained to Jules many times, their kids used to hang out. But they've never talked about Claire Wakeman.

"That woman? She's insane," Jules proclaims. "Anyway, I hear their marriage is on the rocks. An affair." Affairs are sadly unsurprising within the Wesley community. The typical formula was one parent having an affair with an office coworker, resulting in a split or divorce. Take for example Devon Heart (mother of Alex, and nationally known political campaign manager) who had an affair during a Senate race with the candidate in question. Alex was found stone-cold drunk and passed out in the girls' bathroom, though Wesley was able to keep this under wraps. Even Aki knew about this particular drama, but only because Jules was the one who found Alex in the bathroom cradling a bottle of Goldschläger, flakes of gold dried on her lips.

Example number two: Parents having affairs with other parents. Not unheard of but also made for indescribably awkward confrontations. Aki heard from another teacher about how one irate mother sent her boyfriend in her stead to attend a parent-teacher conference with her ex-husband, who had cheated on her with her best friend (also another parent at the school), whom he later went on to marry. Then there were the rare teacher-parent affairs, scandals of a completely different stripe on an unrelated species of tiger. Missy Langley, the former girls' lacrosse coach and a twenty-something UVA grad, at least followed the etiquette of waiting to step out with Stevens Young (father of Tracy, and head of a DC polling firm) until Tracy graduated and enrolled in Middlebury. In addition, Stevens and his wife had been separated for years. Even then, there had been fallout: Meg, who had been on debate team with Tracy, told Aki that Tracy eventually dropped out of school and was currently working in an ashram in Bangalore. For her part, Missy had been more than happy to quit her coaching job and join the Washington, DC, social set, getting pregnant and informing everyone how she *couldn't wait* to enroll the twins at Wesley, illustrating her newly found and quickly adopted sense of entitlement that she could jump the line that forms behind the 7 percent acceptance rate for an unquestioned place at the school.

"Why are you asking about Ice Queen all of a sudden?" Jules had asked, and Aki vowed to fill her friend in later.

"You pick," she mumbles to Ian as she stuffs kung pao chicken into her mouth.

"Captain Lee and his merry band of questionably qualified sailors it is!" Ian declares, pressing play and happily starting on his own dinner as the buzzer rings. Aki can't help but groan.

"Just ignore it," she pleads as Ian hops up to check the monitor.

"I think it's one of your students?" Ian says quizzically.

"On a Saturday? At nine?" Aki asks incredulously, feeling suddenly awake. "It's not Ousmane, is it?"

"Why would it be Ousmane? I think I'd recognize him, by the by," Ian says. Aki hadn't bothered to tell him about Ousmane's drop-by, only that Meg's suspension had been extended. After years of Ian being stationed in this country or that port, Aki has learned to navigate many parental issues on her own, and perhaps, on some subconscious level she does it because deep down, she knows that Ian isn't Meg's biological father. She knows it's silly to think that way—Ian has never given her, or Meg for that matter, any reason to think that he is anything other than the father that Meg was supposed to have, but it's still Aki's reflex to try to take care of things by herself as they relate to Meg.

Ian peers into the monitor again. "It looks like they're wearing Wesley gear. Maybe they're meeting Meg?" he suggests, though Aki knows that Meg would never have a friend ring up to their apartment for fear of mortal embarrassment at the hands of her parents. She struggles to get out from underneath the coffee table and looks over Ian's shoulder.

"No," she says under her breath when she realizes who is on the screen. "No," she repeats.

"It's not a student?" Ian asks. "I'll just tell them to scram, then."

"No, I mean, yes, it's a student. But you know what, I think I should handle this," she says as she buzzes the student in. "I think maybe you should do some work emails in the bedroom, honey." *And maybe I can get some answers.*

Ian, knowing when to intervene and when to escape, takes his food and shuffles down the hallway to the bedroom. "Let me know if I can help!" he calls back.

There is a knock on the door, and Aki steels herself as she grips the doorknob. When she finally collects herself enough to open the door, she tries not to react when she sees Aaron Wakeman standing in the hallway.

★ ★ ★

"Hi, Ms. Brown, Ms. B," Aaron says in a drawl. "I mean, Ms. Hayashi-Brown. Ms. H and B," he says, laughing before wrinkling his face. "Does it ever bother you that people don't call you by your full name?" he asks, slumping against the frame of the doorway.

Aaron is quite clearly drunk.

"Come in," Aki says quickly, looking down the hallway. She isn't sure how wise it is to invite a current student into her home, but she doesn't want him doing something stupid in his current state. "Go sit on the sofa while I get you some water," she says bluntly.

Aaron stumbles into the living room and slumps on the sofa, looking around the room in a daze. Aki returns with a glass of water and says to him, "Drink."

Aaron takes a gulp of water and places the glass on the coffee table. He looks up plaintively at Aki. "I messed up, Ms. B. I messed up big time." He hangs his head and runs his hands through his hair. "I shouldn't have . . ." He trails off. "I am so dumb."

Is he talking about the graffiti? Aki feels strangely energetic but also very exhausted as she sits in the chair next to him. She picks up the glass of water and tries to give it to him, but he waves it away.

"My dad is going to kill me," he says, closing his eyes before he leans back on the sofa.

Aki knows she should be calling his parents to pick him up, but she can't help herself. Instead, she hears herself asking, "Why? Have you done something, Aaron? You can tell me," feeling guilty as she does, since she knows she's not doing this to help Aaron out. She's doing this to see how involved he is with the vandalism and any possible threats to Meg.

Then Aaron does something Aki isn't sure how she should react to. He starts crying.

"I'm so stupid," he wails. "Why did I do that?"

Ian peeks his head out of the bedroom with a look of alarm. Aki shakes her head and motions for him to go back inside.

Aaron's faucet of tears stops as quickly as it started as he stares into her eyes with a frightened look. "Please don't tell them I was here," he whispers. "Or that I was drinking," he pleads. By *them* she knows he's referring to his parents, clearly part of the reason for his emotional anguish.

"Aaron, I don't think you can get home on your own," Aki says, now more concerned with how to get him out of the house before Meg gets back, and she certainly has no intention of having a drunk Aaron Wakeman in her car.

"I don't know who to call," he whispers, his eyes filled with panic.

Aki sighs and thinks. Then she crosses the room to retrieve her bag from the closet and takes out her phone, quickly sending off a text message. She puts the bag back in the closet, trying unsuccessfully to close the door on the overflowing storage space while grasping her phone and willing it to send her a response that will magically resolve the evening's growing problems.

"Ha ha, that closet is so full of crap!" Aaron cries out merrily. "I think I put a coat in there once and it like, ate it." He takes a gulp of the water. "Can I use your bathroom?" he asks as he starts down the hallway.

"First door on the left," she calls after him as she looks down at her phone, and almost shouts *Yes!* when she sees an affirmative response from Aaron's potential rescuers. It should only take them about ten minutes, less if the traffic is light.

Bzzzzz.

The monitor on the wall lights up, alerting Aki to an arrival, which she hopes is Aaron's ride. She leans in to see who it is, realizes it's not who she wants it to be, and slams both hands against the wall on either side of the monitor out of panic.

Bzzzzzz.

On the screen she sees Meg yelling at the camera to let her in, which Aki knows will be a spectacularly bad idea given who is in their bathroom. She must have forgotten her key.

Aki is content to just let her daughter wait outside, but she sees on the monitor that one of their neighbors has propped open the door for her daughter. Meg sticks her foot in the door then shoots a look at her mother via the camera that says *What the hell?* and disappears from the frame.

The monitor goes black and Aki rushes down the hall. "Aaron!" Aki calls out. "Are you done in there?" There's no response. She wonders suddenly if he's passed out in the bathroom and knocks on the door. "Aaron?" She knocks again.

The door swings open, and a sloppy-looking Aaron looks at her forlornly. "You didn't call my parents, did you?"

Aki shakes her head. "No, no, I didn't, but maybe we should wait outside, come on," she says, motioning to join her. He moves slowly through the hallway, and it takes everything in her not to drag him by the collar of his Wesley warm-up jersey. She can't help but peek at the number, which is 27. She's hoping she can get him down the stairs of the building before her daughter appears.

Just then there is a loud banging on the door. *Meg.* Aki panics. She thinks briefly about the fire escape and looks toward the windows, but knows it's too far of a jump to the ground below. As she contemplates throwing Aaron out of the window, she's failed to notice that he's flung open the door to an angry, snarling Meg.

"Meg!" He says in surprise, as if he forgot she lives here.

"*Aaron?*" she spits back. "What are *you* doing here?"

Aki scurries over toward the two of them, knowing she'll need to intervene—and quickly.

"Oh my God, Meg!" Aaron cries out again. "I'm—"

"What the hell, Mother!" Meg looks at Aki then back to Aaron. "Are you seriously *drunk* right now? Super 1990s of you."

"He just showed up!" Aki cries out defensively. *Where is Ian when I need him?* Knowing she's being somewhat hypocritical, needing Ian sometimes and keeping him out of the loop at others. She thinks about calling for him, then decides it will only add to the chaos.

"Meg, I'm so sorry," Aaron starts.

For what? Aki is dying to know. *For dumping Meg? For the graffiti?*

"Shut. Up. Aaron," Meg looks at him in disdain. "Stop. Talking."

"But—"

"No. You have everyone fooled but me," Meg snaps at him as Aaron hangs his head.

"Dude, what is going on?"

Everyone's head swings toward the doorway where Zach and his mother Holly stand, both with looks of surprise and confusion. Zach is in a Wesley sweatshirt, and Holly is uncharacteristically dressed in sweatpants, her hair in a ponytail.

Aki pushes Holly out into the hallway and whispers, "He didn't want me to call his parents, and you were the only ones I thought he might actually trust enough to leave with," she says conspiratorially, knowing Holly will like feeling as if she is the only one Aki can depend on. What Aki really feels like saying is *please take this drunk kid home and have him dry out in your guest room.*

"Of course," Holly says in a hushed voice. "Poor thing, waiting for college letters must be getting to him." She leans closer to Aki and adds, "I think his parents might be having some difficulties right now." Holly gives Aki a knowing look.

"Mm-hm," Aki says noncommittally while thinking about what Jules had said to her. She really just wants Aaron out of her house so that she can talk to Meg and confirm her suspicions, which is that Meg somehow has definitive proof that Aaron is the vandal. But she can't help but wonder, if Meg has more evidence, why not use it?

"Zach," Holly calls out. "Prop him up, help him to the car."

Aki looks back into her apartment and sees Meg saying something to Aaron in hushed tones. His head is bowed, and as she finishes, he looks up at her and is about to respond when Zach hoists him up by his arm, making Aaron lean on him as they walk toward the exit.

"Thanks, Ms. H-B," Aaron says softly. "You're a good dude, Zach," he says as he stumbles out the door, leaning on his friend. "You and Felix, man, you're my bros," he mumbles.

Holly squeezes Aki's arm and says goodbye as they make their way toward the elevator. Aki steps into her apartment and closes the door, turning around to see Meg standing right behind her, arms crossed and face fixed in an ugly expression.

"*What* did he say?" she demands.

"Not much, considering the state he was in," Aki responds coolly. "Meg, I need to talk to you about some things that are concerning me."

"Like what?" Meg shoots back.

Her daughter's belligerent tone combined with the fact that Aki has yet to eat dinner while the clock runs past ten causes her quickly diminishing patience to thin even more rapidly.

"For one, why did you quit the paper? That's a stupid decision for a junior!" The moment the statement leaves Aki's mouth, she regrets it.

"That's all you care about, isn't it?" Meg sneers. "Who cares that there's a white nationalist in the school as long as you get into Harvard! Who cares that Wesley is happy to look the other way. *Mother*," she pauses for emphasis, "there are more important things in life than college!"

"And what about Aaron?" Aki asks. "Were you two in a re—"

"Aarghhh!" Meg cuts Aki off with a guttural scream.

"Is everything OK?"

Meg and Aki swing their heads toward the doorway where, this time, Double stands. Aki can't hold back her look of surprise, despite what Holly had said about Meg and Double being an item.

"She let that *cretin* in our apartment!" Meg bellows. "We are going *out*," she adds, rifling through the closet, flinging things out and around trying to unearth an unknown object. She hunts in a jacket pocket and holds up her key, looking at Aki to try to defy her. "And *yes*, I *did* quit the paper!"

"Why?" is all Aki can say.

"You'll read about it in tomorrow's issue. But Yeardly Ward is a *bitch*, and please don't ever let Aaron Wakeman into our house ever again!" She grabs Double's hand, who gives Aki an apologetic look, then pulls him down the hallway with her before disappearing from sight.

Aki thinks for a moment about chasing after her, then reminds herself of something Ian always says: *The biggest fallacy in parenting is thinking that you can make your kid do anything.*

Instead, she stares at the front hallway, the closet door looking like a gaping hole in the earth, vomiting out a trail of clothes, shoes, bags, and an assortment of empty plastic bags.

She examines the mess, and it strikes her that it's like a parable for her life. So she shoves everything back into the closet and shuts the door, just as Meg shut the door on her.

♦ 15 ♦

"How do we even know these posts are real? They could all be made up. Whoever started the account is probably just looking for attention. We've been very happy at Wesley, no complaints."
— Current Wesley parent, dcparentzone.com

IAN IS THE MORNING lark in the marriage, and he is always up with the birds at first light, reading the paper. He knows not to wake Aki any earlier than necessary, but this morning he nudges her with his foot. "Aki, I think you better take a look at this."

Aki rolls over and rubs her eyes.

"Do you mean the *Quaker Newsman*?" Aki asks, thinking about Meg's reference. "Does it explain why she quit?" she grumbles sleepily.

"No, I mean the *press*," Ian says in a tone that makes Aki sit up in bed.

He places his laptop on her lap, and she sees that multiple tabs are open, one headline screaming: "Liberal Faculty Calls for Extreme Racial Justice Initiative."

Then she sees multiple news articles—mostly negative, many national—screaming similar headlines:

"Teaching Kindergartners that White People Are Racist"
"Private Schools to Dictate Conversations Around Race in
    Your Home"
"Student Civil War Brews at Hoity-Toity Wesley Friends"

Shit.

First, she realizes that the list of Elliot Associates recommendations that they had made to the school, the full list, has been leaked to the press, and they have hungrily seized upon and grossly extrapolated from it. Toggling back and forth between the recommendations, none of which have been officially adopted by the school, and the news headlines, Aki grudgingly acknowledges there really is no way to win when you're as famous as Wesley. She marks some of this up to the McKinsey-fication of private schools. Need a problem solved? Hire an overpriced Ivy League consultant. Worried you might look prejudicial? Make sure an outsider gave you a recommendation for issues you're better off figuring out for yourself. Either way, you get bruised in the press for anything you end up doing. As she sees headline after headline about Wesley and the fallout from the vandalism, all she can think is that karma has invited schadenfreude over for breakfast. Then she remembers Meg and how she quit the paper and has a sinking feeling that the last headline of the day—the one about a student civil war—and her daughter's resignation are somehow connected.

Ian, looking at her with an expression that reads *I have boundaries and will not involve myself with this Wesley drama,* says, "You can just use my computer until I'm ready to leave," then gets out of bed to take a shower.

Aki hurriedly navigates to the *Quaker Newsman* website and scans the headlines but finds nothing explicitly offensive. "Wesley Set to Accept Bids on Campus Expansion," says one. "Gap

Year Seminars Coming to a High School Admissions Office Near You," says another. And then she sees it: "The Racial Divide at Wesley: A No-Problem Problem." Her eyes bear down on the article, which starts:

> A leak within the school has outed Wesley's plans to implement a radical shift in the curriculum in response to vandalism of school property, the ensuing student protests, and the social media account, PoC@wesley.

How did they find about the Elliot Associates recommendations too? Aki panics.

> These so-called problems involving equity and diversity are evident only as a construct, one that the school promotes in order to placate certain members of the community. Wesley, in fact, does *not* have a race problem. As the *only* area school with a minority-majority student body

Aki scrolls through the article. Was the article really arguing that the school is *making up* the allegations of racism?

> and one of the few academic institutions with a PoC Upper School Head, Wesley hardly has a "race problem" in need of such dramatic response. The online community has indicated its own rather than accept the notion that perhaps WFS does not have a problem with race.

Oh, Aki thinks as she rereads the last few lines of text, *Meg certainly would disagree with this. It sounds like they're defending Aaron?*

> It is still unknown if it was incited by a Wesley student.

> It is unfortunate that the school's immediate reaction was mea culpa. First, there is no way to validate anonymous posts that are left online.

Well, I guess that's technically true, thinks Aki.

Second, the best way for Wesley to understand and address race relations is not to start from a place of apology and not to start with the assumption that all Whites embrace racist ideology.

Oh yikes.

We encourage the school to take a more measured approach with respect to the changes in the curriculum and any future decisions and around explicit expectations from families and utilization of "woke" language for the purpose of deflecting criticism. (See: Companion Opinion Article by Opinion Editor Megumi Brown)

Aki clicks on the link and sees an op-ed written by her daughter. The title asks, "What Would Lucretia Mott Do?"

In 1883 in Philadelphia, Lucretia Mott and Hetty Reckless, along with sixteen other white and Black women, formed the Philadelphia Female Anti-Slavery Society after women were barred from being part of official abolitionist movements of the time.

Hmm, maybe the Quaker studies class was good for something, Aki thinks.

Fighting against twin evils of the patriarch and slavery, these women taught community activism skills to its members regardless of race or gender.

Wesley Friends School, though quick to parrot these ideas, repeatedly refuses to protect the rights of minorities and students who identify as female. The continual desecration of the school at the hands of white supremacists and refusal to adopt racial equity directives provided by outside consultants proves this point. (See: Elliot Associates Recommendations)

No, Meg! Aki realizes that Meg has not only leaked the whole list of recommendations, she has undoubtedly gotten them from Aki's own laptop.

Mott once said, "Any great change must expect opposition, because it shakes the very foundation of privilege." We must demand change of Wesley Friends School.

To further paraphrase Mott, the denial of duty to act makes us slaves to those in power. I refuse to be a slave to this institution as long as it stands for prejudice and misogyny.

With this last op-ed, I officially resign my position as editor until the school addresses what any other fair-minded institution would consider a hate crime.

Aki stops reading as her heart slowly sinks to the soles of her feet. She understands that the first editorial has a byline from the Editorial Staff, and that Meg's is an in-kind response. Both have profited off of a document meant only for a small group of administrators to see. The school is not going to like having an internal debate laid out so publicly for the world to examine. Not only that, Aki can't help but worry that the administration will react particularly poorly to Meg's op-ed, since it so aggressively highlights, in the most forceful way possible, the tacit involvement of the school in events that are antithetical to everything it sells itself to be.

Aki jumps out of bed and marches into Meg's room, but it's empty.

Aki runs back into the bedroom and starts throwing on her work clothes as Ian appears from the shower. She looks at him and simply says, "I have to go," then runs out of the apartment.

★ ★ ★

"Meg!" Aki hisses. She's standing outside of the student lounge and knows that Meg will either ignore her or berate her, depending on her mood. Meg looks at her with a blank expression and resumes talking to Aiko. "Meg!" Aki hisses again.

Meg sighs and saunters over to the doorway. "Yes, Mother," she says with a smirk on her face.

Aki motions for Meg to join her outside. She doesn't even know where to begin. "The paper . . ." she trails off, feeling panicky.

Meg opens her mouth, then closes it, narrows her eyes and spits out, "Yeardly Ward, that bitch, she just steamrolled over me." Yeardly, the paper's executive, is of course part of the Aaron Wakeman fan club. Meg continues, "There was no way I was going to let her take over *my* op-ed page. I didn't want my name on that."

"I see," Aki starts, unsure of where the conversation should go. She knows instinctively that her daughter is more likely to share the less Aki contributes.

"I'm not the only one who quit the paper because of this," Meg adds. "Four of us did."

Aki feels a bit of relief chased by a generous helping of annoyance that it's Meg and not Yeardly who quit. She feels her face twitch. Should she say something about college applications? *Only if I want to die here in the school today*, she realizes, keeping her mouth shut.

Meg stares at her mother and puts her hands on her hips. "I'm not putting out another issue with Yeardly and her minions blowing smoke up Aaron's ass so that she can score an invite to the loser prom."

"And how," Aki asks slowly, "did the press get a hold of both op-eds?" *Show no fear*, she says to herself as she looks at her daughter.

"How should I know? Maybe it was a slow news day," Meg shrugs.

"Aki, Meg," a stern voice enters the conversation. They turn around to see Ousmane and a visibly annoyed Amanda standing at his shoulder. "We need to see both of you, please."

★ ★ ★

The moment Ousmane shuts his office door, Amanda immediately starts on one of her patented PR lectures. "So, we can't get the horse back into the stable in terms of those op-eds, but we're going to need you to take down that PoC Instagram account," Amanda says, zeroing in on Meg.

"Sounds like a plan. Hope you know who the account manager is," Meg shoots back.

Amanda, ruffled by nothing and probably the best person in the room to take on the teenagers of the world, continues undaunted. "Well, then, we're going to ask you to take charge of the new Wesley account," and with that, she places her phone in front of Meg, who peers at it as one would a small stain on a large piece of fabric, then guffaws. Aki leans over to see a white circle with the account name: Wesley Unites! with a photographic array of the best, brightest, and most diverse students that Wesley could ever hope to exhibit, all making personal affirmations about the school.

"I would literally rather die," Meg spits back.

"Meg," Ousmane interjects. "You have been suspended not once, but twice in a very short span of time," as if Meg or Aki needed reminding.

"Let's cut to the chase here, "Amanda interrupts. "Harrison is *pissed* and you are in some deep shit." Aki looks at Amanda in surprise. She has never heard Amanda use anything other than toothless threats and multisyllabic words glossed in a meaningless sheen. She peeks at Meg, who is either pretending not to care or really doesn't, Aki isn't sure which. Amanda, on the other hand, looks like she's about to breathe fire. "The op-ed and Elliot Associates leak was a huge embarrassment. Either make a public statement supporting the school and help with the account, which by the way will go a long way with college admissions," she says looking at Aki as she does before continuing, "or else the school will have to get *punitive*," Amanda emphasizes.

"What do you mean by that?" Aki asks in alarm. She looks at Ousmane, whose face is set in an indiscernible expression.

"We've asked students to find better academic homes for lesser causes," Amanda intones.

Counseled out? Aki panics. *My kid?* She thinks about how she threw away her dreams of a PhD in order for Meg to get a solid education. All the terrible parents and boring meetings she's endured for the discounted tuition. The passive-aggressive comments from her own mother.

"She'll apologize," Aki says quickly. *I did not sacrifice everything for Meg to get kicked out,* she thinks feverishly.

"What?" Meg shouts. "No, I won't!"

Ousmane clears his throat and they all turn to look at him. "Amanda and I have just come from a meeting with Harrison, who believes it is of the utmost urgency to show the school community, as well as the greater community, that Wesley is committed to its core values."

Aki stares at him. She understands what he's saying. That the school is willing to use Meg to make itself look better or toss her if she keeps making them look worse. Aki feels very foolish in this moment, realizing just how little the school cares about who vandalized the school compared to how much it cares about protecting its reputation. But she still can't seem to push back against her boss, and she's perpetually overshadowed by her own daughter.

"I'd rather be suspended again than do something I don't believe in. That's *my* core value," Meg announces. "Can I go now, please?"

"No," Aki and Amanda say in unison.

"Ousmane, there must be something we can work out. She hasn't technically done anything that goes against the student code of conduct," Aki pleads. "What can I do here?"

"Perfect," Amanda crows. "I forgot about you," she says to Aki, managing to sound both dismissive and patronizing before narrowing her eyes. "You're right, we *can* use you."

Great, thanks so much, I feel so special, Aki thinks, trying not to roll her eyes in frustration.

"Mother, don't do anything that will compromise your principles," Meg objects. "Or what's left of them, anyway," she can't help but add.

But Aki already feels her head nodding at Amanda. Meg is a junior. She has to save her chances at college. She has to get through Wesley. Otherwise, all the sacrifices that Aki made were for nothing.

"This will work out well," Amanda announces. "I'll set something up, like an interview. A prestige magazine, maybe the *Atlantic*. You can speak in your official capacity as interim director," she decides. "We may not be able to figure out who leaked that consultant report or make those op-eds disappear, but damage control can make it all go away." She turns to Meg and says curtly, "You're lucky. My mom would have hung me out to dry."

I believe it, Aki thinks, as Meg glares at Amanda.

"I feel it might be best for both of you to take the day off," Ousmane announces. "I'll have someone cover your classes, Aki. Please go home with Meg," but Aki knows what he really means is *please go sort this out*.

★ ★ ★

Aki's mind races as she and Meg walk silently back to Aki's car. She's never been able to adopt Ian's Zen-like attitude toward parenting, and she can feel herself hurtling toward emotional panic as they get in the car. Raising a teenager is the world's most exhausting occupation, she decides. As they both buckle in, Meg turns to look at Aki with a look of contempt and disgust.

"Mother, the real reason I'm in trouble is because the PoC@ Wesley account is holding a mirror up to the school and people don't like what they see, same with the op-ed," she announces, as if she's solved all the world's problems.

Everything in front of Aki goes blank and she hears her blood rushing to her ears, a loud pounding sound like when she's lying on her side, trying to go to sleep but can't. She feels a burst of adrenaline shoot through her body and before she can help herself, she's screaming at her daughter.

"What were you thinking, Meg? *What?*" Aki shifts into reverse and pounds on the gas, making both of them lurch forward. She shifts into drive and speeds out of the garage, only to stop abruptly at the red light onto Wisconsin Avenue.

"Jesus, Mother, are you trying to kill us?" Meg shouts, making Aki even angrier. The light turns green, and she jerks the car to the left and barrels down Wisconsin. "Mother!" Meg shouts, putting her feet up on the dash to steady herself, something she knows will drive Aki crazy.

"Get your feet off the dashboard!" Aki screams. "I do so much for you! I do *so much* and—"

She pounds on the brake, and they screech to a stop at a red light in front of Cactus Cantina, making Meg scream again as she lunges forward and snaps back with the seat belt.

"All you ever think about is *yourself!*" Aki yells, feeling an anger toward her child she has never experienced, which makes her feel unsettled but also strangely powerful. "I quit my PhD for you! I took this *job* for you! I committed myself to Wesley so that you would have an education I never could! And here you are posting *idiotic* things to a *stupid social media site*," she roars, stomping on the gas again as the light turns green. "Not to mention *hitting* other students in school!" She pauses and repeats, "*Hitting!*" She knows she's speeding, but her adrenaline is overflowing at this point. "It's like you *want* to get kicked out of school!"

She looks at Meg, whose eyes are shining with rage and tears of indignation. *Good,* Aki thinks. *Maybe it's time for her to feel a little bad.*

Instead, Meg lets out a guttural "Aaaarrrgghhh!" and pounds her feet on the bottom of the car like a toddler. "I *never* asked you to teach at that school! And I never asked you to give up your career! You did that on your own! And by the way, I never asked to go to Wesley!" she bellows.

Aki slows down, taking in her daughter's violent reaction. She is so used to smug Meg, nonchalant Meg, the Meg who shouts a sentence and flounces out the door. But this Meg is different. This Meg is engulfed in long-held anger that she didn't even notice. Meg's eyes flash with indignation. "You never asked me, not even once, if I was happy. Are *you* even happy at this place?" Meg demands, then continues before Aki can respond. "You, all of you, you're all so in love with the image of Wesley you can't bear to not be part of it, you would hate not to be able to say your kids went there! You're all the same!" she shrieks.

"Meg—" she starts but is cut off quickly.

"Admit it, Mother. You're just as bad as the rest of them," Meg says coldly, staring at her with what can only be described as contempt. "What you did back there, it wasn't because you thought what I did was right, but because you can't stand the idea that I'm not the perfect Wesley student."

Aki is about to object when Meg says something that makes her heart drop to her feet.

"You never should have had me! Then you never would have ended up there and neither would I!" she screams as she reaches for the door handle.

Aki panics. She lurches across Connecticut, running a red light and careening down Calvert, nearing their home.

"Mother! Jesus Christ!" Meg shouts, bracing herself with her hands.

Now Aki feels herself tearing up. Out of rage? Anxiety? Sadness? She grips the steering wheel and says to Meg steadily while fighting back tears, "You may not believe it, but I don't regret the choices I made because I tried to make the best ones I could for *you!*" She looks at Meg out of her peripheral vision and sees her daughter, still crying, looking at her lap.

They arrive in front of the condo, and Aki parks the car, takes a breath, and looks at her daughter. "You only have a year and half left at Wesley. Is it perfect? No. Will it help you get to where you need to go? Yes. I am going to get you out of this mess. But Meg," she says, taking her hands off the steering wheel and grasping her daughter's hand. She considers it a good sign when Meg doesn't pull away. "You have to tell me what is going on with Aaron, and if you have concrete evidence that he is the one who vandalized the school, you have to give it to me."

Meg lifts up her tearstained face and says in a low, small voice, "I'm sorry, Mother. I can't."

Aki watches as Meg gets out of the car and enters their home, knowing that she is the only one who will be able to protect her daughter, but that she might fail at that as well.

16

"Too much emphasis on equity and justice and all this. Let kids be kids."

—*Current Wesley parent and considering applying out,*
dcparentzone.com

AKI TAKES A BREATH before swinging open the door of the Black Squirrel, a local bar in her neighborhood. She's just spent a good half hour in her car crying, and when she finally wiped off her mascara-stained face and redid her ponytail, not wanting anyone in her building to see her in disarray, Jules sent her a text with a meme of a squirrel and an emoji of a cocktail glass. Not wanting to go upstairs and get into another tangle with Meg, she figured drinks with her friends might take her mind off things, at least temporarily.

When she enters the long, darkened space, she sees Jules furiously waving a highball glass, making its contents slosh onto a flushed and happy-looking Grayson. Percy also sits with them, enjoying his usual tequila soda. "Hayashi! Over here!" Jules cries out.

Aki makes her way over to them, inhaling and telling herself that a change of scenery and a friendlier crowd will be good for her. As she sits down, Jules pushes a drink in front of her. "It's a Painkiller, just what you need," she winks.

Aki peers at the drink, which smells like pineapple, looks like orange juice, and feels like the solution to her problems. She takes the straw out of the long glass, tips her head back and downs half of the drink.

Jules, Grayson, and Percy all watch her wordlessly, exchanging glances among them. Percy squints. "Hayashi," he says seriously.

Aki looks up at his concerned expression and burps.

Jules and Percy exchange looks. "Want to fill us in, lady?" Jules asks bluntly.

Aki puts the straw back in her glass and sips aggressively as she waves down the waitress and points to her drink. "That was good, what was that, a Penicillin?"

"Painkiller?" the waitress asks quizzically.

"Right, another one of those but a double. And a burger," Aki announces. As the waitress trots off, she focuses her gaze on her friends. "Teenagers are God's punishment for man's sins," she announces, swiping Jules's old fashioned and taking a swig, then picks up a bowl of nuts and pours half into her hand before gobbling them down.

"Hon, I hear ya, Felix just totaled Jasper's Tesla," Jules says with a nervous laugh. "But slow down. You get mean when you're drunk."

"Well, don't let me get drunk then," Aki says between sips.

The waitress reappears with her second, stronger drink, but she can already feel the alcohol settling into her body. She feels warm and, for the first time in days, relaxed. She points to herself. "Do I have the glow? The Asian glow?" She chuckles. "Just kidding. Obviously, that's a racist stereotype. Except it's true," she jokes.

Percy and Jules look at one another. Percy moves a glass of water across the table. "Aki, come on now," he says. "Slow down."

She gulps down the water and slams the glass on the table, making the people around her turn to stare. She starts feeling angry again, and she just wants the incessant worrying to stop.

"I know who vandalized the school," she announces. "And I know who runs the Instagram site." She waits for a reaction, but getting none, continues, nearly shouting, "and Claire Wakeman is a *bitch*!" She nurses her Painkiller and takes another long sip before chewing on the straw. "Don't you guys want to know who did it?" She asks, not that she has any solid proof—she just desperately wants to feel a sense of resolution.

"Sure, whatever you want, sure," Grayson says, as if talking to a deranged stranger in order to placate them and escape.

"It was Aaron Wakeman," Aki says in a low voice. "He did it."

No one says anything. Finally, Jules coughs. "Hon, everyone knows that he lost his jersey. That's not him on the video."

The waitress returns with Aki's burger and a glass of beer.

"That isn't hers—" Grayson starts, but it's too late. Aki is eating the burger with one hand and drinking beer with the other.

"Well, he showed up at my house, *drunk*," Aki insists, taking a bite and a gulp, "and he was telling me he did it, and he was *drunk*," she says again for emphasis, then stops to reconsider her words. "Well, he didn't *say* he did it, but he *hinted* he did it." Then she adds, "He basically admitted to it."

"*He* was drunk, huh?" Percy asks, raising his eyebrow and trying to conceal a laugh as he watches Aki make a mess of her meal and drink. Jules hits Percy's arm.

Despite feeling slightly woozy, convincing them that Aaron is the perpetrator becomes desperately important. She decides that this will make all her problems go away. "We should just tell Harrison he did it and have him kick the kid out!" she announces. Looking at Percy's dubious expression, she says belligerently, "I thought you'd be *thrilled*," she says.

"What's that supposed to mean?" Percy asks casually while taking a slow sip of his drink, placating Aki.

"He's the perfect villain for you," Aki offers. Feeling slightly ill, she pushes her empty glasses and remaining burger away.

"I'm sorry?" Percy furrows his brow.

"Come on!" Aki insists, feeling hot. "You hate kids like him! Rich! Entitled! White!"

Despite the rancor in the bar, their table suddenly feels very quiet.

"Sort of like me, you mean?" Grayson says quietly.

"Hayashi," Percy says, "slow your roll." She knows he's referring to her attitude and not her consumption of the bar food.

"What?" Aki counters. "You hate kids like Aaron. I thought you'd be thrilled at any excuse to get rid of him."

Percy stares at Aki. "I know this isn't you talking, but for the record, I don't dislike kids because they're rich, or because they're white. And I think you owe Grayson an apology."

"No, hey, it's OK. I know Aki's under a lot of stress," Grayson interjects.

"The Wakemans are trying to get Meg kicked out, or me *fired*. Or both," Aki says. "Hey, your dad is on the board, right? Can he pull some strings?" She looks at Grayson. "Not that that's how you got your job," she says clumsily.

Grayson gulps and looks at Aki, then at Jules. "I think, uh," he stammers. "You know, I think I better get home. I have a lot of grading to do." Grayson stands, gives them a sad look, then goes to the bar with a credit card in his hand. He returns and says quietly, "I settled the bill for everyone. Thanks for the night out." He tries to give them a small smile, then backs away from the table before turning around and leaving quickly out the exit.

"Hayashi, that was not cool," Percy says, shaking his head.

Jules intervenes quickly. "Honey, this is not you," she says kindly. "Come on now, drink your water," she urges.

"No!" Aki violently rejects her friends' advice, slapping her hand in front of her and making the water glass tumble from the table.

"Messy," Percy says, standing up. "Bye, you two."

"Of *course* you would leave," Aki says meanly. "You *always* just leave when things get a little rough." Percy stares down at her silently. She wants to stop but can't. "Can't help me with the diversity stuff, which you claim is so important! Can't help me get rid of these consultants, which was basically your idea! Can't help with anything other than your precious art!"

Without another word, Percy turns on his heel and starts walking away from the table, then abruptly turns around and stomps back toward Aki and Jules. He puts one finger on the table, as if he's trying to hold it in place. "I don't dislike people because of their race or their income, because that would be prejudicial and hateful." His eyes bear down on Aki. "I dislike people for their beliefs when they harm others." Then he turns and walks out of the bar.

Aki stares after Percy for a while, then reaches for the rest of her food and stuffs it in her mouth, not sure what else to do.

After over a decade of friendship, Jules knows exactly what is causing her friend's spectacular meltdown. "Why don't you tell me what's going on with Meg," Jules says. "And fill me in on Claire Wakeman."

Aki looks up forlornly at Jules. Where to start? *Meg smacked Aaron Wakeman. She probably runs the Instagram site. She almost wrecked her high school record and got kicked out on the same day. She hates me.* Thinking about all of this, Aki suddenly feels hot and ill and like she needs to leave.

Aki looks up at Jules and whispers. "I don't know," then retches, making the other customers look at her in alarm.

"Oh, honey, let's get you home," Jules says sympathetically.

Aki lets her friend put a sweater around her shoulders as they walk home in silence.

"I guess I should apologize to Percy and Grayson," Aki says miserably as they reach her front door. She fumbles with the keys, and Jules patiently takes them from her, opening the door to the apartment.

"You can do that tomorrow, come on, give me your bag, take off your shoes," she says, opening the closet door.

"Oh, no, don't open—" Aki warns her friend as a jumble of clothes, bags, shoes, and boxes come tumbling out of the closet.

"Marie Kondo is your *friend*," Jules says, laughing as she starts to pick up the contents of the closet.

"It's OK, just leave it," Aki says to Jules. "My life is already a mess as it is."

FEBRUARY

FEBRUARY

17

"We are moving to the area from Chicago and have been hearing a lot about Wesley . . . not all of it good. Is its reputation good anymore?"

—*Moving from the MW, dcparentzone.com*

AMANDA SITS PRIMLY IN an ergonomic desk chair swathed in all sorts of J.Crew crispness, and it strikes Aki that no one at the school bothers to invest in formal work wear other than Harrison, Ousmane, and apparently whoever is in charge of the one-person shop of the Wesley Office of Communications. Aki wonders if there really is enough for Amanda to do all day, but she is nothing but business. She is perched at her desk resembling a small bird of prey, her dark eyes looking at Aki past a cascade of perfectly blown-out waves.

"Hello again, Aki," she says sharply, and it strikes Aki how Amanda's greetings often sound like a threat. "Please sit," she says as she nods to a knock-off Philippe Starck Ghost Chair across from her. Amanda's office has been shoehorned into what used to be a larger office for three finance officers by adding a wall. In contrast to her favorite taupe-colored heels and gray and blue outfits, the room is painted blush with a faded dark pink oriental rug on the floor and yellow accents on her stark white desk. "Since your daughter seems uninterested in assisting us, I've set up that interview we discussed," she says as Aki shuts the door behind her and pulls the chair back, squeezing herself from behind it in order to sit down. "It's good we can finally do something meaningful with your position," she says with disdain, suggesting that Aki has been as useless to Wesley as Aki feels the position is to the cause.

Aki rubs her temples. The interview, the one she agreed to do in exchange for Meg being spared from further punishment. She sighs, still feeling slightly ill and slightly hungover from the previous night's binge. She knows she has to make amends to Percy and Grayson, but she feels nauseous thinking about it, knowing how wrong she was for her behavior. As for Meg, she and her daughter rode to school in silence, as if nothing had transpired the day before. Aki has to figure out a way to get her daughter to talk to her, even though that seems like a fool's errand chased by a fruitless pursuit if there ever was one. Aki gives a long sigh and looks at Amanda, generating just enough energy to give a feeble nod.

Oblivious to or ignoring Aki's current state, Amanda gurgles on. "But you must, *must*, be prepared. No going off script," Amanda demands, fixing her gaze steadily on Aki as if what she is about to say will coax her troops into battle. "It's important, *very important*, that we take responsibility *without* taking responsibility for everything that has transpired."

This comment reminds Aki of former secretary of defense Donald Rumsfeld's confusing axiom about things we know we don't know and things we don't know we don't know. Amanda clicks at her screen and reads: "We at Wesley feel a communal sense of sadness as we take this moment to reflect and apologize for any unintended motions that may have inadvertently led to this terrible outcome.'" She looks up at Aki expectantly.

Sounds like a nothingburger wrapped in a don't-care taco, Aki thinks, but nods seriously, in tone with Amanda, who is acting like they are rewriting a victory speech for Churchill. What else can she say? They can hardly admit to the world, *well, it could be Wesley's own prodigal son, Aaron Wakeman, or maybe it's my very own daughter, Meg Hayashi-Brown! Everyone get on board this express train to Crazytown driven by two consultants who seem to be uniting the faculty and parents only in their disdain for them!*

"Hmm, maybe you should also talk about this," Amanda murmurs, ignoring Aki while typing furiously. "Our blueprint for future dialogue within our community will include three pillars." She looks up at Aki, "I love the word blueprint." Aki nods, feeling like a lost buoy in the vast sea of Amanda's verbiage. "First, a formal office for complaints," Amanda says, ticking off a list that has clearly been curated for her by the consultants. Something about Amanda makes Aki nervous, like if she reaches out and touches her, she'll break into a million pieces from being so tense. "How about we call it . . . the Center for Equity?" Amanda looks triumphant.

"Uhh—" Aki starts before Amanda cuts her off.

"Well, the *name* is incredibly important," Amanda interjects. "We can't call it 'some office with another person.'" Aki feels like she's being reprimanded. "It has to *sound* like the school is taking it seriously."

"The school isn't taking it seriously?" Aki asks facetiously, raising an eyebrow.

"Oh well, of course it is! I meant the name needs to reflect the gravity of the office and its undertaking!" Amanda sputters. "Maybe the consultants can name it," Amanda decides.

"Center for Truth and Power?" Aki offers sarcastically, feeling punchy even though she knows she should be taking what Amanda is saying seriously, since this interview with the press is the one thing saving her daughter's place in the school.

"Center for Diversity, Equity, and Justice. C-DEJ!" Amanda announces triumphantly before continuing. "Finally, this third point, about sensitivity training. We'll have to massage that a bit since you all couldn't seem to handle it," Amanda says as if looking at a dead fish. "Or!" she snaps her fingers. "Maybe we should partner with an HBCU!" she says excitedly while gazing at something behind Aki.

"A historically Black college or university? For curricular development or something?" Aki asks, wondering if she should turn around to see what Amanda is gazing at.

"What?" Amanda's attention snaps back to Aki. "No, I mean, more like a symbolic partnership," she says.

Aki wrinkles her nose. "Why would they want to do that?"

"Because we're Wesley," Amanda says, as if that should be explanation enough. "Anyway, it's important, *very important*," Amanda warns Aki again like one would a toddler near an open flame, "that you *stay on script* during the interview."

Aki nods obediently.

Amanda starts cleaning her desk and stacking her papers. "And I'll send out a formal statement to go along with the interview for board approval, then we'll send it out to the school community from your email."

"Wait," Aki says more loudly than she planned. "I'm putting my name on an email you write? I usually—"

"I think under the circumstances, you might be able to understand why Harrison and I are a little worried about what is coming out of the school," Amanda says pointedly, referring undoubtedly to not just the social media site but Meg's op-ed. "So I'll draft things, but they'll come signed from you as interim director of equity and justice."

Aki nods miserably. She also can't help but ask, "Is the school any closer to finding out who did it?" while wondering how much more cover she needs to provide for her own daughter.

Amanda looks at her sharply. "Let's focus on cleaning up the mess in front of us," she lectures. "We've got upset parents who think the curriculum is being overhauled overnight and rabble-rousing students making claims about the school that aren't true."

Aki looks at the floor.

"Frankly, we can't just go on pointing the finger at a family who has been nothing but a generous and stellar part of our community," Amanda adds, speaking presumably about the Wakemans.

Aki looks up. "Even if their son did it?" she asks, trying not to sound hopeful at the idea.

Amanda stares at Aki. After what feels like a long silence, she says, "Just remember, we want the same thing you do, which is to have Meg graduate from Wesley. So make sure to read the notes for the interview, and stay on script." She adds, "Thank you," with a look that suggests that Aki should be on her way, then asks pointedly, "Don't you have an auction meeting to attend?"

★ ★ ★

"I am so excited that you all are here today!" Holly trills, always and inexplicably happy to command the helm of any Wesley committee. Aki eyes her, still irritated from the Holly-hosted ambush with Claire, not to mention her contentious meeting with Amanda. Thanks to yet another one of Amanda's questionably useful ideas, fueled no doubt in part by the consultants, Aki is there not just to offer Grayson's summer home for auction but to perform an "equity review" of the items being sold that year, part of her never-ending penance for Meg's transgressions and in order for the school to say it does care about equity. When Aki asked what an "equity review" meant, Amanda informed her that there had been discussion within the consultants and advancement office and they decided that it looked "bad" that all the items being auctioned off were so expensive, and that it sent the wrong message about the school.

Then why don't you start with the price of admission? Aki asked. A ticket to the auction cost $200, though families on financial aid were given tickets for free. But Aki knew plenty of double-income parents who still couldn't foot a $400 bill for bad food at the Omni Shoreham, including herself, and if tickets for faculty weren't comped, she'd never go. Amanda informed her in a clipped tone that the item list *has to look a certain way*, and Aki realized it really had nothing to do with access or equity, as usual.

Holly smiles at Aki and continues, "I'd like to welcome Ms. Brown, who is here representing the Wesley diversity and inclusion program!" She nods to Aki, who doesn't bother to correct Holly on the name of her position. A few people applaud politely as Holly continues, "She's going to make sure we're inclusive in our offerings this year," she explains.

Aki looks around the table. It's mostly the same parents from the task force meeting she was forced to run, proving yet again that the school relies on the same set of parents for any volunteer work because they like parents who make the least amount of fuss. With the exception of Liz Everett.

As if on cue, Liz's hand shoots up. Aki groans internally as Holly points at her to speak. "I thought the point of an auction is to raise money?" Leave it to Liz to cut to the chase.

"Liz," Holly starts in a soothing voice, "our mission is of course to raise as much money as we can to increase the amount of financial aid the school can award."

Aki has to admit she sort of wants to watch another Holly versus Liz throwdown, because that would make this meeting a lot more entertaining and possibly take her mind off of everything that has happened in the last twenty-four hours. A few years ago, the auction theme was "In the Enchanted Garden," and both women had shown up dressed as "queen bees" with tiara-topped French twists and yellow and black balloon bottoms (complete with long black stingers), all of which made Jules whoop with delight and ask out loud if it meant that one of them had to die that night, since only one queen can rule the hive.

Liz snorts. "Right, but why do we have to feel guilty about the auction selling things for certain prices?" Liz is not unlike Jules's old English bulldog, Grumbles. When someone gives him a lamb bone filled with peanut butter, he stares down anyone within his field of vision, places one heavy paw over the bone, and growls if you go near what is his. "The point is to make money, *Holly.*"

The auction has historically been the playground for the rich at Wesley, a place to show off all that they can give: "Look! I have a beach house!" "Look, I have front row seats at Madison Square Garden!" Simultaneously, of course, it provides a public stage, the Roman Colosseum in which to show their consumption prowess: fifteen grand for dinner with Harrison and the director of the last *Jurassic Park* movie? No problem! Two grand for a reserved parking space on campus? Cash, check, or direct deposit from my personal charitable trust? It never really bothered her in the past, being a recipient of the largess of the attendees, but Aki also grudgingly concedes her own daughter's point about how the auction might just be another public square for the flaunting of wealth. It makes her recall a passage she read in graduate school about the court of Versailles, about hunting and eating and partying and otherwise not doing very much other than those activities that keep the wealthy busy.

Of course, not all of the families at Wesley are wealthy. Nathan Richter had pointed that out. As a beneficiary of the auction, Aki agreed with Liz: *Make it rain.* But why should any parent feel like they have to pay $200 to attend an official school function? She wonders now, looking out at a sea of privileged faces, if the auction creates an unnecessary cleavage within the parent population, one that continues to make it too obvious who *has* and who *has not.* At the school play, or at homecoming, parents mix with one another, and no one can tell, or at least, everyone pretends not to guess. At the auction, however, only the rich can play.

Liz clears her throat to get everyone to refocus their attention on her. Like Grumbles, she can't let go of her metaphorical bone. And she certainly does not care about the cultural connotations of a massive party. "The auction is what *helps those people* . . ." she trails off, looking momentarily self-conscious, before flipping her hair.

Nonwhite kids get to attend so that Wesley can say it's diverse. Say it, Liz, I dare you, Aki thinks, almost gleefully. She wants to see Liz expose all her biases, if only because she hopes another parent will bite back. *I wonder,* Aki stops to think, *if I am not the absolute worst person for this job,* though she already knows she is. *How can the school,* she thinks with disgust, *proclaim itself to be the academic progenitor of racial equity, then refuse take the steps needed to weed out actual racists from its community?* But she already knows the answer to that. She takes out her phone to shoot off a text, knowing that she looks incredibly rude as she does, but she decides that it is more important than what is going on in the room at the moment.

Then, as if to answer the very question that had just popped into Aki's mind, Liz starts up again. "Wesley relies on wealthy parents to foot a lot of the bills. Why do we have to be made to feel badly about being able to pay full freight? Because we're white? It's not a crime to be white, you know."

"Oh, my Lord," someone says under their breath.

"What?" Liz demands, before jerking her head in Aki's direction. "And what's she here to do? To make sure we make things 'accessible'?" she says, using air quotes. "Just remember *who* is actually helping to make that happen. It's not just some person the school hires."

All heads swivel toward Aki, including Holly, who blurts out, "Aki?" looking at her, apparently, to mediate.

WTF, Holly! Aki thinks before clearing her throat and giving herself a moment to think. "Liz is correct that the generosity of the parent community bolsters financial aid in ways the school alone cannot achieve," she says, watching Liz nod with a Cheshire cat grin on her face. "But the practice of being mindful of how we can make the school more self-reflective is a good lesson for the students as well as the parents." *It is amazing*, Aki thinks, *how I am sounding more and more like Ousmane.* "The auction is one of those, I wouldn't say *evils*, but it is a necessary exercise, and we just want to make sure we don't bar people from attending because of ticket prices, and make sure to have items at all price points," she finishes, feeling like Amanda is feeding her lines, and also like she needs to go take a shower, because what she really feels like saying is *Liz, bite me, you racist Karen.*

"We're so appreciative of your insight here, Ms. Brown," Holly says graciously but with odd formality. Aki's new title means little to her but apparently a lot to the parents around her, though clearly not enough to keep Holly from orchestrating that horrible meeting with Claire, Aki seethes.

Her phone lights up with a response that makes her smile. She quickly types out another text, hoping the group won't need her to contribute any further.

"Maybe you can get rid of the Chick-fil-A cups, though," Beth Morgan comments. Everyone looks to Beth quizzically. "You know, the kids who carry the cups around?" she asks again, twirling her blond dreadlocks around her fingers. Aki assumes that Beth must be the only member of the Morgan Stanley clan with anything less than an expensive every-other-day blowout. "Those red and white Chick-fil-A cups," Beth repeats, looking at Aki.

Everyone's head swivels around back to Aki, who is taken aback. *Taking a wild guess that they're not talking chicken sandwiches,* she thinks and sighs. "Can you catch me up? I don't think I'm the only one who's in the dark here?" *At least I hope I'm not.* Her mind immediately goes to the PoC@Wesley site. It sounds like a post right up their viral public shaming alley. And the account has been strangely silent. *I wonder if it's because I finally called Meg out on it*, Aki wonders.

Beth crosses her thin legs on the chair like a slender Buddha and sits up straight. "So, I heard from my daughter that there is a contingent of kids who have been walking around campus with those cups to make a point."

"And that point would be?" Aki asks, though she's not sure she wants to know.

"Well, as you know, the company isn't LGBTQIA friendly."

"That's an understatement," Melinda Hardy (mother of twin soccer recruits Jason and Todd, stay-at-home and proud of it) interjects.

Beth nods and continues, "So they walk around with the cups, you know . . ." she trails off.

Aki realizes where she's seen those cups before: the day of the hastily christened safe space room, she remembers the lacrosse team showing up at the ribbon-cutting holding the very Chick-fil-A cups that Beth is talking about. She tries to remember if Aaron was holding one but can't recall.

"They eat there and bring the cups back to campus to make a statement, which is that they don't support the LGBTQIA community on campus," Melinda explains to all of them as if speaking to a group of toddlers. "They do it on purpose. They could just go to Panera, you know."

What assholes, Aki thinks to herself as she shakes her head.

"What assholes!" Beth declares bluntly, and Aki tries not to laugh out loud.

"They're just kids," Liz offers, but apparently, she can't stop there. "It's just a fast-food chain."

"How can you sit here and say that? In fact, why do you even send your kids here?" Melinda demands. Melinda is not one to back down from Liz.

"OK, I think we should—" Holly tries to retake the reins, but the horse has not only left the stable, it has jet engines on its hindquarters and the wind at its back.

"No! No!" Melinda insists. Aki thinks she sees a smirk on Liz's face and remembers how Roger also loves to stir the shit, as it were. "*This* is the problem with Wesley! Not that the rich parents go around shining their expensive cars and buffing their conspicuous consumption, it's that they *know* they can get what they want and say what they want, because the school is so desperate for money and standing. It's *disgusting*," Melinda says, though everyone knows what she really wants to say is *Liz, you're disgusting*.

"Melinda, I hardly think you should be one to talk about being *rich*," Liz spits back. Melinda's husband is a partner at a K Street law firm and personal advisor to several tech CEOs. But Jules always points out that Melinda is "nice rich," opposed to "obnoxious rich," like the Everetts and the Wakemans. Aki supposes the distinction is worth something.

"OK, I really need to remind everyone about how we speak to one another while on campus!" Holly is so desperately trying to keep the room from imploding that Aki feels almost sorry for her, except that she never really wanted to be here to begin with. Thinking about it more, she knows she should probably be the one mediating this conflict.

"Well, if you want to talk about conspicuous consumption," Liz says calmly, "maybe we should talk about how much the school is paying for things like the equity and justice program."

Aki bolts upright. "Excuse me?" she asks, then immediately regrets taking the bait, which Liz has very clearly laid out just for her.

"The school is making it an official position with a pay grade almost as high as Ousmane's," Liz says coolly. "And they're going to build, I don't know what, a shrine to cancel culture and political correctness? A new building? The Center for Equity and Justice? Now *that* sounds like a waste of money, if you ask me," she huffs.

Aki can feel her mouth opening and closing and opening and closing. How did Liz already know about all of this?

Melinda throws up her hands. "The fact that you even know all of this just proves my point! The donors all get the inside scoop from Harrison himself, because he depends on them to build his empire," she says disgustingly, before conceding, "though this one might be worth it."

"I was going to say," Liz chuckles, "I thought this would be an altar you'd be willing to pray at. So, Aki, how much are they paying you to tell us to be nice to one another?"

The words are so cutting, they momentarily take Aki's breath away. In all her years at Wesley, she's never had a parent be so openly impudent. Then she realizes the real reason for Liz's ire.

"Liz," she says, making sure to make eye contact. "I know it's difficult for you to accept that Sibley didn't do well in my class, but I wish you wouldn't make this personal." The second she says it, she regrets it, and she knows that Ian would be so disappointed in her for lowering herself to Liz's level, but she has to admit that the look of horror on Liz's face was worth it for at least three seconds.

The other people in the room gasp and squeal, some of them ecstatic to have Liz Everett finally put in her place, others undoubtedly questioning Aki's professionalism. *Oh well, if Meg gets kicked out, I won't need the tuition discount anyway, might as well let loose on Liz*, Aki thinks. She knows it's not good to cross a couple like Liz and Roger, and talking about a private-school student's grade in public is akin to admitting to manslaughter in a police station.

Liz narrows her eyes and glares at everyone around the table. "Well, I'm happy to have everyone know that I went straight to Harrison to complain about how you treated Sibley."

"I treated her fairly. She deserved to fail." *Whoops, TMI?* Aki thinks as more gasps and whispers surround her and Liz.

"No, she didn't! And the only reason your child wasn't kicked out of this school after assaulting another student—and the reason you weren't fired for your complete incompetence—is because . . . *you're minorities!*" Liz screams.

"This is totally unnecessary. I really need to ask everyone to—" Holly stands up, more agitated than Aki has ever seen her, but Liz interjects.

"Sit down!" Liz yells at Holly, who does so only because she's so shocked. Liz refocuses her angry expression back on Aki. "The only reason Harrison hired you in the first place is because he took pity on a single mother with no background in teaching, dirt poor, and no husband," Liz spits out. All untrue, of course, since Harrison wasn't even head of school when Aki was hired, but what's the point of correcting Liz? Aki merely rolls her eyes, making Liz's expression change from dismissive disgust to magenta-hued wrath. "And," Liz screams, crossing her arms and narrowing her eyes, "your poor kid, *who knows where she came from!*"

Aki doesn't know what comes over her, but it is as if the ghost of one of the many *Real Housewives* that Jules loves so much inhibits her body. She leaps across the table at Liz, making everyone recoil and scream, with the exception of Melinda, who pulls Aki back, whispering in her ear, "She's not worth it, come on, Aki, just remember, she's wrong, and you're right."

"Well, now we know where your daughter gets that temper," Liz says, pretending to dust herself off. "If it's so important to everyone, maybe I'll just have to let Harrison know he should speed up the hiring for the *new* head of—what do you call it? *Equity and justice*?" She laughs. "Maybe I'll get some lunch at Chick-fil-A before I do," she says, standing up, hoisting her enormous Louis Vuitton bag on her shoulder and looking around at the room. "You all may hate me, but I have news for you. It doesn't matter what you all think." She gives a little smile and leaves the room, leaving everyone in it totally silent.

◆ 18 ◆

"All of you need a life. Why do you think posting anonymously will get you anything?"

—*Sick of You, dcparentzone.com*

AKI KNOWS THAT SHE should have stayed and said something in her newfound capacity as an administrator, not to mention something meaningful about tolerance, but after watching Liz stomp out of the room, all she could think was *Get me out of here* and ran straight to her office. She didn't even bother trying to help Holly pick up the pieces with another Ousmane-approved quote about finding common ground. She knows that not every parent is like Liz, but what bothers her is how there are *any* Lizes at Wesley.

Aki sits in her desk chair and pulls up a document on her computer, an official proclamation with the Wesley logo at the top. This is a badge of honor, the heads of the lower, middle, and upper schools, along with Harrison, Amanda, and the head of the parent association being the only ones who can send out an emblazoned message. As the interim director of equity and diversity, Aki has also been granted this small but oddly significant mark of power. She stares glumly at her computer, knowing her first official email with this very masthead will be the announcement that Amanda had labored over, the one outlining the school's "Blueprint for Community, Equity, and Justice," the minimized yet also somehow exaggerated list of action items born from Elliot Associates' expensive hourly rates.

She stares at the statement that has been expertly chiseled into rhetorical nothingness, which includes a promise to "investigate" current equity practices, "invigorate" sensitivity training across the school, and "install" the new Office of Diversity, Justice, and Community (Amanda likes alliteration, along with her favorite number three, apparently). The last paragraph is a promise to do better, the "non-apology apology," that Amanda inserted, and closes with the usual "move forward into the light" sign-off, but instead of Harrison's name, it proclaims *Aki Hayashi-Brown*.

Aki reads and rereads the statement, thinking about how she will not only have to sign her name to this but also conduct an interview about it, and she feels anger growling inside of her. She can't let go of Liz's hateful words: *dirt poor . . . incompetent . . . minority . . .* and of course, the final dig at Meg. The long running list of things she hates about Wesley moves through her mind like the scroll underneath a news program: Liz and Roger Everett. The entitled kids who think they can get away with anything. Harrison Neal and his stupid back-slapping politician smile. Amanda and her wrinkle-free face and wrinkle-free suits. Teachers like her, who complain and stay. Teachers like her, who are dutiful for no reason. Dutiful to her mother, dutiful to the school, and dutiful to the parents who throw around their money and expect to get what they want. How did the roads and intersections of her life end up here?

"Arghh!" she stands and cries out. The room—no, the school—suddenly feels claustrophobic, and she needs to get out of her office.

Not wanting to make eye contact with any students and definitely not wanting to run into Meg or Aaron, she barges through the double doors of the upper school and out into the courtyard, which is thankfully empty. *Dirt poor . . . incompetent . . . minority . . .* the words keep repeating themselves in Liz's nasally voice. Desperate to keep her mind off them, she trots through the courtyard, takes a left, and decides impulsively that her destination should be the gym. There, she makes her way to the overhead indoor track, thinking that if she can just move her body a bit, she'll feel better.

Realizing that even low-heeled loafers aren't going to cut it, she kicks off her shoes and tosses her sweater aside and starts running at a brisk pace. How long has it been since she's run? The track, which is housed in the new athletic complex, is unlit save for the shallow rays of sun filtering in from the narrow windows on one side of the gym, casting strange shadows through the cavernous space.

"Mrs. Hayashi-Brown?" a young voice calls out.

Aki looks back to see Aiko, dressed in Wesley athletic warm-up wear, running behind her. Aiko catches up to Aki, and the two continue to run in unison.

"I've never seen you here during the day!" Aiko says.

"Ha ha, yeah," Aki starts awkwardly. She can't very well tell her that she's here to blow off steam, because that seems wildly unprofessional. She goes into teacher mode and asks a battery of questions instead: "How is track season? Am I going too slowly for you? How are your classes?"

Aiko gives Aki an oddly knowing smile, as if she can sense Aki's stress. "If I have a free period right before or after lunch I come and get in a little run. Helps me focus, actually."

"Mmm, yeah," Aki says, feeling slightly uncomfortable at their pace, which has quickened. *Dirt poor . . . incompetent . . . minority . . .* she shakes her head to try to get the words out of her mind again. "Don't you get sweaty?"

Aiko laughs. "I just shower, then go to class," she says gently, then pauses. "I've been wanting to ask you how your new role is as director of equity and diversity."

Aki looks at her daughter's best friend, realizing that—despite almost a decade of sleepovers—she knows very little about Aiko. She remembers that Aiko loves poetry and avocados, hates crickets and AP physics, and can't live without cross-country and track. Aki is grateful for this young woman, Meg's emotional stanchion, always willing to listen and support Meg's litany of breakdowns and emotional upheavals. The two of them are foils for one another; Meg is tempestuous and impulsive yet strong and persistent, Aiko is softer, more thoughtful, and more considerate. But beyond what she hears from Meg and the frequent hellos and goodbyes, she's never had a substantial conversation with Aiko.

"I'm just the interim director," Aki starts. "It's been—" Aki trails off. *A sham?* She can't say that, though Meg probably will.

"You know," Aiko says seriously, "I almost left the school."

Aki almost stops midstride and has to double-step to keep up.

"It was back in eighth grade," Aiko says as their feet pound rhythmically on the rubber track. "There were some kids, they thought it was funny to call me *mulatto*."

The gym holds only the sound of their running, Aki unable to say anything in response. She feels ashamed for not knowing something so hateful had happened to her daughter's closest friend at a school she's been a teacher at for so long.

"Meg defended me, of course," Aiko recalls, laughing. "I think she even got in trouble for hitting one of the boys."

Aki looks at Aiko, dumbfounded. How had she never heard of this? But extracting information from Meg, secrets or otherwise, is a wasted effort and always will be.

"We both know that the school has had a problem for a long time," Aiko says softly. "And Aaron Wakeman and his friends are a big part of that problem," she announces.

Aki pauses, but can't help but ask, "Do you think they had anything to do with the graffiti?"

Aiko keeps her eyes straight ahead on the track. Aki isn't sure if she's offended by the question or doesn't want to respond, and she's about to ask something else when Aiko announces, "I know Meg tried to give him a chance but look where that ended up."

Aki knows she shouldn't pry too much, but she is now dying to know what Aiko means. She tries to conceal her curiosity by acting like she knows what Aiko is talking about. "Riiight, it didn't end up well, did it?" she says, hoping she doesn't sound too fake.

"I told her it was a bad idea," Aiko starts, then stops abruptly, looking at Aki. "Not to sound like a bad friend or anything. I mean, I really was trying to look out for her."

Aki can't beg Aiko to tell her more without revealing that Meg is quite obviously trying to keep something from her. But before Aki can muster up the courage to ask for more information or the creativity to somehow trick her into telling her more, Aiko pipes up and announces, "What a mess!" as Aki concurs silently. "I better finish this set before science," Aiko adds, which Aki understands is her way of telling her she needs to run faster. "It was nice running with you!" Aiko adds as she zooms off.

* * *

Despite returning to her office sweaty, Aki feels better. And though Aiko had divulged a disturbing story about how she was treated as a minority, Aki feels a bit more peaceful as she sits back down at her desk, having forgotten about Liz and wondering if she should try to clean herself up somehow in the bathroom, when the phone on her desk gives off a demanding *Rrrring!*

The display says *Head of Upper* and she knows it's from Ousmane's assistant, Alice. The phone trills persistently and Aki grabs the receiver and blurts out a curt "Hello?"

"Ousmane needs you in his office," Alice says, before adding quietly, "right now."

Aki hangs up the phone and speed-walks down the senior hallway, again trying to avoid eye contact with anyone. How many times has she been called into Ousmane's office in the last few months? More than the person who actually graffitied the school, she thinks to herself bitterly.

"Hey, Ms. Brown, what can I pay you to give us a free period?" someone calls out, as she pretends not to hear them.

She enters Ousmane's reception area and waves nervously at his assistant, who motions for Aki to go into his office. When she enters, she sees Ousmane with his head in his hands, looking much like how she feels. He looks up as she takes a seat in front of his uncharacteristically cluttered desk.

"Aki," he starts, rubbing his eyes. Then he shakes his head and removes his phone from his desk drawer, placing it before her. It shows a picture of Meg and Aaron kissing.

Aki stares at the picture and inhales before looking up at Ousmane, making sure to give nothing away with her expression. The photo is, for lack of a better description, an unsurprising surprise, but it's still a jolt to the system. For his part, Ousmane simply looks at her with a raised eyebrow, and they stare at one another for what feels like a long time. Ousmane finally clears his throat and says, "Do you know what this is?"

"A picture of Meg and Aaron?" she asks obliquely.

"Do I need to ask you about what she is wearing?" Ousmane asks quietly.

Be calm. Aki tells herself. She had noticed this herself upon further inspection. The picture is of Meg in a warm-up jersey with the number 18 on the back, leaning into Aaron for a kiss at what looks to be the homecoming game back in October.

"Well, it appears she is wearing Aaron Wakeman's jersey," she croaks, "But . . ." she pauses to swallow, looking again at the photo. "This doesn't mean . . ." *that she is trying to set up Aaron,* she thinks, not even able to convince herself at this point.

"So you didn't know?" Ousmane asks without a trace of judgment. "About their relationship?"

"Ousmane, Meg tells me very little. I am sure you understand how that feels." Ousmane is but one of the many faculty members with teen children, though unlike Aki, his son doesn't attend Wesley but goes to the French school. From the rare bits that he shares with her, it sounds as if his son is very much in equivalent throes of teen-related melodrama, most of which involves forsaking studies for a future in professional soccer. Aki tries to change the subject, asking what she really wants to know. "Where did you get that picture?"

"Aki, the person who sent me this photo clearly wants to highlight their relationship, but also, I am assuming, to try and obscure any line between Aaron and the vandalism by shifting the focus onto Meg," he explains calmly, as if describing the solar system to a small child. "Suggesting that she was indeed seeking revenge of some sort," he clarifies.

"So, you don't know who sent it? It could be Aaron trying to prove a point, or even one of his friends," she squeaks, doubtful that Ousmane hasn't already thought of this. She stops and looks at Ousmane. "Why are you showing this to me?" She realizes that he must have brought her here for some other reason, since they seem to be covering the same ground repeatedly.

He looks slightly embarrassed, an expression she rarely sees on his usually assured face. She has to hand it to him, she has not seen him at all flustered except that one day in front of the students, when he was just plain angry. "Aki, I am not one to give parenting advice," he says sheepishly, "but I would really encourage you to try and get Meg to talk to you." Aki is about to object when he raises his hand and continues, "I think we can both see that this photo is a warning, and at some point, the school *is* going to have to take some action."

Then, *ding!* Like a single clear bell beckoning an absent con-
cierge in an empty hotel lobby, Aki realizes exactly who sent the
photo to Ousmane.

Ousmane picks the phone up and returns it to his desk
drawer. "Obviously I am not interested in involving myself in
unsubstantiated accusations. What I *do* wish for is to move forward together, and I know that you are working very hard with
Amanda in your role as interim director. I trust you, Aki," he
says, not unkindly.

Aki simply nods, but a white-hot anger burns in the pit of her
belly, and she knows exactly where she needs to head next.

★   ★   ★

Kenwood is a small part of Chevy Chase, a suburb located right
across the Maryland-DC line. While Chevy Chase is made up
of "villages," with a mix of both modest and larger homes, Kenwood is what Jules likes to call "Kardashian-adjacent." The lots
are sizeable and the houses grand, with $3 million marking the
entry point price. The streets are all lined with cherry trees,
bringing thousands of blossom-seeking tourists to the neighborhood every spring, much to the chagrin of the residents but to the
joy of entrepreneurial children charging $10 for cold brew and
organic lemonade. The original charter of Kenwood famously
forbade Jewish families from settling in the neighborhood, with
the assumption that, of course, neither could Black families.

Aki pulls up in front of 5850 Sunset Lane, an address she
found by using the school directory. The house is, for lack of a
better word, gigantic. Neo-Georgian in style, perfectly symmet-
ric, showing off a gleaming white exterior and surrounded by lush
landscaping, the house sits upon a vast lawn. The front door looks
to be at least thirty yards from the street, and as Aki walks from
her Prius and onto the lawn, she feels less sure of what she's going
to say—or if anyone will even be home. Why did she think this

was a good idea? Maybe Meg really does get her impulsive habits from her. Aki stops in the middle of the walkway, abruptly swiveling on her heel, facing her car. Then she turns back again to the door and sighs. Looking at the expansive lawn that encircles the house, she notices a lacrosse net set up with a turquoise semicircle painted in front of it. She realizes that it's set up for practice, and stops and stares at the lines, surprised anyone who lived in a house like this would allow their child to use such a garish color in front of their picture-perfect home. Aki curses at herself when she sees a car pull slowly out of the long driveway from behind the house. She strains to see who it is, as does the driver, who stops the car and lowers the window of their white Range Rover.

"Aki, what a surprise," Claire Wakeman says as she leans over the passenger seat and pulls off her sunglasses, giving her a prim smile.

"Really? Is it really that much of a surprise?" Aki can barely conceal her annoyance, despite the fact that Wesley teachers are practically trained to be obsequious with parents.

"Well," Claire looks amused, "it *is* still school hours. I was about to drive to watch Aaron at his game. Pre-season, of course," she adds as if Aki cares about the distinction.

Aki's impulses take the reins of the conversation again. "Why did you send Ousmane that picture of Meg and Aaron?" she snaps.

Claire sighs. "It's just so unfortunate. I held on to the photo for quite some time because I thought we were friends," she says, staring off at a spot behind Aki's head.

We are not friends! Aki wants to scream. Instead, she screeches, "Why are you doing this *now*?"

Claire feigns a look of surprise. "I just wanted Ousmane to have all the facts. I do feel badly that Aaron dumped Meg, but I always liked Yeardly. They're probably a better fit, long-term, you know?"

Aki ignores Claire's passive-aggressive right hook. Maybe Meg was right about Yeardly pandering to Aaron and using the editorial as a lure.

Claire gives a low laugh. "You don't think it curious that she's somehow always involved with the accusations against my son?" Aki stops and stands still. She can hear her heart beating loudly in her chest. "Why did they choose the number 18 at the town hall? Why does she keep insisting that he is somehow involved with defacing the school despite not having any real proof?" Aki hesitates a moment too long. She wants to spit back that the video footage of the person with the number 18 jersey is pretty damn incriminating for Aaron—except she also acknowledges that her daughter's behavior that day in the multicultural center suggests that Meg does in fact have a clear vendetta when it comes to Aaron. "You've thought about it too," Claire says smugly.

Aki looks at Claire Wakeman, her thin body looking like it's being swallowed by the belly of the car's huge leather interior, and realizes that there is really no way that Claire Wakeman would do anything that wasn't solely for herself.

Aki finally laughs and retorts, "You didn't send in that photo just to protect your son, you did it to go after my daughter. You did it because you're spiteful and entitled," she spits out angrily. "Because I didn't kowtow to you like you expect everyone to."

Claire smiles and puts the car back into drive. "Well," she says as she puts her sunglasses back onto her face, "I'm sorry you feel that way. Hopefully nothing more comes out that hurts either one of our children, but I'm sure you can appreciate a mother trying everything she can to protect her own child." She makes the last comment while staring at Aki through her Chanel glasses, then closes the window on their conversation and drives off of her property, leaving Aki gaping at the retreating SUV as it kicks up gravel and speeds down the wide street. Aki's phone starts vibrating in her back pocket, and she notices her hands shaking with rage as she reaches for it.

Then, belying the anger she had just felt a moment ago, everything around her goes silent and blank, and the world falls away. On the screen is a text from someone who she didn't even realize knew how to text: her father.

Come home, your mother is in the hospital.

♦   19   ♦

"Sometimes I really question if it was all worth it after all the stress and hatred. I remember my freshman year when there were swastikas drawn in the bathroom and the school barely winced."
— *Wesley Senior, PoC@Wesley*

IT'S BEEN A WHILE since Aki's been in the Bay Area. Ian had taken Meg to visit colleges, so it's been almost three years since she herself has been back, she realizes. Her tiny rental car grumbles as she presses on the accelerator, reluctantly merging onto 280 toward Daly City. She booked the first flight she could, leaving DC in the early evening and arriving at SFO well past ten PM with the time difference. She was exhausted, but not tired enough *not* to be irritated. No matter how many times she tried to call her parents, neither of them answered their phones—and she had been trying since she received her father's text on Claire Wakeman's front lawn. Ian took the Metro over to school in order to drive her to the airport, then turned right back around to get Meg, but every time she called to see if her parents had called *him*, he apologetically told her no. Ousmane was incredibly supportive, as was Grayson, who gravely said he would do his best to fill her shoes while she was gone. She couldn't even tell either of them how long she would be out here, though she furiously hopes it won't be for long, knowing she should feel a little more guilty for not wanting to stay longer.

She sighs as she passes by Golden Gate National Cemetery, which is of course not near the Golden Gate at all but across the highway from the San Bruno Golf Club. She's not far from home, and once she passes the bigger strip malls, she'll turn off and meander through the narrow streets until she gets to her parents' house. Unlike San Francisco, most of which has been gentrified beyond recognition, her neighborhood remains an ode to the 1950s, identical mod-looking Doelger homes lined up neatly like Monopoly pieces in muted shades of tan and blue. As the rental car travels through the roads in her old neighborhood, the old Pete Seeger song about Daly City runs through her mind: *Little boxes made of ticky-tacky.*

She finally pulls into the driveway and sees that her parents' car is there, a small Honda boasting 200,000 miles on the odometer. She had offered to buy them a car the last time she visited, but they waved her off saying *next time, next time.* Here next time was, and she wasn't even sure what was going on, or God forbid, if her mother would ever drive again. On the plane, a list of worst outcomes ran laps through her mind. Cancer . . . stroke . . . heart attack . . . given her mother's age, none of these would be a surprise.

She slams the door of her rental and locks it twice before hoisting her backpack on her shoulder. Ian had thoughtfully packed a bag for her, telling her, "I'm hoping you'll only need to be out there for a few days." She hugged him close and prayed for the same. She nervously knocks on the door, then rings the doorbell, waiting for footsteps to come down the front stairs. As she waits in the chilly evening air, she looks at the house next door. The lights are on in their living room, and she sees a cat curled up on the back of a chair. She wonders if it's the same neighbors there, the Wu family, or if it's someone else.

Just then the door flies open and Aki sees her mother standing before her.

"Mom!' Aki cries out in surprise. "Aren't you in the hospital?" she sputters.

"Ara, Aki-chan. Masaka otousan kara henna meru ga kita toka?" (I hope your father didn't send you some strange email?)

Um, yes, he did, Aki thinks as she stares at her mother. She looks unchanged, except that her hair is a little mussed. *"Okasan doushitano?"* (Mother, what happened?)

"Hora, haitte, tomaruno? Haitte, haitte." (Are you staying? Come in, come in.) Her scurries around Aki to shut the door. As she does, she winces in pain.

"Mom!" Aki cries out. "What's wrong?"

"Sonna taihen na koto janaiwayo!" (It's not that big a deal!) Her mother pushes her up the stairs.

"What is it?" Aki feels scared. Now that she thinks about it, she can't remember the last time her mother was ever sick, not even with a cold.

They arrive at the top of the stairs and into the dining and living area. Her father stands at attention in front of the sofa looking uncomfortable, as if greeting strangers. *"Mouchou,"* is all he says.

"Appendicitis?" Aki asks. Do people this old get appendicitis?

"Chotto itakatta dakenanoni otousan oogesa yo," (It just hurt a little but your father overreacted.)

Her father proceeds to collapse on the floor, rolling around and clutching his midsection, moaning and shrieking in alternate measure. He suddenly stops, looks up at them, and points to Aki's mother. *"Uso da."* (Liar.)

Aki can't help but chuckle at her father's reenactment.

"Ara yada. Otsan hitori de omise ni itakunai kara amaeteru dakeyo. Okasan heikidesu." (Your father just didn't want to work in the store by himself while I recovered. I'm fine.)

Aki looks at her father, then at her mother. She assumes the truth lies somewhere in between their two narratives, and that her mother is in more discomfort than she looks, but that her father was not totally honest in why he called her out there. Standing in her old living room, she feels her shoulders drop as all the worry and anxiety drains from her body.

Her mother commands, "*Tukareteru mitaine. Ofuro haitte nenasai!*" (You look tired. Take a bath and go to bed!) It is very much like her mother to tell her to go to bed, but not without taking a bath. A bath is nonnegotiable, Aki knows.

As she shuffles down the hallway, her mother says, "*Ofuro irete agerukara.*" (I'll fill the bath.)

Aki's father has settled back on the sofa, watching basketball. Aki hears the hum of the water filling the tub and she realizes that she should probably just enjoy this unexpected vacation from work and Wesley. She smiles at the back of her father's head and, feeling not unlike her teenage self, trots down the hall with her backpack on her back, strangely excited to be free of any real responsibility. Maybe a trip home is exactly what she needs.

★　★　★

"*Irashaimase!*" (Welcome in!) Aki and her father call out as a bell alerts them to a new customer.

Over her mother's protestations, Aki is today's replacement worker at the register. They arrived an hour before opening, and by eleven the store is comfortably busy. It took Aki an hour or two to remember her long-forgotten arsenal of retail moves—checking inventory, restocking, answering phones, operating the register, and packing groceries, all motions that used to happen naturally. She's very much out of practice, and after only three hours, shockingly tired. She can also feel her father's judgment casting an invisible net across her back as she hurries to pack grocery bags and answer the phone for take-out orders. Since he's in the kitchen behind her, he can see everything going on in the store, including all her mistakes. This sense of surveillance, not to mention the expectation of perfection, is familiar from her adolescence but for some reason stresses her out more as an adult, as if she should have learned something in the interim.

"Hey, do you guys have gojuchang?" a young man asks from one of the aisles.

"Yes, next aisle over," Aki informs him. The funny thing about having a Japanese grocery in Daly City is that you have to be pan-Asian: a little Korean, a little Chinese, some Filipino, some Vietnamese. Japanese is never the majority, in the region or otherwise, and their selection reflects the diversity of cultures in the area.

"Thanks, hey, cool selection of Poki," the guy says, admiring multiple rows of Japanese cookie stick boxes in an assortment of flavors.

"Thanks!" Aki says brightly; it was her idea in high school to make their store a little hipper, though half of her ideas were shot down instantly by her mother. But the compliment still makes her smile, even after all these years.

"Aki Hayashi?" a voice calls out.

Aki, still smiling from the compliment, looks around to find the voice calling her name.

"Oh, my gosh, it *is* you! You haven't changed a bit!" A very tall brunette in her early forties comes rushing over from the candy aisle, laying out a generous assortment of gummies and rice crackers she's apparently planning on purchasing. "You don't remember me, do you? I guess we're not all lucky enough to have genes like yours," she says cheerfully as Aki continues to stare and riffle through her mental rolodex. Is it a past Wesley parent?

A Berkeley classmate? The woman picks up three more types of gummy candies that line the register table as she prattles on. "We all wondered where you disappeared off to!"

With that sentence, Aki freezes, because she realizes that it's a classmate from Penn. What was her name?

"It's Paige Howard! We were in 'Revolutions and Rebellions' together! Gosh, you were so brilliant!"

Ugh, Aki thinks. *Paige Howard.* She remembers her now. Competitive, sycophantic, type-A Paige. Always busy either rewriting drafts of papers to submit to journals or hunting for a Wharton boyfriend. "Hi, Paige, how are you?" Aki asks, trying to summon any niceness she has in reserves.

Paige continues to grab rice crackers and seaweed packets, creating a mountain of snacks in front of Aki as she talks. "We were wondering where you disappeared to!" Paige says again, looking at her expectantly, as if she deserves an explanation, while Aki tries her best to look like she doesn't care. She never stopped to think about what people said after she left the program. Did they know about the affair? About Meg? She thinks about how hurt she was when her advisor rejected her, so hurt that all she could do was pretend it never happened, despite the growing child inside of her. Her mind goes to Meg. Could Aaron really have hurt her that much too? Hurt her so much that she would try to frame Aaron for the graffiti and imperil his college acceptances, as Claire claimed?

Paige punctures her introspection with a chipper question. "So is this *your* store? Or . . ."

"It's my parents' store. I'm a history teacher at Wesley Friends School." *There, happy now, Paige with the flawless four-carat diamond?*

"Oh! Where the president's kids went!" Leave it to Paige to make that particular association. Then she asks the inevitable question that all social-climbers are dying to know. "Did you teach them?" Paige continues to add to her ever-expanding pile of overpriced Japanese junk food.

This is going to be a big ticket, Aki thinks happily. She loves big spenders because it puts her mother in a good mood.

Aki scans Paige's items and adds, "Yes, and I'm also the head of the new diversity and equity program." She says this while feeling like a sham but also knowing that for people like Paige, titles mean everything. "And I suppose you're tenured somewhere?" she asks.

Paige blushes.

No way, Aki thinks.

"I was tenure track at Santa Clara, but I got pregnant with twins, and Hunter and I decided that it was just too hard . . ." Paige trails off. "So, what's it like at Wesley? Is it as intense as it's made out to be?"

Aki, relieved that Paige has seized on a topic unrelated to why she exited their grad program, nods vigorously while thinking about all the afternoons that Meg decided to go rock climbing instead of studying, to no real consequence in terms of her grades. "Pressure cooker," she says simply, knowing that's what Paige wants to hear.

Paige sighs. "Hunter is so dead set on sending the kids to the University Collegiate," Paige says, name-dropping the most selective co-ed prep school in San Francisco and sounding much like a Wesley parent. "We love the small class sizes, the focus on diversity, the emphasis on the whole child," Paige ticks off a list that literally could have come from Wesley's own application brochure. "But I'm worried the twins are going to get overlooked. The smartest kids in their class . . ." Paige trails off and looks at Aki, who raises her eyebrows, unsure of what Paige is trying to say. "Well, you know," Paige finishes lamely.

Ah, Aki realizes. *She means Asian.* She stares at Paige, waiting to see what she'll add. She sees why her mother told her to ignore acts of racism, flagrant or otherwise: because they never end. She also feels a small sense of pride that despite this fact, Meg goes and fights the good fight every day.

"I mean," Paige adds quickly, "I always thought it was great how our department was so supportive of you, since history is such a . . ." she trails off again.

White department, Aki finishes in her head.

"Not that that's why you got the Kellogg fellowship!" Paige declares.

Aki stares at Paige. How did she know, much less remember, that Aki had been the recipient of the one full fellowship in their department? And why did it sound like she was marking it up to affirmative action rather than merit? But of course, Aki already knows the answer: because people like Paige think they deserve everything, and when they don't get it, they blame it on things like race. Otherwise, how could someone like Paige lose out to someone like Aki? Though she sees a line forming behind Paige, for some reason all Aki can see is everything she hates about Wesley in a five-foot-eight package sheathed in JMcLaughlin: white privilege masquerading as wokeness, and narcissism disguised as liberalism. She thought she could escape it for a weekend by leaving DC, but here it is manifesting itself on the West Coast.

"Aki. *Hayaku*." (Faster.) Her father's stern voice booms from behind her.

"*Hai*," Aki says as she speeds through Paige's mountain of conspicuous snack consumption.

"Well, if you ever get into the city, give me a ring, I'd love to catch up," Paige declares, handing Aki her credit card, not even flinching at the three-digit figure Aki has rung up.

"Would *love to*, Paige," Aki says in her well-trained Wesley voice. *Would rather die*, she thinks as she watches Paige sign her name on the transaction slip.

"Guess we both didn't end up quite where we thought we'd be, did we?" Paige asks as she accepts two bags filled with imported carbs. She smiles and exits the store as the line that formed behind her shuffles its way up to Aki.

"*Omatase shite orimasu*," Aki's father says loudly to the waiting customers, reminding her to keep working. (Sorry to keep you waiting.)

Aki watches Paige's departing figure as she scans the next customer's items. She can't shake the lingering irritation and whips around to face her father. "I have to check my work email!" she announces, giving him an excuse she knows he won't counter.

Her father merely nods, then in a gruff voice calls out to their part-time worker. "Joe, ring for Aki!"

Joe stops unpacking boxes of ramen and takes over at the register as Aki whips off her apron and heads toward the storage room, retrieving her phone from her bag, ready to text Jules with an expletive-filled missive about Paige Howard. Instead, she sees an alert for an email on her screen—*From the Desk of Aki Hayashi-Brown*. Aki clicks on it, unconsciously holding her breath as she scrolls through the message with the official Wesley header. The words *pillars* and *blueprint* jump out, and she realizes that Amanda has gone ahead and sent out the email from Aki's account. But what happened to the heads-up and Aki having "editorial input?" How did Amanda even have access to it? She thought Jules was paranoid in insisting that the school regularly checked faculty email, but now Aki thinks her friend might be right. She is so utterly exhausted—tired of being told what to do, what not to do, disappointed in herself for not being more aware of what is going on with Meg, her parents, her school . . . and frustrated at herself for ignoring the unending tide of problems in her life and her lack of power in responding to people like Liz and Paige.

"Um, Aki?" Joe knocks softly on the door. "Your dad wants you to come back."

"OK, thanks, Joe. I just have one more thing to do," she says as she looks up at Joe, who nods and retreats back into the store. *Actually, I have many.*

+ 20 +

"Does anyone know if Harrison Neal is going to retire any time soon? I feel like the school needs new leadership as evidenced by this whole debacle."

—*Curious Wesley Parent, dcparentzone.com*

IN THE END, AKI was only in Daly City for three days. She flew back on the red-eye on Sunday, her mother insisting that she would be fine, especially since the store is closed on Mondays. Her mother didn't let her leave the house, however, until Aki assured her that yes, Meg would get into a great college. After a satisfactory discussion on the topic, she waved Aki off to the airport, making her promise that she'd be back soon. Aki didn't want Ian to have to wake up early and pick her up, so she caught an Uber from the airport.

Looking and feeling crumpled, Aki sits at the café right in front of Wesley, waiting nervously for her guests. When Aki first arrived at Wesley, the area around the school was mainly residential, with the majority of shops and eateries located a mile or so down the road at Tenleytown. In the last few years, new condos and cafés have appeared, and even an upscale supermarket had found itself on the redeveloped grounds of an old federal building right across from campus.

"Hi, hon," Jules says perkily. "This place is great, how French!" She squeals. "Ooh, look at everything you ordered! I'll be right back." her friend promises as she goes off to find the restroom.

Aki looks up, feeling nervous at who has entered with Jules and stands in front of her.

"Hey, Hayashi," Percy says, nodding.

Aki gulps and smiles. Before she had left for California, and during the catastrophe of an auction meeting, Aki finally gathered up the courage to contact Percy and Grayson and ask them to breakfast in order to apologize. To her relief, they both quickly agreed, making their messages the only pleasant thing about that day.

"Hi, Aki," Grayson says cheerfully, making Aki feel both grateful and guilty at the same time.

"Hi, guys, I didn't know what you wanted so I ordered a bit of everything," Aki says, slightly embarrassed. It looks like she has ordered the whole store.

"Wow, this looks great!" Grayson says graciously, taking off his well-worn baseball cap and Patagonia fleece and sitting down. "You didn't have to go to all this trouble," he adds as he pours himself coffee from a carafe.

Percy stays silent as he removes his coat and helps himself to a morning bun.

Jules rushes back and sits, smiling at everyone and asking, "What's good? What should I start with?"

Aki smiles at her friend; she knows that Jules is trying to keep the mood light.

Aki clears her throat. "I want to apologize and let you know that I haven't been honest with you guys," she starts.

Grayson stops eating and looks at her with great concern. "Are you sick?" he asks kindly.

Aki smiles at him. "No, I'm not sick." She looks at Jules for emotional support. "I'm sorry about last week. Meg got suspended again—"

"Meg? For what?" Grayson asks. Aki is surprised he hadn't heard about the second suspension, but maybe he's just being polite. Or he's just being Grayson, which is to say out of the loop.

"Where do I start? After smacking Aaron upside the head, she was the one who uploaded a picture of him onto the Instagram site," she explains, watching Grayson's jaw drop. "Then after she wrote that op-ed that ended up in the mainstream media, the school said the only way they'd let her stay is if I would smooth things over."

Percy's eyebrows lift, but he remains quiet.

"Tell them what you told me, about Aaron Wakeman's mother and what Aiko said," Jules prods.

Aki describes her frosty run-in with Claire at Holly's house, the photo sent to Ousmane, and Aiko's claims that Aaron is not what he seems and Meg's ongoing fury at Aaron. She finishes with Claire's insistence that she was merely trying to protect her son.

"Claire Wakeman is certifiable," Jules interjects. "But her crazy has nothing to do with Aaron. I heard she was running around town with the guidance counselor."

"What?" Aki wrinkles her nose.

"Oh yeah, Cash is stepping out with some pretty little thing, so Claire gets back at him by hooking up with Tim," referring to the school's guidance counselor, a middle-aged, soft-in-the-middle, not to mention very forgettable member of the administration. "Anyway," Jules prattles on, "Cash got Tim fired so Claire is just out for blood, including yours and Meg's," she concludes. "She's a hot mess."

Percy, who has stopped eating at this point, looks at Jules, then at Aki and starts shaking his head. "I knew the school's priorities were out of whack, but this is *insane*," he declares. "So, when Harrison promised he was going to root out the problems in the school, he decided that problem was *Meg*?"

"I *know*, right?" Jules pipes up again. "Can't blame their biggest donor, so blame the biggest donor's targets."

"I guess that's why I was so intent on making you guys believe it was Aaron that day at the bar," Aki says, ashamed. "The school never really was going to try and root out who did it, because if it was a student, it would make them look bad no matter who it was."

"We know you and Meg are on the right side of all of this," Grayson exclaims. "And everyone has a bad night, Aki, it's OK."

Aki smiles at him, feeling terrible at the joke she made at his expense. "I'm really sorry, Grayson," she says. Grayson smiles and shakes his head.

She looks at Percy. "You were right not to volunteer for any of this diversity business. Just like Meg said, I'm just being used. And now I have to do some interview and make Wesley look good," she adds, somberly.

"Look," Percy says suddenly as he points out the window. The café, located right across the street from Wesley, provides them with a panoramic view of the school, and what they see is a mass of students gathering on the front lawn.

"Come on, I have a feeling we want to see this," Percy says, finishing his croissant and grabbing another one for good measure. Grayson does the same, as does Jules.

They rush out onto Wisconsin, crossing at the light as more teachers and students gather on the field. Aki can feel her heart beating as she surveys the group, now fanning out into a long line. They are mostly upperclassmen, and Aki scans the line for Meg—and there her daughter is, standing in the middle of the line flanked by Double on her right and Aiko on her left. For a second, she worries that this will be the final nail in the coffin that represents Meg's academic career at Wesley. She sees all the students linking arms and walking backward, step-by-step, pressing their backs up again the chain-link fence that borders

Wisconsin Avenue. She has no idea what is going on or what's about to happen, but she's been at Wesley long enough to know that something eventful is about to unfold, particularly since it's an unsanctioned event.

"Did you know about this?" Percy asks her as they line up with the faculty and remaining students, watching the line get longer across from them.

"Did you?" she asks as Percy shakes his head. Then she hears something she doesn't expect. She whips her head around to find where the sound is coming from, and she sees a clump of students, also seniors, standing near the faculty and looking out at the lawn with hardened expressions. Then she hears the surprising sound again. It's the sound of a snort.

"They just want attention as usual," says Yeardly Ward, her eyes narrowing into tiny folds. When she catches Aki eyeing her, she covers her mouth with her hand and leans into Kiya Emerson, a senior on the soccer team. In the small cluster also stands Zach Henderson-Hinds, Sibley Everett, and to her surprise, Jules's son Felix. Aki realizes that she is looking at a small group of anti-protesters, the few less-than-progressive members of the Wesley student community. There are always a few politically conservative students, some who make themselves more obvious than others.

A few years ago, a student named Michael Finely, son of a Black senator and a white investment banker, caused an unwanted stir (for Wesley, natch) when he published a *Medium* article supporting the confirmation of a Supreme Court justice whom his mother had openly vilified during the confirmation hearing. Being such a flagrant middle finger to his liberal mother, and the press gobbled up the "mom versus rebellious teen" angle and spit it out on several websites in true inside-DC schadenfreude glee. Michael was, for lack of a more suitable word, brilliant, and given his political leaning surprised no one when he was admitted early to Stanford and went on to become editor of the *Stanford Review*, a conservative student publication.

"Can we just go to assembly, please?" Yeardly whines to no one.

Aki feels like snapping at her when another sound forces her to refocuses her attention to what is unfolding on the field.

"Today was supposed to be Senior Skip Day!" a loud voice calls out with the help of a megaphone. Aki, along with everyone else, swings her head back toward the seniors lined up against the fence. Double yells into the megaphone and continues. "But instead, we are having a senior sit-in!"

Senior Skip Day is a long-standing tradition at Wesley, a day when the senior class announces, usually with great fanfare at morning assembly, that they are skipping classes for the day. It is never advertised in advance and always concocted under the cloak of secrecy. One particularly memorable year saw a set of low-flying drones flying a long banner through the campus with the words "Senior Skip Day!" on it. Another public declaration came in the form of oil cans filled with—of all things—oranges, spelling out the same words on the football field.

"What the hell is a senior sit-in?" an incredulous Blake Heston asks, joining Yeardly and her friends. Blake comes from a family that owns a famous hotel chain, and Wesley's new wrestling arena is named after it.

"We will protest *again* until our voices are heard!" Double yells out.

"We can hear you," Zach says, making the others laugh.

Aki shoots them a look, which they ignore.

Percy announces, "I think I know why they're lined up like that!" he says, lifting his chin and motioning toward the students. "Go back across the street, you'll see it," he says, smiling, making Aki confused. He looks over at Yeardly and her friends, shakes his head, and adds, "Your daughter is on the right side

of history." Though she and Percy rarely cross paths during the
school day, at this moment she feels close to him, knowing he
supports his daughter's actions even as they scare her as a mother.
"Come on, Aki, go back across the street," he prods.

Aki looks at Percy's face and without a word scurries away
from the field, down a set of concrete stairs that lead down to the
garage, where she makes her way out to the sidewalk. She can
hear Double yelling into the megaphone as she waits impatiently
for the walk signal to change. As she crosses the street, she sees
Joanna Javier-Hernandez preparing to do a stand-up, her cameraman swinging his camera away from her and back toward the
school. At first Aki is afraid that Meg is going to give another one
of her vitriolic press conferences about her thoughts on Wesley
Friends, but when Aki follows his gaze and looks back up at the
field, she sees it. The seniors, standing, arms linked, backs pressed
up against the fence. Where they had once crudely taped the
number 18 to their hoodies, today they had large red signs on the
backs, each one emblazoned with a letter. It takes Aki a moment
to see what all the letters together spell out:

WE WONT STOP UNTIL THEY LISTEN WE WONT
STOP UNTIL THE HATE STOPS

Sixty students, their backs literally to the wall, demanding
the school take action. She looks at Joanna Javier-Hernandez,
who calls out to her.

"Hey!" Joanna starts, but Aki holds up a finger and catches
the light turning green and runs back toward the garage and
up the stairs, returning to the field out of breath. When she gets
there, she sees that more students and faculty have gathered to
watch.

"Aki," a gravelly voice booms. Aki looks up to see Harrison
Neal standing in front of her, dressed in his usual uniform of
khakis and blue shirt, topped today with a Wesley Friends fleece.

"We're hoping you might say a word to these . . ." he trails off, looking behind him at the protesters, "students . . . about per- haps . . . becoming part of a more conducive discussion about these issues," he says smoothly.

Aki narrows her eyes at him. She looks behind Harrison to see a frazzled Amanda on her cell phone, thwarting press inqui- ries, she presumes, and a somewhat sheepish Ousmane standing a few feet behind Harrison.

"Why me?" Aki asks innocently, though she well knows the reason why he is asking her.

"Well," Harrison coughs. "As head of equity—"

"*Interim* head of equity and diversity," Aki corrects him for no real reason.

"Yes, well, in this important role, we find it is best if you act as a conduit between the administration and the students—"

"Because it would look bad to have a white person tell them to stop a peaceful protest, right?" Aki says bluntly. "You could ask Ousmane," she says, rudely, she knows.

"You already agreed to this," Amanda reminds her.

"Not for *this*," Aki responds curtly. "For a sit-down inter- view with a *script*," she points out.

"Opportunity has presented itself this morning," Harrison says, furrowing his brow. "To engage with the protesters directly. And for you to show what Wesley really is."

"Or maybe you do want to find a new school for Meg," Amanda says coldly, "and maybe even yourself."

Aki looks at Amanda, then at Harrison, then starts across the field, feeling the eyes of the faculty, Yeardly Ward and her merry band, and the rest of the upper school student population on her back.

Meg's eyes are wild with fury as she watches her mother cross the field.

If you want peace, prepare for war.

Aki walks right up to her daughter.

"We aren't going anywhere!" Meg says defiantly. "I don't even care if they suspend us."

Aki's heart does a little flutter, as she looks at Meg, Double, Aiko, then down the row of seniors, their arms still linked and some shivering from the cold. She looks past petite Aiko's shoulders and sees Joanna speaking furiously into her microphone across the street. Aki goes to Meg and Aiko and grabs both girls' forearms.

"No, Mother!" Meg begins again.

Then Aki does something she never thought she would do. She tucks her hands into each girl's elbow and links her arms with theirs. By standing with them, she is finally standing up to all the Paiges of the world and their prejudicial insinuations. By joining them, she is rejecting the racist Lizes of the world. By being part of the protest, she is rejecting a lifetime of swallowing her anger and instead becoming part of the solution rather than propagating a system that created the problem to begin with. And even though "old" Aki might have lurked on the sidelines, more anxious and harried than supportive or vocal, she feels like a new person today, angry but resolute in her righteousness. Is she worried that both she and Meg might not be back at Wesley? Yes, she is fucking terrified. But at least she'll leave knowing she not only supported her daughter's beliefs but she finally stood up for herself.

She looks across the field and meets Percy's eyes, and even from far away she can see his lips curl up into a smile. Then he breaks into a jog to join the end of the line of seniors. She watches as Grayson also break ranks, as it were, to cross the field and pledge his allegiance. A steady trickle of faculty walks across the threshold toward them, making the line along the fence grow longer and longer. Harrison Neal and Amanda have disappeared, leaving Ousmane to round up the remaining faculty and herd them back into the building. Aki looks down the row and sees the other history teachers, realizing then that there will be no history classes today, unless Ousmane decides to cover all of them himself, but she lets go of her usual worry. The frigid air is no match for the sudden exhilaration she feels when Meg leans over to her and whispers in her ear, "I love you, Mother."

"Why does it feel like Wesley hates White people?"
                                        —Just asking, PoC@Wesley

"I WAS SO PSYCHED to get your email," Joanna says as she sits down in a flimsy plastic chair across from Aki. "Hey," she calls to an assistant director off to the side. "Can I get some Red Bull?" She winks at Aki. "A girl's gotta eat!"

When Aki was in Daly City, holed away in her parents' storage closet, angry at Paige, Wesley, and the world, she decided that she was going to "reframe the narrative," as Amanda would say. She sent an email to Joanna Javier-Hernandez, offering to speak with her on the record, with zero plans for staying on Amanda's script, not to mention any high-minded notions of a sit-down with the *Atlantic*. This was going to be Aki's way of telling people what she really thought. No more Mrs. Nice Aki.

"Thanks," Joanna says to the AD, who has scurried back with the can of Red Bull. She turns back to Aki with a thin smile. "It's been a while since we first aired the story, but a new hook is great," she says, more to herself than anyone else.

Aki watches as the AD scurries away, his task completed, then turns back to Joanna. "Right, so we can focus on what we discussed in my email?" Aki presses. She may not be versed in crisis management or press releases, but she knows enough not to trust Joanna to quote her correctly. "And it's not a long segment, right?" Aki asks, suddenly nervous that her great idea might turn into a really bad one.

"Won't be more than two or three minutes." Joanna leans in and winks, "That's average for a local news program, in case you're wondering."

Aki mentally calculates just how much damage Joanna Javier-Hernandez could possibly do in three minutes and can't decide if it's going to be along the lines of spilled milk in aisle seven or full-blown nuclear meltdown. Then again, Aki is the one giving her the milk and the nuclear codes.

"OK, why don't we start?" Joanna says peppily as she motions to the cameraman and raises an eyebrow to a young man standing behind him. "That's one of the producers at the station," Joanna explained. "He went to Albany Prep down the road," she supplies, as if that is supposed to explain something to Aki. All she knows about Albany Prep is that one of the vice president's sons went there, got bullied, and ended up at Wesley, which was more than happy to have him.

The producer nods at Aki, then at Joanna. The lights in the studio move and shift toward the two women, and Aki momentarily squints at the glaring rays. Joanna inhales deeply and gives three short puffs out of her mouth before someone yells, "Rolling!"

Joanna turns abruptly to the camera and begins, "I'm here with Aki Hayashi-Brown, the interim director of equity and diversity at the Wesley Friends School. Aki—" she turns to her and cocks her head slightly. "Three months ago, the terrifying words 'make Wesley white again' were scrawled on the walls of your school, one that is known to embrace liberal values and counts several presidential children as alumni. Can you talk to us about what the school is going to do to finally address the hate crime?"

Leave it to Joanna not to mince words. Aki inhales, bracing herself before she speaks. "Wesley's response has been all smoke and mirrors at the expense of truth and inclusion, that is the fact of the matter," she says, knowing these words will be a dagger through Amanda and Harrison's neatly worded but ultimately empty defenses. "They've squandered cash to hire consultants who did nothing but create division among the faculty and parent community, and they're no closer to figuring out who did the actual crime." Aki pauses. "And I'm not sure they really want to know."

Joanna pounces. "Why not? Why wouldn't they want to know who did it?"

"Because it might be inconvenient to the school to find out the truth," Aki explains. This much is true. It would be hugely embarrassing if it was revealed to be the son of the school's biggest donor. Her mind flashes to Claire Wakeman's icy blue eyes, *I think we both know that Meg is behind this*, and Aki has to push back the thought that it wouldn't look too good for anyone either if it turns out the daughter of the interim director of equity and diversity was, in fact, trying to frame the son of the school's biggest donor.

Aki shifts in her chair. "The students who were protesting are right. The school protects the privileged, sometimes racist parents instead of protecting its own students, many of whom still experience everyday racism. It's not just an embarrassment, it's plain wrong."

Joanna's face exhibits such surprise, Aki can't help but feel a deep sense of satisfaction.

"Can I add one more thing?" Aki asks.

"Of course," says Joanna, as if granting a wish to Cinderella.

Aki looks directly into the camera, trying not to squint at the bright spotlight in her face. "Wesley is the Potemkin village of liberalism," she starts, trying not to giggle at Joanna's confused expression. "It's all a façade," she explains driving home her main point. "The students have known all along, and now it's time for the adults to admit it and do something about it."

Joanna, for her part, almost looks impressed. She turns to the cameraman and purrs, "I think we've got all we need," then looks back at Aki. "Old story: The school is a victim. New story: The school is the criminal. I love it!" she declares excitedly, as if finding a designer handbag on sale.

Aki isn't sure how to take that but gives Joanna a small smile and fiddles with the wired mic on her sweater, antsy to get to school and away from this crime scene, or maybe her own guilt.

"Oh, let me get that," the AD says as he removes the mic. "So have you met Jack Topper?" he asks casually. Jack is one of the more famous parents at Wesley and has his own network news program. He is also easy on the eyes, as Jules likes to point out, and unlike the Wakemans, generous without the expectation of special treatment.

Aki looks up at the AD. It never ceases to amaze her how everyone in this town knows who sends their kids where. "Oh, uh, yes," she says, trying to remember if she has actually met him or not.

"What's he like?" the AD persists, the tiny mic in his hand, an eager expression on his face.

"Um, he's nice," Aki responds, thinking of his antics at the auction. Jack likes to auction off a live taping to his show and never lets the crowd bid less than $10K. He famously likes to jump on stage and sing and tap dance with every $5K bid. "Nice to have as part of the community," she says standing up. She's assuming the next question will be whether or not she has his number. Typical DC, where everyone is always hustling someone.

"Hey, thanks again for reaching out," Joanna interrupts, then looking at the AD, barks, "Stop trying to job hop and go grab me a coffee!" She turns back to Aki. "Just FYI, since it's a follow-up segment, we'll recap the incident, but this time we get to add you, so that's good. We'll run it sometime this morning. So, you really don't know who did it?" she asks hungrily, spitting out her words in rapid fire.

"You've seen the video, I presume," Aki responds offhand-edly, trying to cover up mounting multiple fears for her daughter. "There's not much to go off of."

"Sure, but the kids must know *something*. You're just not asking the right people," Joanna muses. "Well, if you hear anything else, you know where to find me," she whirls around and yells out to no one in particular, "Where's Rachel? We need to edit this puppy and have it give birth! March is almost here, people! In like a lamb, out like a ratings lion!" She then turns back to Aki and gives her another wink before stomping off in her black patent heels.

*   *   *

Aki yawns. Turns out subterfuge is exhausting. Her interview with Joanna took place at the local studio in Maryland at five-thirty AM, so she's been awake since well before that. She managed to placate her ravenous appetite with a hearty breakfast at a bougie café in Bethesda right near the station before hopping on a bus and taking it down a mostly empty Wisconsin Avenue back to school. After that, the day had been long, but she's about to round third base and slide into the last period of the day, which is a free period anyway.

Sitting in her office, she looks at the schedule for her upcom-ing classes and realizes that the timer is winding down toward March and the college acceptance waiting game. In a few weeks every one of Wesley's seniors will know where they are headed in the fall, and every teacher will no longer be able to command the attention of their students. Senioritis had already set in for roughly half of the class and it was coming for the rest of them. She calculates that she has to finish out her syllabus in the next three weeks. She tries to forget that Meg will be leaving their home in a year.

Her inbox lights up with an email message, but from a sender she doesn't recognize, one that simply says Wesley Parent.

Curious, she clicks on the message. The body of it simply says:

This is not spam, but evidence that Meg is out for revenge.

Aki immediately feels her throat seize. She knows she shouldn't, but she clicks on the video attachment. On the screen is a dark room, and Aki squints to see what is going on. The camera tightens in on Meg, who is holding up her hands and screaming at someone.

"I will fucking end you, Wakeman!" Meg screams.

Aki's eyes grow wide, and she stops breathing.

She watches Meg scream, "I will get you kicked out of this school if it's the last thing I do! Don't believe it? Watch me, you douchebag!"

The camera moves slightly to the left, where a clearly inebriated Aaron Wakeman leans against a wall, half-smiling at Meg as she screams at him. Then the screen goes black.

Aki sits back in her chair. She knows she shouldn't admit this, but she's not particularly surprised that her daughter would say something like that. She also knows that if Meg was already in deep trouble, she can now definitely say goodbye to a senior year at Wesley Friends. She also assumes this video originated from the house that Claire built, since Claire has made it clear that she will do anything to throw Meg under the bus—or multiple buses—for that matter. And Aki knows that if she's been sent this video, Ousmane has been as well.

* * *

"Enter," Ousmane's voice says from behind his door.

Aki had managed to slip past Ousmane's assistant and knock on his door, hoping to cut any phone call or lecture off at the pass. When she enters the room, Ousmane eyes her for moment, says nothing, then finally instructs her to close the door.

"I think you probably know why I'm here," Aki begins.

Ousmane gives her an indiscernible look.

Aki has rehearsed this next part in her head. "Ousmane, how long have you been here?"

"Eight years," he responds.

"Can you honestly say that in those eight years, the school is in a better place than it used to be? I'm not holding you account-able, by the way. I've been here that whole time as well," she says, watching his eyes, which at first reveal nothing, then flutter a small twitch of acknowledgement. "Ousmane, we have been foot soldiers in a movement that *says* it's one thing but really is another. We've been told we're at a place that values integrity and equality, but when you look around, it's a shrine to wealth and, frankly, the perpetuation of wealth."

He says nothing, and she continues. "We are both wholly qualified in our roles, but for some reason I still feel like I'm here to check a box." She raises her eyebrow and leans back in her chair. "And it's not my colleagues that are making me feel this way, or the students, by the way."

Ousmane quietly uncrosses and recrosses his legs, clasping his fingers and resting his hands on his lap. "And you believe that making a statement to this effect to the press will drastically alter that path of the administration to your liking?"

Aki doesn't blink. The interview must have just run.

"Ousmane, have you ever asked yourself why Harrison doesn't want to make any significant changes? Why he has some-one like Amanda always deflecting criticism?" She goes for the jugular. "Is it right for him to protect people like Cash and Aaron and forsake all others?

"Aki," Ousmane says sharply, "I hope that you have enacted these measures as a way to improve the school community and not due to some personal vendetta you have against Harrison or the Wakemans," he warns. Aki opens her mouth to object, but Ousmane ignores her and lowers his voice. "I will never admit to saying the following, but I do not disagree that forcing his hand is a good idea."

Aki stares at Ousmane, a sachem of propriety, never one to openly advocate this way or the other, happy always to wait for equilibrium, surprised that he is acknowledging her flagrant middle finger to Harrison Neal and Amanda Nutley.

Ousmane stands and makes his final declaration. "There is already discussion of your replacement, so do what you can with the role. In the interim, you would be wise to find out who is sending me these photos and videos, as I suspect this is the path toward resolution with the vandalism. Better yet, figure out who the real vandal is, as this will mostly likely be the only thing to protect Meg."

Aki is too afraid to ask if anything will happen to Meg as a result of the last student protest or the video in their inboxes, and instead, nods and thinks about his words. As she exits his office and into the hallway, she runs into Grayson, ever cheerful, his mop top in usual disarray and coffee steaming in his YETI mug.

"Aki! How's your mom?" he asks affably. "Hey! I saw you this morning on TV, you were great!" he adds, holding up his mug as if giving her a toast.

Aki is slow to respond to Grayson's greeting, her mind still on Ousmane's advice but also on the video that was sent to her earlier that morning, still playing in a loop in her mind. Out of nowhere, Aki realizes she might have something to help Meg.

She panics for moment, then impulsively asks Grayson, "Hey, I don't have my car here, can I borrow yours?" Ian had taken the car in for service while she was in Daly City and hadn't gotten around to picking it up from the dealership. Grayson nods and jams his hand into his pocket, extracting a key and what looks to be odd bits of string.

"Thanks! I'm a great driver, don't worry!" Aki calls back as she tears toward the parking lot.

♦ 22 ♦

"Why is Wesley still talking about a campus expansion? Shouldn't they be using their money on other stuff?"

— Just Wondering, dcparentzone.com

"COME ON, COME ON, come on," Aki chants, willing the light at Connecticut Avenue to turn green. She had expected Grayson to drive a Subaru of some sort, but after realizing that the key in her hand had a Mercedes insignia on it, it appeared that the only car in the staff parking lot that could be his was the black G-wagon. Equally as shocking as his choice of vehicle was how clean the interior was, but she laughed out loud when she turned on the car and from the satellite radio station came the soothing strains of Celine Dion.

"Finally!" Aki shouts out loud as the light turns green and she tears down Wisconsin and into Maryland, finally screeching to a stop in front of the Wakeman's *Architectural Digest* worthy house. Aki feels lightheaded as she plows up the walkway. She jabs the doorbell, two, three, four times. *Shit.* Her shoulders sag, and she furtively looks around to make sure the neighbors aren't watching. As she turns, she notices the lacrosse goal, which she remembers seeing the last time she was here. Aki cups her hand above her eyes, blocking out the sun in order to get a clearer view. Faint circles on the grass linger on the lawn, though much of the spray paint has washed away. Turning on her heel, she grasps her key and makes her way back to Grayson's car. But before she starts the engine, she collects herself, and she calls Jules.

★ ★ ★

There is a sizable crowd for today's boys' lacrosse game against Albany Prep, arguably Wesley's biggest rival. On one side of the field stand both teams, Wesley in white and maroon, Albany in dark blue with red and white details. On the other side of the field is a hover of helicopter parents, many decked out in either Wesley gear or Albany Prep blue, cheering on their sons as if they were going into battle at Antietam.

Aki has a bird's eye view and scans the crowd. Holly and Claire are standing together, bundled up in shades of gray, maroon, and white. Aki hardly even notices the lacrosse game, which is going on at high speed on the grass, as she storms toward Claire and Holly, rage in her heart and her head focused on one thing. Out of her peripheral vision she sees Jules making a beeline toward her, waving two cell phones dramatically.

"Holly!" Aki barks. She barely recognizes the tone in her own voice.

Holly turns around. She's dressed in expensive jeans and a Wesley sweatshirt, though her oxford shirt pops up from the collar. In her ears are shiny oversized pearls. "Hi, Aki, how are you?" she asks affably. "I never see you at lacrosse games!"

"Did Zach host a party in the fall?" Aki demands, ignoring the niceties. "Maybe right before Thanksgiving?" she yells over the cheering crowd while dismissing Claire's cold, silent stare with what she hopes is a withering look of her own.

"Hmm, maybe?" Holly says, one eye on the game and the other on Aki, trying to be polite. "Jeremy and I were out of town most weekends."

Jules places herself next to Aki, while catching her breath. "I found what you needed, friend," Jules says, giving Aki a knowing glance.

"Attack! Zach! Go!" Holly suddenly yells, her usually elegant demeanor making way for overzealous sideline coaching. "Guard that short side! GUARD IT!" She screams like a donkey, momentarily making the other women stare at her.

Out of the corner of her eye Aki sees Zach and Aaron tearing around the goal with breathtaking agility. Holly turns back to them and smiles serenely. "What is this about?"

"I found something on my son's cell." Jules unlocks a newer iPhone model and opens the photo app, scrolling through it expertly before clicking on a video, setting it to pause, and handing it to Aki.

"We think you might be interested in this," Aki says to Holly, though her comment is really directed toward Claire.

Aki presses play, and Holly looks down at the screen. Jules's mouth is set in a tight, straight line, and Aki sees Claire pretending to ignore them while looking back and forth between the game and the phone. The crowd roars as someone from Wesley— Double apparently—scores a goal.

"Doouubbblle!" The sideline roars. Claire looks away from the game, no longer centered around public adulation of her son, to view what is on Jules's phone. On it is a video of a darkened room—Holly's living room and Meg's figure in the center of the screen.

"Shut up, Aaron!" Meg says in the video.

Aki's eyes flit to Claire's expression, which is mixed with satisfaction and rage. A wave of anger rises up in Aki's belly as the crowd around them roars again, and she can't help but look at the field: Albany Prep is now on Wesley territory, and they are dangerously close to the goal.

"What are we looking at?" Holly asks innocently.

When Aki first viewed the video in her office, she recognized the room that Meg was standing in: the linen sofa, the abstract painting, the tasteful colors on the walls; it was Holly's living room. She waits for Holly to comprehend what is on the screen.

"Is that my house?" Holly suddenly realizes.

"You shut up, you bitch." On the video, Aaron slurs as he slumps against the living room wall, bumping the abstract painting that hangs on it.

"What is this?" Claire says crisply as if she hadn't been paying attention when it it's clear she had been.

"Stupid bitch," Aaron says again, nearly toppling over as he grabs at the wall behind him, clearly drunk or high if not both.

Holly gasps, then looks up at the game again as the crowd roars. She quickly looks back at the phone.

Watching the video for the first time, Aki also noticed that the entire boys' lacrosse team was present at the party. And for better or worse, where Aaron was, so too would be Zach and Felix. She also knew enough to assume that if one kid was filming the encounter between Meg and Aaron, so were many others. She called Jules and begged her to retrieve Felix's phone and instructed her how to search for it by date and media type, which she did. Jules immediately sent her a copy, then Aki asked her friend to meet her on the field for moral support.

As if to prove Aki's point, the next part of the video showed multiple students with their phones out, recording the quarrel, but inadvertently documenting the detritus of indulgence as well: Solo cups, empty bottles, bongs, cigarettes, cast-off clothing and random undergarments, some students passed out while others were hooking up—the typical weekend bacchanal of a DC private-schooler.

"Take back what you said!" Meg screams at Aaron as he bumps against the abstract painting on the wall and drunkenly tries to straighten it, only to cause it to go crashing to the ground.

"Oh my God, what is this?" Holly screeches, finally realizing that the party on the screen is in her house.

"You racist shithead!" Meg screams at him, while other kids close in on their conversation, phones overhead.

God, Meg, how many times have I told you that video is forever? Aki thinks as she watches her daughter spiral in anger. Claire's reaction, which registers satisfaction, one that says, *see, I told you she was crazy*, makes Aki want to lash out, but she holds the phone steadily, letting the video continue playing.

"What did I say?" Aaron taunts her, wiping his nose repeatedly and clearly enjoying Meg's attention.

"Apologize!" Meg screams again.

"What, that your mom's a massage parlor whore and you're a Chinese bastard?" Aaron screeches, eliciting a laugh from several boys in the video.

Claire's face freezes.

"Well, that's just *so* sweet," Jules mutters.

With Aaron's words, every racist memory filed away in Aki's memory, from her father on the golf course to Paige and Liz making insinuations about her race, rush to the front of her mind, making her furious and hurt all over again.

"You're just jealous!" Meg screams in fury, this time pushing his shoulders against the wall, making Aaron grin and stumble. The fact that he is not scared of Meg is clearly infuriating her.

"Of what?" Aaron jeers. "Your new boyfriend?"

Aki assumes he's talking about Double.

"Come on, Meg, let's go," Aiko steps into the frame and pulls Meg off of Aaron.

"And *you*," Aaron slurs. "*You* don't deserve to be here anyway," Aaron says, struggling to stand straight. Someone hands him a shot, which he downs quickly.

"Why don't I deserve to be here?" Aiko calmly asks, stepping in between Meg and Aaron. A voice whoops excitedly at the new confrontation.

"There used to be standards," Aaron says. The subtext of his taunting now clear. "Like, how in the fuck did Double get a verbal offer from Princeton? Sus."

Aiko looks Aaron squarely in the face as she holds Meg back behind her with one arm. "Aaron, you are a small, racist coward," she says in a low voice before taking Meg's arm and retreating into Holly's cavernous living room.

"Oh, my God," Holly says under her breath.

"They're the reason we can't get into the Ivies, you know," another voice yells out.

Meg whirls back around, looking for the voice.

"He has a point, white men have the hardest time getting into college now," the voice holding the camera adds, making Aki hold her breath, because this is Felix's voice. She looks at Jules, whose expression is tense, eyes narrowed as she watches the video.

The camera jiggles as Aaron claps Felix on the back and says, "Exactly, Wesley used to have standards, but now it's just filled with pussies," Aaron declares sloppily, making Zach laugh. "And *minorities*."

"Oh, my God," Holly repeats, looking ashen.

Claire looks back to the field, breathing deeply. The game is apparently tied, as evidenced by the rowdy crowd, both sides hungry for victory.

"Do us all a favor and just go back to where you came from," Aaron says on the screen. "Go join your *boyfriend* in Africa, Hayashi!" he shouts drunkenly. "Maybe someone will actually fuck you, Aiko, but then again they'd probably have to be drunk."

Then Meg walks back to Aaron and smacks him across his very drunk face. Aki braces herself as Holly and Claire cry out, "Oh!"

Jules, for her part, smirks as she announces, "He deserved it."

"Excuse me?" Claire demands.

Aki turns up the sound as high as it will go for the next part. "I will fucking end you, Wakeman. Watch me. I will get you kicked out of this school if it's the last thing I do! Watch me, you douchebag!" she screams.

This was the only part of the video that had been sent to Aki and Ousmane.

Then a quiet voice and someone's back enters the frame. "Meg, come on now, let it go." It's Double's voice. She watches as Aiko steps aside and Double pulls Meg back from Aaron. Then what she sees next makes her gasp. Aaron steps right up to Double, gives him a drunken smirk, and spits in his face. Then the camera goes dark.

The four women stare at the phone for what feels like an eternity.

Finally, Aki speaks. "Someone sent Ousmane a shortened clip of this to frame Meg, then sent a copy to me."

Silence encircles the women despite the crowd roaring around them. Holly keeps looking at Claire, who tosses her hair and watches the game as if she's seen nothing to incriminate her son.

Claire glares at Aki. "What I saw was my son being attacked and him defending himself," she declares, her expression turning to stone. "We all know that your daughter has been attacking him all year, which is the only reason he was lashing out like that. You all saw how Meg was in that video! Someone needed to protect my son," she insists, validating Aki's suspicion that Claire was in fact the one who sent the video to Ousmane, and probably the photo of Meg and Aaron kissing as well.

"You have got to be shitting me—" Jules begins, before being cut off by Claire.

"For all we know, Meg is the one trying to frame Aaron for the graffiti," Claire sniffs.

Aki is about to snap back when the crowd roars in a way that makes all the women look. Instead of exaggerated cheering, people sound angry.

"What the hell! Break up the fight, ref!" someone yells out.

The women look toward the center of the field. Instead of a Prep player and Wesley player having it out, as would be expected, they see two Wesley players locked in a scuffle. Finally, one of them drags the other to the ground and begins pummeling him.

"Wakeman! What the fuck!" the Wesley coach yells.

Aki strains her neck and sees that Aaron is hitting a player on the ground, and just when it looks like Aaron might get in yet another hit, the other player leaps up and punches Aaron in the face.

"Oh!" Claire cries out. "Do something!" she yells to the coach, leaving the women and running toward the team bench.

The Wesley coaching staff runs out onto the field as the ref furiously blows his whistle. The Albany Prep players encircle the fighting boys while their own coaches try to herd them back to their side of the field.

"End him, Wakeman!" someone yells at Aaron—another player. Aki watches Holly's face go white and realizes it must be Zach egging Aaron on.

Just then, the other boy barrels into Aaron, knocking him off his feet. Aki sees Double standing over Aaron menacingly as the coaching staff tries to hold him back.

"Both of you are acting like arrogant turds!" Felix shouts, frustrated. Aki can't help but guffaw at his insult; he sounds exactly like his father, Jasper.

"Red card! For both of you!" The ref voice and whistle scream ceaselessly. "End of game!" The ref starts waving his arms over his head. "Automatic forfeit by Wesley!" he cries out. Aaron hobbles out, the coach on one side and Claire on the other as the rest of the coaching staff tend to Double's wounds.

Holly watches everything unfold on the field, then turns back to Aki and Jules. She blinks, then says, "Is Zach going to get into trouble?" her voice shaking. She pauses, then continues, "College acceptance letters go out in a few weeks."

Aki looks at Holly for what feels like a very long time before simply saying, "Have a good afternoon, Holly."

"They probably just had a little too much to drink!" is the last thing Aki hears before the crowd begins to clap halfheartedly, marking the end of the game.

"It's so like Wesley to use more money on a new building but none to support students of color."

—*Wesley freshman, PoC@Wesley*

"THANK YOU FOR HELPING me back there," Aki says as they slip out of the bleachers and head toward the parking lot. "You OK?" she adds.

Jules clears her throat. "I am," she says, quietly, "wondering where I went wrong with Felix."

Aki knew Jules enough to know this would be deeply upsetting. While Jasper is fiscally conservative and Jules doesn't agree with all of Wesley's cultural commandments, hearing her son sound like just another privileged private-schooler was bound to wound Jules's black-and-white sense of right-and-wrong.

"Jules, he was drunk," Aki says, sounding a little too much like Holly. "Kids this age, they're just trying things on for size to impress their peers," she adds quickly.

"Meg doesn't," Jules replies.

"Every kid grows at their own pace, you know that, Jules," Aki says, trying to cheer her friend up. She doesn't want to believe that Felix meant what he said in the video, for her friend's sake.

Jules sighs. "I'll be fine once I give Felix a little whooping. You're sweet to check on me," she says as they reach Grayson's G-wagon. "A verbal whooping, that is. I know how Wesley feels about corporal punishment," she jokes, making Aki feel a little better. "Shouldn't you be trying to find Meg, though? I have a feeling she's the only one who's going to be able to explain that video."

Meg. Aki had been so busy cornering Holly and Claire she had forgotten about her own daughter. How maybe, just maybe, she will finally make things clear for Aki.

"Go find her," Jules says kindly.

★   ★   ★

Stalking Meg via find-my-phone, she sees her daughter is at Starbucks on Wisconsin Avenue right by school. Aki, who still has Grayson's car keys, jumps in his car and careens down Wisconsin in order to intercept her. She speeds down the busy street and sees on her phone that Meg has just left Starbucks. Once she spots her, she rolls down her window and waves to get Meg's attention.

"Nice ride, Mother, did Harrison give you a raise?" her daughter jokes.

"I'll give you a lift back to school, get in," Aki prods, happy that Meg doesn't appear to be in an awful mood.

Meg opens the door and jumps in. "Black interior and wood burl, nice, Mother," Meg jokes. Aki has to admit that it's a nice change to be on her daughter's good side. Meg has been respectful, if not outright friendly in the twenty-four hours since the protest and the TV interview.

Aki clears her throat and uncharacteristically gets to the point. "Meg, I was shown a video of you at a party getting into an argument with Aaron Wakeman."

Meg gives her mother a blank look, then turns her head to stare silently out the window.

Aki continues. "Meg, I also saw the picture of you in Aaron's jersey. Kissing." She looks sideways at her daughter's expression, which has yet to change. "I need you to tell me what's been going on."

To Aki's great surprise, and instead of being met with a usual stone wall of silence, Meg bursts out crying. At first, the tears are merely falling silently from her eyes, but then a wail is followed by a series of guttural sobs. Aki, so taken aback by this foreign scene, pulls Grayson's car abruptly over to the side of the road, eliciting honks and angry noises from the cars behind her.

"God, Mother, you seriously need to go back to driver's ed!" Meg exclaims tearfully as she tries to catch her breath between sobs. Aki waits patiently, knowing that if she says anything more, Meg is likely to revert to a state of silence. Meg sniffles and finds a napkin in the passenger-side cupholder, blows her nose, and shakes her head like a dog shaking off a wet coat. "Aaron and I slept together," she says dully. "Over the summer."

WHAT WHAT WHAT WHAT WHAT?! She wants to yell. *Keep calm*, she tells herself instead. Far be it from her to tell her daughter what to do with her body other than to use protection, but even this seems like a crazy idea. She searches her daughter's face, which is blotchy and red from the crying.

Meg looks at her mom. "You know how I had that internship?" Aki nods, thinking about how Meg had spent the summer working for an arts foundation and wonders what this has to do with her daughter sleeping with Aaron Wakeman. "Well, he was at a lacrosse camp at the boys' school right near there."

"Prep Academy?" Aki asks out loud, even though she knows that's what her daughter is talking about. Not only is it famous for its lacrosse program, but it is also literally across the street from where Meg was working.

Meg nods. "He found out I was working there, and he always wanted to eat lunch together." Aki thinks about Claire's bemusement at her son's dalliance with Meg, insisting it was more Meg than Aaron who was smitten. "He would text me, buy me lunch, and we'd meet on the field in front of the foundation. A lot of times he'd drive me home even though it was completely out of his way," Meg says, sniffling. She looks at her mother. "He was . . ." she trails off.

"He was?" Aki asks softly.

"He was nice," Meg says, gulping. "At school, he's so popular, but he actually doesn't like it, like he's been thrust into some role he didn't ask for," she explains. "He's really well-read. He's really funny," Meg says softly, like she's defending her choices to herself.

Aki nods, hoping her daughter will keep talking.

"Like I seriously think if he could go back to being in the manga club and hanging out with the geeks, he'd be a lot happier," Meg concludes. "But his brothers, his parents, it's a lot of pressure to be someone else," she starts sniffling again, and the tears have restarted.

"What happened?" Aki asks, fearful why her daughter is crying so much.

Meg's expression changes like a hot afternoon in the summer when it's about to storm. "What do you mean what happened? We slept together, and I'm an idiot," she says, blowing her nose and now looking angry. "I am so, so stupid."

How could this have transpired without her knowing? Aki wonders. She scans her mind for how she could have been that clueless, but gives up. It's been a long time since she's been in control of her daughter's schedule, much less known what has been going on in her personal life. Then she remembers how her mother told her to listen to what Meg wasn't telling her. Is this what she had been talking about? Is this what Aiko hinted at when she said she had warned Meg not to get involved?

"Don't worry, we were safe," Meg says, which makes Aki slightly more relieved.

"So, the argument at the party?" Aki asks, suddenly remembering why she started this particular conversation.

"Ugh, he was being such a grade-A jerk," Meg says, now just looking plain irritated. "How could he go from being great one minute then turn around and become such an asshole the next?"

"Meg," Aki starts slowly, trying to fill in the holes of Meg's story, "I'm trying to help you," she finishes lamely.

"With what?" Meg snaps, making Aki annoyed. The conversation hadn't been too adversarial up until this point, but now old Meg is back, snarling and confrontational.

Aki pauses. If she tells her daughter that a video clip has been sent to Ousmane, Meg will undoubtedly go nuclear on Aaron. But what Aki really wants to know is how Meg went from clearly being in a relationship with him to *this*.

"So, you were together, and he decided to break up?" is all Aki can come up with.

"I broke up with him," Meg shoots back before looking out the window again.

Well, that explains some of Aaron's actions in the video, Aki thinks.

Then in a low voice Meg says, "It was never going to work anyway. It was fun for a while, but . . ." Meg trails off, looking out the window, speaking as if in a trance. "We're just too different."

"So, what was Aaron talking about?" Aki asks, thinking about Aaron's drunken tirade. She understands now how much everyone knew but her. "About you having a boyfriend?"

"Oh, that." Meg says flatly. "He's talking about Double."

More information that comes as a shock to Aki, despite all the rumors. "So, you and Double are dating," she says, knowing that Meg and Double make a lot more sense as a couple, but it's yet another thing Aki doesn't know about her daughter's life.

"Double and I are friends," Meg says, looking at her mother. "But we also don't need labels."

"Meg," Aki starts slowly, not sure how much to give away to her emotionally volatile daughter. "If Aaron gets blamed for the graffiti, you know he'll be kicked out of school, and it feels like you've been pointing everyone in that direction for months."

"Good," Meg says without a hint of remorse or sympathy. "He deserves it. You saw how he was," she says bluntly.

"OK, but Meg, if people think you were out for revenge of some sort, either because he dumped you or because of the way he was talking to you in that video—"

"What?" Meg interrupts, now in a rage. "You think *I'm* trying to frame *him*? I told you; *I dumped him*." Meg looking disgusted, adds, "And you saw how he can be a racist, sexist pig." Meg declares, though looking somewhat unsure, "Of course he did it."

"Meg," Aki starts again. "The video of the graffiti proves nothing other than someone in his warm-up jersey did it," Then she adds fearfully, "And there's a picture of *you* wearing the jersey."

"Mother! That was at the *beginning* of the season!" Meg yells exasperatedly.

Aki tries again. "You obviously liked him enough to have some sort of relationship, so why break it off?" Aki desperately tries to make sense of her daughter and her daughter's line of thinking.

Meg looks squarely at Aki's face. "He goes against everything I stand for."

"Then why . . ." *sleep with him*, she doesn't finish.

"Because I knew I could." Meg says bluntly, answering her mother while staring out the window. "Because all the Yeardly Ward's of the world want him, but he wanted me."

Aki is momentarily speechless. Was this Meg's father speaking? A person who could sleep with a person one day and break up with them the next?

"So you dated him . . . then—"

"Slept with him, yes," Meg supplies, making Aki wince. "And then we broke up. Simple."

Aki opens her mouth, thinks a bit, then starts again. "I feel like there is a lot of anger still directed toward Aaron—"

"ARGH! Mother! I hate myself enough already! I hate myself that I did this, that I slept with such a jerk! Aiko was right, I never should have gotten together with him!" Meg shouts at her and breaks down into tears again, weeping, Aki realizes, like an adult, not crying like a child. Watching her daughter sob into her lap, Aki understands what the real problem is. Despite everything, part of her daughter is still in love with Aaron Wakeman. And she also knows now why Aaron came to speak to her that day—not because Claire had sent him, but because he had been—and perhaps still is—in love with Meg. She looks at her daughter and the cyclone of emotions she's just witnessed and realizes something else: she's not sure that she trusts her daughter at all.

★ ★ ★

After her conversation with Meg, Aki knew that it was time to come clean with Ian. The fact that he was gone for six weeks then home for two is a handy excuse to keep him clueless, but Aki knows it's time. She begged Meg to come home with her and talk to Ian as well, but Meg insisted that she needed some time to think, so Aki dropped her at Aiko's house near school, then doubled back to Wesley just in time to see Grayson parking the mini school bus.

"Thank you so much," Aki says, trotting over to him, holding out his key.

"Sure, but hey, how are you going to get home?" Grayson asks.

"I'll just take the bus, it's not a big deal," Aki replies as Grayson starts shaking his head.

"I'll take you home," he says. Aki starts to object, but he waves her off, saying, "Let me just grab my stuff from the office. Wait here," he commands. Ten minutes later, he returns with his backpack and grins. "Come on, hop in!"

Aki gets back in the G-wagon, this time on the passenger's side. She sits primly as Grayson starts the car, and realizes she has no idea where he lives. "Are you sure this isn't too far out of your way?" she asks.

"It's fine, you live in Adams Morgan, right?"

Aki nods. "On Crescent."

"Right-o, let's go!" Grayson says cheerfully, and in that moment, Aki realizes that in a few years, or perhaps a decade, Grayson might make a very good father. "So, Aki, why did you decide to become a teacher?" he asks.

Aki is momentarily taken aback by the sudden personal question and thinks about how to respond. "Well," she starts slowly. "It was sort of chosen for me. I got pregnant with Meg before I could finish my PhD, but I always loved history and I knew I wanted to teach." Grayson nods solemnly. "And you?" she asks. She had assumed this whole time that teaching was a placeholder for Grayson while he decided what he wanted to do with his life.

"I had a teacher who saved my life," Grayson says, making Aki look at him in surprise as he nods solemnly. "I went to St. Paul's for a PG year. I was so messed up, Aki," he says seriously.

A postgraduate year was typically reserved for athletes and underachievers who need an extra year to prepare for college. She was surprised, given his lineage and Yale degree, that he would have needed one. "Oh yeah, so messed up in high school, *so messed up*," he emphasizes. "Too much pressure, too much money, too many drugs, not enough guidance, way too insecure, I was a mess," he explains honestly. Aki sits silently, hoping he will tell her more, feeling guilty for assuming he'd lived an easy life. "But my history teacher my senior year, he just took me aside one day and said, 'Listen, you have talent! Don't throw it away! What are you going to do with all the privilege you've been given?'" They stop at a light and he drums his fingers on the steering wheel. "He helped me turn it around and wrote me a recommendation for St. Paul's." Grayson recounts as he nimbly moves between several double-parked cars. He is a surprisingly slow and steady driver, and they make their way leisurely through DC, but Aki is enraptured.

"I mean, I know why I got into Yale, but I decided I was going to work really hard. I'm not going to lie, I slipped a few times and had to deal with some hard stuff, but I knew I wanted to do for kids what my history teacher did for me." He looks up the street and says, "Tell me which one," as Aki points to the red brick building on the corner, disappointed their conversation is drawing to a close. "So that's why I'm a teacher," Grayson says decisively. "I mean, I did take that year off to ski, though," he says jovially, like the Grayson she knows and has grown to love.

As Grayson expertly parallel parks his oversized and out-of-character SUV, Aki sits and considers what he has just told her. The irritation she's feels toward Wesley is due to a slurry of resentment she feels toward an administration that has slowly veered off path combined with an increasingly difficult paren- tal population, a slurry that has grown thicker and more potent in recent years. She has more sympathy for the children, know- ing how it feels to coalesce around an overbearing parent's will. Aki looks at Grayson's face: handsome and youthful, but now she notices worry lines that probably shouldn't be there and a sadness in his eyes.

"I think you're an amazing teacher, and you will one day make an amazing parent," she says truthfully. She's surprised to see his eyes well up, then watches as he catches himself and gulps.

"That means a lot, Aki, because I respect you so much," he says quietly.

"Well, maybe you shouldn't," she says, thinking about everything that has transpired with Meg and her faltering and short-lived directorship, which was, of course, a sham and has devolved into a personal vendetta despite insisting to Ousmane that it is anything but.

"I've also been meaning to tell you, Aki, that I really appreciate the changes you've been trying to make at Wesley," Grayson says earnestly. "I know that things need to change."

Aki looks at his thoughtful expression and for once in a long time feels hopeful. Maybe everything she is doing is not completely in vain if the future of the school believes in it too. But something tells her that might not be the case.

MARCH

◆ 24 ◆

"Can we please get back on topic about how hostile the Wesley community is? My daughter recently came out and instead of acceptance some kids call her names in the hallway."

—*Shocked Parent, dcparentzone.com*

A YOUNG ASIAN WOMAN appears in the doorway of Aki's classroom. It's early, and as usual Aki is bent over her desk trying to catch up on things she should have done the night before.

"Ms. Brown?" the woman says.

"Ms. Hayashi," Aki responds, surprising herself.

"I'm . . . I'm sorry," the woman stammers.

"Yes, I'm Ms. Brown," she says, sighing. Aki peers at the woman wearily, she's never seen her before.

"I've been sent over here to ask you to come to Harrison's office," the woman responds peppily.

"Now?" Aki asks. She can't help but look at her students, who stare back at her, undoubtedly praying they'll get out of class early.

The woman nods her head, and Aki's sigh serves as a dismissal bell, because all of her students rush to collect their things, as if any hesitation on their part will make the magic offer of a free period disappear. Aki gathers her own papers and joins the

nameless woman—an administrator of some sort, she assumes—
in the hallway.

"My name is Sarah Hashimoto, by the way," the young Japanese woman—in her late twenties from the looks of it—says as
she extends her hand to Aki, who shakes it hurriedly.

"What is this about?" she asks, trying not to sound annoyed.

"I'm taking over your role as DEI director, and Harrison
wanted us to meet," Sarah explains.

Aki isn't sure whether to laugh or cry. She feels like she's
looking at her twenty-six-year-old self and wondering if Harrison really is this transparent. She supposes this is the school's
response to her interview with Joanna Javier-Hernandez.

"But Harrison also wanted me to come find you because a
Mrs. Wakeman is in the office with him," Sarah says.

"What the hell is with that woman?" Aki says under her
breath. "So, you're taking over my role, huh?" she asks.

Sarah nods. "Harrison and Amanda asked me to shadow you
for the next few days." Then she cocks her head and asks, "They
asked me if I'd like to teach some classes on Asian history. Do
you do that too?"

Guillotine has fallen, Aki thinks as they rush through the
mostly empty hallways, students tucked away in their classrooms, except for her own of course, who loiter and lie on the
floors looking happy to be free. They cross the courtyard and up
the hill to Hartwell House. When they get to Harrison's office,
Aki knocks on the door gingerly, looking Sarah up and down
as they wait. It's like the school went out of their way to hire
her doppelgänger. Maybe that way people won't ask where Aki
disappeared to.

"Enter, please," Harrison's voice says from inside the room.

Aki takes a breath and strides into the room. As she enters
the office, she is surprised to see Aiko's parents, who sit with confused expressions on their faces.

"Aki, hello, please take a seat," Harrison says, gesturing to the one empty chair in front of him. His expression today is less used-car salesman and more TV detective bearing bad news. "I see that you've met Ms. Ha-ha-sh . . ." he trails off pathetically.

"Hashimoto!" Sarah says brightly.

Aki glances at Claire, who is dressed shoulder to ankle in a palette of all white—white wool slacks, a crisp white shirt topped with an oversized white wrap, and white pearls. She looks shiny, like the inside of a shell, and fuzzy, like the belly of a sheep. Overall, of course, the ensemble screams *expensive*. Aki nods hello to Aiko's parents, Kwasi and Anna, who appear to have come from work, Kwasi in a sharp suit and gold tie, Anna in a chic wrap dress and overcoat. Being a Wesley teacher means often feeling underdressed in the presence of the "clients," as Harrison considers them. Aki takes a seat in the front row while Sarah disappears into the oversized sofa lining Harrison's back wall.

"Thank you all for coming during a busy day," he says, nodding to the Oseis. "I will try to be concise and clear. There have been allegations of bullying against Aaron Wakeman by Aiko and Meg."

Aki snorts out loud. Everyone turns to look at her in surprise, but Aki can't stop what is rapidly becoming laughter. Perhaps it's due to a general lack of sleep, or the stress from the last few days, but she feels a spark of a howl running through her body like an electric shock. Actual tears begin to roll down her cheeks as Claire, Aiko's parents, Amanda, Sarah, and Harrison openly gape at her reaction.

"I'm sorry," Aiko says, wiping her eyes. "But Aiko and Meg bullying *Aaron*?" She hoots.

"Ms. Brown," Harrison warns.

Aki calms herself down and sits straight in her chair, trying to look sober. *This is what my life has come to. Sneaking around high school lacrosse players' backyards, taking on positions I know nothing about, begging my own child to let me in on her life, yelling at my boss at work.* Before she can stop herself, Aki says, "Who the hell cares?"

"Excuse me, but *I* care," Claire huffs.

"I bet you do. You care *so much* about your son you 've been sharpening the guidance counselor's pencil," Aki chides. Everyone stares blankly at her, making her guffaw. "She's *fucking* him!" Aki clarifies, making Claire and Aiko's parents gasp. "At least she *was*," she adds for clarification, not that it matters.

"I have *never*—" Claire begins, before Aki cuts her off.

"Lady," she spits out, enjoying Claire's shocked expression. "You don't think I know what's going on? You keep sending me and Ousmane an assortment of photos and videos trying to frame my daughter for vandalism that is pointing straight at your racist son and you come in here telling me that my daughter and her friend are bullying *him*? Ha! And where is Ousmane, by the way?" Aki shouts. She knows that he's more likely to be her ally, probably the reason why he's not in the room.

Claire looks down at her lap and smooths out her slacks.

I have to hand it to her, she's as cold as ice, Aki thinks as she continues. "Look, I get it, you see me, you think, 'Ooh, docile Asian lady who won't kick up a fuss,' not to mention you're so rich you're used to getting every single thing you want—except of course, a faithful husband."

"Ms. Brown, *please*," Harrison pleads before shifting his attention to Claire. "I assure you we take these bullying allegations seriously."

"Stop acting, we both saw the whole clip, the one where Aaron is drunk and saying disgusting things to the girls, not to mention spitting on Double. So what if she says she'll 'end him'? I'd say it's even-Steven in terms of the bullying." Aki's eyes dart from Claire Wakeman to Harrison and Amanda, who look like the see-no-evil-hear-no-evil monkey statues. She feels like she's going crazy. How much gaslighting can one woman be involved in? "Where is Ousmane?" Aki asks again.

In the silence following her question, Aki starts laughing. She closes her eyes and lets out a roaring laugh, and it feels good letting out the stress that's been bottled up inside for so long. *This is all so stupid*, she realizes as her laugh subsides into a chuckle. *Why could I not see the forest for the trees?*

"I don't think my son receiving a death threat from your daughter is anything to laugh about," Claire says coldly.

"Death threats?" Aki spits. "Fine, suspend her again, but what about Aaron? He clearly vandalized the school."

"And where is that evidence?" Claire demands. Aki stares at Claire, her unlined face, and glossy shampoo-commercial hair. A house so perfect that not even a lacrosse marking in such a garish color could diminish it. She steels herself.

This is it.

"On your lawn, lady. And on the side of the school," Aki says with a sense of delight. "Same ugly shade of turquoise. What is it, more expensive than plain white?"

For a moment Claire pauses, then waves her hand at Aki. "Please, anyone can buy spray paint. For all we know your daughter stole Aaron's old jersey and used it to frame him," she says, shooting out of her chair. "I expect a quick and fair resolution to the threats against my son, Harrison!"

"What she really means, *Harrison*," Aki says, "is that she's rich and she wants the school to do what she says. That's how it works, after all, right?"

"Enough!" Harrison says loudly, making Claire and Amanda jump. "Ms. Nutley, what do you suggest?" Leave it to Harrison to get anyone else but himself to do the dirty work.

"Well," Amanda says, standing up straight and pursing her lips. "Per the school handbook, with instances of bullying, the students in question should convene with the help of a mediator to discuss their issues."

"My son *will not* be in a room with these girls," Claire spits out.

Anna and Kwasi exchange a look of worry, and Aki doesn't blame them. It's easy enough to tell that Aiko is barely involved in any of this. Then Anna clears her throat.

"May I ask, what is it that Aiko is said to have done? Does this have to do with the Instagram page she runs?"

Oh no, no, no, no, Anna! Stop! Aki screams in her head.

"Your daughter runs the PoC@Wesley page?" Amanda asks with incredulity. "What the actual fuck!"

Claire looks up triumphantly. "So, you see, Harrison, both girls used all means possible to torture my son."

"Please, you do that yourself," Aki snaps.

"Ms. Brown, I think it is time for you to return to classes. I will meet with you privately later," Harrison says, openly excusing her from the conversation.

Aki looks at Aiko's parents. "Aiko has a First Amendment right to run that account, and she never posted anything from inside campus," Aki says as she stands to go. "Just remember that, Anna!" she says as Anna nods gravely. "She did this school a favor by pointing out how hypocritical it is!" She understands how much Meg's thinking has infiltrated her own, possibly for the better, she realizes now.

"GOODBYE, MS. BROWN," Harrison says loudly. His desperation makes Aki feel strangely satisfied, and she has to stifle a laugh when she sees Sarah Hashimoto's unblinking, wide eyes. *Good luck, kid,* she thinks to herself.

Aki exhales to signal her annoyance with the conversation, then gives Claire a fake wave and smile. As she exits Harrison's office, she whips out her phone, and starts texting as she walks down the hall.

"Hey Ms. B, no phones!" Ethan calls out to her jokingly.

"Oh, fuck off!" Aki says back, making everyone, including Ethan, howl with laughter in the senior hallway. She types out a text to Ian.

> I found out who spray-painted the graffiti and I may have just gotten fired.

*   *   *

Ian surprised Aki by picking her up from school, or rather, waiting for her at her car at the end of the day. She feels her shoulders release the tension that has built up throughout the day as she falls into his chest.

"Bad day?" he asks, enveloping her in a hug. "Better than catastrophic global warming, though, right?" he jokes. "Come on, I made a dinner reservation," he says, taking her keys and opening the car. She says nothing but thankfully settles in the passenger seat, ready to be gone from Wesley for the day. They drive down Wisconsin Avenue toward Georgetown, and Aki watches the school recede in the side mirror. Minutes later they're seated at a small Thai restaurant on the edge of the shopping district, Aki sipping on a Thai beer as Ian licks the salt off the rim of his margarita. "I asked for no salt," he grumbles.

"Where's Meg?" Aki asks, though she already knows the answer.

"Aiko's. So, what happened?"

Aki recounts the story, Claire's allegations, Harrison's fluster, her lack of decorum, her general anxiety about Meg's involvement in unresolved issues, and her TV interview. She wonders what Ian will say, and if he'll reprimand her.

Ian sighs and takes a gulp of his drink. "I've thought for years that you should leave Wesley."

Aki is glad he's not angry. "I know, but that idea isn't really helpful right now," she says, feeling defeated.

"Aki, I'm being serious. I feel like you've lost who you are at that school," Ian says, looking genuinely concerned.

"What do you mean? Being a history teacher? Or the new position?" Aki asks, confused.

"No, I mean *you*, as a person," Ian says, looking up at the server and thanking him as he leaves their dishes. "You used to be less afraid. Over time, it's like the school has made you too careful," he says thoughtfully before taking an enormous bite of pad thai.

Except I've just screamed at everyone who is my superior, and the week isn't even over, she thinks as she watches him attack his food and considers what he's said. She was certainly not timid in graduate school, often arguing with her peers in class, and of course, having secret affairs she shouldn't. But when she started at Wesley, she felt defeated, like she started off owing something to them. Maybe that weighed on her over the years. Taking orders was her childhood, after all. Is her recent spate of aggression a reaction to all of this? She ponders these ideas as Ian motions to the green curry.

"Aren't you going to eat?" he asks.

"What are we going to do about Meg?" she says quietly. It's easier to focus on her daughter than herself, a crime shared with so many other parents mired in personal problems.

Ian gulps down some food and takes a drink. "Aki, we can't control what she does, and we can't control what happens to her. She'll learn from her mistakes, and she'll be fine."

"Ian, they're actively trying to kick her out during her junior year," she says, knowing she sounds overdramatic. *Even Wesley won't do that, will it?*

"You just said Aaron is the one who spray-painted the school. Meg will be able to fight her way out of anything she did to expose him. She's smart," Ian says calmly.

Aki can't help but feel annoyed at Ian's Zen state of mind. "What has made you all West Coast cool all of a sudden?" she demands.

Ian grins, looking boyish and handsome, making Aki momentarily less stressed. "I have some news," he says.

"Please let this be good news," Aki says reflexively. It feels like every conversation she enters into these days is contentious.

"*I* think it is, though I'm not sure about how you or Meg will feel," he says. "I got a huge grant," he says, his eyes excited.

Aki feels a trickle of happiness for him, but also assumes this is yet another project that will keep him away for weeks at a time. *We'll definitely both miss him, maybe that's what he means*, she thinks sadly.

"I'm going to hand the Greenland project off to Lisa," he says, referring to his co-investigator. "Because they just gave me Point Reyes and Bodega Bay!"

Aki's mouth opens, but nothing comes out. Point Reyes and Bodega Bay are an hour and a half drive north of San Francisco, a barren but beautiful national park with rolling yellow hills that drop dramatically into a lonely part of the bay. He's talked about studying pollution control in the area for years, but with the land being heavily regulated and researchers vying to do things in that region of California, she had forgotten about it. "What about ice samples?" is all she can muster to ask.

"We've finished with that work," Ian explains. "Lisa and I still have to write up a final report, but she's going to do the wrap-up, you know, closing up shop," he says energetically with a hint of margarita, "and I get to set up a temporary research station in Reyes," he says dreamily. He never understood why Aki was so opposed to the Bay Area. He couldn't get enough of the hiking, the marine life, and the food.

Aki chews on a clump of rice. "Is this why you were called back to Silver Spring a few weeks ago?" Aki asks, realizing that his surprise visit home hadn't only been a surprise for her. "So, six weeks on, two weeks back here, as usual?" she asks listlessly. She can't remember a time when Ian wasn't off doing research. Sometimes she wishes he would just take a job at a federal agency and stay in DC, but she knows that would make him miserable.

"Yes, but here's the thing," Ian starts slowly, which means he's going to try to convince her of something. "Now don't get angry." This is the other thing he likes to preface arguments with, which also happens to be what she likes to say to Meg, not that it ever works. "I think we should all move."

Aki feels the rice on her chopsticks fall on her plate. "Move?" she says forcefully. "Like *move*?"

Ian laughs. "If all goes well, Meg will be on the West Coast for college. And Aki," he says gently, "I think it's time you consider saying goodbye to Wesley."

Aki stops completely. She's complained about Wesley intermittently in the past, and she and Meg have both been miserable this past year. But leaving has never seemed like a real option. She knows why, and it's the same reason that despite everything, she's so scared to watch Meg graduate. It's because they both grew up at the school.

"Just promise me you'll think about it," Ian says.

◆ 25 ◆

"Can we please address how Wesley is going to move forward from this?"

—*Perplexed, dcparentzone.com*

QUAKER MEETING IS A ritual Aki used to shrug off as a good excuse to stare into space for forty minutes. There are other private schools that engage in these types of activities, of course. Some of the Catholic schools have weekly mass, and the Episcopal school down the street had both chapel and services at the National Cathedral. Aki remembers asking a friend who is Jewish what her daughter does during the school's chapel service. Her friend shrugged and said, "She naps."

Aki trails the long line of students and faculty to the meeting house, a newly built structure where the old gym used to be. Five years ago, it was a basketball court built in the fifties with glass blocks in the place of windows and stands that pulled out from the walls. Now demolished (like most of the older buildings at Wesley), in its place stands a soaring structure with arched wooden beams and skylights that wash sunlight down over rows of simple wooden benches.

Before the new meeting house was built, students sat on the floor of the gym, faculty on the bleachers, collectively staring into the middle of the wooden floor. Girls would lean on girls, boys would lean on walls, and couples would sit with intertwined legs. Aki liked the simplicity of those meetings in the gym, everyone in one place, focused on the same thing and all different things at the same time. The new meeting house is larger and more beautiful but has done nothing to bring them closer together as a community.

As per usual, everyone sits facing the middle of the room, the absence of a pulpit being one of the hallmarks of a Quaker gathering. Students rarely stand to speak, though the point of any Quaker meeting is to wait to feel like you should rise and contribute, and Aki has grown accustomed to making the forty-minute silence part of her week. This week, she's grateful for it. She knows she's in real trouble with Harrison, and she's worried Meg might be too. Despite Ian's optimistic cheerleading ("School is almost over! Just hang in there!"), she knows that regular decision notices will roll in soon, and there is still enough room for someone like Claire to keep making her daily life at Wesley as uncomfortable as possible until she makes sure her precious son is into somewhere like Princeton.

Faculty always sits in the back of the meeting house, mainly to keep an eye on students who try to sneak in cell phones or the more brazen ones who dare lay down on the benches. Aki sees that Jules has grabbed their usual seats and walks over to join her.

"How's Meg doing?" Jules leans over to ask.

"She's good, thanks," Aki whispers, knowing that's a lie. Meg, who had been warm toward her after the protest, had reverted to her normal moody self after their talk in the car. Aki leans back on her bench and closes her eyes. She thinks about Ian's suggestion to leave Wesley for the West Coast. What would she do? Teach at another school? That's a reasonable option, of course. She had never considered it, assuming that Meg would graduate from Wesley but that she would stay. She starts to list all the private schools in the Bay Area in her head: *Urban, Collegiate, St. Mary's* . . . none of them will take Meg as a senior, she knows. Maybe she can just graduate from Westmoor, Aki thinks, then laughs despite the irony of the situation. So desperate to get out of Daly City and a place like Westmoor High School, she ended up on the East Coast and determined to give Meg the education she wanted for herself—only to have her daughter end up at the very place she had tried to escape.

"I've never spoken in meeting before," she hears a timid voice say. Aki opens her eyes and looks around the room. She cranes her neck and finally sees someone with their back to her. "The student body has been traumatized. Traumatized by the school's past inactions at addressing racial divides, and now by the clear racism that has left a literal mark on its buildings."

Aki realizes that it's Aiko talking.

"But . . ." Aiko trails off. "I . . ." her voice starts to quiver, and students begin to whisper among themselves. Aki watches her back straighten. "I am the one who defaced the school, and I take responsibility." Aki looks at Jules in shock, as audible gasps fill the enormous space. "I did it to see if the school would finally step up and address the deep-rooted problems with racism it has," she says. "And—"

"She didn't do it!" Another figure jumps up next to Aiko. Aki looks to see who it is as her body goes numb. "I did!" The voice who is speaking now is Meg.

Jules grabs Aki's arm as Meg continues. "She's trying to cover up for me," Meg says, adding defiantly, "I hate this school and everything it stands for." She glares as she stands next to Aiko, her dark eyes piercing the assembled crowd now all watching her. "You all pretend to be all 'I'm an ally' but you don't know *shit*!" Her face is contorted with anger and anguish. "When I started here, no one could spell my name, my *real* name. MEGUMI. I've been here twelve years and most of you still don't care what my real name is!" Meg is yelling now, and Aki is instantly taken back to Sruthi telling her how Thomas Feller called her "Yucky" behind her back. She viscerally feels her daughter's pain. How could all these years pass with no progress? She is ashamed to think that she has been part of the inaction. She watches as her daughter waves her arms, commanding attention. "You all call me Meg and act like my friend, but you don't care at all. You only care about getting into your stupid Ivies and not about what's going on in the world outside these fucking walls and how racism affects all of us, SO I REMINDED YOU!"

Gasps are followed by even louder whispers. Aki jumps up out of her seat, trying to push past the rows of knees in her path to get to her daughter. Then another voice calls out, making her stop midstride.

"They didn't do it. I did it. I know all of you think I did it anyway, and you're right."

It's Aaron Wakeman.

He pauses and looks at Meg. "You're right."

Students and faculty alike stand from their seats to identify the three students at the middle of this public confession. The room erupts into murmurs, then into loud talking, some students even starting to cry while others call out to Aiko, Meg, and Aaron.

"Sit down, Wakeman!" a voice calls out. "This isn't *Dead Poets Society*!"

Aki tries to get out of her row, frantically trying to figure out how to get Meg out of the room. She sees people closing in on Meg and Aiko, and she's frightened, unsure how the girls' statements are being received. She does the only thing she knows to do.

"Stop!" she screams. "Stop!"

The room stops moving and goes silent. "Just stop!" she pleads, swinging her head around and looking at everyone in the meeting house. She feels the attention of the crowd on her, so she continues. Then like a crumbling brick wall, the months of stress and invisible weight of anxiety brought on by watching her daughter struggle, her colleagues bicker, and plagued by her own self-doubts, she feels her inhibitions and reservations disappear.

"We need to ask one another," she starts, her voice shaking as she looks around at the faces in the meeting house. The freshmen are just out of middle school—many of the boys have yet to grow, with mere shadows of fuzz above their lips. Even the seniors, who are more adult in their demeanor and stature, still look like babies to her. She has known so many of them since elementary school, running around, playing tag, and getting skinned knees. When did they change so much?

She continues, this time more loudly, "We need to ask ourselves, 'Have we all caused what is wrong in this community?' We say we value certain things, but do we really? What if we're the ones who have perpetuated this? This hatred and intolerance and anger?" Aki wonders if Aaron will ever be able to redeem himself for what he did, but before she can think through what she's going to say next, she asks, "Are we all completely full of shit?"

She feels like she already knows the answer, but before she can dwell on that, she hears a single clap echo in the room and feels grateful for sole source of support. Then she hears a few more. She looks around and sees some of her colleagues standing: Percy and Grayson stand, clapping loudly. Then more clapping, this time from students who are seated on the benches. The applause grows louder, the sound bouncing off the ceiling and walls. As more people stand, Aki searches the room to find Meg and Aiko. Their backs are to her, and they look to be heading out the exit opposite her.

"I agree with Ms. B," a loud voice booms through the meeting house. Everyone swivels to identify the speaker. Felix. "Frankly, I don't like who I've become this year," he says, hanging his head. Aki looks down at Jules next to her, who is biting her lip and trying to hold back tears. Felix looks around the room and adds softly, "I'm sorry," then sits back down quietly as his friends pat him on the back for his contribution.

Aki watches Meg and Aiko look back at Felix before exiting the room and feels panicked. She pushes past people in her row, some standing and talking, others sitting, trying to catch her daughter before she disappears completely. A hand on her forearm stops her from leaving. Aki looks down to see Jenni Pai from her history class.

"We know it wasn't Meg," Jenni says in a soft voice.

I hope you're right, Aki thinks, giving Jenni a tight smile and rushing out of the meeting house as fast as she can.

★ ★ ★

Where are you?

Aki looks at Jules's text. She's driven home from school and pushes the elevator button in her lobby before deciding she doesn't want to wait, then races up the stairs to the third floor, feeling faint as she slams open the front hall door and bombs through the hallway. Ian is out, thank goodness, because she doesn't want any questions as to why she's home before lunch. She throws open Meg's bedroom door, scanning the room and feeling crazed. She starts with the drawers, flinging out everything inside—underwear, bras, socks, shirts, jeans—nothing resembling a jersey. She moves to the closet. She drags Meg's desk chair over to the closet so she can go through the upper shelf. Her phone dings from inside her pocket, and she hastily retrieves it, reading the text on the screen.

Where is Meg?

Aki doesn't know where Meg, Aiko, and Aaron were herded off to, but she imagines that the terminus was most likely Ousmane's office, given their public confessions. She reaches up to the shelf in Meg's closet—there is so much junk but not anything she's trying to locate. Old yearbooks, textbooks, photos—she keeps chucking everything onto the floor. She hopes she doesn't find what she's looking for, that it was just Claire's mind games getting to her.

Her phone rings. It's a Wesley prefix, and she can guess who it is, but she ignores it, throwing her phone on her bed and refocusing on the shelf. She sees a rolled-up poster board to her left and yanks it out. But something is stuck on it, and she pulls harder. An object flies out of the poster board, rattling on the floor and rolling lazily under the bed. She jumps off the chair and gets on her hands and knees, looking under the box frame, reaching for the object that is just out of her reach. She strains, pressing her shoulder and chest against the floor, finally touching it with her fingertips. She irons her body as flat as she can, finally coaxing the object into her palm. She pulls back her arm and sits up. When she looks at what she's retrieved, she stops breathing.

It's a can of turquoise spray paint.

★ ★ ★

"Aki," Ousmane starts, looking uncharacteristically frazzled. He rubs his palms on his temples as he drops his head into his hands, elbows on his desk.

Aki had sped back to campus after her discovery but only after disposing of the incriminating can of paint in the dumpster behind their condo building. She paused for a moment, standing in front of the enormous blue dumpster, thinking about how many times she had seen Meg out on the condo parking lot, making banners or completing an art project, knowing very well the spray paint really could be from that but also that she doesn't want to ponder alternatives. At least if Aki got rid of the spray paint, she wouldn't have to think about it. When she made it back to campus, there was an email from Ousmane's assistant asking her to swing by his office as soon as she could.

Aki sits across from Ousmane, watching him massage his head. "What did they say?" Aki asks. "The kids," she clarifies. She assumes she's been brought in to defend Meg after her revelation at that morning's meeting and hopes she can sound convincing considering what she's just found. *It doesn't mean she's guilty*, she reminds herself, even though she had just used the very same evidence against Aaron while shouting at Claire, also disposing of said evidence just like any good Wesley parent would do.

"They each continue to insist they acted alone," he says, sighing. "Which I find impossible."

"Well—" Aki starts before Ousmane cuts her off.

"What do you think we should do?" Ousmane asks her plainly.

"Me?" Aki is taken aback. "Ousmane, I don't know if you heard, but Harrison Neal has replaced me with my twenty-five-year-old doppelgänger so maybe you should ask her," she says, feeling a twinge of guilt. It's not Sarah Hashimoto's fault, and Aki certainly doesn't envy what this role has in store for her.

Ousmane clears his throat and closes his eyes, rubbing his temples again.

"Ousmane, what is it? It's not like you to look so . . ." *stressed*, Aki thinks.

"Please do not talk about this to anyone," he starts, waiting for her to acknowledge his words. She nods quickly to get him to start—or maybe to stop—talking. "Harrison Neal has been asked to step down."

Aki's eyes widen with surprise, since this is not what she was expecting him to tell her. Finally, she blurts out, "Why? Hookers?"

Ousmane laughs. "No, nothing as interestingly lurid. It has come to light that he has been—" Ousmane stops, clearly searching for the appropriate phrase. "Let us just say that if he has had an inappropriate relationship, it has been with Cash Wakeman."

Aki doesn't know what to say but thinks about how the conspiracy theory that the rich parents are shadow rulers of private schools rings very true right now.

"The board was alerted to the fact that Harrison made a deal with Cash to build the campus extension and new athletic complex without appropriate bidding. They were then going to pack the board with Cash and his compatriots to guarantee an OK for the project."

That was supposed to be a $200 million contract. Aki opens her mouth, but nothing comes out. All she can think is that Joanna Javier-Hernandez would love this scoop, and now she understands why the school never intended to pursue Aaron as a real suspect in the graffiti.

"Some sort of coup d'état was in the works," Ousmane sighs.

"And the board found out?" Aki asks, still trying to wrap her head around what Ousmane is telling her.

"Yes, here is where we come to something of a . . ." Ousmane looks up from his hands, which have been massaging his head again. "Change."

Aki looks at him, totally confused. Are they still talking about the kids?

"The board convened again last night and decided that I will take over Harrison's responsibilities until a suitable replacement can be found," he announces.

"Oh, wow, Ousmane," Aki starts, unsure of what to say. "That's great!" she decides. "Congrats!"

"As you know a search for a new head of school typically takes two years," he explains. "So I expect that will be my tenure as well."

"I think they should appoint you permanently," Aki says forcefully. "I think it would be good for the school."

"Well, that brings us to you," he says, suddenly sitting upright, no longer as haggard looking.

"Me?" she asks. "Are you going to kick the newbie to the curb and reinstate me as equity director for your first act?" she jokes.

"No, Aki," Ousmane says seriously. "The board has decided you should be the new head of the upper school."

EPILOGUE

"D R. HAYASHI-BROWN?"

"Yes," Aki says, smiling. "You don't have to call me that, you can just call me Aki, it's OK," she adds.

She is standing in a classroom in Dwinelle Hall, the building that houses many of the undergraduate classes on the Berkeley campus.

"We don't need to call you professor?"

Aki smiles. "Not until I finish my PhD, no. Until then I'm just your TA," she says happily. She stares out at the small group of undergraduates attending her office hours. "Anyone have any other questions?"

A hand shoots up. "Is it true you used to be a high school teacher?"

Aki laughs. "Guilty as charged. I regretted never finishing my degree, so here I am." She turns to the white board behind her. "So, should we turn to the paper?"

"Is it weird being so old for a grad student?" someone asks.

"That's rude!" another rebuts.

Aki laughs again. "No, it's OK. Yes, it does feel strange being so much older, but I'm grateful to be here. I don't know what I'll do after this, but just remember, regret is the worst curse in life."

She pauses to look at their youthful faces, many the same age as Meg. They look back at her, probably wondering what regret even is. Aki answers questions about the paper for thirty minutes before wrapping up her office hours, saying goodbye and making her way out of the history building and onto the quad.

"Hey, you hippie dippie grad student!" a loud, high voice calls out. "I thought someone was going to try to sell me pot, but wouldn't you know, they tried to sign me up to become a member of the Socialist Party while they were at it!"

"Jules!" Aki cries out, running toward her. "Jules!"

"Good grief, girl, this is not *The Notebook*," Jules replies, laughing while hugging her.

It's been months since Aki saw Jules, longer than any time in the ten years they had been at Wesley together.

"Are you wearing *hemp*?" Jules cries.

Aki laughs and tugs at her shirt. "J.Crew. Let's get some coffee," she says, pulling her toward Telegraph Avenue. "Tell me everything!" She steers Jules toward the campus gates and the shops. "What's up at Wesley?" she asks.

Grayson emails her from time to time, filling her on gossip and news: Sarah Hashimoto lasted for exactly one semester before she left for a job at Google; Percy was on the verge of becoming a famous artist and was considering leaving Wesley; and Grayson was hanging in there. He promised to visit soon on his way back from Tahoe over winter break.

Jules gawks at the tidal wave of students and dodges multiple oncoming bikes. "Well, our friend Ousmane has his hands full, that's for sure," Jules replies, pulling out her sunglasses. "I don't get it, is there no autumn in this part of the country?"

The Berkeley sun is hot, and students rush about in shorts and T-shirts. "Hands full with what?" Aki asks.

"Oh Lord, you know," Jules says, waving her hand. "Parents, the board, students, the usual."

Aki thinks about her last conversation with Ousmane before she resigned from the school. For months she had been so curious but never found a good time to ask him: that day when he interrupted Meg's interview with Joanna Javier-Hernandez on the street and whispered in Meg's ear, what had he said to make her stop talking?

Ousmane looked at Aki, his eyes wrinkling ever so slightly with what looked like delight.

"I told her that I might have to call her grandmother," he said, giving Aki a knowing grin.

Aki chuckles at the memory. She hopes Ousmane is well and knows he must be doing a better job than Harrison, because he cares about the right things.

"Do you ever see Meg on campus?" Jules asks.

Much to everyone's relief, and despite two suspensions her junior year plus a transfer to a public school in her senior year of high school, Meg had been accepted to Berkeley. Aki and Ian decided to tell Meg about their move to San Francisco at the end of her junior year in order to soften the blow, but to their surprise and relief, Meg was upbeat and excited about the move, even though it meant saying goodbye to Aiko.

"It's all good, she'll visit. Like I could go back to Wesley after all that anyway," Meg said reasonably.

What Aki didn't tell Meg was that she was "in conversation" with the chair of the Berkeley history department to complete her long-discarded dissertation and that she had secured her own funding for it. When she had applied for a grant, the thinking was that she might take a sabbatical from Wesley, but upon leaving her job, she decided there was something else she really wanted to do instead. Berkeley had agreed to accept her long-unused credits from her old program, and she found a professor willing to take her on as an advisee and teaching assistant. While Aki wouldn't have to take any classes, when she told Meg right after her own acceptance to Berkeley, and her daughter's reaction was simply, "Why can't you go to Stanford?"

Aki laughs at Jules's question. "I did run into her once at the school store. Her eyes murdered me." They arrive at a coffee shop and Aki opens the door.

"Is this place *clean*?" Jules sniffs as she steps daintily inside. "OK, it is," she confirms before striding to the counter. "Oh, and it's Manhattan prices, I see how it is."

"You didn't need to pay, you're my guest!" Aki pleads.

"Oh Lord, I am so happy to be away, are you kidding me? Ever since Felix left for Vandy, Jasper expects me to watch cricket with him! The Claremont is *gorgeous*, by the way," referring to the spa and hotel she's staying at for the weekend. Aki and Ian had found a three-bedroom bungalow not far from there in the Berkeley hills, but Jules insisted she should stay in a hotel, which Aki suspected was her way of getting a little vacation for herself away from Wesley. As for her daughter, Meg had come over a grand total of once since starting school—and that was only because Aki's parents were there for dinner.

"How's Felix?" Aki asks.

"Lord, I'm assuming drunk and failing out of his classes," Jules responds before accepting a tray of their tea and baked goods. "But I think he's made some friends. Nicer ones," she says, walking over to a window seat before changing the subject. "Let's people watch. Will we see Bernie Sanders?"

"He's from Vermont."

"Same thing," Jules says. "So, are you so happy to have escaped the third ring of hell?"

Aki laughs. "Wesley?" she asks, knowing full well what Jules means. "There are things I miss . . ." Aki says, trailing off as Jules raises her eyebrows.

"Like what, the demanding parents or the jaded students? At least Harrison and the Wakemans aren't there," she concedes, taking a bite of her muffin. "Ooh, yum. I can get behind the vegan thing, I guess," she announces while stuffing it in her mouth zealously.

Aki laughs, happy to be with her friend after such a long absence. She knew that the Wakemans had left, of course. After the triple confession in Quaker meeting, Ousmane had no real recourse but to punish all of them despite not believing any of them. She's sure he had his suspicions, though he never made them obvious to her. Just as Jules had insisted, there had been surveillance video that the school had kept under wraps, and rumor was that Josh Fayer had hacked into the school's security to download it and sent it to PoC@Wesley. But it ultimately never showed more than the shadowy figure in the incriminating jersey. As for the can of spray paint, Aki simply tries to keep it out of her mind. She never asked Meg about it, because by covering up the crime, she had become as bad as whoever had done it, if not a party to it, and no longer had the moral ground from which to preach or interrogate. It was also the reason why she finally decided to leave Wesley. Though she had told Jules that teaching made her feel like the best version of herself, more and more, Wesley was clearly erasing what was left of her.

In the end, Ousmane suspended Aaron, Meg, and Aiko and decreed that they would make a public apology and speech to the student body. The Wakemans cried foul, of course, saying Aaron shouldn't apologize for something he didn't do, not to mention something the school couldn't prove, but Ousmane ignored them, knowing what he did about Cash and Harrison and having viewed the video of a drunk Aaron spewing racist and hateful things. The Wakemans quickly pulled Aaron out of school to prevent such public flagellation, and rumor was that he enrolled at a boarding school in New Jersey. He also ended up getting into Princeton, but his entry had been deferred a year—by the school or by Aaron himself, no one knew. All of this of course unfolded during the debacle that was Harrison's resignation. Citing the desire to "spend more time with his family in Maine," Harrison left as quickly as Aaron did, exiting without even a note from his desk or bothering to clean out his office. The school guidance counselor, Timothy, who had been fired thanks to Cash Wakeman in an act of revenge for sleeping with his wife, apparently had tried to be reinstated, but ended up at the girls' school down the road. She later heard from Holly that Claire moved to Santa Barbara and was seeing a film producer.

"Did you hear about Aaron?" Jules asks suddenly.

"That he ended up at a boarding school?" Aki asks.

"No, after that," Jules says, finishing her muffin and slurping her tea. Aki shakes her head, assuming he went to college like everyone else. "He joined the army."

"He did not," Aki says, honestly shocked. "I thought he deferred a year before Princeton!"

"He did, but I guess the army was his last stand against his parents," Jules says. "I mean, what could get a set of parents like the Wakemans angrier than their child not going to college? I have to hand it to him."

Aki lets this idea, and the image of a closely shorn Aaron Wakeman, sit in her mind for a moment. She hopes he'll find his way like Grayson did. She wonders if he ever will, though she concedes that the one selfless thing he did was to try to cover up for Meg's confession that day during Quaker meeting. She still hopes it was Aaron who had actually done it.

"Do they keep in touch?" Jules asks softly.

"Meg and Aiko?" Aki asks. Aiko is at Brown, in Providence, a whole country away.

"No," Jules says. "Meg and Aaron."

Aki is taken aback.

"I don't think so," Aki says slowly. "But who knows," she admits. Aki conceded that it is totally normal for an eighteen-year-old not to confide in their parents, but it still pains Aki that she did not succeed in having a closer relationship with her own daughter. More than staying at Wesley for so long, this was her greatest regret. She also knows that any repairs to their relationship might end up taking longer than the lifetime they spent together at Wesley.

"Who did they hire to take over the upper school?" Aki suddenly asks. She knows she can just as easily look it up, but she never bothered.

"Oh, Darius Redd is filling in while they do a search," Jules says, referring to a universally beloved humanities teacher. "I suppose you know they were grooming you to take that position all along?"

Aki doesn't correct her as she remembers Ousmane's proposition right before she left Wesley. It had seemed impulsive and poorly planned, but he later explained that Harrison had originally planned on making her middle school head, not that she was at all qualified for it. Just another misdirected attempt by the school to live up to its own ideals. After Harrison's exit, the board hastily conferred and decided to appoint her interim upper school head instead, though of course, she turned it down. But all the times that people called her Ousmane's "right-hand woman" made more sense after those particular events.

"Did they ever make any changes? The school, I mean," Aki asks, and can't help but feel hopeful, if only because she wants some change to have happened and wants to believe she and her colleagues' efforts—not to mention the students'—weren't completely in vain.

"Well, they replaced Elliot Associates, thank the Lord! Did you know that after some social media reconnaissance they found out that one of the consultants is seriously anti-Semitic? Wesley was shitting itself! Elliot Associates filed a wrongful termination suit, but of course Amanda somehow made it go away."

"Amanda is still there?" Aki asks incredulously as Jules nods wryly.

Jules downs the last of her drink. "I have to admit, they've changed some things for the better, probably because Harrison left." She waves her hand as if to chase away a fly. "Enough about work! Are you being a dutiful daughter and seeing your parents more?"

Aki nods, but the truth is, Ian and Meg go see them more than she does, mainly because they want to be fed.

"Oof, I gotta get back to the hotel!" Jules cries out. "I wanna get changed before dinner!"

Aki laughs as she follows Jules out the door, her heels click-clacking away. "It's not fancy, you don't have to worry!" she calls after her.

"I'm here to celebrate, come on now," Jules calls back.

"Celebrate what?" Aki asks.

Jules turns around and looks at her seriously. "Your freedom!" she cries back. "You got a do-over!"

Aki thinks about this; it's true, of course. She was finishing something she started eighteen years ago. And she's hoping to restart her relationship with her daughter.

"Some people wish they could change their lives. You went out and did it," Jules says, smiling. "Come on, girl, get moving! I have a salt scrub and massage reserved for us!"

Aki laughs and follows her friend down the street, thinking about Jules's comment. She could be stuck back at Wesley, running on the hamster wheel, desperate to get off or believe falsely that she was making progress toward change. And even though it may be too late for her to change some of the things she did when she was at PENN or when she was teaching at Wesley, she knows she can make things better for herself and with Meg now. Jules is right, she did get a do-over. After almost twenty years of feeling stuck, she finally feels in control of her choices, and she's determined not to waste them.

ACKNOWLEDGMENTS

T HERE IS A TERRIBLY clichéd and hackneyed stereotype of little girls who dream about their weddings from the time
they are very young, but as a first-time author, I have fantasized
about writing an acknowledgement section in the back of my
very own book for *years*. As my kids would say, *cringe*. But I am so
grateful to be able to thank the many people who helped me
along the meandering path that is my adulthood and professional
life.

Let me start by saying that I always wondered why actors and
authors open their speeches and acknowledgements by thanking
their agents, but now I know why. Your literary agent is not only
the person who champions your book and finds the perfect pub-
lishing partner, they slap you on the back and cheer you up when
you get noes and congratulate you vociferously when you get a
yes. Your agent is your first editor, brainiac business manager,
sometime-therapist, and, if you are lucky, someone you can call
a friend. It is not an understatement to say that this novel would
not exist nor would I be able to call myself a published author
without Melissa Danaczko. For the writers out there dreaming
of selling their debut novels and to the published authors who
haven't yet had the chance to work with her, you would be lucky

to have Melissa on your side. She is not only one of the smartest people I know, she is savvy, kind, funny, and pretends to laugh at my jokes in an incredibly convincing manner. As cheesy as it sounds, I do not know what I would do without her. Listen, sometimes cheese is good, especially on pizza and in thank-you notes.

A tremendous amount of collaborative work went into completing this novel from an equally tremendous group of individuals at Alcove Press. When you read a book, you don't think about all the amazing minds that worked together to create it—it's not just the author! I owe eternal gratitude to Melissa Rechter, who believed in the idea, was one of its first real advocates, and was the best editor a first-time author could have. She was gentle and insightful, not to mention artful in her editing. Her deft touch added not only to the work but how I approached my writing. Thank you also to Rebecca Nelson, Mikaela Bender, Madeline Rathle, Dulce Botello, Matt Martz, Stephanie Manova, Doug White, and Thai Perez, without whom the book would not exist. Your hard work is unheralded but deserves ample appreciation.

It may take a village to raise a child, but it takes a continent's worth of friends to help you believe that you can actually write. In fact, several continents: In the UK, thank you to Maggie Parke and her mother, Peach, who were the first people to ever read and edit my writing. Thank you to Meghan Rogers, whom I met on the sidelines of a humid swimming pool during a club swim practice in London. She enthusiastically read and reread many drafts of this book and gave me critical feedback. Meghan is not only the best beta reader a writer could hope for, she's that amazing friend who volunteers to walk your dog in a pinch and take your child to swim practice because you couldn't figure out your other carpool.

Thank you to the many friends who never once said, "You're doing *what*?!" when I told them about this book (and were also some of the first people to preorder it with enthusiasm). These include many amazing members of the MAPIA API Alliance, my Kennedy School friends Lydia, Alyssa, and Rob, Catherine and Charlotte Swezey, Yvonne Hao, Kim Penn, and Amanda Hewitt. I should include here the best students that I ever had, Ethan Charlip, Scott Glanzel, Josh Fayer, and Laura Fazekas, I love you all very much. Please get married so that I can come party at your weddings.

To the amazing community that I have met through my daughter's school, I am grateful for your friendship and support (and none of you are like any of the parents in this book!): Trish Primrose Wallace, Susanne Salkind, Molly Mattison, Gargee Gosh and Andy Chasin, Priya and Dan, Kate and Kevin Bertram, Travis Allen and Paloma Adams-Allen, Ann Sun, Lilly Liu Minkove, Mika Shannon, Sumi Choi, Heidi K (with whom I am leading the revolution), Chanelle Blackwell, Mich Black, and Paige Smith (SST!). Thank you also to Dominic and Christina, who were early supporters of my novel. You are both incredible educators, and my children were lucky to have been under your guidance.

Finally, thank you to the people whom I am lucky enough to call some of my best friends: Sarah and Dave Nesbitt, Hope Stevens, Elise Colella, Sunday morning walking companion JK, my running partner and coconspirator Tisha Schestopol, and favorite carpool pal Bram Schestopol. Shoutout to our family's favorite travel companion Callie Wallace. To my wonderful friends in Japan who may never read a translated version of this book: Maiko Sagara, Hideko Ishibashi, and Madoka Koyama, I miss and value all of you more than you will ever know.

To my father, who left a legacy of writing one hundred nonfiction books (many on political topics that I didn't agree with, but I respect his tenacity nonetheless), and to my mother, who told me I could be whatever I wanted. Thank you to my extended family, Eben, Jeenah, Lia, Roberto, Brian, Rachel, Dick, and Ellen (the latter who came to my dissertation defense—that is true loyalty, folks).

And finally, thank you to my husband and children—I love you very much. And to Wilby, the best writing companion a person could ever have.